Cold Kill

Cold Kill

DAVID LAWRENCE

Thomas Dunne Books
St. Martin's Minotaur
New York

THOMAS DUNNE BOOKS.
An imprint of St. Martin's Press.

www.minotaurbooks.com

Library of Congress Cataloging-in-Publication Data

ISBN 0-312-34741-3
EAN 978-0-312-34741-3

First published in Great Britain by Michael Joseph
An imprint of Penguin Books

First U.S. Edition: June 2006

10 9 8 7 6 5 4 3 2 1

To Stephen Kovacevich

I

The sky is darkening but not yet dark; it shows a vibrant, unbroken blue, so deep that if you stare at it long you might take it to be the onset of blindness . . .

It's the moment in a wilderness when all birdsong suddenly stops. The moment when you're out on a four-lane highway with your thumb cocked, fifty miles from anywhere, and you know that the cars won't pull over now, and the big trucks are hammering through, already lit up against the failing of the light.

It's the moment when the creatures of the night shift in their sleep, then wake and sniff the air.

The time between the dog and the wolf.

There were starlings roosting in the Holland Park woodland, their feathers fluffed because there was frost in the wind. In among the trees, the scene of crime team had pitched a four-sided blue PVC screen, and halogen lamps were sending up a cold, white glow that flooded the interior and rose in a broad beam to cut the half-light. When the wind caught the edge of the screen, it furled and slapped; the starlings rose in a little cloud, then settled again, softly. A crowd of hard-edged shadows moved on the blue backdrop.

The shadows were a forensics team, a scene of crime officer, a police doctor, a stills photographer, a video man and two officers from the AMIP-5 murder squad. DI Mike Sorley and DS Stella Mooney were the shadows on the far side of the screen – either keeping their own counsel or staying out of the way.

Valerie Blake was also there, but you couldn't see her shadow because she was lying in it.

Everyone was wearing white coveralls, almost disappearing when they moved through the crossbeams of the fierce halogen glow. The tented area enclosed a single silver birch. As the workers in that space passed and re-passed its pale, slender bole, it seemed the only one of them given over to patience and thoughtfulness. The doctor had a fleece-lined climber's jacket under his coverall, with a woollen beanie beneath the hood; his fingers were white to the knuckle. He got off his knees and moved to join Sorley and Stella, shoving his hands into his armpits for warmth.

'Difficult to say how long she's been dead. Taking the ambient temperature and the wind chill into account, I'd say more than three hours, less than ten.'

'That's a big window,' Sorley observed.

'You'll get more from the pathologist. Sorry, it really is a tough call. She's very cold.'

Stella looked at Valerie where she lay. Of course she was cold; it was no weather to be out wearing nothing but a DKNY T-shirt and a pair of cross-trainers. The search team had already found the rest fifty feet away: underwear, matching grey sweats and a hoodie for extra warmth. Her door key and mobile phone were in a zipper pocket. They bagged the phone separately and handed it to Stella, who would take it back to the AMIP-5 incident room and rifle the address book for the names of people who didn't yet know that they were 'relatives of the deceased' or 'grieving friends'.

Or 'suspects'.

In the same way, Stella didn't yet know the dead woman as Valerie Blake, but that wouldn't take long.

The doctor was running down a checklist of notes. 'Female, mid to late twenties, largely unclothed, dead at the scene, secondary trauma to the head, almost certainly the result of a blow with a blunt instrument, though the cause of death is clearly strangulation.' Despite the thin rime of frost coating her skin, the mark of the ligature lay on her throat like an amethyst necklace. 'Possibility of sexual assault.' He amended that: 'Likelihood.'

The wind had risen with the encroaching darkness: raw-edged, carrying the sort of chill that settles and seeps in. A bird had flown into the tented space and couldn't find its way out, despite the lack of a roof. It cannoned back and forth, just above head level, flapping against the plastic, twisting in the air, sometimes rising on the brilliant columns of halogen light as if they were thermals, but then dropping down again, unequipped for night flight. As Stella watched, the wind shook the lamps and the light shifted crazily. The bird grew more frantic, wings whirring as it flew past her face.

Sorley said, 'Let's leave them to it.'

Their shadows slid on the screen, then they emerged and, despite their overall whites, were almost lost to darkness, though the man watching from cover was sufficiently sharp-eyed to pick them out from the backdrop of trees; just enough light left in the sky, just enough backwash of light from the tent.

The watcher was standing close to a plane tree, any silhouette of his own absorbed by the tree's bulk. The leafless branches thrashed above his head. He was motion-less, barely breathing, though his eyes were wide and unblinking. A smile on his lips. He was trying to picture the scene on the inside: all that lively activity round a still, lifeless centre; the quick and the dead.

The watcher saw the two of them, a man and a woman, he guessed, talking a moment, their heads close together; then the man turned, moving out of the treeline and starting across the open grassy space towards Kensington High Street. The headlights of cars shone like markers on the park road. As he watched, a gust of wind toppled one of the lamps and a shout went up. Shadows scattered, then swarmed towards the hotspot on the screen where the lamp had fallen.

Stella went back in. Two forensic officers were righting the lamp, while another attended to the doctor, who sat with his back to the birch tree, knees raised, head down, blood showing blackly on his forehead and also on his wrist where he'd raised an arm to block the worst of the impact.

Stella said, 'Get him out of here.' The scene of crime officer was DC Andy Greegan and he was already on the case, nudging the forensics man aside, getting the doctor to his feet. What worried Stella was also worrying Greegan: corruption of the scene; the doctor's blood and DNA as compromising evidence. Greegan hustled the doctor out of the tent while a forensics man taped off the small area where he'd fallen.

When Stella re-emerged, the watcher was still in place. He saw her strip off the white coveralls and ball them up; saw her start down towards her car; saw her drive away. She was only of passing interest. His real attention was to the tent and the picture in his mind's eye of Valerie Blake as she lay sprawled on her back, her skin paper-white, dark hair tied back in a pony-tail, the blue-black line of the ligature across her throat. The picture was satisfying to him, even though it was incomplete: her face was blurred, her physical build difficult to determine.

He stood there a long time, watching them work, watching the shifting shadows, never feeling the cold.

2

Area Major Investigation Pool 5's incident room had been set up in a police overspill property off Ladbroke Grove, close to the admin centre and holding facility of Notting Hill police station. AMIP-5 was a fluid affair, just like all AMIP groups: cops are pulled off this job or that when a detective inspector requests them. The DI would have been appointed in turn by the Senior Investigating Officer managing the case: in this instance the SIO's choice had been DI Mike Sorley.

Sorley had asked for DS Mooney; Stella had asked for DC Andy Greegan, DC Susan Chapman and DC Pete Harriman. Greegan was the best scene of crime officer Stella knew and Sue Chapman's coordination skills included an eye for detail that, in the past, had often meant time saved. There would also be an exhibitions officer and two other street cops; they were taking a little time to find because a flu virus was taking its toll of available officers. The exhibitions man wasn't an issue, Stella considered, as long as he was anally retentive; someone who shaved twice a day and lived with his mother would be just fine.

One of the street cops she asked for – one of her opposite numbers, in effect – was DC Maxine Hewitt. Stella had worked with Maxine before, and knew her to have the kind of instinct that bypasses the ordinary. But the other street cop, Pete Harriman, was her first choice. He and Stella had worked a number of cases together and they understood one another. It was the kind of understanding that proceeds from having shared danger and shared laughter.

Extra officers might be drafted in if needed, and local uniformed help could be asked for, but Sorley and Stella had got the people they wanted: their core team; their murder squad.

Stella copied the names and numbers from Valerie Blake's mobile phone, rebagged it and put it in the exhibitions room, ready to go for forensics testing along with the other items from the scene of crime. That was the easy part. She looked at the list and knew there was only one first choice.

'Home.' That was the tough part.

It was almost six thirty. Greegan was still at the scene; Sorley was on the phone to the SIO with his initial report. The other members of the squad wouldn't arrive till next morning. Stella made a call, but it wasn't the one she ought to have made. When John Delaney picked up, Stella could tell from his preoccupied tone that he was working.

She said, 'I'll be late.' It was what people involved with cops often heard. Delaney didn't mind. Freelance journalists have their own time-tables.

He said, 'If you were to join me for a curry, what time would I get to the restaurant?'

'Make it ten o'clock.'

'Perfect.'

She could hear the rattle of his fingers on the keyboard.

'How easy is this?' she asked. 'A girl is murdered. Young woman. You don't know who she is, but you've got a list of contacts for her. One says "Home". You make the call. Someone lifts the phone and says, "Hello."'

'The problem being . . . ?'

'The problem being what to say next.'

'How many times have you done this?'

'Surprisingly few.'

'Say what you said the last time.'

'Last time I didn't get it right.'

He laughed. 'Right? How in hell would you ever get it *right*?'

'Exactly.'

'Which restaurant?' he asked. He lived in Notting Hill Gate and there was no shortage of curry houses.

'The one you can get into. Give me a call.'

'There's nothing you can say that can make a difference: nothing right.'

'I know.'

She hung up and called Pete Harriman on his mobile. When he answered, she could hear the voice of a commentator rising above a background din. She said, 'You're in the pub.'

'Big screen,' he advised her. 'Big game.' She told him about the phone list and he said, 'Only one choice, Boss.'

'You're right. But I could phone, or I could take a less direct route: get BT to trace the address from the number and go round there.'

'It would be kinder.'

'It would. Not only that, we'd be there to gauge the response.'

Harriman laughed. He'd picked up on 'we'.

Stella said, 'Strictly speaking, you're not on the strength until tomorrow morning.'

'I know,' Harriman said, 'but look at it this way: we're two-nil down, and the bastards are all over us like a rash.'

'Home' could have been husband and kids, but it was parents. As when people say, 'I'm going home this weekend.' The house you grew up in; the streets you played in; the place you could always go back to, but not the place where

8

you wanted to live when you were in your mid to late twenties. Which is why, when Valerie Blake's father opened the door, he didn't look worried; not for a second or two anyway; then he saw the expression on Stella's face, and realized who she was and why she might be there. He took a step back and said something, but no one quite knew what it was: less a word than a little cry of fear. He sat down heavily in the hallway, suddenly and without knowing it was going to happen, driving the breath from his lungs. In the same moment, his wife emerged from the kitchen to find Stella and Harriman at the door and her husband bolt upright on the hall carpet, his mouth gaping, his ribs heaving with effort.

Stella hadn't spoken a word; there was no right word to say.

The bookies had shortened the odds on a white Christmas to three-to-one. The Notting Hill stores had fairy lights and pint-sized Santas and seasonal two-for-one offers. The all-glass frontage of the Ocean Diner had been sprayed with fake snow. The Notting Hill late-shoppers weren't smiling, though. It was too cold for a smile. They were wondering what the fuck had happened to global warming.

Stella stood on the far side of the road from the Light of India, waiting to beat the traffic. She could see John Delaney at a window table, pouring the Cobra beer that a waiter had just brought and reading through a sheaf of manuscript: the work he'd done that day. He was a features-writer and his current project was winter and the homeless. Like holly and tinsel and cheap perfume, it was a seasonal bestseller.

She liked the way he ran his fingers into his hair, then rested his head on his hand to read. She liked the way he looked: the narrow planes of his face, the slightly uneven mouth. She liked his wry humour. She liked the way he held on to her after they had made love. All this was new. Until a couple of months back, she had lived with a man called George Paterson, though her relationship with Delaney had started a while before George had discovered it and left home.

Stella and Delaney had first knocked into each other when Stella was involved in a murder inquiry where Delaney had an interest. And 'knocked into each other' about summed it up: their attitudes had been somewhere between confrontational and outright aggressive. The aggression was the flip-side of sexual attraction, though they had kept sex out of things for quite a while, and Stella had thought that she and George might make it after all. Then sex had become the issue and there was too much heat between Stella and Delaney for George not to notice.

Now Delaney sat at the window table, reading and waiting for her, and she looked across, catching glimpses of him between the passing cars, and thought that she was in love with him and that he was definitely trouble.

'Attacks on women in London,' he said. 'It's an old story that keeps coming up new. Five in the last twelve weeks. Was she raped?'

'Not sure yet. Looks like it.'

'So not thrill-kill.'

'You know all the tags, Delaney.'

'I read the papers.'

She still called him Delaney sometimes, as if it were a sardonic reference to the days when they were at loggerheads, or as if she half expected those days to return.

Harriman and Stella had taken Valerie Blake's parents to the morgue. The father sat in the car, back straight, hands in lap, like a stone statue. From time to time he said, 'She's an only child.' The remark seemed to come at evenly spaced intervals, as if the man were counting. He was sitting directly behind Harriman, and each time he spoke the hair rose on Harriman's forearms.

'She's an only child.'

The morgue was bright and cold, light coming back off steel tables, steel bowls, steel doors. Both parents went in to make the ID. A morgue assistant rolled the body out of its steel cabinet and for a long time no one said a word. The father swayed slightly, but never took his eyes off his daughter and never made a sound and never blinked. Stella looked at the mother; a nod of the head would have been enough.

Finally she spoke breathless, dry-eyed: 'She's an only child.'

After the attendant rolled the body back, the mother turned to leave, but the father remained, his eyes fixed on the space where his daughter's face had been, as if it had left a ghostly print on the air. It was Pete Harriman who took his arm and led him out.

In an ante-room to that hall of death, Stella sat with Valerie Blake's mother and father and asked questions. Valerie's mother gave the answers. Her husband's name was Howard, hers was Mary. Valerie had a boyfriend called Duncan Palmer. She lived alone. She worked in a gym: as a PA, not an instructor, but that's where the keep-fit culture came from. She had no enemies. She hadn't been acting strangely. She hadn't seemed worried recently.

Rows with friends? No.

Money worries? No.

Relationship with Duncan seem okay? Seemed fine.

Easy questions. Mary Blake gave her answers like someone ticking the box. Howard Blake said nothing; Howard had gone somewhere. Not that he'd left the room, but he had made a trip inside his head and either he'd found a place that seemed safe and had decided to stay there, or he'd got hopelessly lost. You couldn't have told which by looking at his eyes; his eyes were as hard and reflective as the steel trim on the chairs they sat in.

It was a short walk to Delaney's flat and Stella had found a parking space. It was the kind of combination that made an automatic choice of 'your place or mine'. Stella was still living in the basement flat in Vigo Street that she had shared with George Paterson. It wasn't a good arrangement: even though George had been back and taken everything he owned, he hadn't taken everything of himself. But some kind of inertia that Stella couldn't properly explain kept her there. The idea that she and Delaney might live together was one of the great unspokens. Stella needed her own space; she also needed to keep her own company from time to time; and she assumed that Delaney felt the same. She told herself that any sane person would.

He made them a drink and, when she reached for it, drew her in, sliding his hand under the waistband of her jeans at the back. His touch never failed. Hadn't failed yet. They made love whenever they were together.

Stella woke in the middle of the night; a sound had disturbed her. She walked naked out of the bedroom and into the living space: stripped floorboards, rugs, a galley kitchen, Delaney's desk, a circular table where they ate, a big area sectioned off by two large sofas, an open fireplace, a television he only ever switched on to get the news. Good for one person; good to visit.

The sound that had woken her came back: someone

playing electric guitar in another apartment, a bluesy sound, long, weeping lines. She went to the tall casement window and the light from streetlamps seemed brittle, as if it had hardened as the temperature dropped. You could almost see the frost taking hold.

Stella leaned against the window-frame, her naked body half in shadow, half in lamplight, a sketchy blue cross-hatching by the underside of her breast, the crease of her thigh, the bevels of her cheekbones. She had dark hair and blue eyes, a combination that you noticed at once. She was in her early thirties and still slim enough and pretty enough to catch glances from men who passed her in the street, though when she looked in a mirror, she saw someone who could benefit by dropping a few pounds, fixing her hair and calling by at the gym. Someone had told her that, after forty, women became invisible. Three storeys below, some party-goers went into the All Nite to buy breakfast, or maybe for something to keep the party going.

London is never dark – there's always that luminous glow: the light-mix from storefronts, from cars, from streetlamps, from the windows of the city's raw-eyed insomniacs. Over the rooftops, less than a mile away, Stella could make out a smudge against the skyline: the trees in Holland Park. She saw Valerie Blake's pale body, down and lifeless; saw her own pale, naked reflection in the long window.

The guitar wailed and rose, then bottomed out. A police siren took on the note and modified it. Stella went back to bed, shifting into Delaney's warmth. He stirred and rested a hand on her flank.

'So am I,' she said, as if he could hear. 'So am I – an only child.'

3

'It's just another day,' Stella was saying, 'and you've done this before: put on your DKNY T-shirt and your sweats and your running shoes. You've probably got a few different circuits according to how good you feel or when you last went for a run. Do you always go out at the same time? Probably. Different at weekends, maybe. How often do you go? That depends on whether you get home from work early, whether you have a date, whether you think you need a drink more than you need exercise. Today, you'll run. You put your mobile phone and your house key into a zipper pocket. You've already decided that you've got time to run through the park – time before it closes, that is. It closes at dusk: that's what the sign at the gate says. So it's still light when you set out. How much time do you allow? That depends on how fast you run. A slow jog – you'll leave twenty minutes or even half an hour; if you're an experienced runner, you could make it in ten to fifteen. These are things we'll be asking about: how often she ran; what routes; how fast.'

The team briefing was being videotaped: Stella's idea. All briefings would be taped so they could be used to chart the investigation, the way it progressed. The essential factors in any briefing were clarity, shared information, inspired speculation, coffee, chocolate bars, salt and vinegar crisps and a thick, hanging pall of cigarette smoke. Stella had quit smoking some while back, which meant that, given the rough calculation that applies to secondary inhalation, she was down to a pack a day.

In addition to Andy Greegan, Pete Harriman, Maxine Hewitt and Sue Chapman, the team had acquired an exhibitions officer in DC Nick Robson and a gofer in DS Jack Cuddon. Cuddon's job was to act as Sorley's bagman: an information officer, in effect, and a link between AMIP-5 and the people who controlled the budget. Stella thought he'd be good at that; he had the look of a bureaucrat about him – thinning hair, a narrow face, almost prim, a subdued tie. A couple of civilian computer operators would join the team in a day or so, though they would be doubling up on other jobs.

'Just another day,' Stella said, 'just another run. Except you never get through the park. Someone stops you and kills you.'

The stills of Valerie Blake were pinned to a whiteboard. She was dead from all angles. The DKNY T-shirt was pushed up and you could see that Valerie was still wearing her sports bra. Somehow, that detail made her near-nakedness all the more startling: the white torso, the thick pubic vee, long legs slightly bent at the knee. Her head was turned to one side, as if better to show off the line of bruising at her throat. Also on the whiteboard was the beginnings of a list of contacts and interviewees. Two carried a single tick: Valerie's parents. There was provision for many ticks: many repeat interviews.

'We'll get uniform to put an incident board up in the park,' Stella said. 'There'll have been other runners, walkers, people with kids, people taking a short cut either over the hill to the Avenue or down to Kensington. DC Harriman and I are going back to the parents. When we've got a list of the victim's contacts, we'll organize a division of work. In the meantime, someone had better organize a search team for Valerie's flat. I don't imagine they'll find much, but we'd better take a look. Andy?'

Greegan nodded. 'Okay, Boss.'

Maxine Hewitt was looking at the stills. 'Five attacks in twelve weeks,' she said.

Delaney had offered the same statistic. Each of the AMIP-5 officers had noted the earlier killings and had kept track of the resulting investigations. Different teams were involved, although a single term kept cropping up to describe the murders: 'thrill-kill'. Mostly it cropped up in the tabloid press. Sue Chapman had liaised with other teams, obtained the crime-sheets for each case and distributed them to the members of AMIP-5.

'Same method,' Harriman observed. 'Attack with a blunt instrument, probably a hammer, then the garrotte.'

Maxine lobbed her coffee carton into a bin. 'Wasn't one of the attacks also a rape . . . or an attempted rape?'

Sue Chapman said, 'A girl on the towpath between Richmond and Kew. She'd been hit on the head too; then garrotted. And a couple of the others who died the same way were missing items of clothing.'

'Okay,' Maxine said, 'Valerie Blake was hit and strangled. Possibly raped. This is our man.'

'The others were more hurried,' Harriman observed. 'On one occasion, he was actually disturbed at the scene. No description, just the usual short, tall, fair, dark, twenty to fifty years old sort of thing. But he seems to be getting better at it.'

Maxine said, 'If he wants to spend time with them – if rape's on his mind – he'd be thinking about how best to allow for that. He'd be doing a bit of forward-planning.'

Stella used the term in her first report: first layer in the colour-coded strata that would build to a mountain of paperwork. Someone sitting down to think about how best to do the thing: someone choosing a time, choosing a method, choosing the killing-ground.

Forward-planning.

Harriman was smoking to keep warm and no one was going to persuade him that it was a lost cause. As they walked across the car park, Stella said, 'If you smoke in the car, I'll have to open a window.'

'You sound like an ex-smoker.'

'I sound,' Stella advised him, 'like your superior officer.'

Harriman said *fuck* under his breath, then took a massive last drag and sent out a long plume of smoke and frosted breath that clouded his face as he walked through it. He was wiry-thin, a narrow gypsy face and dark, curly hair; there was more than one woman in his life and each of them knew that, and expected it.

Stella drove, which gave Harriman nothing to do with his hands. She said, 'Any worries about the parents?'

'I don't think so. I think the parents are in the clear.'

'Me too.'

Despite the growing fashion for thrill-kill and death-by-stranger, most murders are domestic issues: a row on the stairs, a row in bed. Rows in the kitchen always gave scope – there are knives in the kitchen.

'Listen,' Stella said, 'I don't need to come back with you. Talk to the mother: she's more or less functioning. Get a list of contacts. Did anyone locate the boyfriend?'

'Not so far.'

Mary Blake had told them that Duncan Palmer worked as a headhunter. Stella had conjured a picture of a man with a loincloth and a nose-bone.

'You take it,' Stella said. 'You take the parents.'

The traffic was slowing for a red light. Stella changed down and blipped the accelerator to pull away from the line of vehicles, then cut straight across three lanes to the nearside. A chorus of horns said *Bitch* in unison. When the lights changed, she turned into a side street and made a call to the morgue. She expected to hear Sam Burgess's assistant but got the man himself.

'I'm prepping,' he said. 'You can be first up if you like.'

To get to Sam Burgess's world of steel and tile and frigid air, Stella descended two flights of stairs, then, down below street-level, walked through a series of rooms that held evidence of the frailty of flesh: specimens, spare parts, the body's leftovers. The rooms all had slap-flaps instead of doors, as if the trick was to get in fast and leave faster. She was always conscious, when she visited Sam, of how easy it was to die: a glitch in the machine; a bug in the system; foreign matter, like a blade or a bullet.

Sam was a small man in his mid fifties with deft hands and a monk's tonsure of white hair. He liked to work to music and today it was a symphony, Brahms 3. Sam's assistant was called Giovanni; Giovanni smiled but didn't speak. They seemed at ease in their underworld: the music, the tools of their trade gleaming and laid out for use, the body of Valerie Blake between them and waiting to be tended to. Sam had already made his preliminary, external examination. He'd taken swabs; he'd been into the secret places; he'd combed her hair. It was clear to see that she had been more than just pretty: the trim, toned body, the dark hair and pale skin, the clean planes of cheek and chin, the small, straight nose. It was possible, Stella thought, that Valerie had been beautiful, though with the life gone from her it was no longer possible to tell. In part, beauty lay in movement, in laughter, even in anger, and those things had left her; there was just a stillness, an absence.

'He's a big guy,' Sam said. 'Or so it seems to me.'

'Who's big?'

'The killer. Strong.'

'Why do you say that?'

'Throttled her with a ligature: made a hell of a mess of her thorax. Small bones broken, ruptures ... I could see that without cutting. No doubt about the cause of death: asphyxia by strangulation. Takes strength to kill that way, unless you hang your victim, of course.'

'And he didn't –'

Sam shook his head. 'Well, the abrasions and internal fractures don't seem right for that, but I'm not saying didn't until I've been in there for a better look. One thing ...' He beckoned Stella over and pointed to the ligature mark. When she nodded, as if to say, *Sure, she was strangled*, he said, 'No, just there.' He touched Valerie's neck at the very edge of the bruising. Alongside that mark, almost, in its shadow, was another, thinner line.

'More of an abrasion,' Sam said, 'nothing to do with the ligature.'

'She was wearing a necklace?'

'Something ... Just a chain perhaps, given the configuration. Or something on a chain. They didn't find anything at the scene?'

'No. Forensics are still there but hoovering and dusting. We'd have found something as obvious as a chain. He must have taken it.'

'Not robbery, surely.'

'No,' Stella said. 'Keepsake, more likely.'

Sam looked up and sighed. 'I can deal with her as a clinical puzzle. When she becomes the victim, it gets tougher.'

'She was found just after four o'clock,' Stella said. 'Do we know when she died?'

'Not long before that.'

'Not long, meaning . . .'

'An hour, maybe ninety minutes. There was very little insect invasion: too cold. I'm relying on the doctor's report to some extent: she was out of rigor mortis when found. Then there's the pattern of blood-puddling and the post-mortem developments in the trauma to the thorax and neck.'

'Was she raped?'

'Not sure –'

'Why?'

Sam had been talking while he worked: toothcombing Valerie's body for evidence, going to places that even a lover might have been denied. He said, 'Everyone knows about DNA these days. It's tough to leave no evidence at all, but there's no need to leave anything as helpful as semen.'

'You mean he could have used a condom.'

'Could have. I'll take a swab: the laboratory people will look for traces of lubricant. There's no real evidence of rape: no vaginal tearing, no anal trauma. Certain amount of bruising on the left upper thigh, but that could have happened in any number of ways. Of course, not all rape provides evidence of actual physical injury, but you know that.'

'It depends on the level of intimidation,' Stella observed; 'how frightened the victim is, so how ready to comply.'

'There's another possibility.'

'Go on.'

'There's a significant trauma to the left temple and to the cranium over the left ear; bruising to the ear itself as well. It's in the scene of crime report and it's clearly visible. But there's also bruising to the back of the head. She was struck down before she was strangled.'

'Meaning he could have knocked her out, then raped her, then killed her.'

'Yes, he could.'

Sam picked up a scalpel and began the big 'Y'-incision that would open Valerie from clavicle to pubis. Stella had seen it before, but that moment of awful drama never failed to bring a rush of giddiness. She watched as Sam worked, revealing Valerie for what she was – what we all are, Stella thought. Skin and bone, cuts of meat, a toothy smile and a hank of hair.

The music hung in the air.

Sam and Giovanni worked at the same rhythm, handling her with care. Now and then, Sam would speak into the mike, but the two men had no need for instruction or question: they were deft and practised, mechanics of the flesh. Sam was removing the thorax, the trachea, the lung-tree – all of a piece; Stella half expected to see a tap-root. He laid it out for inspection, then paused, looking back at the shell that had once been Valerie Blake. He lifted her hair away from the scalp flap and looked again at the ligature mark on her throat, then beckoned Stella over.

'See that? I hadn't noticed before.'

Stella could see nothing but spare parts and a semi-dismantled machine. 'What?'

'The ligature mark stops short on either side. And I'm thinking now about that bruising to the back of the head: less of an impact bruise than a pressure bruise.' Sam picked up the SOC notes and found the place he was looking for. 'There was a tree near by.'

'That's right,' Stella said. 'Inside the SOC tent.'

'A silver birch.'

'Yes.'

'A tree with a narrow bole.'

Stella waited.

Sam said, 'I think the bruising to the back of the head, the pressure bruise, is where her head rested against the tree. I could have guessed it from the way the eyeballs were turned in to the skull and from the pattern of blood suffusion, but I didn't notice the difference. I can see it now. Her torso was upright when she died. I think he stunned her, sat her up against the tree, then garrotted her – a ligature put loosely round the throat and going right round the tree, then a short length of wood or whatever inserted into the loop to twist it, using the tree as the strangling pole.'

'A method of execution.'

'Or a method of torture.'

'Except she was unconscious when he strangled her.'

'Was she?' Sam asked. 'How do you know?'

Stella was silent on that one.

Sam continued, 'I think it's likely that Forensics will find grains of tree bark from my combings – on her hair, on her T-shirt, on her back.'

'How long?' Stella asked. 'How long for her to die?'

Sam shrugged. The music came to an end and the room seemed suddenly brighter, steelier.

He said, 'As long as you like.'

4

Stella entered the post-mortem information as bullet points on the squad room whiteboard and circulated Sam Burgess's initial findings. Forensics had taken a first look at Sam's combings and taken samples from the bole of the silver birch; there were grains and fibres that looked right. They hadn't been fully analysed yet, but no one was in much doubt.

Pete Harriman lit a cigarette, having forgotten the one burning in his ashtray. He said, 'Lethal injection.'

Andy Greegan had the PM report in his hand. 'Bullet in the brain,' he suggested.

Jack Cuddon was on his way to DI Sorley's office with a sheaf of costings-sheets. He said, 'Crucifixion. Have the bastards lining Oxford Street. Watch the murder rate drop.'

When Stella spoke, other people's tobacco smoke fluttered on her breath. 'Let's look at the patterns here. Five attacks on women, two of them fatal. That's excluding Valerie Blake. We've all had a chance to look at the crime-sheets: where are the similarities? All the attacks were made out of doors; in a public place. Two in parks, two in the street, one on the towpath. That fits with the attack on Valerie. In one case, the victim's clothing had been disturbed or partially removed. That was the towpath attack; the victim died without recovering consciousness. Murder weapons: a blunt instrument and a garrotte.'

'The first incident,' Maxine Hewitt remarked.

'The first, yes. Then came an attack in a park. The victim

recovered, but remembers nothing of what happened. Blunt instrument only. No attempt at rape.'

'No apparent attempt,' Sue Chapman remarked.

'Meaning?'

'How does anyone know what was in the bastard's mind? He was disturbed.'

'That's an assumption,' Stella said.

'Stands to reason. No time to use the garrotte. Only reason she survived.'

'Good point. Third attack was in the street, late at night, the victim was walking home from a local disco. Blunt instrument and garrotte. She'd said goodbye to friends just a few minutes earlier. Again, clothing disturbed but no certainty of rape. In fact, like the others, no motive that anyone can find.'

'That's when the tabloids started talking about thrill-kill,' Harriman observed.

'Same with the fourth and fifth attacks,' Stella continued. 'One in a park, midmorning, lots of people about, no one saw or heard a thing. The other in the early hours: a girl who'd gone out for milk from the Eight-til-Late and was taking an alleyway shortcut back. You get a picture of this guy walking up behind his mark, taking out the hammer, or whatever, striking to the head – what –?'

'Usually twice,' Greegan offered.

'– okay, twice, then applying the garrotte.'

'If he gets time,' Harriman said.

'And does he strangle them after the sexual assault or before?' Maxine wondered.

Greegan said, 'Well, like the others, Valerie was strangled; she was also struck.' He was reading Sam's report. 'The PM talks about "a clearly delineated depression twelve centimetres in diameter, possibly a hammer-blow". That puts her alongside the others. I don't think this guy is a rapist, not really. He's a killer. He likes to display them: a way of saying I've been here; I did this. That's why their clothing is removed or disturbed.'

Harriman said, 'Which makes it attack by stranger – thrill-kill – whatever you want to call it.'

Stella said, 'Garrotting takes time. A hammer-blow, a stabbing, it's done and you're gone. This keeps you on the scene for a while. Why?'

'Certainty,' Maxine offered. 'Two victims survived the attack. Okay, one died without regaining consciousness and the second suffered memory loss, but –'

'But it's risk,' Stella agreed. 'Hit-and-run is a risk: his victim might survive *and* remember.' She paused. 'And there's another possibility.'

Pete Harriman's remark tailended Stella's, as if he had been anticipating her. 'The guy was enjoying it.'

How long for her to die?

As long as you like, that's what Sam Burgess had told her.

'Yes,' Stella said, 'that's what I had in mind.'

'There's another pattern,' Maxine said. 'Geography. They were all in west London.'

Andy Greegan opened his mouth to speak and was ambushed by a sneeze. He turned his head aside and sneezed again.

Stella said, 'Don't get sick.'

'I'm fine,' he said. 'Where's the boyfriend?'

'Was in America. Now on his way back. We got to him through his office. He'll call in as soon as he lands.'

'So he was in the States when she was killed?'

'That's right.'

'Verifiable?' Greegan asked.

'Absolutely.'

'This isn't a domestic,' Harriman said. 'This is some bastard with a hammer, a garrotte and a fucked-up brain.'

Ask coppers what they like least about the job and they'll say paperwork. Everything has to be down on paper. Paper comes first and last. There's a form for everything, and everything needs its report. Paper's your back-up. Paper's your fail-safe. Paper is the all-purpose, cover-your-arse proof-positive.

Stella was hacking out a report when Sue Chapman came over with some more paper: a folder holding that day's confessions. On average, there were four confessions a day.

I did it. I killed her. Bitch deserved to die. How good it felt. You can contact me at the above address/phone number/email/try and find me fuckwit copper.

Sue had wild hair and a calm manner: methodical, organized, a coordinator's brain. Stella could almost believe that Sue didn't mind the paper; that maybe she had worked out some kind of a relationship with the paper. It gave a whole new meaning to the word 'ream'. She put a note down on Stella's desk.

They were all followed up, the letters from crazies, the phone calls from crazies, most often by uniform because the local guys could check the usual names, the serial confessors, the eager inadequates. But they went to the SIO and the team leader first and the originals were all forensic-tested, copied for the handwriting experts and the profiler, then bagged in clear plastic folders. The note Sue had given to Stella was a copy, but she had the plastic-covered original in her hand. Stella looked first at the copy, then at the original.

T-shirt . . . dark hair tied back in a pony-tail . . . I stripped her off . . . I threw the rest away . . . strangled her . . . got my hands round . . .

It was signed: 'Robert'. Robert: as if Stella ought to know who that was; as if they might be less than close friends but more than mere acquaintances.

The papers had reported a body in the park and named it as Valerie Georgina Blake. They added that she had been strangled. There had been no physical description, nor any mention of the fact that she had been jogging or that she was found almost naked. The crank letters and calls used what they had to hand and invented the rest. Sue Chapman had read and logged them all: some of the inventions were pretty banal; some had turned her stomach.

'Hair colour,' Sue said, 'and the clothing.'

Stella nodded. 'This guy knows more than he should.' She got up. 'I'll take it down to DI Sorley. In the meantime, copy and circulate, okay? Also, send a priority notification to every front office in the Met area. If this guy shows up at a nick, I don't want some bored copper kicking his arse and showing him the door.'

Sue nodded. She seemed a little distracted and Stella looked at her again, more closely. Her face seemed pale amid the cloud of hair. 'Are you all right?'

'Fine,' Sue assured her. Then: 'Truth to tell, I feel very slightly off.'

Stella grimaced. She said, 'Don't get sick.'

5

The sky was the colour of zinc with a livid purple underglow and you could smell snow in the air. Sadie had been out by the Notting Hill Gate arcade for two hours. She'd started by playing the three tunes she knew on the penny whistle. She had learned 'While Shepherds Watched' by trial and error because it was Christmas; it wasn't a difficult tune to play, but maybe she'd made a bad choice, because it wasn't earning her enough for a fix either. Sadie had a streak of pink in her hair and a streak of green. You might think they were reflections from the shopfront neon. She had a nose-ring and a lip-spike. She had a tattoo of a swallow on her neck, just under her left ear.

A little later, after dark, she would move away from the shops and down to the Ocean Diner. She had staked out a patch by the alley door: it was where she bedded down when she was too tired or too cold to go on. Sometimes she would try for a hostel bed, but there was always the chance of getting busted and, anyway, she needed the money for scag. Now and then, the kitchen staff at the diner would come to the door for a smoke and maybe give her something to eat.

Just recently, though, there had been another source of money. At first, the street-people had been wary of him: he could have been Drugs Squad, he could have been the Revenue, but he wasn't; he was exactly who he claimed to be – a journalist writing a piece about street-people and Christmas. Tidings of comfort and joy.

Sadie switched to 'Lord of the Dance'. She had on every

piece of clothing she had scavenged or stolen. She would have liked to have wrapped her sleeping-bag round her shoulders, but she was sitting on it: folded three times as protection against the deep chill rising from the pavement. People went past, heads down against the wind, their hands in gloves, their money unreachable in pockets and bags.

Come on, Sadie thought. Come on, for fuck's sake. It's Christmas. It's Christmas and I need to jack up.

She looked over to where Delaney was hunkered down and talking to a skinny, red-headed street-sleeper called Jamie. Talking, but getting little back. Jamie was lying full length, his head poking out of his bag like a turtle's. Delaney handed the boy his business card as if he were trying to establish credentials; he also handed over some money. Jamie stowed both of them somewhere in one of his layers of clothing.

That boy's head is wrong, she thought. Not the look of it, but what's inside. He's living inside his head and things in there are a monster mess. Come and talk to me, Mr Writer-man. Give me some money, I'll tell you whatever you think you want to know.

From where she sat she could see the minimum-wage boys and girls in their paper hats and paper bow ties, working the queues in BurgerLand. For Christ's sake, she thought, don't anyone buy me a burger. People did that. It meant: if you're hungry eat this; don't expect money for drugs. A BMW four-track drew up right by her. The driver got out carrying a fistful of cash and thumbed most of it into a parking meter: enough to buy him ten minutes. He walked past Sadie, putting the spare cash in his pocket. The parking meter was earning more than the BurgerLand kids.

Delaney squatted down, his rear just light of the pavement, his forearms hanging from his knees. He looked very uncomfortable. Sadie could see that he was holding a twenty-pound note.

He said, 'Hi, Sadie. We talked before, remember?' Either Sadie had about her a faint tang of urine, or the pavement did.

She nodded. *I remember. Give me the twenty.*

On that earlier occasion she had told him that she had come to London from Scotland looking for work, waited tables, had some bad luck with bosses who wanted a side-order of sex, lost the jobs, started drinking, got in with a bad crew, experimented with drugs, moved from flat-share to squat to streets. She had told him that she was clean now, and was hoping to find a hostel bed for the night; maybe a job; then maybe a way back into the real world, wherever that was. None of it was true of her, but some of it was true of people she knew and it made a good story, the kind of story that his readers would enjoy. She particularly liked the phrase 'experimented with drugs'. Her experiments made Glaxo look small time.

Delaney told her he was just touching base and she nodded again, smiling at the note in his hand.

He asked her where she was sleeping and she told him about the kitchen door of the Ocean Diner and the kindness of the sous-chefs.

He asked her whether she'd had a good day, meaning money, and she told him that the citizens of Notting Hill Gate seemed not to be overburdened with Yuletide cheer or a seasonal spirit of generosity.

He mentioned the weather and they agreed that it was cold.

He wondered where she might be spending Christmas and she let him know that she hadn't completely made up her mind on that one.

He gave her the twenty pounds.

She asked him what Jamie had said, and he told her that Jamie was expecting Christ to celebrate his birthday by descending to earth trailing clouds of glory and that this event would be clearly visible from the Portobello Road.

It wasn't an opinion Delaney had come across before, though he'd heard Sadie's story several times and didn't believe a word of it. It was street-people stock-in-trade.

'Anything you give them, anything anyone gives them,' Stella informed him, 'they use to buy drugs.'

Delaney was cooking. There were half a dozen things he could make and he was making one of them: grilled chicken and salad. He found cooking slightly irritating – its smug conventions, its plans and maps, its arrogant insistence that you could knock together ingredients costing fifty pence and ask twenty pounds. He paused to sip his seven o'clock whisky. Seven o'clock was when he stopped work for the day.

He said, 'I know that.'

'They live on the fly.'

'I know that too.'

'Outside the law.'

'I like outlaws.' He smiled. 'So do you.'

She was sitting at the circular table, hunched over reports and case notes, a drink of her own to hand. Since George had left, since Delaney had become a permanent part of her life, her secret drinking had almost stopped. At one time, she would hole up in the pub after work, glad to be on her own, a ritual vodka-rocks on the bar. She used to like it poured into a shot glass, one cube of ice only, and she would flirt with it for a few moments before taking the first hit, getting that first lift. She was never a drunk, but she'd had a clear view of what that would be like. Now, she had made a deal with herself: if she was with Delaney she drank only moderately.

Of course, she wasn't always with Delaney; that was the deal-breaker.

He wandered across and looked over her shoulder. The note from 'Robert' lay on top of the pile. Stella was staring at it like a code-breaker whose decipherment system has just gone belly-up.

'It's privileged,' she advised him.

'I've stopped hacking for the day.' He continued to read, then asked, 'Did he do it?' When she didn't reply, he said, 'It's a loony letter, right?'

'You'd think so.'

'Which means it's not.'

'It looks as if he knows things he shouldn't know.'

'What?'

'The hair and the clothes.'

'It's not in the same class as a birthmark in the shape of an elephant above her right buttock, is it?'

'Perhaps not; but it's accurate.'

'Could he be guessing? From press reports, or something – creative thinking?'

'Just possible. There's an outside chance that he could be lucky. Some of these nuts like to give detail in the hope that they'll hit the jackpot. We had a confession letter once that mentioned a tattoo on the victim's right shoulder.'

'And she had one.'

'She did.'

'And this was the killer.'

'No, this was a quadriplegic with a voice-activated software programme and a dream of mayhem. The killer was the husband, as we so often find.'

'Or the wife.'

'Or the wife. Poor woman.'

Delaney laughed and moved away to the worktop to open some bag-salad.

'It's an identification thing,' Stella said. 'He wants us to know that it really was him. Wants us to believe.'

'Then why doesn't he turn up in person?'

'He could. The letter might be one step in a sequence. First step.'

'Other steps being?'

'More letters. Phone calls.'

'Why not just keep quiet about it? Why the need to talk?'

'It's a big thing, killing someone. Big thing to keep to yourself.'

Delaney heard the catch in her voice. Stella had killed a man. She hadn't meant to, but when he'd attacked her she'd lashed out with a wheel-nut crank and taken him in the neck. He'd been wearing a new pair of sneakers, bright white, and Stella had always thought of him as Nike Man. When the crank had connected, he'd gone down hard and she had been grateful for that, because another man had been closing fast, intent on hurting her badly.

It was the vagus nerve, she learned later: she wasn't sure of its function, but its location in the neck, apparently, gave it a direct route to the heart. The incident had taken place on the Harefield Estate, a place where you could get scag, flesh and guns; a place where you could get slammed, knifed and shot. Stella had grown up on the estate, but she was no longer at home there.

She had hit the first guy, then run from the second. By the time she found out that her attacker had died, Harefield had taken care of its own: the body had been bagged up, shipped out and rendered down. No fuss. Stella had never reported the incident. Only Delaney knew it had happened.

In the corner of his eye, he saw her empty her glass and look round for a refill. Bad memories bring on bad habits.

They ate the chicken and salad, talking, touching hands now and then; afterwards, they went straight to bed: it was still that fresh between them, still that urgent. It wasn't late, but, after a while, Delaney fell asleep.

The sounds from the street were yells, sirens, parties relocating, the rev and roll of traffic. Stella dozed, slipping in and out of a dream in which Nike Man waved at her from one of the high, bleak walkways on Harefield. He was saying something, but the wind took his words.

Phone me, she shouted up to him. Phone me. I need to speak to you.

Her mobile rang and she picked it up, still carrying the dream in her head. It was Mike Sorley. He said, 'Robert's come to visit.'

6

Robert said his full name was Robert Adrian Kimber. He wasn't eager to give an address, but he was very eager to tell Stella and Harriman and Sorley exactly how it had felt to kill Valerie Blake. It had felt good. It had felt thrilling. In fact, it had felt so special that he wished he could do it all over again.

He smiled when he said this and the smile seemed genuine and open. Stella could see how he would be attractive to women: mid thirties, fair hair parted to flop on the side, a longish face but with regular features, green-grey eyes; perhaps the lips were a little too feminine, pink with a slight pout. No one else was in the squad room at that time, so Harriman had logged on to the national police computer and run Kimber's name through the database – and come up empty.

'So that was why you killed her,' Stella said. 'Because it felt good.'

Kimber nodded; the smile came back. 'Same as before.'

'Before?'

'Same as with the others.'

'Let's talk about the others.' Stella avoided his eyes and kept her voice low: it said, *Tell me anything, tell me everything; I'm here to listen and believe.*

'I like that way of doing it,' Kimber said. 'I reckon that's the best way of doing it.'

'What is?'

'So you're close. Close up. With a gun or a knife . . . well, no, I've never thought about that way. You stand off, don't you? No contact. Bit closer with the knife, perhaps, but it's not that *personal*, is it? Think of a gun, now. You point, like pointing your finger, and you're way back, aren't you? Think of a knife. You've probably got to stab any number of times and so you're busy, aren't you? *Busy*. My way, you're able to see what's going on. You can feel things; you're using your hands. Close up.'

'How did you pick her?'

'Valerie? My Valerie? Well, there she was. You see some-one, you take a shine —'

'Tell me how you happened to find her.'

'On the tube.'

Stella paused. It wasn't what she'd been expecting.

She and Harriman were at the interview table with Kimber. Sorley was sitting in but saying nothing. Inspectors don't make good interrogators: too much time spent pushing paper and balancing budgets. You lose the nose for it; a good liar can hold you off for hours.

Harriman said, 'When was that — on the tube?'

'A while back.'

'You've been following her.' Kimber spread his hands and smiled, confirming the obvious. 'Answer for the tape,' Harriman told him.

'Followed her, yes. Of course.'

'That day? That week?'

'For a while.'

Stella took over. She asked, 'Why?'

'I used to have a place,' Kimber said, 'a place with a big window that looked down on to a street. Busy street. Shops and pubs and so forth. People coming and going most of the time. To and fro. Back and forth. Couples and friends and people on their own. I used to sit there and watch. Yashica seven by thirty-five with a six-point-five degree field.'

'What?'

'Binoculars,' Harriman told her.

'Binoculars. I was about thirty feet up from the street and the glasses brought people right up close. Next to you. As if you could touch. Couples and friends, they're not what you're after. Not really. They're talking to each other, looking at each other, laughing and joking and you're shut out. People on their own, that's different. That's what you're looking for. Singletons. You're beside them. They're walking along and you're there, looking into their faces, reading their expressions, reading their thoughts. They're inside themselves and you can see that. And, if you think about it, there's no other time you can do that, is there? Not even with people you know well.'

'Do what?'

'Study them. Study their faces. Imagine someone walking down the street and you're there – really there – on the street with them, and they're walking forwards and you're walking backwards but just in front of them.' He paused. 'Got the picture?' Stella nodded. 'Just in front of them and looking directly at them. You couldn't do it; they wouldn't let you. Or on the tube and you get up and go to the person opposite and you crouch down and look them right in the face.' He smiled at the self-evident silliness of the idea. 'I shouldn't think anyone's done it ever; I mean, however well you know someone you couldn't just decide to get close, get really close, and look into their face, could you? Anyway, they'd know: they'd react; they wouldn't be themselves. But with the glasses, there you are. Your face next to her face – like nose to nose. The invisible man. And she doesn't know. She hasn't got the slightest idea. Except –'

'Is it –'

Stella started to speak, then tried to check herself when

she realized he hadn't finished. Kimber looked at her, waiting. She looked at him. Face to face, if not quite nose to nose.

'You said "she". Was it always women? When you looked down on the street – always women you watched?'

'Oh, yes. Women, always. Of course.' Stella waited, not wanting to offer a prompt. Finally he said, 'Except . . . yes . . . I was explaining, wasn't I? She doesn't know, the woman in the street, except, sometimes, she can feel you. And she looks round. Like when you stare at someone and eventually they start to look round to see where it's coming from. She does that because she can feel you in the air. She can feel your eyes. And sometimes she looks up, and even though you're really a long way off and she could never find you, your heart leaps because she seems to be looking straight at you.'

He was talking to himself now. Stella and Harriman were sitting very still so as not to break the moment. Sorley was a statue in the corner of the room.

'Then she goes out of sight. She's walking towards you and, at first, you get everything, the way her body moves, the way her breasts move and her hips move and her hair floats a bit in the breeze; then she's just head and shoulders; then it's just her face . . . the binoculars make a circle like a cut-out – a circle of light – and you can't see anything outside of that and her face fills it, and then she's gone. And you can wait for another, I mean, you can probably already see another, especially if the shops are open and it's a weekend or something, but then she'll be gone, and so will the next one, and the next and you wonder what they're doing and where they've gone and what their lives are like when you're not there.'

He closed his eyes, as if picturing the circle of light and the woman walking towards him, then disappearing.

After a moment he opened them and asked for a drink of water. Harriman went to fetch it and Stella announced to the tape that DC Harriman had left the room. She also announced that she was switching off the tape and that it was 12.03 a.m. She and Kimber sat opposite one another, silent and strangely edgy, like actors waiting in the wings, their lines on hold. Sorley shifted on his chair and Kimber looked across as if registering him for the first time. The lights in the room hummed slightly and a phone rang in the outer office, fifteen rings or more before it cut off. Harriman brought water for everyone: a large bottle and four paper cups.

Stella said, 'Twelve fourteen, DC Harriman has entered the room, you saw her on the tube?' It sounded seamless, as if the question had been too long backed-up.

'That's it.'

'And you followed her.'

'I followed lots. You want to know more about them, that's the point. Watching them through the glasses, that's fine and good. That's one thing. It's great because of the nearness, but then you lose them.'

'How many?'

'Lots.'

'Ten?'

'Oh, yes. More.'

'And did you kill them?'

Kimber shook his head, but it wasn't denial. 'I'm not talking about that. Not about them.'

'Okay. Let's talk about when you saw her on the tube. Valerie.'

'Valerie,' Kimber agreed. 'I followed her to her office. So I could go back there any time, any weekday, and wait for her to come out. Then follow her home.'

'Where was that?' Harriman asked.

Kimber gave an address in Penzance Place; it was the right address.

'You followed her when she went jogging,' Harriman observed. 'You jogged along behind her, did you?'

Stella detected the edge in Harriman's voice: irritation or disbelief. She said, 'You knew her routes.'

'Short run: Holland Park. Long run: Hyde Park. I didn't need to go. I could wait until she got back.'

'But you were in the park. She died in the park.'

'Well, I always walked that way to get to her flat. Sometimes I saw her running through. That was wonderful. As if she was coming to find me, you know? Putting herself in my way.'

'You wanted to be up close when you killed her: is that what you said?'

'That's right.'

'Tell me about that.'

'Why not kill her in her flat?' Harriman asked. 'Break in, kill her there.' Stella dropped her head and turned it a fraction to the side, as if Harriman's interruption had arrived on a cloud of bad breath.

Kimber was looking at Stella. He said, 'She had alarms.' Then, 'Up close in the circle of light; up close when she died. How could it be any other way?'

'You took a risk.'

'It was almost dark.'

'There were people about.'

'The park was closing. It was dusk: everyone making for the exits.'

'Other joggers.'

'Joggers don't see anything. They're running. They hear their own breath, they think about the next step. Why do you think it was so easy to catch her?'

'You strangled her.'

'Up close. And you can see the life going. The light going from her eyes; a stillness coming over her.'

Kimber's eyelids drooped. He looked a little dazed.

Stella's voice was low, almost a whisper. 'How did you do that?'

For a moment, Kimber didn't react; then he looked at her, eyes wide, as if startled. 'Do what?'

Stella could see the change. *Lost him.*

'You strangled her.'

'Yes.'

'Tell me how you did that.' Then, in the hope of finding her way back, 'What was it like?'

Kimber folded his arms and placed them on the table, then bent over and rested his head.

He said, 'I'm tired now.'

'If I'm trying to sneak in through the window,' Stella said, 'I'd prefer you didn't kick down the fucking door.'

Harriman shrugged. 'Sorry, Boss. It seemed like a good question at the time.'

'I lost him.'

'He'll talk some more; he's a sicko.'

'You've got him down as a time-waster . . .'

Harriman shrugged. 'He'd been following her, so he'd know her hair colour, know she tied it back when she went jogging.'

'But wouldn't know she'd been stripped.' As if she were reading his mind, she added, 'I know it's slim.'

'What will you do?'

'Call this his statutory rest period, talk to him in the morning.'

'Not charge him?'

'Not yet. We need to find out where he lives: internet

search, listings CD, old-fashioned electoral register. Get down there, toss the place, find something helpful.'

Sorley had gone to his office to sketch a report for the case-log: just the bare bones. They had taken DNA samples with the suspect's permission: a mouth swab. They had suggested he might like to have a solicitor present and told him that they could provide him with one if necessary. The suspect had declined. He had smiled and declined. Sorley made a call to say he was on his way home. He was in a newish second marriage after a bad divorce and was still edgy about the hours he had to keep, since it was absence that had made his first wife's heart grow colder.

He was shrugging into his coat as he went through the squad room. 'Think he did it?' he asked. Before Stella could respond, he said, 'I think he did it.'

Pete Harriman lit one cigarette from the butt of another and hit the speed-dial on his mobile. Like Sorley, he needed to check in; unlike Sorley, he didn't expect complaints. When his call was answered, he said, 'Did I wake you?' There was just enough of a pause for the woman on the other end to say 'Yes' before he added, 'Good. It's so much nicer when you're awake.'

Stella said, 'Nine a.m. briefing. Text everyone.' As Harriman made for the door, she said, 'Sooner rather than later.'

'I'll do it in the cab.'

'You came by cab?'

He smiled. 'You called me at nine thirty. I'd been drinking. In fact, I'm a bit pissed, to tell the truth.'

Which is why you kicked down the door. I understand that.

'Do you think he did it?'

'He stalked her, he knew certain details, he's fucking crazy, so why not?'

'He mentioned others. He said, "Same as with the others."'

'I noticed. We could be closing a whole rack of case-files.'

'Talk to people on the squads that handled those cases. More than that, talk to anyone who's worked on anything like the same MO. Take DC Hewitt with you.'

Harriman smiled. He said, 'Maxine Hewitt. What *is* her story?'

Maxine and Harriman had worked together before and he'd hit on her. No surprise there, but she'd fended him off and he wasn't used to that. Not rejected him outright or turned him off like a tap; just deflected him – a smile, a joke. The joke lay in the fact that Maxine was gay and Harriman hadn't spotted that yet. Stella knew: she'd seen Maxine one night, leaving the movies with a woman. They had kissed on the street: the kind of kiss that goes way beyond skin-deep. Maxine knew that Stella knew, and that was fine; but she didn't go out of her way to tell people any more than Harriman walked into the squad room and said, 'By the way, I fuck women.' Though, in truth, it was a ploy he'd sometimes thought of using.

'You mean the story that doesn't include you,' Stella suggested. 'Maybe she doesn't get wet every time you smile at her.'

'Difficult to believe.'

'It's a first.'

They walked out to the car park. A frost had settled and they could feel the bite of the cold on their faces. There were alarms going off somewhere: the rolling note of a house alarm and a couple of two-tone car alarms. Just part of London's background noise; Stella and Harriman barely registered them.

'She'll be asleep again by the time you get back,' Stella advised him.

'I know. I'll try not to wake her as I go in.'

Harriman laughed at his own double-entendre. He was lighting a cigarette as he walked away. He left black footprints in the frost.

Stella used a credit card to take the worst of the rime off her windscreen and side windows, then sat in the car for a few minutes to give the heater time to work.

Robert Adrian Kimber . . . If you didn't do it, you certainly wanted to. Like a taste, like a smell, like something right at your fingertips.

She gunned the car out of the AMIP-5 car park and the rear wheels took a little shimmy on a patch of black ice.

It was just after 1 a.m. and the streets were busy. People were coming and going at drinking clubs, at casinos, at all-night supermarkets; parties were working up to full volume; there were still vestigial queues outside a couple of dance venues. It was Christmas, and the Christmas story was spend, drink, dance, spend, jack up, spend, enjoy, get down, go down, spend, face off, face down, get off your face and don't forget to spend.

The whores had hearts of gold, frankincense behind their ears and myrrh in the dinky flasks that they kept in their clutch purses next to a strip of condoms and a mobile phone. Snatch purses, they called them. At this time of night, in these temperatures, you could always get a deal: they were happy to get into anyone's car.

Stella drove back to Delaney's flat, past houses that marketed at three million and stood just on the fringe of high-rise estates where the jobless, penniless and hopeless lived in their three-room hutches.

The rich had window-bars and gated estates and direct-link alarms.

The poor had nothing to lose.

When she got in, Delaney was awake, sitting at his laptop, playing old-style jazz, drinking whisky, eating ice-cream. Stella stole his drink and read a couple of the notes he was making for his article.

'Have you got him?' he asked.

'Not sure. Could be. Who are Sadie and Jamie?'

'Street-people.'

Stella tapped him on the arm, then pointed at the window: a view of rooftops and a quarter moon in a cold sky. 'They're out there now.'

'Bound to be.'

'Panhandling the late-nighters, looking for a warm spot over a kitchen-grating.'

'I expect so.'

'Low-tog sleeping-bags in sub-zero temperatures.'

He retrieved his glass and took a sip. 'And here am I in the warm with my single malt getting a series of articles out of it. Well-paid articles. What a shit.'

Stella got a drink of her own: vodka-rocks. Their journo/cop routine wasn't a new thing, nor was it particularly adversarial. Well, a bit, maybe. Just a little edge to it: Hands On vs Hands Off. In life, cops needed journalists, and vice-versa. Cops wanted to manipulate journalists, and vice-versa. Cops went eyeball to eyeball with journalists, and . . .

Stella and Delaney were not blind to the ironies and parallels in all this.

'Maybe you ought to be down there with them,' she said. 'Sleeping out, jacking up, pissing into your bag.'

'I've done all that,' he told her. 'Didn't you notice I'd gone?'

She drank her vodka, pushed his computer across the desk, sat on his lap and kissed him open-mouthed. She said, 'I can't get enough of you.'

Sadie sacked-out over the hotspot by the back door of the Ocean Diner. Jamie was tagging along for the kitchen leftovers, but he wasn't bedding down. He seemed to be always on the move.

'Christmas,' he told Sadie, 'the birth of Our Lord. The time is surely approaching when we will see Him again.'

'Yeah,' Sadie said. 'I'm counting on it.'

'In all His glory.'

'Absolutely.'

'Come to separate the sheep from the goats.'

'Good idea.'

'The Son of God come to send sinners to hell and the righteous to Paradise.'

A sous-chef came out for a smoke and to catch half a minute of the frost-laden air. When he exhaled, the smoke billowed with his breath and seemed to go on for ever. He went back, then re-emerged with the remnants of unfinished meals and a two-thirds-full bottle of Tŷ Nant.

After they had eaten, Sadie turned in her bag and pulled the flap over her head. She'd been trying half the night to make a connection, but she hadn't raised enough money, and her regular dealer, who might have extended a credit deal, wasn't on the street or at home.

'The Son of God,' Jamie asserted, 'born in a stable and risen in glory.'

'Okay,' Sadie said. Neither spoke for a full five minutes, then Sadie added: 'You know what, Jamie? Fuck the Son of God.'

7

Duncan Palmer was raw-eyed and looked a little ragged round the edges. You might have put it down to jet-lag, were it not for the fact that his girlfriend had been murdered. Sue Chapman had phoned to let him know that Stella and Harriman would be arriving at ten; even so, he took a long time to get to the door. He was wearing grey sweats – like Valerie's, Stella thought – and his hair was up in a coxcomb: not a fashionable cut but the result of having just climbed out of bed.

Stella's thoughts extended to: *So you slept well.* And, as if answering her, he said, 'America: the flight out's no problem; coming back's a killer.' He took them into the kitchen, switched on the kettle and put coffee into a big cafetière. As if it were an afterthought, he said, 'Okay to talk in here?'

'It's fine,' Stella said. 'Wherever you like.'

'In here, then . . . get some coffee.'

They sat on metal café chairs round a metal fretwork table. The kitchen was yellow and green, and there were occasional Italian tiles with fruit and vegetable paintings. It looked as if it had been copied from a lifestyle magazine.

Stella said, 'We want to say how sorry we are about Valerie.' It was textbook and often brought tears. Even if it did, you still watched them; you tried to look through the grief.

Palmer didn't cry. He nodded as if in agreement. He said, 'I can't take it in. It doesn't seem real.' Also textbook.

Harriman said, 'We know you were in the States. It's just

elimination: same for everyone that was close to her. Don't worry.'

Palmer got up and left the room.

Harriman looked at Stella and shrugged. She got up and took a tour of the kitchen. Palmer lived in a Kensington redbrick; the windows looked straight down a narrow road to the big high street stores, the crowds, the inch-by-inch traffic. The intersection allowed just a cut of the action: fifty feet maybe. Stella could see a panhandling Santa outside a designer clothes store, offering his good-cause box to the passers-by. She watched until Palmer came back, and Santa hadn't made a single hit.

Palmer put a small appointments diary down on the table in front of Harriman, then crossed the room to add hot water to the coffee. 'My time in New York,' he said. 'Breakfasts, lunches, dinners, office and boardroom meetings. It was a full schedule. Will you catch him?'

'We'll try,' Stella said. 'We hope to.' Then, as an afterthought, 'We expect to.'

'But you don't always.'

'Not always.'

Harriman asked about arguments, enemies, resentments, grudges: the textbook coming out again. Palmer crossed all the boxes: none of these. 'It's a random killing, isn't it?' he asked. 'A crazy person.'

'We're not sure,' Harriman told him. 'We're looking at that.'

'All the attacks on women recently.'

'I know. We are looking at that.'

Stella said, 'Did Valerie wear a chain, or a chain with something on it? I mean something she always wore: in bed, in the shower, when she was jogging?'

'A cross.'

'Can you describe it to me?'

'A plain gold cross on a gold chain.'

'Was it a religious thing?'

'No. Well, only in the sense that it was a cross. But Valerie wasn't religious. I think she'd always had it: from when she was a kid, I expect.'

'A confirmation present, perhaps.'

'Sort of thing. It had her initials on the reverse – VB.' The line of questioning caught up with Palmer abruptly. 'He stole it?'

'Yes.'

'How do you know?'

'He . . . pulled it. Left a mark.'

The information seemed to bring Palmer suddenly closer to Valerie's death: its nature, its detail. He half turned and looked away. Then he said, 'That would be after she died.'

'I would think so,' Stella said.

'Why would he do that? Not to sell it?'

'No.'

Palmer thought for a moment, then said, 'Keepsake.' When Stella didn't respond, he added, 'Yes. That would be it.' Then he said the weirdest thing. 'Something to remember her by.'

Palmer walked them back through the living room to the door. Harriman was out in the hall and Stella halfway there, when Palmer said, 'Was she raped?' He asked it in a low voice, almost a whisper, as if it was something that might remain a confidence between them.

'We're not sure,' Stella said. Then, 'It's possible.' She didn't mention Valerie's near-nakedness, the sweats found a little way off. Palmer nodded. Stella stepped back into the room as she added, 'There had to be a post-mortem. I don't think it'll be possible for you to see her.'

49

'See her?'

'To say goodbye.'

'Oh, yes.' Palmer backed off a little: Stella's move back into the room had brought her close to him, inside his body-space. He said, 'She's gone, though, hasn't she? Why say goodbye to someone who's already gone?'

Palmer's flat was five minutes from the park. As Stella and Harriman emerged, a string of joggers went by, then a woman on her own, pacy and stylish in Lycra leggings and a washed-out pink-and-grey top. Valerie Blake in another life. Harriman put the key into the ignition, but Stella motioned him to stop.

'When you look out of his window,' she said, 'there's a clear view front and left, but there's a plane tree off to the right. See?'

Harriman turned to look. 'Okay. And –?'

'Drive round the block and park on the blind side of the tree.' Harriman drove, waiting to be told why. When he parked, Stella bent down in her seat to check the eyelines. 'I doubt he noticed the car, even so . . . he can't see you from the window, but you can see the street door. You might have a bit of a wait.'

'Go on.'

'There's a woman in his flat.'

Harriman was silent for a moment, thinking back to what he might have missed; finally he asked, 'How do you know?'

'He was wearing her perfume.'

'What?'

'I don't mean intentionally. It was on him; he smelled of her. It was in the air, but when I got close to him, it was stronger . . . skin-contact made it more pungent.'

'I didn't smell it.'

'That's what forty a day will do for you.'

'So where was she?'

'In the bedroom. Where else?'

'I haven't got a camera,' Harriman warned her.

'Well, I think it'll be pretty easy to find out who she is.'

'How?'

'We'll ask the bastard – when we're ready.'

Robert Adrian Kimber was talking technique: how you picked your mark, how you stayed with her, close but discreet, how you paced things by having several in hand at the same time so you could switch and change if one of the sisterhood seemed to notice you. He used those terms: *in hand*; *sisterhood*. Stella was running the interview, with DS Jack Cuddon sitting in. She said, 'We need an address, Robert. We need to know where you live.'

'People often walk looking at the ground,' Kimber said; 'have you ever noticed that? Looking at the ground or looking straight ahead. Getting where they're going. Sometimes a woman will stop, though: something catches her eye, something in a shop window, something she wants. It's tricky. Do I stop too? Do I walk past and wait?'

'You say you killed Valerie Blake.'

'That's it, you see. That's the culmination. That's the end of things: the first meeting.' He smiled at her, then at Cuddon, and the smile became a chuckle. Cuddon's eyes were dark with anger.

Stella said, 'How did you do that? Kill her.'

'She was strangled – you know that.'

'Yes. So she was jogging . . . you were – what? – waiting for her?'

'I knew where she went. I knew the route.'

'What was she wearing? Do you remember that?'

'Running clothes.'

'What?'

'Jogging gear.'

'Can you tell me the colour?'

'She always wore the same.'

'Did she? What was it?'

'The usual thing.'

Stella paused for a moment. She was biting the inside of her cheek. The tape spooled on. Kimber wore the trace of a smile; he looked at Stella and nodded, as if to encourage her.

'What made it different, Robert? You follow her, you like doing that. Why kill her?'

'There were others to follow.'

'But why kill her?'

'The first meeting,' Kimber said, as if she might not have heard the first time, 'that's the end of everything.'

'So you're waiting, you've picked your place, she comes by, she's running –'

'Looking at the ground,' Kimber offered, 'or straight ahead.'

'Okay. Then what?'

'You know what.'

'Yes, but I need to hear it from you.'

'She was strangled, wasn't she?'

'Detail. I'm asking for detail.'

'What sort of detail?'

'How you killed her, how difficult was it, did she struggle?' Stella knew she was leading too strongly: this wouldn't be a good tape to take into court. 'She was attractive, wasn't she?'

'My Valerie? Oh, yes.'

'The place where you killed her –'

'Among trees. Trees and bushes.'

'No one could see.'

'No one.'

'Did you rape her?'

A silence fell. The tape-spool gave a little creak. Cuddon closed his eyes. He could hear sounds in the silence, as if the air were chafing against the walls.

'That's pretty personal, isn't it?' Kimber asked. He sounded affronted. 'That's pretty personal stuff.'

They took a break. Cuddon punched the wall hard enough to make Stella wince. He said, 'That prick. That shitehawk.'

'You'd like to have him humanely destroyed.'

'Well . . . destroyed.'

Cuddon went to the coffee machine. On the other side of the room, Maxine Hewitt was raiding the AMIP-5 chocolate hoard. The coffee was a cruel practical joke that everyone kept falling for. Andy Greegan was sitting at his workstation with his head in his hands; he'd been running through lists of names and addresses from the internet, from the register of voters, from a listings CD called Info-04. He said something indecipherable as Stella walked past his desk. Maxine lobbed her a Twix and raised a questioning eyebrow.

'DC Robson's with him,' Stella said. 'He's playing games.'

'The same games?'

'The same. As soon as you get to details, he starts side-stepping.' Stella shrugged. 'I'm going to have to charge him or let him go.'

Andy Greegan spoke again but louder. He said, 'I think I know where this guy lives.' He still had his head in his hands and he sounded like a man speaking from under a mudslide. 'The name's right, including the middle name. Must be him. He's on Harefield.'

Stella said, 'How did you get him?'

'Utilities. Electricity, to be specific. He doesn't vote: not a good citizen.' Even from a distance, the high flush in Greegan's cheeks was noticeable.

'Print it out and go home.'

Greegan shook his head. 'I'll be all right, Boss.'

'Go home,' Stella told him, 'you've got the flu.'

Greegan clicked 'print'. It took him a while to get the mouse-pointer settled because of the shivers chasing down from his shoulders. He said, 'You're right. I feel like shit. I'm really ill.'

Stella flapped a hand at him. 'Get out of here, Andy, for Christ's sake; you're a fucking germ factory.'

Mike Sorley glanced through the interview transcripts, stopping briefly to read more carefully the passages that Stella had highlighted.

He said, 'He's taking the piss.'

'I know. Still think he did it?'

'He had information not contained in any press release. I like him for it, yes.'

'Okay, well, we've had him for fourteen hours. He's due another rest period. It looks like I'll be asking you for an extension. And a search warrant: we've got his address.'

'There was a time,' Sorley said dolefully, 'when a confession would do it for you. The guy owned up: that was that; a couple of hours in court, then straight to the gallows. Case solved, on to the next.'

'The good old days,' Stella observed.

'One less on the streets.'

'And if he didn't do it?'

Sorley shrugged. 'They've all done something.'

8

Between the street and the treble-racked, four-sided arrangement of high-rise blocks that made up the Harefield Estate
was a no man's land that Stella thought of as the demili-
tarized zone. The DMZ. It was a little waste land littered
with waste objects that spoke of wasted lives: gutted cars;
white goods leaking their CFCs; soft furnishings soaking up
the weather; a ground-cover of fast-food cartons and used
syringes and condoms and cola cans that had doubled as
crack pipes. The tower blocks were arranged round a circular
space known locally as the bull ring. When Stella had lived
there, her mother would send her down eighteen storeys to
the convenience store for groceries and a quarter of vodka.
Nowadays, the shopfronts in the bull ring were boarded and
graffitied, save for a KFC and a liquor store. You could still
get the vodka.

For some, Harefield was simply a place to live: they got
by as best they could by hearing nothing, seeing nothing
and saying less. They behaved as if they were under martial
law; under curfew. For others, the place was a vast business-
incentive scheme. The businesses in question included dealing drugs, dealing flesh, dealing cards. There were specialist
outlets for passports and visas. Armourers were finding
business so hot they were waging a price war. The dealers
were on the landings, the whores were on a rota system,
and the spirit of free enterprise, like the spirit of Christmas,
was in the air, bringing the scent of money.

Two vehicles stopped in the bull ring: the first a car carrying Stella, Pete Harriman and Jack Cuddon, who was doubling for Andy Greegan, the second a people carrier bringing a forensics team. Some spare uniforms would be along later to secure the flat. Stella got out and felt a little lurch of alarm, as if the ground had dipped beneath her. The bull ring was where Nike Man had died – Stella backed up against a car, a second man closing in, and a hot reflux of fear rising in her gullet. The wheel-nut crank had been in the well between the seats, and she had swung it without picking her target. A couple of inches higher and her man might have survived; and couple of inches lower, and he'd have shrugged it off for sure.

She looked up and saw faces on the high walkways, the estate's foot-soldiers in their uniform of estate chic: baggies, hoodies, beanies. They stood unmoving, watching, confident on home ground. Cops came to the estate often, but they would be Drugs Squad or Vice Squad or the SO19 gun team: and mostly they would be expected. The Harefield Estate operators understood that good business practice involved a little industrial espionage. A pay-off here in exchange for a phone call there and, overnight, product would be shifted. Product and livestock. These cops weren't here to raid. The soldiers knew that. They were the wrong side of the DMZ for sure, but, as long as they kept their distance, things would be fine.

You can name buildings after local dignitaries or poets or Cumbrian lakes. The man who'd designed Harefield was a realist. The blocks went from A to L. Stella and Harriman stepped out of the lift in Block C and on to the walkway of Floor 16; they were looking for Flat 31. Two dudes sat on the walkway rail, their backs to the sheer drop, sharing a spliff.

They said, 'Hey, motherfucker. Hey, bitch.' That was as far as it went.

The sound of a Hatton gun taking out the door-hinges of 16/31 went round the circle of tower blocks: sharp echoes hanging in the air. Kimber's flat was stone cold. Everyone in the team was wearing white coveralls, and Jack Cuddon was doing Andy Greegan's job of organizing an uncorrupted path from the door to the search site. The flats were basic clones: a passageway from the front door led to one or two bedrooms, a living room, a kitchen. But you can customize any space – make it your own, make your mark.

Pete Harriman walked into Kimber's living room and stopped dead. He said, 'Holy Christ.'

Stella joined him; she said, 'This guy's a case. He's a real *case.*'

Harriman stood in the centre of the room and did a slow revolve. The walls were black and they were papered with ten by eight candid-camera shots: all women, all young, none of them posing or smiling for the camera because they weren't aware that they were being photographed. A space had been left beneath each photo where Kimber had used a pen with silver ink to record the time, the date, and then to give to each an embellishment, a little story. His handwriting was small and fastidiously neat, the lines evenly spaced. If you stood a little way off, you might be persuaded that this was design: wallpaper that borrowed its ideas from the photograph album; a touch retro-chic for a sink estate, perhaps, but hey . . .

Then you might take time to read what was written; you might read the *details*.

'Kimber, you sick fuck,' Harriman said.

Stella was looking at the pictures.

A woman sitting at a pavement-café table, smoking, staring at nothing in particular, her hair drifting across her cheek.

A woman sunbathing in the park, the camera taking in a long length of leg and probing under her skirt.

A woman peering into a restaurant, searching for a friend maybe, her own reflection looking back at her.

A woman walking down the street, all purpose and urgency, her coat making wings either side, her hair flying.

A woman on a park bench leaning back to drink from a bottle of water, her throat arched, sunlight among the water as it flowed.

A woman preparing to dress a naked mannequin in a clothes-shop window, her arms round the dummy from behind, her face looking over its shoulder.

A woman leaning forward to attend to a child in a buggy, her blouse falling forward, the soft slope of her breasts.

And women framed in windows at night, or at dusk, some part-clothed, some naked, some in motion so slightly blurred, some on the far side of the room so muddled with reflections, some removing clothes so indistinct, some closing the curtains so sharp and defined. Many such women ... though it would have taken time and trouble to find them and catch them like that: trapped for a moment inside their own lives.

Times and dates logged ... and then the little stories, which were brief and dark and terrifying; stories of blood and pain and desecration. As Stella read them, they dizzied her; her throat tightened and the blood sang in her ears.

'You think he did any of this stuff?' Harriman was reading too.

'I don't know.' She shuddered. 'Jesus Christ, I hope not.'

'We can check some of them. Some of them have names.'

*

58

Jack Cuddon was going from room to room like a man with a purpose, but, in truth, it was just nervous energy taking him forward. He was muttering to himself. Stella could feel the anger – as if he were shedding flakes of fire. He stared at the photographs in turn. He read the vile little stories word by word. He was breathing through his mouth like a man who had just stepped off a running track.

He said, 'This is bad. This guy has to go down.'

Stella was staring at a photograph of a woman who was turning to look over her shoulder, almost as if she had spotted her follower or heard the sound of the shutter-release. The movement had brought her into half-profile, the curve of her breast, the sweep of her hip; her dark hair was back in a pony-tail and she had clean, delicate planes to her face, a small, straight nose.

Harriman moved to stand next to her. He said, 'It's Valerie Blake.'

In the bedroom, they found more photographs, both on the walls and in a long row of albums. They found a laptop computer. They found locks of hair, fifty or so, arranged on a black display card, time and date carefully recorded.

They found a notebook.

9

```
I will call this one Anthea.
I will call this one Beatrice.
I will call this one Cherie.
I will call this one Davina.
```

The book was spiral bound and close ruled. The writing was as neat and evenly spaced as the writing on the walls. There were faint traces of dusting-powder on the covers. Forensics had done a rush job on the book, principally for DNA samples; Stella would let them have it back for dye and heat tests, ink analysis and so forth. It was a book you could buy in any stationer's and the ink was fine-point fibre-tip.

Harriman turned up at her desk with bad-joke coffee and a couple of report-sheets. She said, 'Who's cross-referencing the women in the pictures?'

'Maxine and Sue. They're getting some help from the indexers.'

'Tell them that the names are not likely to help much. He's naming them himself: going through the alphabet.'

'Some might be right.'

'Might be. But, if not, there's nothing to go on except the faces; in other words, nothing to go on.'

'The missing persons files.'

'Missing persons with no names to match.' She picked up his report-sheets and glanced at them. 'How long before she came out?'

'Two hours. Let me tell you how many people knocked on the car window and complained about pollution.'

'You had the engine running.'

'Two hours? An airflow coming in straight from the Arctic. They're calling it an ice-wind; listen to the weather forecast.'

'Duncan Palmer lives in a very middle-class area. People recycle; they ride bikes.'

'They drive fucking great SUVs that never see a rock or a patch of mud.'

Stella was reading Harriman's description. 'Tall, sexy, blonde, slim.'

'I didn't say sexy.'

'It's between the lines.' She put the report down. 'You followed her to where she lives?'

'She went back to Palmer's flat.'

'Did she now. And before that –?'

'Went shopping. Picked up some bits and pieces in a food hall: something for the rest of the day. Pâté, pasta, salad, two swordfish steaks. And etcetera. Me next in the queue with my cheese and pickle sandwich.'

'Then she went back.'

'No. She went to a place called Filigree. It's a jeweller's in the Hypermarket. She was looking at a 1950s Rolex Oyster.'

'Did she buy it?'

'They're trying to find her a Patek Philippe, whatever that is.'

'Did she give a price range?'

'Up to fifteen hundred.'

'No kidding . . .' Stella picked up Harriman's report again and glanced at it, as if for confirmation. 'A Christmas present,' she said.

'Could be for her father, brother . . .'

'For her husband.'

'There's a thought,' Harriman agreed.

'But we think it might be for Duncan Palmer, don't we?'

'We're thinking along those lines.'

'Did you get her name?'

'They took her number and said they'd call her. Lauren Buchanan.'

'What were you supposed to be doing?'

'Browsing. The place was pretty full: it's Christmas. She didn't notice me, don't worry.' He paused a moment, then added, 'Listen, he was in America. The appointments check out. A few cancellations, but nothing that would give him time to get back to England.'

'I know,' Stella said. Then, 'Men can be bastards, can't they?'

'I don't know,' Harriman said. 'Why ask me?'

The DNA reports from the scene of crime and from the post-mortem were still backed up in Forensics. Stella called the lab and asked for a cross-check on Kimber's mouth swab. She was told it was going to take time. The guy on the phone sounded weary.

'How much time?' Stella asked.

'Difficult to say.'

'How difficult?'

'It's a process, you know? A process. Also it stands in line.'

'What's your name?'

'Davison.'

'Okay, Davison. This is a murder case and I've got a suspect – good suspect, really handy – but there's a problem. He's confessed.'

'That's lousy luck.'

'Yes, it is. I've got some promising circumstantial evidence but nothing to nail it down with. You've got the DNA reports from the scene of crime and you've got the suspect's DNA.'

'Which scene of crime?'

'Valerie Blake.'

'That wasn't me.'

'What?'

'I didn't do the work on that. Might have been processed, might not.'

'But it's there. Someone's got it. I mean, it's in the lab, isn't it?'

'Oh, yes. But it's not me.'

'In about three hours, I'm going to have to ask for a superintendent's custody extension on the guy; after that, I'll have to go to a magistrate and I might not get what I want. If I release him without charge and you come back some time later with the information that his DNA's all over the victim and all over the scene of crime, I'm going to be unhappy.'

'And you are –'

'Detective Sergeant Mooney.'

'Tom.'

'What?'

'My first name: Tom. What's yours?'

'Are you flirting with me, Davison?'

'I don't know. What colour underwear have you got on?'

'Black,' Stella said. 'Lacy thong. Silk panels.'

'Phone me in the morning.'

When Stella looked up, Sue Chapman was standing a few feet away and smiling. She said, 'Don't you find they ride up?'

'I'm wearing M & S. There's a "process", it seems, and I want a quick result. Forensics should get out more.'

'We've been in touch with the teams handling the other attacks. No matches that we can find. We've covered attacks further afield, too, and murders of women going back five years. If the faces are among Kimber's photos, we can't see them. No luck with missing persons either, not so far; but that's a much bigger job. You asked me to update you.'

'Keep them looking.'

'About two hundred and ten thousand people are reported missing each year,' Sue said. 'Most return within seventy-two hours, but that still leaves twenty thousand. A lot of those are kids; some are men. Bring it down to women under thirty-five living in London and the south-east and, okay, you're only talking about three thousand but he had a couple of hundred photos in that flat. Trying to make a match –'

'I know it's a long shot.'

Sue started back towards her own desk, then paused a moment; she turned and spoke from where she was. 'The thing is . . . you look at Kimber's pictures – those women being spied on. They don't know they're being watched. There they are, wearing their everyday faces. Then you look at the missing persons shots and they're a section out of a family photo more often than not: a holiday snap or something taken at a party; and they're laughing or smiling at the camera.' Stella waited. 'You've got the private face and the public face, haven't you? They don't look like each other.'

'You're right,' Stella said. 'I know you're right.' She went back to Kimber's diary. 'Keep them at it.'

10

I will call this one Anthea.
I will call this one Beatrice.
I will call this one Cherie.
I will call this one Davina.

I could be anyone thats the point. Davina walking down the street she thinks whos following
me? She turns around to look. There are twenty
people following her. Fifty. A whole streetfull
of people. I could be anyone.

Look at how she walks my Elaine. My Fenella.
Look at how things move. You can get in front sometimes and watch her go by then drop back again to
let her lead the way. You can take risks let her
go round a corner and out of sight then find her
again.

She stops for a coffee or she goes to a park with
her lunch to catch the sun or she stops to look at
something in a shop or she stands by the side of
the road waiting for a cab.

You can be a long way off. You can be almost out
of sight. Fast telephoto lens 500mm F4 800 ISO
film. Its as good as binoculars you get right up
close.

See her make a cup of her hands to shield the
flame when she lights a cigerette.

See her undo the top two buttons of her blouse

and hitch her skirt up to her thigh turning to put her face to the sun.

See her put out her tongue to catch a drop of mayonase that falls out of her sandwhich down along the side of her hand.

See her hook back some hair that the wind has blown across her face when she sits with her knees up reading her book.

The book is called *Experience* thats how good the lens is. Thats how close I can get.

See how she sits crosslegged in those jeans her hands resting between her legs the croptop the little pucker-up of her belly the silver ring.

This is where she lives my Gina. My Harriet. Now I know I can come back and find her here. Come back tonight. You need fast film. You need somewhere to stand.

Important to work out the gography. Wheres the bedroom? Wheres the bathroom? And the timing thats important. When does she go to bed? Does she take a shower in the morning or at night?

~~If she lives with a man~~

~~If she lives~~

If someone else is around I wait. I bide my time. If she draws the curtains I wait. I bide my time. If she goes out again if she gets into her car if a taxi calls I wait. I bide my time.

See her in the bedroom as she goes back and forth unbutoning shaking her hair free.

See her in the bedroom in her panties and her bra deciding what to wear.

See her in the bedroom turning naked thinking that perhaps she ought to draw the curtains. Maybe coming over to draw the curtains. Now she comes over.

See her in the bathroom the window a little foggy. The windows not overlooked. Why worry?

Or you can go up to the Strip. Sometimes I go up to the Strip. The girls on the Strip are okay for some things but theres nothing secret about them. Nothing private. I fuck them. I fuck them really hard and I make them do things and thats OK but you cant really get close to them because they can see you. You can fuck them but you cant get right up close like you can with the binoculars or the supertelephoto. You can fuck them and there giving it come on come on baby thats great and there right in your face but it doesnt matter who you are. Theres one called Nancy is what she says shes called. Ive used her a few times. Shes got a room upon the Strip. They dont all have rooms some want to do you in the car or in a doorway. Some go into the cemetry. They suck you off there just inside the gate. I tried following her but it didnt work. There wasnt any danger in it. Danger for her I mean. I followed her back to where she lives and I took a photo through the window but what good was that when she had already taken her clothes off in front of me? Also they are prostitutes and anybody can do anything they want to them.

See my Irene walking to the tube station. I'm a long way off. Supertelephoto 500 F4. Long way off and right up close. See the way the wind lifts her hair.

I will call this one Jennifer.
I will call this one Katherine.
I will call this one Lavinia.

I I

Stella and Maxine Hewitt passed Jack Cuddon on their way to the interview room. 'He's had a chicken curry,' he told them, 'and he's had his rest period and he's all yours.'

Stella started the tape, gave the date and time, then announced herself and Maxine. She let Kimber know that they'd found his flat and they'd looked at the walls. He smiled at her. She told him they'd found the locks of hair. He smiled again. He said, 'Is that all you found?'

A breath of the ice-wind crept into the room. 'What did I miss?'

'My little keepsake.'

It was the same word that Duncan Palmer had used. Stella let the tape run. She could feel the pulse in her own wrist. 'A keepsake —'

'Valerie's cross. Gold cross on a chain. Gold chain.'

Stella lowered her head as if in thought; she was pacing herself, trying not to rush him or offer a lead. When she looked up, she asked, 'Where is it?'

Kimber smiled at her, then redirected the smile to Maxine. He looked pleased and excited. 'Where is it?' he said. 'That's for me to know.'

They went back to the flat with a full crew; they took the place apart. Maxine went as a fresh pair of eyes. She looked at the photos on the walls and what was written beneath them. She didn't speak until she and Stella were back in the car. Then she said, 'It's a man's world.'

They'd pretty much dismantled the flat and everything in it. Under the floorboards they'd found a collection of dull porno tapes and a trunk-tracking police-base scanner, but they hadn't found a gold cross on a gold chain.

'He knows about it, that's the important thing. The jogging sweats and the chain.'

'He was logging police calls,' Sorley said. 'He's got a hundred-channel, twelve-band Bearcat scanner, for Christ's sake. He probably knew what the scene of crime guys were *thinking*. Look at the transcripts. See if there's anything on them about the sweats and the chain.'

'There couldn't be anything about the chain. Sam Burgess picked up on that and Duncan Palmer confirmed it later.'

'About the sweats, then.'

'He did it,' Stella said. 'He's playing a game. Maybe he thinks he can withdraw the confession later, get a smart counsel.'

'Has he signed a statement?'

Stella shook her head. 'That's something else . . . he's teasing. But the chain's real evidence: on the tape, loud and clear.'

'DNA,' Sorley observed. 'That's *real* evidence.' He glanced at his watch and lit a cigarette. Stella wondered whether the two events were causally connected: a sixteen-hour, forty-cigarette day would allow him a cigarette every twenty-four minutes. He looked hungry for it. 'What else do we know about this guy – apart from the fact that he's a self-confessed killer?'

'Nothing. No form, no social services record. He lives up on Harefield. His neighbours have collective amnesia. But it's not his background I need to know about.'

'No?' Sorley drew on his cigarette so hard that his cheeks dimpled. 'What, then?'

'How he thinks.'

'And –?'

'There's someone who might be able to tell me about that.'

'A friend of his?'

'She's never met him.'

Anne Beaumont spread copies of the forensic search-site photos of Kimber's flat out on her conservatory table and looked at them one by one, moving as someone moves at an art exhibition: comparing, judging, looking for continuity and style. Photos of photos; they took in three or four areas of wall and were sufficiently detailed to make legible the stories Kimber had written beneath.

Stella asked, 'You read the book?'

Kimber's journal had been scanned into a computer and printed out.

'I did. I'd sooner have seen the book itself. I'm not a graphologist, but there are certain signs that can't be missed.'

'He's very neat.'

'That's one of the signs.'

'He had a computer. Why would he write this in a notebook rather than use a word processor?'

'More personal. Also it's unique. I suspect he likes the process of writing these things down in longhand, likes forming the letters. Handwriting's sensual. Here's another thing: no one can hack in.'

Anne Beaumont was a shrink; also a criminal-profiler. For a short time she had been Stella's shrink, when a case had collided with Stella's personal life with all the velocity and concomitant damage of a car-crash. That relationship was over, though Stella always used Anne as a profiler if she needed one and if the budget allowed. She liked Anne's wryness and her sharp sense of humour; she liked the fact that her approach to life was on a nil-bullshit basis.

'What can you tell me?'

'Well, first off, he's a collector. Trophy-hunter. In the days of washing-lines he'd've been stealing underwear. He puts the women up on the wall – on display – like the heads of buffalo or antelope in the trophy room of a man who shoots big game. He's captured them. Same with the locks of hair.'

'How did he do that?' Stella wondered. 'How did he get close enough to cut their hair?'

'You think he did it after they were dead?'

'There's no evidence for that. Fifty locks of hair – fifty deaths, all unnoticed? It's not possible.'

'In the movies,' Anne suggested. 'Sitting behind them on a bus. In a crowded tube. Simply walking close behind in the street. The hair might not belong to the women he regularly stalked. In effect, he's collecting two different kinds of trophy: a lock of hair – which is one sort of capture, a token – or else he's stalking – when he gets not a token but the woman herself.'

'People would see him do it: cutting the hair.'

'You'd be surprised at how little people see. Ever see.'

'What about the things he writes under the photos?'

'Yeah . . . Twisted bastard.'

'Is that a detached psychoanalytical assessment?'

'About as detached as I felt when I read them.' Anne paused. 'They represent a slight problem, in that collectors are usually pretty harmless. They possess the item instead of the person. Of course, things can go from bad to much worse. This guy's collecting is tied in with stalking and there are classic escalation patterns involved in that activity. I'm interested in the way he keeps talking about being up close, liking to be close, using binoculars and the long lens.'

Stella mentioned what Kimber had said in interview: how the binoculars brought him almost nose to nose with his quarry; that he was the invisible man; the way a woman might look up as if she had sensed him watching.

'Yes,' Anne said. 'It's all about power. How are you? How's John Delaney?'

Stella smiled. In their patient–shrink days, Anne had often asked unprofessional questions; Stella had come to recognize it as professional trickery. 'I think we're okay. Lots of sex. Is that a good sign?'

'Who cares? Have you moved in together?'

'No.'

'Why not?'

'I have a feeling that we'd need more space. There's something adversarial about the way we joke with each other.'

'Is there? God, Freud would have loved that.'

'Is he a killer? Did he kill Valerie Blake? Has he killed others?'

'I'm an analyst, not a crystal-gazer.'

'Is it likely?'

'It's possible. Look, some stalkers set out to oppress their victims, they hang about, make a nuisance of themselves, they phone, they send letters, they apply pressure. Others begin by simply following. It's a way of being intimately involved with someone without their knowledge, a bit like contact-free rape. Then they want to get closer. This guy talks about that all the time. When he says he's the invisible man, he's enjoying a common power fantasy. Where is he – the invisible man? He's in the next seat on the bus, he's breathing down her neck in the street, he's slipping in with her when she enters her flat, he's in the bedroom when she undresses, in the bathroom when she takes a bath. Ever had that sort of thought yourself?'

Stella shook her head, then said, 'I suppose so.'

'Everyone has at some time or another. Following is a physical manifestation of the fantasy. Obviously, you have to be disturbed to take things that extra step; and the real problem arrives when intimacy at a distance isn't enough.'

Anne's consulting rooms were in Kensington Gore opposite the park, a first-floor room with high windows and lightly scented with fresh flowers. There were a few books but not textbooks; there were two big abstracts – planes of soft colour combined with harsh, white spaces; there was a small wire sculpture of a leaping hare. No trace of any influence in the room save hers.

'Why has he confessed?' Stella asked.

'Because he did it?'

'Well, he knows about her clothes – the jogging things, sweats, that she wasn't wearing them, and he knows about the gold cross and chain she was wearing: actually, he says he took it.'

'You're not sure, though.'

'It's shaky; it's not difficult to dispute. He hasn't asked for a lawyer, so we haven't been challenged on specifics yet.' She paused. 'I'd like to have him for it.'

'I bet you would.' Anne went out of the room and returned with a bottle of wine and two glasses. 'I call it the Judas Syndrome,' she said. 'Confessing is also unburdening, isn't it, in the Catholic sense? The religious sense.'

Stella took the offered glass and sipped her wine. 'What usually happens is that we get a few crazies calling in and owning up. Some are just nuts: we hand them over to social services. Others haven't got the first idea how the crime was committed, or where, or when. A few are up to speed but shaky on small essentials. Now and then, we get someone who's pretty convincing, which is why we usually keep back some detail or another.'

'It's a form of glory-seeking,' Anne observed. 'For a time, they'll be the person they claim to be: the ruthless killer, the rapist, whatever, and they'll get all the attention that goes with it, but they'll hope to be found out. Generally speaking they retract, don't they?'

'Yes. Anyway, you never hear of anyone going to trial on a confession, not these days. If there's no independent evidence, they're likely to walk. Robert Kimber would have been shown the door a while back if it wasn't for the fact that he seemed to know things he shouldn't.'

'And now you've got this stuff: the photos, the horror stories in silver copperplate.' Anne got up and began to roam among the young women Kimber had snapped and captured, pausing now and then to read, her expression bleak.

'Whether he did it or not,' she said, 'he'd be better off dead.'

John Delaney was trying to avoid patterns: patterns made him feel boxed in. He wasn't used to someone coming home and he wasn't used to this evening-meal routine and he wasn't used to cooking it. He called Stella's mobile and got her just as she was parking. He said, 'We're eating out.'

The sky was clear and the pavements were slick with frost. London generates its own heat, but even that big city glow couldn't keep the temperature above zero. The cold amplified sound: sirens three streets away, a store alarm, a little chorus of car alarms like the call-and-answer patterns of exotic birds.

They went to a Chinese place just six doors down from Delaney's flat. The waiters greeted him as if he'd been away too long. The restaurant was warm and cluttered and noisy. Stella told him about the trophy walls in Kimber's flat and the locks of hair taped to display boards. She was still worried about the technique involved in that.

'On a bus,' Delaney suggested. 'At the movies.'

'That's what Anne Beaumont said.'

'Who?' Then he remembered: Stella's shrink when she was having dreams of dead babies and drinking too much and seeing Delaney but still living with George Paterson.

'She asked about you.'

'What did you say?'

'I told her you're a great fuck.'

'Did she need to know that?'

'She's interested in my well-being.'

'Which involves your orgasm count . . .'

'Who's counting?'

'What did she say about your crazy person?'

'Did I say he was crazy?'

'He walked into a police station and confessed to a crime – how sane is that?'

'She mentioned something called the Judas Syndrome.'

Delaney looked delighted. 'She called it what?' He took out a small notebook and wrote the term on a blank page.

'It's a piece, isn't it?' Stella asked. 'You can see a piece in it. Well, you can't have my profiler.'

'I bet she'd be intrigued to meet me, knowing what a great fuck I am.'

A waiter arrived and they ordered what they always ordered: both the food and the wine. Delaney recognized it as a pattern and it made him edgy. Stella called the waiter back and asked for water chestnuts.

'You don't like water chestnuts,' Delaney observed.

'They're not for me, they're for you.' Stella could recognize a pattern as well as anyone.

'Actually, it's not your profiler I'm after, though she'd be good background. The piece would have to contain a Judas point of view.'

'Dream on.'

'If you release him, he's free to talk to anyone, even me. If you charge him and he goes to trial, I'd have to wait, but I could do the groundwork – the investigation, the confession, the trial.'

'It's too close to home.'

'Therein lies my advantage.'

He smiled his off-centre smile, which normally did the trick but, just now, brought a little rush of anger.

'You're in possession of privileged information. I can't come home every night and worry about what I should or shouldn't say.'

His smile faded and the words *come home every night* were strung out in the air between them. Stella could almost see them glow: her very own Christmas message.

Their waiter returned bringing the wine. The muzak was seasonal selections; just at that moment, 'Mary's Boy Child', a traditional Chinese favourite. Stella lifted her glass. She said, 'Listen, we can work something out. We can have a few basic rules about things like that.'

Delaney nodded. 'Sure. Of course.' He closed his notebook.

'You've got very neat handwriting,' Stella observed. 'Very neat, very small.'

'Sign of –?'

'Sign of a great fuck.'

They talked about other things and laughed together and ordered a second bottle of wine. Delaney mentioned Jamie and his certainty that Christ was on his way from celestial realms and would surely arrive on the anniversary of his birth, come to smite sinners and exalt the virtuous. Stella said she was all for sinners being smitten; she hoped they might get smitten shitless.

They enjoyed their meal, though neither ate the water chestnuts.

Later, Stella sat on a counter stool with what some people might think was a drink too far and read through the day's reports.

No matches had been found between any victims of recent attacks and the photos on Kimber's wall.

No matches had been found between those photos and

any of the faces from the missing persons files, though that search was long and continuing.

The superintendent's custody extension on Kimber had expired, but a magistrate's extension had been successfully applied for. This carried a note from Sorley, telling Stella to charge the man or let him go. He'd given a time-scale: it was brief.

The text of a phone message from Davison at Forensics mentioned that he was on the case. It carried a rider from Sue Chapman letting Stella know that she hadn't bothered to transcribe Davison's request for Stella's age, hair colour and cup-size, which formed the greater part of the message.

Delaney switched off his computer, then got up and passed behind her to make coffee. She was still reading when he came round to stand in her eyeline, waiting for her to look up. He was holding a pair of kitchen scissors and a lock of her hair.

'See?' he said. 'That's how.'

13

Driving in London is a matter of attitude: face this guy down, cut that guy up, never give way, never look back. You can run a red light on a count of three but a count of five will get you sideswiped in the grid. When Stella emerged from Delaney's flat next morning and looked up towards Notting Hill Gate, an ambulance, a tow-truck and a traffic patrol car were trying to solve just such a problem. She walked to work through the crowds of shoppers, office workers, winter-break tourists, beggars and lost souls.

Sadie was playing the penny whistle outside a shop that sold cards and cola and the sort of brightly coloured gewgaws that bought Manhattan from the Delawares. Jamie lay alongside her on his bag, asleep. Most druggy panhandlers had a scabby-looking dog and Sadie was thinking that Jamie was no substitute – she'd made three pounds in two hours. Robbing was a better bet: she'd finally got last night's fix by rolling a drunk, but those were scant pickings.

Stella went by, thinking of other things.

Mike Sorley lit a cigarette and tossed the pack down on the desk. The government caution reminded him that SMOKING CAUSES A SLOW AND PAINFUL DEATH. Stella saw that someone had underlined the large, black type in red pen. Second wives are often younger wives and carry certain responsibilities.

Sorley said, 'They'll be putting health warnings on prostitutes' arses before long.'

'Or the kite-mark,' Stella said. 'I think we charge him. I think there's enough.'

'It's not against the law to take pictures of people in the street.' Sorley's job was to be devil's advocate. 'Or to write obscene stories on your own walls.'

'The journal –'

'Okay, say you're his brief. What's your line on that?'

'Fantasy.'

'Exactly. He's made up the names, hasn't he – alphabetical order? So he made up the rest.'

'But all of those together, plus his confession, and knowing about the sweats and the cross and Valerie Blake being one of his trophy snapshots –'

'The sweats were given over the air, weren't they? One of the SOC guys.'

Stella had checked the transcripts. 'Yes, they were.'

'And Kimber's got a state-of-the-art scanner.'

'The sweats but not the chain.'

'As soon as he decides to appoint legal representation, the confession's out the window, you know that. The Crown Prosecution Service knows that. He's never signed a statement. Blake being among his snaps and knowledge of the chain – that's more helpful, but one is entirely circumstantial and he could have known about the other, about the cross, from following her.'

'But not that the killer took it.'

'Guesswork. Imagination. It's little enough.' He added, 'Why did he wait?'

'For what?'

'To tell us about the cross.'

Stella remembered Kimber's excited smile, the way he'd tempted and teased her with it . . . *My keepsake*. Something new to offer, something he'd decided to hold back . . . or something he simply hadn't thought of before. It made her uneasy, but she wasn't sure why.

'How long before I have to charge him?'

'You may as well make a decision now as later. Nothing useful on his hard disk, I suppose?'

'Straight porn. No paedo.'

'Okay, well, it's your call.'

'Let's take it to the wire,' Stella said. 'I'm waiting on Forensics.'

Two hours later Harriman picked up a call and patched it to Stella's line.

Davison said, 'I asked around. People say you're hot.'

'They don't know me.'

'A significant number ratified the black thong with silk panels.'

'I'm afraid I made that up, Davison.'

'Please! That thong is at the centre of an entire dream-world.'

'It doesn't exist. What do the tests show?'

'It's not him.'

Stella closed her eyes as if to concentrate better. 'Are you sure?'

'I'm a scientist. I have certificates.'

'I need detail.'

'The pathologist – it was Sam Burgess, right –?'

'Sam, yes.'

'Okay, Sam had gone over the body very carefully, he's meticulous, always does a thorough job. We looked at the scene of crime findings, DNA on her jogging clothes mostly, because the open nature of the scene meant that there would have been more individual traces than stars in the sky. So, we've got the SOC traces and we've got the traces that Sam picked up from her in the morgue. There are significant rogue traces, that's for sure: on the sweats and on her body, especially in her hair.'

'What were they?'

'Other hairs. Hairs not her own. We shed hair all the time, not least during exertion.'

Davison went silent. Stella said, 'Hello?'

'Drinking coffee,' he said, 'sorry. Now, you can pick up a DNA trace through any normal human contact, so in a case like this we look for a preponderance. We found one, but it doesn't marry with the swab you took from Robert Adrian Kimber.'

'Not Kimber.'

'Not.'

'Definitely not?'

'We've got close to a million profiles on our database; every week, we make better than sixteen hundred positive matches. We know what we're doing. If he was at the scene of crime, he was wearing a full-body condom.'

'Is he on the database?'

'No, sorry.'

'Is the DNA you *did* find on the database?'

'Sorry again.' She was about to hang up when he added, 'DS Mooney, I'm on your side. I'd nail the bastard for you if I could.'

Sorley and Stella headed up the briefing. The team members had equipped themselves with coffee and cigarettes and salt-and-vinegar crisps; it was only ever salt-and-vinegar; chocolate bar of the week was Kinder Bueno.

Stella said, 'We're releasing him. He's going.'

'The DNA test,' Harriman guessed.

'The DNA, yes; it doesn't match. And he's not on the database.'

'What about his special knowledge?' Maxine Hewitt asked. 'The sweats and the cross she wore round her neck.'

'The sweats he got from scanning exchanges between SOC officers and Notting Hill nick. The chain's a more difficult issue.'

'Because he had to be there to know.'

'No. Because someone told him.'

A silence fell. You could hear the fans in the VDUs and the rumble of a plane settling into the Heathrow flight path.

Harriman said, 'You mean someone here, don't you?'

Sorley was leaning against the exhibitions board. Valerie Blake lay half naked and dead just behind his right shoulder. He said, 'We've looked at the photo of Valerie Blake that was on Kimber's wall: the cross isn't visible. It's possible that he'd seen it on another occasion and decided to mention the sweats first and the cross later, keep us on the hop, but it just doesn't feel like that. Suddenly he's got this new information for us and he's very pleased with himself. As if the information was new to him as well.'

No one spoke.

After a moment, Stella said, 'He didn't kill Valerie Blake. He couldn't have decided to confess until after her death. He wasn't planning it. Why would he remember the cross? He had a scanner. The information about the sweats came from us. The information about the cross came from us too.'

Sorley looked round the room. He said, 'In your own time . . .'

*

84

Kimber waited while his possessions were brought up from the exhibitions room. The contents of his pockets, a Bearcat police scanner that was not, in itself, illegal, some videos, a box-file of photographs, locks of hair taped to display boards. Nick Robson was the exhibitions officer, but Stella had sent Jack Cuddon down to get the stuff.

Cuddon wasn't speaking; he wasn't saying a word.

Kimber smiled at him winningly and said, 'Listen, you can keep the videos. I've finished with the videos.'

You could see the tremble in Cuddon's hands; violence reined in.

To Stella, Kimber said, 'I did it, why don't you believe me?'

Stella said, 'Many sad people kill themselves; it's a good solution.'

'You ought to believe me.'

'Some take pills; some jump off tall buildings.'

'You'll be sorry that you didn't believe me.'

'Some slash their wrists; some hang themselves.'

Kimber said, 'You'll see.'

Four thirty and already dark. Or what passes for dark in London: city-twilight. Stella stood by a squad-room window and watched Kimber as he flagged down a cab. Jack Cuddon was standing behind her, also watching. She walked out to the car park and Cuddon followed. He lit a cigarette against the chill. Neither had bothered to collect their coats. The wind brought tears to Stella's eyes.

'You were seconded,' she said.

Cuddon nodded. Stella noticed that the face she had previously thought prim could become closed, etched with hard lines. His eyes were dark-rimmed, as if he hadn't slept.

'Where from?' she asked.

'Drugs.'

'Never seen anything like this?'

'Dealers and suppliers kill each other all the time: Yardies, Triads, Snakeheads, Turks. There's a daily rate for the job.'

'Anything like *this*?'

'No.'

'And you were never up close, were you? It was always admin, never the sharp end of things. You wouldn't have been in the interview room or at Kimber's flat if DC Greegan hadn't keeled over with the flu.'

In the car-park lamplight, their faces were smudged with shadow under the eyes, their cheekbones pinched white with the cold.

'He'd be better off dead.'

It was what Anne Beaumont had said. Stella shook her head. 'He didn't do it.'

'He's walking the streets now.'

'Jack, he didn't kill her.'

'He did other things. You were in that flat.'

Stella said, 'You've got something to say. Say it.'

He walked off a little way, disputing with himself, then came back. 'My wife was raped, it was before I met her, he stalked her for a while, that came out later, but she hadn't known about it, then he raped her, he'd done it to five other women, stalking at first, it always started that way, then raping, they didn't catch him, not when my wife was attacked, they caught him after that, after he'd attacked two other women, this was seven years ago, she was twenty-eight, but I didn't know until a few months back.'

He stopped as if he'd run out of story or out of breath, then shrugged suddenly and dropped his cigarette and trod on it and lit another.

'When did you get married?' Stella asked.

'Four years ago.'

'What changed things for her?'

'He was released. Simple as that. They let him out. She couldn't take it.'

'A few months back,' Stella guessed. Cuddon nodded. 'How is she now?'

'Difficult to tell,' he said. 'She doesn't live with me any more; she lives in Prozac Land. A happy place where happy people smile happily all day long.'

The wind had a real edge. Stella wiped away tears with her cuff. 'You wasted my time, Jack. I was an ace off charging him. Worse than that, whoever did kill Valerie Blake has been given more time.'

'He's walking the streets now,' Cuddon said. 'Kimber's away free.'

'Go home, Jack. You're looking lousy. There's something going round. We'll have to find someone else. I'm really sorry.'

'Are you?'

'Believe me.'

'He's walking the streets,' Cuddon said again. 'Who knows what could happen?'

Mike Sorley was swimming in paper. He raised a hand as Stella came in: not waving but drowning. He said, 'He's gone –?'

'Coming down with the flu,' Stella said.

'I'll ask for a replacement.' He checked his watch and lit up. 'Why did he do it?'

Stella told him.

He said, 'It wasn't on his file.'

'I'm not sure anyone knows.'

'It should have been on his file.' After a moment, he added, 'It is now.'

*

Stella was in the women's room. She emerged from a cubicle to find Maxine Hewitt washing her hands for the fifth time.

'They sent you,' Stella suggested. 'The rest of the team.'

'They sent me, yes – to ask what's happening.'

Stella mentioned Jack Cuddon's illness and Maxine observed that there was definitely something going round. Stella washed her hands and held them under the warm-air dryer; they were still cold enough to tingle slightly.

'Why did he do it?' Maxine asked.

Stella told her.

Maxine said nothing until they were walking down the corridor to the squad room. 'I suppose we're lucky he didn't kill the bastard.'

Stella said, 'I suppose so.' Then, 'Of course, he still might.'

14

Robert Adrian Kimber: Hello. We've never met, but I've been reading about you. Now that the police scene of crime tape has gone and the police have also gone, I thought I'd drop you a line. Throw you a line, you might say. Life-line of sorts.

I know how you feel. I know why you did what you did. If you want to know more about that – if you want to know more about me – put a card in the message-mart at 'Store Twenty-Four' in the North End Road about a missing cat called Nero. Also use the words: 'Smoky-blue with a white tip to his tail'. Put your email address.

I hope you don't mind that I took a look round. Finding you was easy. You just need contacts. I've got lots of contacts. The replacement door wasn't very sturdy. In fact, a number of people had been in before me, but they didn't find anything to take, of course, because the police had done that. I'm afraid someone pissed in your hallway. Some people are too stupid to live, aren't they?

It was a shame they took the photos away but I enjoyed your stories. If you like the fiction you'd like the real-life version even more. You must have been thinking about that, haven't you? I bet you have.

I would love to see your photos.

Can you guess who I am? I was so surprised when I saw Valerie's name and yours linked in the press. It would be nice to have a chat about Valerie and what you told the police and what they said. You had them guessing for a good long time, I have to hand it to you.

Valerie. You were following her and the thing is I didn't know. That's the odd thing, the really odd thing – I didn't know.

Don't forget the cat's name is Nero.

15

There were no roses in Rose Park. Winter roses, summer roses: you'd wait in vain. Maybe there had been once; maybe a rose garden had existed where now there was a scabby acre of grass and four chain-and-tyre swings. Maybe roses had once flourished next to those starved ornamental trees and the tangle of overgrown scrub.

Rose Park had a bad rep. You could check out the recreational tendencies of those who used the park from the litter of syringes and condoms. Dog-owners from Harefield would bring their pets along for a run and a dump. Now and then, young mothers new to the area might spot the swings and take their kids in, but they never went back. The locals, especially those from the Harefield Estate, used it as a short cut between the shops and the maze of small roads that led in and out of the bull ring.

That's why Sophie Simms was walking through. It was a regular route for her and she wouldn't have worried about Rose Park's reputation anyway, as it was still light and there were people around in the streets. She was thinking about the guy she had spent the night with: a new guy – she'd been seeing him for a couple of weeks. She liked him, but there were problems, and she was having a little debate with herself.

He's good looking but you know he's into bad stuff.
Everyone's into bad stuff.
No, really bad stuff.

He's sweet when he's on his own.
Meaning you don't like his friends.
I'm not sleeping with his friends.
It's drugs and it's not now and then.
Good, I could use some drugs.
Me too. But it's how deep he's in. Those Yardie boys . . .
I can keep him clear of those guys.
You can?
Sure.
Tell me how.
Easy. I'll never let him —

Sophie never finished telling herself how, because that was when the light suddenly faded to grey and things around her seemed to fly away. Seemed to scatter. She knew she was falling but didn't know what had made that happen. There was a noise like a machine in her ears. She registered the pain a moment later, like a shout on the wind. It was bad, it struck every nerve in her body, but in her head it was immense: a red and white explosion too big to allow her to cry out. Then the noise stopped; the pain billowed; the grey became black.

She went on falling long after she hit the ground.

He pulled her into the scrub and knelt beside her. He hit her with the hammer twice more, bringing the blows down from as high as his arm could reach, then propped her against one of the ornamental trees and looped a length of woven cord round her neck but didn't pull it tight. He stripped her from the waist down; he pulled off her leather jacket and pushed her sweater up under her chin. He was wearing a reversible coat, red one side, black the other. He switched the red for the black, then took a pack of babywipes out of his pocket and cleaned his face and hands very thoroughly. As he left, he dropped the clothes he'd taken from her into a skip.

She could have been anyone. In fact, he had picked out several other women, but something had happened to keep them safe: one had answered a mobile, another had taken a path that led away from the scrub-cover, on a couple of other occasions someone else had come into sight.

Sophie had been on her own in the park, just for a minute or so. She had taken the path near the scrub. A minute or two was what he needed. The first hammer blow had taken no time at all and he'd been in the scrub with her twenty seconds later. People can die that easily; they can die that fast.

But Sophie wasn't dead.

It was dusk when Stella walked into Rose Park. There was a light drizzle on the wind, rain turning to ice. Back on the road there was a light-show of roof-bars and blue domes, their beams sweeping the bare branches of the ornamental trees. Sorley had put out a panic call and found a scene of crime officer to deputize for Andy Greegan. The guy had gone straight to the scene; now he was organizing halogens and nominating an entry/exit path to the site.

Stella could see he was doing a good job. She said, 'You are?'

'DC Silano, Boss.' He had thinning hair, a long widow's peak greying at the sides, but a boxer's build. The straight nose and strong chin were masked a little by fleshiness; at a stone lighter, he would have been good-looking.

'First name?'

'Frank.'

'Where did they find you, Frank?'

'Paddington Green.'

'Where is she?'

'Charing Cross trauma unit. We've got some stills.'

'At the scene?'

'Yes.'

'How did that happen?

'Some kids found her. They robbed her and took off. Then one of them decided to call triple nine to report a body. A response team got here before the ambulance; one of the uniforms had a camera. They couldn't risk moving her, so he fired off half a reel while the others were doing vital signs.'

'Where's the response team now?'

Silano nodded towards the road and the mish-mash of lights. 'In the car. One of them went with the ambulance.'

Stella moved closer to the place where Sophie had lain. Forensics officers in white coveralls were going over the ground, moving slowly, sampling and bagging among the spikes and the dog turds. She could see where the grass was matted and sticky. When she stepped back to the path, Harriman was walking towards her, a little silver point-and-push camera in his hand.

Stella said, 'Get someone down to the hospital.'

'DC Hewitt's on the way.'

'Is that the camera?'

'This is it. Be good, I should think: you can't go wrong with these things, self-focusing, automatic flash.'

'Did you get a verbal report?'

'The uniforms say she was propped against a tree. There was a ligature round her neck, she was naked from the waist down, the rest of her clothing had been pushed up under her chin. No sign of the missing clothing as yet. The police doctor went with her in the ambulance. According to the uniforms, the doctor gave it as multiple blows to the head with a blunt instrument.'

'It's the Valerie Blake MO.'

'Identical,' Harriman said.

There were streetlights and shop-window neon and head-lights, but there were no lights in the park. Stella looked up the path towards the exit that led off to the Harefield Estate. She could see the tops of the tower blocks, a more solid grey against the darkening sky. She remembered walking back across the park with bags from the mini-mart: nine, maybe ten years old; she remembered the man who had opened his coat to her; she remembered the gangs of kids steaming through on stolen bikes. How many of those kids had survived, she wondered; how many had escaped?

Stella Mooney, Detective Sergeant, AMIP-5 murder squad. Most Harefield kids went the other route: druggies, crooks, hookers, dealers. Maybe you don't make the choice, she thought, maybe it's all down to chance, a decision so small you can't remember it, a choice based on next to nothing.

A figure was standing at the top of the path. Stella didn't see him at first because his silhouette was muddled with the railings that ringed the park; then he shifted his weight and, for a moment, came clear.

Without looking away from that shadow, Stella said, 'The guys in that response vehicle will know the patch. Tell them to drive to the north side of the park. The path we're on now leads to a side street, then there's an alley, then a main road, then you get into Harefield. Tell them to park across the alley.'

Harriman followed her eyeline. He said, 'Where?', then the shadow moved again. 'Okay, I see.'

'I won't move until he does. Go with them. Leave the

driver in the car and take the other guy with you. Call me when you're in position, then start down the alley. I'll move up from here.'

'Not without some help.'

'I'll take this guy, Silano. He looks handy.'

Harriman started back to the road, walking quickly, resisting the urge to run. Stella moved a little way into the tree-cover, keeping to the tape-lines set out to protect the site. She wanted to maintain a fix on the shadow, but she had the light from the street behind her, so she was a silhouette too. She moved further into the trees, wanting to be inconspicuous. It was a good thought, though others weren't thinking as fast. The guy driving the response vehicle came off the verge fast, saw a gap between a panel truck and a toy sports, and hit the siren. Harriman yelled at him, but by the time the driver killed the noise they had hit the main road intersection and the shadow was peeling away from the railings, now a lower, sleeker shape – that of a man starting to run.

Stella said, 'Oh, shit!' She was wearing jeans and trainers but the guy had a good forty yards start. As she started to run, she called to Silano. He was mapping the progress of the forensic search and half heard his name, but when he looked round Stella had gone.

The guy was clear of the path, clear of the alley, out of sight, and the response vehicle wasn't even close when Stella emerged on to the road. Harefield was a grid if you looked at it from a planner's point of view; it was a maze if you knew it well. Straight roads all converging on the bull ring like spokes in a wheel, with circular roads intersecting, but those plain-and-simple routes were overlaid with rat-runs that took you past lock-ups and maintenance buildings, across the DMZ, back into the surrounding side streets, or underneath the raised tower blocks themselves. Stella knew them all. She didn't think she could overtake the guy by following him, so when she hit the first estate road she ran down it for twenty yards or so, then turned off into a rat-run that would take her straight to Block C, *his* walkway, *his* door. She had no doubt that she was chasing Robert Kimber.

It was dark now, the estate part lit by the orange glow from streetlamps on the main routes. The freezing air hit her lungs and left an ache. She went past a row of garages and came out at the back of the block. Her route would be under the building to the entrance and up the exterior stairs to 16/31. It was a better than evens bet that someone would have kicked the lift doors crooked, so she was trying to pace herself for the climb.

There was light at the perimeter but the walk-space under Block C was a blank. She ran into the deeper darkness, slowing to a jog because she couldn't tell what was in her path. There was a stench: the ripe stew of an inner-city midden. The whoop and wail of a siren was coming at her from the street, but she couldn't tell how close it was. She was looking straight ahead at the far side of the block when she saw the ghost coming towards her.

16

Pale and skinny and seeming to drift in the near-dark, arms extended to draw you in, just the way ghosts are supposed to look.

Stella stopped twenty feet away. Suddenly, the walk-space under Block C was no place to be. The figure seemed to shimmer, coming and going, as if the darkness were washing over it. For a full ten seconds, neither spoke or moved, then Stella said, 'Police officer.'

The ghost came a step closer and Stella caught a little gust of rank breath and piss and beer; then the apparition backed off and faded. Stella continued towards the faint rim of light on the far side, the skin on her back crawling.

The walk-space was a reception black spot. When she came clear, she called Harriman, who was already on his way up to Kimber's flat. She said, 'You thought Kimber too.'

'Who else? There's a response car and driver in the bull ring.'

'Okay,' Stella said. 'Kimber – is he in?'

'I can hear the TV.'

She met Harriman on the walkway. Robert Kimber came to the door with a beer in his hand. He asked them whether they happened to have a warrant that would entitle them to enter his premises.

They didn't.

He asked them how he might help, but he kept them at

the door. He pointed out that he was halfway through a meal and halfway through a television show. It was a cop movie, he told them.

Stella said, 'You can't. You can't help.'

Kimber smiled and nodded agreement. 'I didn't think I could.'

'Okay,' Harriman said. 'What odds it was him?'

'My view? Pretty short.'

'Because he'd have heard the call-in on his scanner. Because he likes to watch. Like an ambulance-chaser except he's a scene of crime freak.'

'Or because he did it.'

'So we get a warrant, go back, toss his place again.'

'And count on finding the murder weapon and some bloodstained clothes?'

'No. Well, toss it anyway.'

'What for?' Stella asked.

'Fun.'

'I've had enough fun on this fucking estate tonight.'

They were making the long trip down the exterior stairway. If you looked out beyond the DMZ, you could see lights from surrounding streets, like the lights from the camp of a besieging army.

The response car was in the bull ring. The driver was sitting very still and watching some kids. The kids were watching him. They were leaning up against the steel window-shutters of a bookie's, a launderette, a KFC carry-out. The shutters bore bright red and green aerosol tags. The only place open was the off-licence, which had a permanent steel-mesh guard up over the plate-glass. The kids had been in and bought some cans.

All boys, early to mid teens. Six of them, maybe eight.

Stella and Harriman walked past the KFC and turned towards the car. One of the boys said, 'Hey, bitch.'

Stella turned, stepped up and backhanded him in the mouth. It was a good, fast hit and the boy had been smiling at her. She'd shut his mouth with the slap and a tooth had cut his lip.

Harriman closed his eyes for a moment; he said, 'Oh, good,' and looked towards the response driver, who had taken a baton out from the door-clip and was getting out of the car.

The boy touched his lip with his finger and brought it away bloody. Stella said, 'Hey yourself.' She walked to the car and got in and waited for Harriman and the driver to join her.

They cleared the DMZ and came out on to the road a little too fast. Stella saw a car she thought she knew: a red Audi with a clutter of books and papers on the parcel-shelf. She looked over her shoulder but couldn't catch the licence-plate. Harriman was looking at her, a smile on his face. He was still thinking of the boy she'd slapped.

She said, 'I know.' Then, 'I'm sick of kids like that. They think nothing can touch them.'

'You touched him. You touched him pretty hard.'

Stella wanted to say: *The last time I hit a guy in the Harefield bull ring, I killed him. I killed the bastard. I killed the arsewipe. I killed him and I think I'm still having trouble with that.* Instead, she took out her mobile and made a call to the locals to let them know that there were eight boys dealing class-A gear down on Harefield. The descriptions she gave would have fitted a hundred kids like that and the copper on the line let her know as much.

'You're right,' Stella agreed. 'So bust the first eight you come across.'

She leaned back and closed her eyes. John Delaney drove a car like that. But there were lots of red Audis in London, of course; and why wouldn't you have a few books and papers on the parcel-shelf?

It had been driving on to the Harefield Estate.

17

You could visit Santa in his grotto. You could win a Christmas hamper. You could buy him/her the gift he/she had been dreaming of. You could stop off at the Ocean Diner for a snowball or sledbanger. You could stand outside Videoland and watch *White Christmas*. Or you could step up to the slick black BMW parked illegally in a residents' bay just off the Saints, carrying a .45 Glock 21 automatic, standard trigger pull, thirteen-round magazine capacity, with the clear intention of killing its occupants.

There were three guys in the Beamer and they really shouldn't have been there. Not because they were in a reserved bay but because that particular half of the postal district was operated by people who expected their drugs and their whores to get exclusivity. Glock Man was on a mission to let them know about that.

The car was throbbing to a low bass: techno-house music. Everyone in the car was bored and the two men in the front seats were reading. They often had to wait and knew to take magazines: they favoured boxing or snatch. As soon as the fourth man came downstairs to join them, they would start cruising the streets round the Strip, handing out street-cut gear to their distributors. The fourth man had hit a streak on the blackjack table just before ten the previous evening and the night had lit up for him after that. This morning, he was a little slow-moving.

The guy in the back of the car said, 'Could you turn that the fuck down?' He would have called himself more of a retro man: old-style R & B. And, in any case, he was making a phone call to a girl who didn't want to listen.

He said, 'We can work this out. We can make it work.'

She said she didn't think so.

He said, 'Listen, who's been talking to you?'

She said she wasn't naming names.

He said, 'Don't believe everything you hear.'

She said she only had to look at his lying bastard face.

He said, 'Oh, *fuck*!' but this wasn't a response to her mistrust. He had seen Glock Man, walking directly towards the car, his hand down by his side to make the .45 a little less obvious. Retro Man dropped the phone and reached into his pocket for his own gun, yelling at the same time. The guys in the front had just enough time to look up before they were hit. Retro Man got off four shots. Two missed, one took the man in the passenger seat in the back of the head, raising a mist of red on the car window, the fourth hit Glock Man in the fat of his waist, spinning him round and dropping him.

Retro Man was halfway out of the car when Glock Man got up on one knee and shot him three times before pitching over on to his side. His gun clattered across the road and went under the Beamer. He levered himself off the road like a man doing the last press-up in a hundred-press routine, got to his knees, then to his feet. You wouldn't call him nimble now; but a hopping lope took him down the street and out of sight in a couple of minutes.

This was around noon and broad daylight. People had taken to doorways or rushed into shops; some had ducked down behind wheelie bins or recycling units; some had hit the pavement and put their hands over their ears. Now, with sirens coming in from two directions, they hurried on.

The front-seat guys had taken ten bullets between them.

They were dead. The windscreen was frosted in red. Retro Man had been shot through the arm, the shoulder and the throat. He lay belly-up across the street with the traffic backed up on either side. He was not quite dead.

The Glock .45 lay under the car.

Sadie had stayed absolutely still during the shooting. When it was over, she'd picked up her bag and found a new pitch two streets away where people were going about their business as normal. She sat down and started 'Lord of the Dance'.

Jamie watched the movie in Videoland. He liked the snow because it looked clean. He liked the look of the big room with its ceiling-high tree decked with trinkets and lights. The people sang and kissed each other. He wanted to be some-one like that. After a while he went to sit next to Sadie. She had learned the first few bars of 'Silent Night'. He put his head in his hands and muttered to himself as she played.

And the angel said, 'Fear not, for I bring you glad tidings of great joy . . .'

The hospital was a sky-high stack of Chinese boxes sleeved in glass. The big windows blanked the outside world. By day, they reflected the 747s bellying down through the high white winter clouds to Heathrow; at night, they reflected the city lights. A system of elevators and a labyrinth of corridors took you to numbered floors and numbered wards. The intensive care unit was 15D. In a curtained cubicle, Retro Man was trying to make a comeback. He wasn't aware of it, because he wasn't aware of anything, but he was about on the brink.

Sophie Simms was in a side ward. She was beyond the brink: she had stepped off and was free-falling.

Stella had taken Maxine Hewitt with her. Maxine sat with Sophie's family and asked questions that no one wanted to answer about friends, enemies, lovers; about bad habits and bad blood. No one mentioned bad luck. The Simms family consisted entirely of women: Sophie's mother, her grandmother, her two sisters. They were blonde. Even the grandmother was blonde, though she needed a little more help with it than the others.

The grandmother and the sisters said nothing. The sisters sat close to one another but at a remove from the others and flicked through the pile of magazines that lay on a low table. They favoured *Sugar* and *Miz*. The grandmother was shredding an empty cigarette pack. The mother told Maxine that her name was Tanya. She had cried her make-up into a thick tideline round her jaw, but now she was stony-faced.

She didn't know who Sophie's friends were.

She didn't know whether Sophie had enemies.

She didn't know where Sophie went at night.

She didn't know whether Sophie had a boyfriend.

She didn't know why anyone would want to kill her beautiful daughter.

She asked whether she could go now; she wanted to sit by Sophie's bed. She thought that Sophie could hear what she was saying even though she wasn't able to respond. There was a special communication, she said, between a mother and her daughter.

Maxine said that would be a good idea. After Tanya had left, Maxine offered her cigarettes to the grandmother, who took three and headed for the street. The sisters put down their magazines and ticked off some boxes.

Did Sophie do drugs? Sure, who doesn't? Nothing heavy. Just Es and dope.

Did Sophie hang out with a bad crew? Just some fit boys.

Did Sophie have a boyfriend? Yeah, someone new. Scuzz? Buzz?

Did Sophie have any enemies? No.

Maxine asked the questions because it was required, but she didn't think Sophie's murder had anything to do with drugs or love or revenge, and neither did the sisters.

One of them said, 'It's that crazy guy, right?'

'We don't have any theories just yet,' Maxine told her.

'The crazy guy. Attacking women.'

'We don't know.'

The other sister had an afterthought. She said, 'We live on Harefield, yeah? It's not a matter of enemies. You don't have enemies, not as such. You have crews, yeah? You have territories. We're not in a crew. We don't have *enemies*, we have *other people*.' She went back to reading *Sugar*.

Stella was talking to Dr Shah, who had flawless skin, regular features and a catwalk figure. Since the woman was also a senior registrar, Stella decided to think of this as overload.

'It's an issue we're going to have to raise with the family,' Dr Shah said, 'and pretty soon.'

'You want to switch her off?'

'Sophie Simms is alive mechanically, but she's brain-stem dead. We have to approach her relatives about harvesting her organs.'

Stella shook her head. 'She's a murder victim. We've ordered an autopsy and a forensic investigation.'

Dr Shah sighed. 'It's a young heart. A young renal system.'

'I'm sorry.'

'Don't apologize to me. Pop into dialysis on your way out.'

'There's no possibility of a reversal?' Stella asked.

'That she regains consciousness, that you talk to her, that

she identifies her assailant? No, none. She's already switched off, in effect. She's a shell. We're effecting a simulation of life, but all it amounts to is inflating the lungs and maintaining the circulatory system. Sophie left a while ago. All we're doing is keeping putrefaction at bay.'

That's one way of putting it, Stella thought. Dr Shah's bleeper sounded and she moved to a phone. While she was taking the call, she looked across at Stella as if to say *That's it; we're done.*

Maxine was coming into the ward as Stella was leaving. She said, 'They're off the estate, just like a thousand others. There's nothing to distinguish her from the other victims.'

'Unless she happened to know him.'

'Why would she?'

'Somebody does.'

They were almost at the door of the ward when two nurses drew the curtains on the last bed space and emerged with a trolley. Stella and Maxine glanced sideways, reflexively, and saw a figure rigged with tubes and drips and wearing a full-face oxygen mask. A monitor showed the sluggish blue blips of a troubled heartbeat. Stella thought he looked like a man who was too close to death to pull back.

She was right. Retro Man would die that night, a couple of hours after Tanya had given permission for Sophie's life-support system to be switched off.

18

From: Angel@langfor.com

Well, Robert, I picked up your message about poor Nero. I wonder – have you had any thoughts about me? About who I am? Now you can tell me. Now you can email me back. All that coverage in the papers about you – I expect you enjoyed it. I expect you enjoyed leading them a dance. DS Mooney, was that the name the papers gave? Did you enjoy your sessions with her?

They always hold something back, don't they? What did you do about that? I expect you stayed vague. I expect you did some ducking and diving. You must have been pretty good because it took them a while to work you out, didn't it? I expect you went in prepared. You must have known something. What did you know?

The thing I really want to ask – how did it feel pretending it was you – pretending you had killed Valerie? I expect it was thrilling. It was thrilling, wasn't it? Did you run through it in your mind? I expect you did. I wonder how close you got to the real thing. I could tell you how close. We could compare notes.

I would love to run through it with you. I would love to take you through it, step by step. I expect you can close your eyes and see the park in your mind's eye, the park that day, Valerie jogging through. I expect you make up a scenario, don't you? Except it's you there with her, you going after her, and it wasn't you, was it?

Do you know who it was?

Email me back and let me know how you feel. Let me know what you see in your mind's eye. The park, the weather, the single figure waiting, biding his time, the risks, the method. The feeling. The way it felt. I expect you thought a lot about the way it felt. I expect you told DS Mooney about that. Now tell me. You can be as detailed as you like. The Devil's in the detail, as they always say.

Let's speak soon.

19

The squad room was decorated with a little tree-chart of progression points and a paper-chain of SOC shots. The point-and-push camera had a hard flash and Sophie looked chalk-white, her features lacking definition. People were smoking and drinking and eating: some were doing all three. The air in the room was thick and blue, but there was nothing else to breathe. Stella wafted her hand in front of her face: a novice non-smoker eating secondary-soup.

'It looks like a replica of the Valerie Blake attack,' she said. 'But it isn't quite. The post-mortem's being done this afternoon, but the doctor at the scene was certain that she hadn't been strangled. The blows to the head killed her.'

'The configuration of clothing,' Maxine asked. 'Do we know whether she was raped?'

'No. I'll be asking Sam Burgess about that.'

'It ties in with the earlier attacks in some ways,' Harriman observed. 'So did Blake: the blows to the head, the attack taking place in an open space, in the street or a park.'

Maxine said, 'Except we spent a day with the team that are looking at those other incidents and the similarities are superficial. Copy cat, maybe. More likely to be men hating women. Nothing new there.'

'And no DNA matches,' Stella observed.

'DNA, yes. Matches, no.'

Frank Silano was breaking the filter off a B & H; Harriman gave him a light. Silano said, 'We've put up an incident board. Exhibits have been listed; they're with Forensics now.

Uniform found her clothes in a skip. The earlier attacks might not fit, but this MO's identical.'

'Two strikes in short order,' Harriman said. 'This guy's going to keep at it, isn't he?'

Stella said, 'I think he is.'

Sam Burgess was working to the Sibelius violin concerto, the *allegro moderato* finding almost the same pitch as the electric saw he was using to trepan Sophie Simms. Giovanni was alongside; he reached in and lifted out the brain. Stella thought of pickled walnuts. Sam took a scalpel and cut a thin slice for forensic examination, as if that sliver might contain Sophie's last thought.

Easy. I'll never let him out of bed.

'She wasn't strangled,' Sam said. 'The garrotte might have been round her neck, but he didn't apply it. No time, perhaps.'

'He didn't kill her either, not immediately.'

'No, but he meant to. The hammer blows were more than enough to do the job. God knows how she survived as long as she did.'

'You're sure it was a hammer?'

'Pretty sure; can't think what else would fit the configuration and blow pattern. But Forensics will have a better take on it.'

'And there's the question of whether she was sexually assaulted.'

'Well, she'd had sex in the last twenty-four hours. Whether it was willingly or not is another matter. No trauma.'

'Clear DNA, though.'

'There will be.'

Sam stood back to allow Giovanni to take the brain to the scales: the sum total of all Sophie Simms had known or thought or felt. Love doesn't live in the heart, Stella thought; why do people think that? It lives in the brain along with doubt and displeasure.

'The hospital wanted her organs,' Stella said.

'It's a waste,' Sam agreed. 'I don't think we're going to find anything significant.' His plastic apron and eye-shields carried tiny red polka-dots. Stella looked towards the dissecting table, where Giovanni was waiting for Sam to make the Y-incision. Sophie had a butterfly-tattoo on her thigh just under the hip bone: something only a lover would see. As Sam made the first cut, Stella half expected to see it lift and fly off.

She pushed through the slap-flaps, going from room to room in that subterranean city of the dead, and emerged to a bright day and cold that bit the bone. Her phone rang as if it had been waiting to find the signal.

Harriman said, 'Two things. Kimber confessed to a crime a couple of years ago.'

'Murder?'

'Murder-abduction.'

'No chance he actually did it?'

'No. They caught the guy with the body in the boot of his car.'

'Jesus. What else?'

'Valerie Blake's flat was burgled two days before she died.'

As Stella walked in to the squad room, Sue Chapman was walking out.

Stella said, 'You look like hell.'

Sue nodded. 'Feel the same way. I'm going home.'

'I ought to say don't come back till you're feeling better.'

'But –?'

'Come back sooner than that.'

Harriman showed her the message forms. The information about Kimber was from DS Reid at Paddington Green. The other came from DS Gerry Harris at Notting Hill.

Her first call was to Harris, who'd been sharp enough to make the connection between the burglary and Valerie Blake's murder. She asked, 'Can I get a copy of the crime report?'

'Give me a number. I'll fax it to you while we're talking.'

Stella gave the number. 'Anything special about it?'

'Just another break-in. We get dozens a day. They work in teams. Kids mostly. You know – pre-teen and upwards. Valerie Blake's place showed some familiar patterns: they'd raided the fridge, had a drink or two, made themselves at home; they'd taken a lot of street-market gear, clothes and shoes and so forth; they've obviously got a buyer for it. We drop in on the local street-markets from time to time, but it's a lost cause, really. They'd been fairly comprehensive, so I reckon they knew her habits. Leave for work, get home from work. A working day would give them a lot of leeway. Most of these little shits go in and trash the place just because. This lot don't. We call them the Clean Machine.'

'How did they get in?'

'Jacked a window. Took the whole thing out. It's easy. People buy alarms and such like. They don't know.'

'You didn't make an arrest, I suppose?'

Harris laughed. 'It's a statistic. I expect she was insured. They only take easily disposable stuff and smallish items. I mean, it wasn't the sort of job where they load the white goods on to a lorry. She gave us a list; it's on the report.'

Stella heard the fax machine on Sue Chapman's desk kick in. She said, 'It's coming through now.'

'Okay,' Harris said. 'I'm here if you think of something else.'

DS Reid wasn't as genial but then DS Reid knew he'd fucked up.

'You didn't log this,' Stella said, 'or it would have turned up as a cross-reference.'

'He was a time-waster.'

'You didn't log it.'

'He was in and out. I done it, no you didn't, goodbye, end of story.'

'You didn't log it and we spent a lot of time with him. We could have been looking at other things.'

'Let me ask you something, DS Mooney.' Reid was talking rank to rank now. 'Did you ever work a long day? Did you ever come in and find yesterday's backlog still on your desk along with today's pile of shite? We were looking for a nine-year-old boy, and the tabloids were running a story that started each morning with big headlines that told the world exactly how many days had passed since he went missing and suggesting that the police were a bunch of incompetent arseholes –'

'You didn't log it,' Stella said, 'you incompetent arsehole.'

Andy Greegan sounded like a man drowning in a glue-pit.

Stella said, 'You were running the search team at her flat.'

'There wasn't any sign,' Greegan said. 'Two days before she died?'

'Yes.'

'So she'd tidied up. They hadn't tagged the walls or kicked the doors down.'

'They jacked a window.'

'Easy to get out, easy to put back. Any builder – five-minute repair.'

Stella was looking at the list on the crime report. 'They took quite a lot of her clothes. She can't have had time to replace them.'

'Okay.'

'No, I'm asking – wouldn't someone on your team have spotted that?'

'They were all men.'

'Andy, they took ten pairs of shoes.'

'Yeah?' Greegan broke off to sneeze. 'Jesus Christ,' he said, 'this is flu. This is *really* flu.'

'How many pairs of shoes has your wife got?'

'God knows. I've got two: one black, one brown. I'll tell you what – I did wonder why she didn't have a TV. But then I wish I didn't have one.'

20

She had been waiting for Delaney to say something, but the time for waiting was past. He came in looking cold and tired and she hit him with it before he'd taken off his coat or poured a drink.

'I saw you driving on to the Harefield Estate. Yesterday, some time after five.'

'Is that right? What were you doing there?'

'It *was* you –'

'Some time after five. Yes, that would be me.'

He went through to the bathroom and didn't reappear for twenty minutes. Finally, he came back wearing a bathrobe and looking for that drink.

'Same as you,' she said, as if the conversation had never been broken.

'Same as me –'

'You asked me what I was doing. The answer is I was talking to Robert Kimber, same as you.'

'How do you know?'

'I'm a detective. I detect.'

The drink was whisky and it was going down well. 'Does it matter?'

'It does to me. It's a case I'm involved in and you're working off privileged information.'

'No, I'm not. The papers carried the story. Anyone could go after a follow-up piece.'

'You're not anyone. Not on this occasion. It's complicated, John, surely you can see that.'

'Sort of but not really. You mentioned the Judas Syndrome. Perfect headline. I just want a few words with the guy. He won't be the only person I'll talk to.'

'It makes me uneasy. Go back to Yuletide street-people.'

He walked over and caught her by the waist and kissed her mouth. He tasted of whisky, which made her want a drink of her own. 'I'm doing that too,' he said. 'It's where I've just been.'

She pushed hair off his forehead and kissed him back, just lightly. She asked, 'How are they doing?'

'Freezing, filthy, impoverished, but hey, they're *free*.'

'Vagabonds,' she suggested.

'Bare-arsed philosophers.'

'I'd prefer you stayed away from him. It would be better.'

He freshened his drink. He said, 'Better for me, for you, for him?'

'Better all round.'

In bed, things were just the same as ever. His look went through her like light through water.

She woke in the night and he woke too, as if she'd called him. They lay quietly, the city still up and running at 3 a.m. but distant and dim.

She said, 'What did he say to you?'

'Nothing.'

'Why?'

'I was sounding him out. He wants money.'

'Of course.'

'Of course.' He moved close and looped his arm round her. 'You can listen to the tape. Whatever he says —'

'I've listened to his tapes. I've had enough of that man's tapes.' After a moment she added, 'He's a watcher. He's got a police scanner. He listens to the call-in, then he goes to the scene of crime and watches. I'm pretty certain he was in Rose Park.'

'Sophie Simms.'

'Good recall.'

'I'm a journalist.'

'He's sick, John. His head's full of . . . black stuff.'

'That's what makes him interesting.'

From: Angel@langfor.com

Are you Robert or Rob or Bob or Bobby? I expect your mother had a special name for you, didn't she? Bobby. Bobby Kimber.

It was good to get your email, Bobby. Full of very interesting things. Of course, you got it wrong about the feeling, about how it felt, what it was like, but then you've never done it, have you, so how would you know?

You were in the right area, though. You'd got the picture. In the ball park, as they always say. There were some things you missed out. Missed them because you weren't there at the time. I expect you would like to know what they were. I could tell you, if you like.

I could tell you if we met up. I sometimes go to a pub down on the river. I expect you know it. The Dove. It's along from Hammersmith Bridge. Perhaps we could meet up there. How would I recognize you? There were no pictures in the paper. Send me an email and say what you look like. I expect you've got a piece of clothing you could wear that would help me to pick you out.

I was very interested in your Bearcat. Do you only go to murders or do you go to accidents too? I expect you like accidents, don't you?

The thing is, Bobby, it's the preparation as well as everything else. It's the being busy. It's the planning. Because that's when you start to think about it. Sometimes you look back and you remember thinking about it being better than doing it – if things go wrong at the time, or you have to hurry, if something spoils it.

The thing is, you get this fantastic buzz, it's like a big tingle, it's like bubbles in your blood. I think it's the risk. It's the risk and it's being the powerful one, it's having the power. Well, you said that yourself. You got that bit right, for sure.

Some item of clothing I'll recognize you by.

Back-up can come in the shape of an ARV team or the so 19 gun squad, or it's forensic help, or it's a five-foot four-inch carroty-haired grease-monkey working out of a lock-up in Shepherd's Bush. Like every detective, Stella had a network of informants. The vocabulary changes: at one time, your contact might have been a grass, or a nark, or a face, or a voice. These days an informant is called a chis: that's Covert Human Intelligence Source. Stella sometimes doubted the 'intelligence' factor when she was speaking to Mickey Wicks, but he was connected and that was what mattered.

Mickey ran a workshop out of the lock-up. It wasn't much of a space, so he was restricted to handling just one car at a time and that included the cars he handled in other ways, such as the executive limos that were lifted from some address on the north side of Holland Park Avenue and wound up on the south side of the English Channel half a day later. A Merc, a Jag or a Lexus would come down to him for a respray, a plate-change and a new chassis number on a fast turn-around basis that left Mickey in possession for no more than three hours, which was why he'd only once been arrested for conspiracy to rob and handling stolen goods.

Stella knew about Mickey's way with top-of-the-range autos, but it wasn't really her business. She had found Mickey through a series of hand-ons from colleagues who were moving from the division or retiring or going back into uniform. She'd inherited him. His vehicle remakes were a fair means by which to threaten him, but way back in the chain someone must have had something really serious on Mickey Wicks, though everyone had forgotten what it was. The relationship continued out of habit. Habit and greed.

She drove down to the Bush amid a clatter of airborne garbage. The wind was still coming in off the Arctic shelf, but now it had some muscle. There were reports of offshore gales and heavy seas. Mickey heard an engine die and looked up from his work to see Stella parking across the open doors of the lock-up. The doors were open to prevent Mickey succumbing to exhaust fumes and he was using three patio heaters to compensate. He was working on a midnight blue BMW seven series and, just at present, it wasn't carrying licence-plates.

Mickey said, 'You couldn't move your car down the mews a bit?'

Stella stood close to the door, within reach of a patio heater. She said, 'I won't be long, Mickey.'

'It's not a good time, Mrs Mooney.'

A number of her informants called her that. It seemed to fall easily to the tongue, probably because a man would have been addressed as mister. None of them called her Stella.

'Someone coming for the car?' Mickey was silent on that one. The gales, the big seas off the south coast, meant that ferries weren't running and the supply lines had jammed, leaving Mickey stranded with a midnight blue BMW and a sick expression. Stella took another step into the lock-up. 'Look, I just need something on a crew robbing over in Notting Hill. The police up there are calling them the Clean Machine. I expect the name's got back to them.'

Mickey shook his head. It didn't mean, I don't know; it meant, I can't tell you.

'I need to recover some property,' Stella said. 'It's a murder inquiry.'

'The person's dead?' Mickey asked. 'Let it go. What good can it do?' Mickey the philosopher.

'We need to run some tests. DNA. It's like' – Stella nodded at the BMW – 'let's say that was stolen and we wanted to know who'd handled it. And let's say we had your DNA sample. We'd test the car, we'd get a match, the jury wouldn't hesitate. Say what you like about Stephen Hawking, science is a wonderful thing.'

'I don't know what you're on about,' Mickey said.

'Clean Machine. If we know, you know.'

'Stephen who?'

Stella was prepared to be patient; prepared to explain. 'Anything you come into contact with you mark,' she informed him. 'A hair will do, a fibre, microscopic stuff. I expect you know all this, though, don't you?' She ran a hand over the BMW's bodywork.

'Your car,' Mickey said. 'Could you move your car?'

'I won't be here long, will I? I hope not.'

Mickey grimaced, showing his teeth. 'Mrs Mooney . . .'

She said nothing.

The patio heaters hissed. 'Five crews,' he said. 'Five altogether. Clean Machine – they're just one of them. If I ever get named for this –'

Stella said, 'Tell me and you won't. Don't tell me and you will.'

'This isn't just a bit of a smack. This is . . . I'm dead.'

'Robbery isn't an AMIP event, Mickey. If they look for anyone, it'll be a chis who talks to uniform.'

'Everyone talks to everyone,' Mickey said, 'that's the fucking trouble.' Stella nodded but said nothing. Mickey was getting set: he was almost there. 'They operate off Harefield. Kids, all of them, but there's a management team. The guys that run them set targets and a work-rate.'

'Why five crews?'

'Five gangs on the estate. The kids won't work with people from a different gang.'

'The guys who run the crews: who are they?'

'Don't know.'

'Please . . .'

'There are people I deal with off Harefield, but they're not these people. I could take a guess, but, unless it really matters, don't make me.'

'Okay. We might talk again on that.' Mickey looked unhappy. 'What happens to the gear?'

'It goes to a warehouse, then it gets knocked out to weekend street-markets.'

'This stuff was stolen five days ago.'

'Monday.'

'Yes. So it might still be in the warehouse, is that right?'

'Could be. They tend to leave it for a while, let it go off, you know?'

'Go off?'

'Like food past its use-by. Fresh gear is top of the crime lists.'

'Where's the warehouse?'

'Please move that fucking car, Mrs Mooney, it sticks out like a dog's bollocks.'

'I'm going, Mickey. I'm on my way.' Stella took her car keys out of her pocket. 'Where's the warehouse?'

He gave her a location off the North End Road. It was two streets away from where Stella had lived with George. From where she still lived.

She trickled up to Shepherd's Bush Green at little better than walking pace. It was four o'clock and office parties were turning out on to the streets from restaurants and pubs. Indiscretion was in the air: the manager unfairly passed over for promotion with something on the tip of his tongue; the PA busy with the tip of her tongue as she whispers in her boss's ear.

A girl in fuck-me shoes got nudged off her heels and into the road as she danced with a drunken colleague. The rest of the crowd laughed and cheered. When Stella braked heavily, the girl palmed herself off the passenger door and her partner caught her, swept her back to the pavement and kissed her open-mouthed: season's greetings.

She drove down to the North End Road and found the warehouse – a tall, red-brick building – then parked across the street among a row of cars on a metered stretch. She got out and walked the perimeter of the warehouse, which ran for a short distance along the two streets on either side, and ended with a high wall and delivery yard at the back.

Harriman picked up her call. She said, 'We're going to toss a warehouse off North End Road. Possibility of finding whatever was robbed from Valerie Blake's flat.'

'Do we need it?'

'We'll know when we find it.'

'You're thinking DNA database.'

'It's a possibility.'

'We'd have found it, wouldn't we – when Andy Greegan went in with the search team?'

'The burglars took clothes and shoes. Who knows where she might have gone in them, or who she might have met?'

'Are we calling uniform in?'

'I don't think so.'

'They won't be happy.'

'You're right. On the other hand . . .'

On the other hand, Harriman thought, the more people who know the greater the risk. One bent copper is all it takes.

He said, 'How many of us do you want?'

'Four. You, me, Maxine Hewitt, Frank Silano.'

'Silano?'

'He looks handy, don't you think?'

'When?'

'We'll do it tonight.'

'You mean after they've closed.'

'I'm looking at the place. It's big. Basically, it's a hardware and white goods storage, so obviously semi-legit. They'll have several exits, a dozen or so people in there pulling orders. It's possible that they'll also have clients from the markets. I don't want to go in mob-handed and stir everyone up. And I don't want issues of territory fucking things up. Uniform can have them after we're through.'

'Is it alarmed?' Harriman asked.

'Are you kidding? This is Harefield-run. I should think every villain in west London knows to stay clear. Anyway, even if some joker did try to do the place, I don't think the owners would want the local cops turning up and asking them for their inventory.'

'Shall I warn the armourer?'

'Maybe. I'll talk to Sorley.'

'Come on, Boss, you're never alone with a Glock.'

'Brief the others. Tell them when but don't tell them where or what.'

'Just get one for me, then. *I'll* have the gun.'

'Tell DI Sorley I'm on my way and need a word.'

'Someone ought to have a gun.'

23

Robert Kimber was counting a wad of banknotes like a teller: they crackled as he peeled them off. Delaney was investing. If you're freelance, you back your own hunches.

Up in 16/31 he had a view of gulls drifting down a leaden sky. The walls looked as if they'd been freshly stripped, ready for new wallpaper. New trophies. The place was under-furnished and very tidy. Over by the window, a small workstation with a laptop computer. Kimber stowed the money in his pocket and smiled invitingly. Narrow face, grey-green eyes, blond hair with a flop to it. The pouty mouth spoiled things, Delaney decided.

He handed Kimber his business card. 'Use the mobile number.'

Kimber dropped the card on to a small table that stood between them, without bothering to look at it. Mister Cool. 'Do you want something? Coffee or a beer?'

'No.' Delaney put a cassette-recorder down on the table. 'You okay with this?'

'Used to it. The police record you.'

Delaney switched on but let the silence ride a minute. Then, 'I suppose the first thing to ask is why you did what you did.'

Kimber was holding the smile. 'Kill her?'

'Confess to it.'

'Because I killed her.'

'The police don't think so.'

'That's why I'm sitting here talking to you.'

'They're sure of it.'

'I know, they told me.'

'Okay, let's go from a different angle. You killed her, then you walked into a police station and told them so. Why do that?'

'To see what would happen next.'

'What did happen next?'

'We had a little game. When will this be out?'

'I'm not sure. I have to sell it first.'

'You said it would be in the paper.'

'It will be. You're too good to pass up, don't worry.'

Kimber's laptop played a five-note tune. He ignored it. Delaney went on asking questions, but he wasn't interested in getting a Q & A interview – he just wanted Kimber to talk. His article would take it for granted that Kimber was a liar, a victim of the Judas Syndrome; what he was after was detail, personal stuff, self-betrayal.

You're too good to pass up. Kimber liked the idea. He talked seamlessly, all the time with a bright little smile on his face. After twenty minutes Delaney said, 'You know, I wouldn't mind that coffee.'

Kimber went to the kitchen. Delaney got up and walked to the window. The city was dim under a low drift of cadmium and carbon monoxide. The laptop was showing Kimber's email window and announcing *one unread message*. Delaney left that message alone. He went to 'Inbox' and glanced at the recent list: some spam, the rest from 'Angel'. He opened one and a name caught his eye.

I expect you enjoyed leading them a dance. DS Mooney, was that the name the papers gave? Did you enjoy your sessions with her?

They always hold something back, don't they? What did you

do about that? I expect you stayed vague. I expect you did some ducking and diving. You must have been pretty good because it took them a while to work you out, didn't it? I expect you went in prepared. You must have known something. What did you know?

Delaney glanced towards the kitchen. He scrolled down.

The thing I really want to ask – how did it feel pretending it was you – pretending you had killed Valerie? I expect it was thrilling. It was thrilling, wasn't it? Did you run through it in your mind? I expect you did. I wonder how close you got to the real thing. I could tell you how close. We could compare notes.

I would love to run through it with you. I would love to take you through it, step by step.

The kitchen door had swung to and Kimber kicked it open, coming down the hallway with two cups of coffee. He found Delaney where he'd left him. Kimber's smile was no less eager.

He said, 'What else do you want to know?'

Mike Sorley's office was a litter of store bags. New life, new responsibilities. He held up a kidskin handbag with a tag on it that read 'Echt Leder'. Stella nodded. 'She'll like it.'

'Like it?'

'Love it.'

'You think so?'

'Trust me.'

Sorley looked pleased. He said, 'I never used to do this. Make the choice. She used to tell me what to get and where to go for it.' 'She' was the wife Sorley had left. 'I didn't know I had taste. I spoke to DC Harriman. He said you'd made a firearms request.'

'And you said –'

'Nothing yet. What's the risk factor, one to ten?'

'Somewhere between two and nine,' Stella told him.

'You expect to find people in there?'

'Not really.' She paused. 'It's possible.'

'I'll authorize it. Someone ought to tell uniform.'

'I thought I'd leave that to you.'

'I'll try to get round to it,' Sorley said, 'sooner or later.'

Stella put in a call to John Delaney. She said, 'I don't know what time I'd be home. I could go to the flat: it might be simpler.'

Home, the flat, your place, my place . . . What do you say when you don't quite belong anywhere?

He said, 'Whatever you want.'

'I'm going to be over there. Over by the flat.'

'Sure. Okay.'

'Just don't put the chain on. Don't lock me out.'

He laughed. 'Never.' He knew that she had to be given a long rope. All women.

24

A Yale can be tricked with a credit card, a barrel lock will give up to a pincer-pick, you can take a gib-saw to a brass lever lock. All these work. So does a Hatton gun, which is the mechanical version of a flat-footed kick from Robocop. It makes a lot of noise, but Frank Silano wasn't worried about waking the neighbours.

Stella had the list of items supplied by DS Harris. They worked in two teams, Maxine and Silano going to the third floor and working down, Stella and Pete Harriman going to the basement and working up. There were neon strips in every room. It wasn't complicated. One floor was white goods, one floor was electrical goods, one floor was any hardware that wasn't in those categories and one floor was clothes. Everything was racked according to type: dresses, coats, shoes. Stella speed-dialled Maxine.

She said, 'We're on the ground floor. There's a lot to look at.'

In the end, though, Valerie Blake's things weren't difficult to find: the descriptions she'd given had been accurate. They had put on latex gloves and were packing the clothes into evidence bags when Harriman touched Stella's arm. Maxine and Silano saw the gesture and paused. All four of them fell silent.

Stella simply nodded: *Yes. I heard it.*

They listened. They took out their guns. They waited. The sound came again, but it was difficult to interpret. A sleeper harried by a nightmare . . . something in pain. Silano pointed to the far end of the room. Beyond the racks of clothes was a rubble of boxes and garments thrown down anyhow: rejects, perhaps, or items yet to be sorted. The noise came again, high and broken, almost musical.

Stella motioned to Harriman, who went left as she went right, each circling in order to get to the space between the boxes and the wall. Harriman walked through, but Stella had to kick down a stack of boxes. It sounded like a landslide. She stepped through, bringing her gun to bear at about head-height, then adjusting when she saw the figures on the floor. Harriman was already in position but holding his weapon at his side.

There were six. Four adults and two children. One of the children was a baby. The mother had the child to her breast and she was weeping; that was the strange, muted sound Stella had heard. The woman's husband still had his hand clamped across her mouth. Some of her pain he could cram back, but some was unstoppable. At first, Stella thought the woman's distress must come from fear and, like Harriman, she lowered her gun. Then she saw that the child was dead.

They looked at Stella, wide-eyed and fearful, all except the mother. She was looking down at her baby and making those terrible noises and offering the child her breast and all the time her tears were falling on to its lifeless head like rain.

It was a mixed convoy: an ambulance, a police security vehicle, two patrol cars, a pair of immigration officers in a standard-issue Land Rover. The mother went alone into the ambulance. Alone, save for her dead child. Her husband called to her as he was put into the security van. He reached out, as if his arm could span the distance between him and his wife, as if he might touch her, and he howled, his mouth wide, his eyes fixed on her. She was holding the child tightly, its head still lifted to her nipple. A smudge of milk lay on its partly open lips.

One of the immigration officers gave a case number to Stella along with his card. Stefan Bowers. He said, 'Just make it Steve. There'll be some forms to fill in.'

'I bet there will.'

'We're going to call in the cavalry now,' he told her. 'The chances are these people were going to be moved on tonight. We might get lucky.' He looked round at the vehicles, the cops, the roof-bar lights. 'Maybe not, though.'

'Where do you think they're from?' Stella asked.

'Eastern Europe at a guess. Romania, perhaps.'

'The child was dead,' Stella said.

Bowers nodded, looking away towards the ambulance as it moved off. 'We'll need to check that.'

'Check what?'

'Cause of death – possibility of contagion.'

Maxine Hewitt was sitting in the passenger seat of her car with the door open and her feet on the pavement. She said, 'I'm being hard-nosed about it. I'm thinking of it as being all in a day's work.'

'Yeah,' Stella said. 'Me too.'

Harriman took the back routes to Stella's flat in Vigo Street. Her sometime home. There were fairy lights in windows and drunks in doorways.

He said, 'It happens every day.'

'I know that,' Stella told him. 'I don't see it every day.'

There was a faint smell of gun-oil in the car.

She jacked up the heating and looked in the fridge, but she'd been away for too long. Things had died in there; had died and were rendering down. The freezer compartment carried a cook-from-frozen American Hot and a bottle of Stoli. She took them out.

This is dangerous.

A shot-glass, a single ice-cube, vodka over the ice to the top of the glass, so a little meniscus formed, thick and clear. She sat on a kitchen stool with the glass on the worktop in front of her and leaned in to take in its scent – just the faintest thing, but Stella could detect the wheat, the rye, the barley malt, the herbs. Or thought she could. The rye, the high, the risk, the rashness, the dreams of dead babies.

Don't go there.

A case where two children had died: Stella's case. It wasn't her fault, but it had felt as if it was. A woman dead, her husband under arrest, and Stella questioning him all night. He had said, 'Where are the children?' He had said it again and again. Stella knew they were safe: they were with his sister. When she went to the house next morning, on a routine call, she had found the children hanging from the banister. The sister had said, 'She's dead now. She's dead, that bitch. All dead.' The social worker had called it a family feud.

Stella had been okay for a while, then one day she'd got into her car and driven away and kept driving. George had found her after a week. On the way back to London, she had started to miscarry her own child. The dream had started after that, always coming at 3 a.m., always bringing her awake, a dream of dead babies and one of them hers. Vodka and the 3 a.m. dream were indivisible.

She waited for the pizza, but then ate only one slice. It tasted old. The vodka tasted brand new.

It was almost possible to hear George's voice. His work-station still in place, his draughtsman's board, his portfolio of designs. He was a boat designer. He'd sent her a letter from Seattle saying how *buoyant* the yacht market was, how it was pretty much *plain sailing*. That kind of corn had been a private joke and she knew he meant something by using it. By running it up the mast.

The past is another country. Don't you know that?

She remade the bed with fresh linen, but couldn't lie in it. Instead she went back to the main room and poured herself another vodka and drank it and then poured another and drank that and sat by the window to watch the winter dawn come up, her face against the cold glass, her eye following the first ragged flocks of birds as they crossed the high, clear, pink-and-aquamarine sky.

She thought of the mother, gagged by her husband's hand, her full breast drooping to the child's face, the smear of milk on those motionless lips.

We'll need to check that. Cause of death – possibility of contagion.

Stella wondered what could be more contagious than sorrow.

25

Pink and aquamarine shaded to blue ice. There were still a few late stars and the frost on iron made pavement railings sticky.

Sadie and Jamie crossed the road by Notting Hill tube and found a sheltered patch outside a newsagent's. People were going in for papers and cigarettes and chocolate. The Christmas spirit was beginning to kick in because Sadie had made enough the previous evening to get off her face, which had made the cold less of a problem for a while. Jamie didn't bother with drugs; he was high on the love of God. Well, he'd smoke a little draw perhaps, but then that was in keeping with spiritual experiences. Jamie had read a book called *Inward Jesus* in which the author demonstrated convincingly that Our Saviour was the Magic Mushroom Man from Galilee. They sat on their bags and Sadie played 'Silent Night'.

Maxine Hewitt went into the newsagent's and bought a pack of B & H.

Pete Harriman stopped for a red light and glanced across at Maxine as she smoked. They were on their way to Harefield to talk to Sophie Simms's boyfriend, who hadn't been hard to ID. Not Scuzz or Buzz but Jaz: Harriman had simply talked to the Drugs Squad and they'd made the connection straight away. Harriman asked whether Sophie had been part of the Harefield drug scene and was told no. 'No' didn't mean she stayed clear of drugs. She took drugs, sure, they all did; it meant that she wasn't connected, that she didn't have anything to do with the importation or distribution of drugs.

The same couldn't be said of Jaz.

Harriman said, 'What do you do when you're not coppering, Max?'

'Very few people call me Max.'

'You don't mind?'

'No, not really.'

'So what's the answer?'

'I do what most people do.'

Harriman hopped the light on amber, pulling towards the kerb in case someone on the right-hand junction was running the red. Someone was: a small Peugeot braked hard and stalled across the grid. A chorus of horns went up. It was London driving, no question.

'You mean go to the movies, go to the pub.'

'Sort of thing.'

'Me too.'

He looked at her and there was a hint of a smile on her lips. He didn't know what kind of a hint it was.

At that time in the morning, Harefield was asleep. There were people on the estate who had jobs and families and lived unexceptional lives, but they went about their business quietly and at night stayed indoors.

Harriman and Maxine were watched as they crossed the DMZ, but this was 9.50 a.m. and daylight and there were two of them. Harefield went on alert when drugs officers came in with dogs and an SO19 gun squad was abseiling down from the tops of the towers to get to the sky-high crack dens. Two cops didn't require an operational response. But they were still an irritant.

A girl came to the door smelling of dope and sex. Maxine showed her a warrant card and she sighed in disgust, then walked back into the flat. Jaz took his time. First he had to climb into some clothes, then he had to visit the bathroom. Harriman wondered how much coke was going down the pan, how much blow.

The living room was furnished with two beaten-up armchairs and a table. When Jaz finally showed up, he took one of the armchairs. His skin was dusky gold and he had sixty-rep biceps.

He said, 'What?'

Harriman asked him about Sophie and Jaz shrugged. 'I knew her.'

'You were seeing her.'

'I see lots of women, yeah?'

'She died,' Maxine said. 'Did you hear about that?'

Jaz glanced up at her. He saw the look in her eye. He said, 'Out in the park. Bad shit.'

'She told her sisters you were special to her. You were together.'

'Nah, man. Why would she say that?'

'Maybe,' Harriman said, 'she believed it was true.'

Jaz held up his hands. 'What do I know?'

'You let her think it?'

'Let her think? I don't let people think. They think what they think. Listen, she wanted to hang out, that was okay, and she liked to fuck. She was good at it.' He laughed. 'They could put it on her gravestone.'

Maxine said, 'What's your real name, Jaz?'

'Why?'

'Because if you've ever been arrested we might have your DNA on the database. In which case, I need your name. And, in case we haven't, I'm asking you to give a sample now.'

Jaz said he was Jason LeGuinnec. He spelled it for them. Yes, he'd been busted. Yes, he'd given a swab. And he wanted them to know that he was on the other side of London when Sophie had been attacked, okay? He was there with *people*.

Harriman said nothing. He knew that Jaz hadn't killed Sophie. Maxine knew it too, but she decided to make Jaz give a second sample for the hell of it. Jaz rubbed the swab round his mouth and over his gums, then dropped it into a glassine envelope.

Maxine smiled at him as they were leaving. She said, 'Not this but something else. Take it from me. You're on a list. It's just a matter of time. We'll fix you up.'

Jaz went to the door with them like an attentive host. Good idea to show a little class. Good idea to let people know that the cops were there to mess you up.

Jaz lived on Floor 16. He watched Harriman and Maxine walk away, watched Harriman hammer on Kimber's door as he passed, then turn, twenty feet further on, as Kimber opened the door and looked out.

'Robert Adrian Kimber,' Harriman yelled. 'Good morning, you sick fuck.'

There was a market in the main street. Stallholders dressed in red pixie hats were offloading Christmas trees and strings of lights and rolls of Santa paper. You could get lookalike YSL and lookalike Rolex and lookalike Chanel. A sound system was playing carols loud enough to harrow Hell.

Harriman nudged along in the tailback. There was only one tailback in London, but it went all the way. He said, 'Movies, yes, definitely. I don't go to the theatre.' He pronounced it 'theahtuh' and waved an expressive hand.

'You should give it a try.'

'Shall we?'

Maxine didn't take his lead. She lit a cigarette and looked out at the laden stalls. 'How much of this would be knock-off, do you think?'

Harriman said, 'You're not queer, are you?' – grinning, making a joke of it.

She was exhaling smoke and a great laugh came with it, making her cough so that she had to wait, reaching for breath. Finally, she said, 'Yes, I am. I am queer. I've been queer since I was seventeen. I'm definitely queer.'

Harriman knew a rat-run. He swung the wheel and juiced the car into a maze of back streets. He made good time. He faced down drivers coming the other way.

Finally, he said, 'That would be it, then.'

26

As exhibitions officer it was Nick Robson's job, after the warehouse raid, to bag, store, catalogue and keep every item that had relevance to the case. Valerie Blake's clothes and shoes would go to Forensics in the hope of a happy match, but then they would come back to Nick. In the meantime he took the gleanings from the pockets of Valerie's stolen dresses and jackets and entered them on the database.

a tube ticket
a 'while you were out' card from the Post Office
a letter
a tube of lip-balm
a blister pack of Nurofen
a hair-tie
a receipt from a petrol station at Heathrow

These items would go to Forensics too, but Stella wanted to look them over first. She was wearing latex gloves and using tweezers to turn the pages of the letter. It was written to Duncan Palmer but had never been posted. It said, *I love you*. It said, *What's wrong?* It said, *Are you having second thoughts?* It said, *Is it the workload, the wedding, the fuss, is it me?*

Stella turned to Robson. She said, 'Get this to Forensics and ask them for a quick turnaround. There's a guy down there called Tom Davison. Tell him I asked after his underwear.' She indicated the Post Office card. 'Someone sent her a parcel. Let's find out what it is.'

Mike Sorley had left a note on her desk: *Call by*. She walked down the corridor to where he was elbow-deep in paper, a cigarette in his mouth, another forgotten in an ashtray. Someone had inked a message round the rim of the ashtray: SMOKING MAKES YOU IMPOTENT.

He said, 'Know why I became a copper?'

'So you could pull people off the street, falsely accuse them and kick them round a cell. It's what career coppers do. I read it in the papers.'

'Yes. So why am I doing admin? Fucking admin. I'm Admin Man.'

'And you don't –'

'And I don't qualify for overtime because of rank. Exactly.' He shoved some reports aside and washed his face with his hands. 'I'm feeling a bit crap.'

'Don't get flu.'

'I will if I fucking want. You had a lively time last night.'

'We got what we went for.'

'What happened to the illegals?'

'They'll be in nick by now, along with a mixed bunch of killers, rapists, GBH specialists and psychos, most of whom will want to kill them on the grounds that they're available.'

Sorley looked at her. '*What?*'

Stella shrugged. 'It's not their fault.'

'It's not yours,' Sorley said. 'It's not mine.'

'Okay.' Stella let it lie. It was politics. Don't do politics. Leave it to the bent bastards in Westminster.

'A view has been taken,' Sorley told her, 'that things aren't going along all that fast. In fact, aren't moving much at all. It's been suggested that Valerie Blake and Sophie Simms get handed over to the team that caught the earlier attacks.'

'And are they close to a result?'

'No.'

'Exactly. We liaised with them. There are certain similarities, but the differences are striking.'

'There's a theory that it's copy-cat. You suggested it yourself.' Sorley started to fish through the piles on his desk, looking for the relevant report.

'If it's copy-cat, then we're talking about different individuals, different thinking. The MO might look familiar, but one line of inquiry isn't going to bring us two killers. Apart from that – DNA. No matches.'

'There's pressure,' Sorley told her. 'You're going to have to give me something soon.'

Jaz was feeling bad. Not ill but not good. It had to do with visits from the cops and Sophie dying and having sluiced some street-cut coke down the pan – and people, he thought, people getting in my fucking *face*.

The girl who'd opened the door to Harriman and Maxine fished out some skins and a block of gold. She put the TV on and Jaz switched it off. She started to speak and he told her to shut up. When she sparked up, Jaz took the spliff for himself, then made a call on his mobile and went out.

The girl said 'Bastard' to his retreating back, though not loud enough to be heard. She rolled another spliff and watched *Bargain Hunt*; it was the high-point of her day.

Jaz picked up three guys in the bull ring. They smoked for a while and drank some high-percentage beers and talked deals. Then they went back up to the sixteenth floor and knocked at the door of Flat 31. When Kimber came to the door, Jaz explained their thinking.

Harefield was a business address and the cops are bad for business.

Kimber was a celebrity now. They'd seen him in the papers.

Celebrities were okay in their place. This wasn't the place.

Now the cops were making regular visits.

This had to stop. It was a problem.

Kimber might think that a change of address would solve the problem.

It was certainly what everyone else was thinking.

They were pretty sure he'd agree.

They were prepared to give him all of two days to agree.

Kimber was dressed to go out. He was wearing a yellow, down-filled jacket and a blue baseball cap with a dark red peak: you'd spot him in a crowd for sure.

Jaz said, 'Okay?'

'Okay,' Kimber agreed.

As he made to leave, Jaz shouldered him back against the door and held him there a moment. Kimber's expression blanked. He stared up past the circle of tower blocks to where a gull was sliding down the wind. It banked, stiff-winged, looking for easy pickings.

Jaz laughed. He was feeling a little better.

Kimber's journey took him through Notting Hill Gate, where he stopped off to buy a pack of cigarettes. A girl with a penny whistle was playing Christmas carols, pinched with the cold, scarcely able to hold a tune. A boy with rank hair and a tangled beard was sitting close by and talking to her; or talking to himself.

When Kimber emerged from the shop, Sadie said, 'Spare some change?' He didn't look at her. As he started down Holland Park Avenue, she added, 'You prick.'

A girl went by in a leather coat and long scarf. Another was wearing a dark blue woollen coat. Kimber noted them. Either would have done: follow her, get close to her, find out about her, take a clipping of her hair. He watched them till they were out of sight, then forgot them. Something more important was happening. He felt alive in every nerve, his heart tapping hard, his fingers tingling with the cold.

Some item of clothing I'll recognize you by.

27

The Dove was busy, but no one was using the deck that overlooked the river, so they took their drinks out there. The river was high and flowing fast. Gull-cry, the sky slate blue, a wind off the water.

'You're not as I imagined you.'

Kimber took off the baseball cap. He said, 'No? How did you see me?'

'More like me.'

Heavy build, squat face, thin lips, high cheekbones, dark hair receding off his forehead, but the eyes a pale blue that seemed almost colourless in the winter sunlight. Not Oriental, not exactly Russian. Something that didn't quite fit.

'And you are?' The man sipped his drink. Kimber asked again, 'I don't know your name.'

'Leon Bloss.' The man held out his hand, the last thing Kimber expected. He went to shake and found himself holding a gold cross on a thin gold chain. The clasp was broken. 'Valerie's,' Bloss said. 'Valerie's crucifix.' He had a high, thin laugh, like a bird's cry.

Kimber closed his hand over it and a shock, like voltage, travelled to his shoulder. He realized he was trembling.

He said, 'Why did you kill her?'

Bloss was looking across the river to the far towpath. A flat-bed cargo vessel went by, lifting a silvery-green wake. He lit a cigarette and let the smoke flow from his mouth and nostrils. Kimber sat patiently, clutching the crucifix, the little cross-bar biting into the palm of his hand. He knew that a decision was being taken, something larger and more dangerous than whether Bloss simply answered his question, though answering the question was a part of it. Or maybe he was being offered an opportunity. Was it too late to walk away?

'Well,' Bloss said, 'she made herself available to me.'

Kimber sighed, relaxing his hand, and the cross caught a glint of the sun.

It had always been too late.

They walked on the towpath, hands deep in pockets, shoulders hunched against the upstream wind.

Bloss asked, 'Do you work? Have you got a job?'

'Made redundant a year ago. I got a package ... there's that, and social security.'

'Good. That's good.'

'I have to move,' Kimber said. 'I have to find somewhere to live.'

'There's a problem?'

'The police ... they know where to find me. They come round from time to time. It makes people nervous. It makes me nervous.'

'Still on the Harefield Estate?'

'Yeah.'

Bloss said, 'We'll find you a new place. No problem.'

'Tell me ... what was it like? Valerie ...'

'How did you select them – the girls you followed?' A question answered with a question.

'If they were sexy. If they looked my way. If they got on my bus.'

'Never anyone you knew?'

'No. Just one time. A girl I worked with. But it wasn't any good.'

'Why not?'

'I liked it that she was there in the office and chatted to me and didn't know that we had, you know, a different *connection*. But I knew her and –'

'What?'

'I wasn't the stranger. She knew my name, all sorts of things about me. It didn't work.'

'You cut their hair. You told me . . . you took a snip of their hair. Why did you do that?'

'You took Valerie's cross.'

Bloss nodded. 'Yes . . .' He held out a hand and Kimber returned the crucifix. He'd been holding it all the time.

The cross and the snippets of hair: tiny power-sources, as if they held a live charge.

'We'll go back and collect your things,' Bloss said, 'I know of a place. I don't suppose you'll have much to move.'

'No.'

'I've got a car. We'll get you out of there. Don't worry: it's as good as done.'

They found a bench and sat there: old friends out for the day.

Bloss picked up a couple of pebbles from the path and lobbed them at the water. Droplets rose and glittered. He said, 'Did you ever think of going further?'

'I broke in a couple of times. Looked around. Touched their stuff.' Kimber paused. '*Smelled* things. Thought I might wait for them to come home.'

'Smell's important,' Bloss said. 'I can vouch for that.'

'I never did what you did.'

'Wait for them, and –'

'I wasn't sure how to do it. Get it right.'

'Wait for them and fuck them.'

'I thought about that.'

'Kill them.'

'I thought about that.'

'How did you feel, being in there, in her place, among her things, knowing she would come back, and even if you weren't there, you'd *been* there?'

'As good as following. Better, in some ways.'

'What did you leave?'

'How do you know I –'

'What was it?'

'It might be . . . something on the pillow.'

'A trace of yourself.'

'Just a trace. Just a smear. Or I'd lick the cups.'

Bloss looked at him, almost startled. 'What?'

'The cups in her cupboard. Lick them.'

Bloss smiled. 'Yes, I like that.'

'But I never did what you've done. How is it? How does it make you feel?'

'You know,' Bloss said, 'I made a bit of a mistake with Valerie. I wanted to make it look like sex. Like a sex thing. I took her clothes off and left them somewhere else. There had been other attacks, I'd read about them, and I'd sort of got the idea that they were about sex as much as killing. He used a garrotte.' Bloss paused; a light smile washed his face. 'Very personal; very *hands on*.'

'That's why you did Sophie the same way.'

Bloss was silent a while, then he said, 'Yes.'

'I knew her,' Kimber said. 'She was seeing a guy . . . a few doors down from me. Well, didn't know her, but I knew who she was. I used to see her go past, see them going somewhere together, see her crossing Rose Park from time to time.'

'There you go,' Bloss said. 'It's all connected. The world works that way.'

'I even thought about following her sometimes. Not serious, because she was an estate girl, but I thought I might get a clipping. She had nice hair.'

Bloss said, 'Is that right? I didn't notice.'

'They kept asking me how I'd killed her. Valerie.'

'What did you say?'

'Boxed clever. Tried to. I didn't know about the garrotte.'

'It's a very personal way of doing it. You can feel them going. And it's up to you how fast. It's an inch by inch thing.'

'But you used the hammer.'

'To quieten her down.'

'No, I mean with Sophie.'

'Ah, yes. To make it look like the others. And I left the ligature to link Sophie to Valerie. So they would think of them as all of a piece – all the attacks.' Bloss shook his head and gave a little laugh. 'I don't usually do things that way.'

'How then?'

'Whatever occurs. Common mugging. Break-in gone wrong. Sometimes an accident if the opportunity presents. You have to be ready to improvise. You know the way a carpenter will go with the grain? Like that.'

A craftsman talking to an apprentice. Kimber could envisage the learning curve.

They walked back in a rising wind. Kimber said, 'Can I have it?'

Bloss knew he meant Valerie's gold cross. He shook his head. 'I'd like to, but it's spoken for.'

'How many?' he asked. 'All in all.'

He meant how many trophies; how many dead.

'I don't know,' Bloss said. 'I try not to look back. Nostalgia's an overrated thing.'

28

Sue Chapman had been replaced by Marilyn Hayes, one of the team's civilian computer operatives. The people working with Marilyn had shared her tasks between them. Paperwork and budget: the operational watchwords. Marilyn was striking. She had good looks, a great figure, a tumble of black curls, and you could only wear those jeans with those fashion boots if you had great legs. The most striking thing about her from Pete Harriman's point of view was the wedding ring.

As Harriman passed her desk, Stella smiled. She said, 'Life is full of little disappointments.'

Harriman was silent on the subject.

Marilyn patched a call through to Stella. Tom Davison said, 'You asked after my underwear, DS Mooney. I can tell you that it's a very full topic.'

'Crowded, I imagine.'

'Packed with good things.'

'What you don't know about me,' Stella said, 'is that I'm a year off retirement and have problems with weight and alopecia.'

'That's not what the hidden-camera shows. I've got a DNA match for you.'

'That was fast.'

'Not the clothes and shoes from the warehouse. I'm talking about the scenes of crime – Sophie Simms and Valerie Blake.'

For a moment, Stella missed the point. Then she said, 'A match?'

'All over the place. The unidentified DNA at the Blake scene of crime is also present at the Simms scene of crime.'

'Does it incriminate?'

'I'd say so, yes. There are traces at the wound sites.'

'Male?'

'What do you think?'

'Stranger things have happened. Have you cross-referenced with –'

'The earlier attacks? Yes. Not present.'

'You're sure?'

'We don't work alone down here.'

'What?'

'These results were checked by two other guys.'

'Can I get this in writing?'

'I'll fax it through.'

'Can you do it now?'

'I'm sitting by the fax machine as we speak.'

Sorley had his coat on. His desk was a swamp, but at least he was walking away from it. Stella came in with more paper and he stood up to read it.

'It's the same guy. It's not Kimber, it's not linked to the other attacks. We've got a series of two, positively linked, apparently random, apparently motiveless.'

'The others were random and motiveless.'

'But they weren't committed by our man.'

Sorley picked up his briefcase, heavy with paperwork. He handed the report back to Stella. 'Okay, he killed our two, he didn't kill the others, it doesn't bring us any nearer to finding the bastard, does it?'

'No, but it means we've got his DNA. It also means that we don't have to transfer Blake and Simms to the other teams.'

Sorley hefted the briefcase, testing its weight. 'Oh, good.'

As she was leaving, Nick Robson handed her a brown office envelope. Nick was tall and had a moustache that was too old for his face. 'The package waiting for Valerie Blake at the Post Office,' he said. 'A video. It was in a padded bag: I've sent that off to Forensics along with the video-sleeve. We dusted the vid and it was clean, so I think it's okay to let it go.'

'What's on it?'

'It was a plain sleeve.'

'But you didn't play it?'

'We haven't got a VCR.' Stella put the envelope in her bag and headed for the door. Robson said, 'How well do you know that guy Davison in Forensics?'

'Never met him.'

'Really?' Robson said. 'He seemed to know a lot about you.'

She walked past her car and straight across the road to the pub. It was instinct more than choice. When she'd been with George, towards the end when going home had seemed either too bleak an option or too cosy, she would hole up in the pub for a couple of early-evening drinks. A couple, or three. She would take the day's reports and browse through them, as if she were there for just that purpose though, in truth, she needed time out of time, a place where she didn't belong.

Maybe it was having gone back to the Vigo Street flat. Maybe it was that she couldn't bring herself to lie in the bed, or it was almost believing she could hear George's voice, or being up at 3 a.m. with a bottle of Stoli.

Old habits.

She ordered a drink: shot-glass, ice, vodka. She had drunk it and its partner when she saw Harriman sitting in a booth at the far end of the bar. She took her last drink, her *final* drink, and sat down with him. He said he was just killing time.

'Until –?'

'I'm meeting someone. No point in going home.' She fished in her bag and handed him the report Davison had faxed through. He angled it to the light to read. The pub was dressed for Christmas and the lamps were covered with a holly and ivy crêpe-paper trim.

'Doesn't help us find him,' he observed.

'Sorley said that.'

'But it lets us know what to focus on.'

'Exactly.'

Harriman sipped his beer, looking at Stella over the glass. He said, 'Don't laugh, okay?'

'Okay.'

'Did you know Maxine Hewitt's gay?'

'Well, I'm afraid I did, yes.' She was laughing despite her promise.

'Thanks,' he said. 'Thank you very much.'

She had walked back to her car when she saw Marilyn Hayes leaving. In the car-park lights it was possible to see that Marilyn had freshened her make-up, and the jeans–boots combination looked as good as ever.

Stella watched her across the road and into the pub.

Never second-guess a class operator.

29

Delaney said, 'You don't look good.'

'I didn't sleep.' Stella was cooking. She had called in to an Eight-til-Late on her way back and picked up salmon steaks and salad, which was as close to the notion of ingredients as she was prepared to get. He'd opened a bottle of wine, but she'd poured herself a vodka.

'Bad dreams –'

'No dreams at all.'

He put his arms round her and kissed her. The liquor had made her breath hot and heady. He said, 'I love you,' which was true and she knew it.

'How are your street-people?'

'They're out in the cold.'

'In both senses'

'Exactly. They're beginning to sense a genuine affinity with the Baby Jesus.'

'But they're good copy.'

'Couldn't wish for better.'

'This case,' Stella said, 'this fucking case is going a step forward and a leap backwards.'

'What's the step forward?'

'We found a DNA match at the Simms and Blake scenes of crime. Exclusive to those scenes.'

'And it doesn't belong to Robert Kimber.'

'No, it doesn't.'

'But that still doesn't help you find –'

Stella held up a hand to stop him going any further. 'It should have been Kimber,' she said. 'He sounded right and he felt right and he had the look.'

'What look?'

'You know it when you see it.'

'Copper's instinct.'

'That would be it.'

'Gut feeling . . . sort of a hunch, really.'

'Shut up.' She hit him on the arm, laughing, and turned to put the salmon into the oven. 'Make the salad. You open the bag and invert it over a bowl; tricky till you get the hang of it.'

Delaney opened his mouth to tell her about Kimber's emails, then closed it again. He wasn't through with Kimber: there was more to be had. But if he let Stella know that he'd visited the man and interviewed him, that chance would be lost. All he'd hear would be the sound of doors slamming and one of them would probably be the door to his flat.

Valerie Blake's video was lying on the worktop. He moved it to find a place for the salad bowl. 'What's this?'

'I don't know yet,' she said. 'Put it on.'

Stella cut a lemon into quarters. She dropped one of the quarters into her drink and splashed a little more vodka into the glass.

Delaney poured vinegar and oil into a screwtop jar. He added a little Dijon mustard and some crushed garlic and shook the jar hard.

Kimber said, 'Hello, Valerie. You don't know me but I know you.'

Stella paused, the glass at her lip. Delaney paused in mid shake. The man on the video was wearing a face-mask made of some thin, glossy material, satin or silk, with holes cut for the eyes and mouth. His lips were slightly pursed and damp and pink. Even though the tape was short, he had a lot to say for himself.

After a while, Stella said, 'It's Kimber.'

Delaney knew it was but couldn't say so. They watched it three times. Later, Marilyn Hayes would make a transcript of it for circulation, and, as she set down the words, she would feel her face burn, feel the nerves in her back jump as if someone had pulled a wet thread in her spine.

Hello, Valerie. You don't know me but I know you. I know where you go and what you do. I know where you live . . . as you can tell, or how could I have sent you this message? What did you think when the postman delivered it? Something a friend had sent? And what do you think now? [LAUGHTER] Well, I am a friend, Valerie. Think of me as a friend you haven't met as yet. A friend in the offing, you might say. I watched you reading on the tube the other day. I don't read much, really, but I might try that book, just to imagine you following the story, just to share it with you. I like it when you go jogging, Valerie. I can see your shape. I can see your breasts move. I like the way your hair lifts in the wind when it's not tied back. When you're walking in the street you look from side to side, look into shops. If you'd known, you might have seen my reflection there sometimes, just behind you, waiting for you to set off again. Sometimes I'll be coming towards you, sometimes I'll be behind you. You never knew, did you? I'm always there. It would be no good looking, because I'm just one in a crowd. How would you know me? You don't know me, but I know you. [LAUGHTER] I think I'll come over and see you some night. I think I'll come round. You'll be asleep. Fast asleep, but when you wake up I'll be there. I'll be there in the room with you. And we'll have such fun. [LAUGH-TER] Let me tell you what we're going to do . . .

After the screen went to blue for the third time, Stella speed-dialled Sorley and held the phone close to the TV while he listened.

He said, 'What do you want to do? We know he's not our man.'

'What we do know is that he's a stalker and he had a lot of fun at our expense. Now this. Intimidation, issuing threats, obscene articles through the post, intent to commit a serious crime, you name it. And he's walking the streets, free as air.'

'You want to nail him anyway.'

'That's right. Bring him in and hand him over to Serious Crimes. He'll have sent other videos to other victims. There'll be crime reports. DNA, voice-printing, shouldn't be difficult.'

'You could give them the video. Let them go after him.'

'Why wait?'

'Is this personal, Stella?'

'Yes, it's personal.'

'Fair enough. Go and get the bastard.'

The message she left on Pete Harriman's mobile said, 'I know what you're doing and I know who you're doing it with, but you're missing all sorts of fun at sixteen thirty-one, Block C.'

She took Maxine Hewitt and Frank Silano and called in two ARV teams to watch their backs. The Hatton gun made a bass-percussion sound as it took the door out, but at that time of night it was one bass-percussion sound among many.

There was a detritus of odds and ends scattered about and, in Kimber's bedroom, the closets and drawers were empty. The scant furniture was still in place, but the small workstation had gone. They made a search anyway, but it was clear there would be nothing to find.

'Think he knew,' Silano asked, 'or got lucky?'

'Lucky. Two hours ago, I didn't know myself.'

Silano took the kitchen. A full rubbish bin, stale food, cardboard sleeves from ready meals.

Maxine took the bedroom. A jumble of unwanted clothes and a dirty sheet heaped on the mattress; she turned them with latex-gloved hands.

Stella took the main room. Circulars, giveaways, pizza vouchers.

John Delaney's business card.

As they were leaving Kimber's apartment, the Drugs Squad were emerging from Jaz's place. Jaz was with them, his wrists snared by plastic handcuffs. When he spotted Maxine, he looked puzzled for a moment, then he saw the light. He showed her his teeth and she smiled back at him.

'I told you,' she said, 'that it was just a matter of time.'

The girl stood in the doorway, looking a little unsteady on her feet. She focused on Maxine and called her a fucking bitch, but didn't know what to do next.

Stella watched as Jaz was hauled off. She said, 'Did you do that?'

Maxine shrugged. 'Someone certainly did.'

'Ask me,' Stella told her. 'Ask me before you call up the heavy squad.'

'I didn't say it was me.'

'No, you didn't,' Stella agreed. She might have been smiling.

In the bull ring, a group of boys had gathered, hoodies pulled forward, diesel denim scuffing the ground. Stella and

Frank Silano got into the car, but Maxine delayed a moment. She pointed at the boys, her thumb cocked.

'You're next,' she advised them, and her thumb wagged: one round, two rounds, three. Blam-blam-*blam*!

30

Bloss and Kimber strolling on the Strip, up among the druggies and the whores, the dealers and the high-rollers. The night was cold, but everyone was out to play. Although it wasn't raining, there was a light mist in the air, a thin cloud of droplets that carried exhaust gases and fast-food stain and ganja-smoke and a rainbow haze of neon. Bloss had taken Kimber to a studio flat on the main road, just before you hit the Strip. It was over a bookie's and faced the cemetery. Just now, they were checking the territory; they were getting the lie of the land.

'Anyone,' Bloss was saying. 'Anyone you choose. But here's the trick: it has to be someone you don't know. Who doesn't know you. As if they were random.'

'They always are,' Kimber told him. 'The ones I follow.'

'We're not talking about following.' Then Bloss checked his stride and glanced at Kimber. 'Are we?'

Kimber looked away to where a girl was making a sale to a punter driving a family hatchback, bending low to give him a good look at what was on offer. She undid the top button of her fake-fur coat and named a price. All the girls were wearing fur: red, blue, pink, black, orange, tiger-striped or pinto.

'Her?' Bloss asked. 'Yes, it could be her. Bit close to home, perhaps.'

Kimber nodded. 'I used to see a girl up here. Nancy.' He looked round as if he might find her. 'I paid her, you know. I like that. It's the best way. I paid and I did what I wanted.'

'And what was that?'

'Games.'

They walked a little further. The whores eyed them but didn't approach. Bloss had a look that said *Not me; not now.* The pimps eyed them too, then shrugged and turned away; these guys weren't punters and they weren't cops, so obviously they had business of their own and as long as it didn't stop the hookers hooking, the pimps would have no complaints.

A spinner with STAND on one side and FAST on the other was advertising a minicab rank. Bloss made a deal with one of the drivers and they went down to Notting Hill and ordered drinks in the Ocean Diner.

He said, 'Here's how it works. You pick your ground, you pick your person, you pick your method. If there's no connection between you, you can't be caught. In order to be caught, you have to make a mistake. That's why I wanted to make it look as if Valerie and Sophie had been done by whoever attacked the other women – because it's likely *he'll* make a mistake. There was nothing between Valerie and me; nothing between Sophie and me.' He was drinking whisky over ice, rolling it round his mouth, savouring it. 'Except that I killed them, of course.'

'Did you follow them?'

'Follow . . . ?'

'For a few days, maybe. A week or so. Beforehand.'

Bloss shook his head. 'Went out. Chose someone' – he made a short, chopping motion with his right hand, the hammer coming down – 'took my chance.'

'I'd follow,' Kimber said. A man with his preferences; a man with his own way of doing things. 'I'd want to follow for a bit. Get to know them, get a good sense of them. Tease myself with it.'

'Riskier,' Bloss advised. 'You can be seen.'

'I'm never seen. I'm the invisible man.'

While they were talking, Kimber had been watching people go by in the street. Bloss followed his eyeline and laughed. 'Sure,' he said, 'any of them. Pick any one of them.'

Suddenly, Kimber seemed feverish. His eyes glistened. 'What should I use?'

Bloss finished his drink and signalled for another. He said, 'You have to look at possibilities, weigh things up. It's winter. It's cold. People are wearing heavy coats and other clothing underneath. A knife could be deflected, or might not go deep enough. Do you see what I mean? You might not get the *depth*. You're probably coming up behind the person, so you want your first move to be decisive. More than that, you'll have chosen your ground. You'll have found the place. So you don't want that person getting clear, getting into the open.'

'A hammer,' Kimber suggested, taking a tip from the expert.

'A hammer's good. A hammer works.' Bloss waved a hand to the barman and held up three fingers – make it a triple. 'Now, there's the question of whether you want to kill that person outright, kill her right there and then, or whether you want to spend some time with her.'

'Spend time . . . ?'

'You see, that can be a tricky thing. You want to spend some time, so you try and get the swing just right, hard enough to put her down but not so she's dead. Maybe not even out, but let me tell you, that's more luck than judgement. Some people have thin skulls.'

Kimber had a schooner of beer in front of him, almost untouched. 'Valerie?' he asked.

'Sophie. Second strike, the hammer went through. Went through and stuck. I had to stand on her shoulder and heave to get it back.' Bloss laughed. 'Here's a tip, Bobby. Get a reversible coat. There's always a bit of a problem.'

'Problem?'

'Splatter problem.'

Bloss's drink arrived and he took a long swallow. Kimber said, 'It's Robert.'

'What?'

'Not Bobby – Robert.'

'And babywipes. Don't forget the babywipes.'

A car alarm kicked in directly outside the diner, started by nothing more than the wind. On the other side of the road, a beggar was sitting on her sleeping-bag and playing the penny whistle, her Christmas carol drowned out by the two-tone shriek.

'Now there's a good hit,' Bloss suggested. 'Street-people. No one knows them, no one gives a fuck.'

'A bit impersonal,' Kimber said.

Bloss looked at him and laughed. 'You're right. Bobby, you're so right.'

Earlier, Bloss had watched as Kimber unpacked. The photos that Kimber had pasted to his walls were in an artist's portfolio along with the card of hair-clippings. While Kimber went round the tiny flat distributing his belongings, Bloss sat quietly by the window holding the card, his finger-tips making the faintest contact with the blonde, the brown, the red, the black. He wasn't looking at the snippets, but his hands moved like those of a blind man, tracing the features of a loved one whose face he'd never seen. He lifted the mounting-card closer and took the scent: still a trace of perfume, he thought, and, somehow, wonderfully, a trace of the girls themselves.

163

Now he took a long pull at his Scotch and said, 'Oh, Bobby, you're so right.'

Anne Beaumont was wearing a top coat and a scarf. She opened the door to Stella and said, 'It's after ten.'

'You're going out.'

'I just got in.'

Anne opened the door a little wider and Stella stepped inside. She said, 'Jesus, it's cold.'

They went downstairs to a basement kitchen and Anne took a bottle of red wine from the rack. She said, 'I was listening to the car radio: someone said it's too cold for snow. Difficult to work that one out, since the North Pole's under about fifty feet of it.' She handed Stella a glass of wine and Stella gave her the video, as if it were a fair exchange. 'If this is a scene of crime vid,' Anne warned her, 'I can't watch it on an empty stomach.'

'It's not.'

'I need to eat anyway. Want something?'

They made pasta, which gave Anne long enough to watch the masked man several times. When Kimber got to the list of things he wanted to do to Valerie Blake, she closed her eyes as if it were a defence against the damp, pink lips pursing through silk and lingering on those obscenities.

'Have some Parmesan,' she said; then, 'This is him, is it? The Collector.'

'Robert Adrian Kimber.'

'He's got a lively imagination.'

'We can't find him. He's gone. What I want to know –'

'Is whether this tape tells us anything we didn't know before. Well, the answer's yes and no.' Anne was hungry. She gathered spaghetti on her fork and ate it while Stella waited. 'Remember I said that matters can escalate? A jour-

164

nal's one thing; it's for his own amusement. The tape is something else; it's to bring him into the life of his victim. While he's following her, the trick is to keep out of sight – to remain unknown. Okay, he doesn't want to be identified, obviously, hence the mask, but he does want her to know he's there. The kind of control he gets from following – the kind of power – is his to know about. Now he wants her to know about it too; he wants her to be frightened. She sees that tape and he's an indelible part of her life, not just when she watches it, not for a couple of weeks, but for ever. That might be the purpose. That might be the endgame. It depends how much closer he needs to get. Whether he needs to see the effect of his power over her, see it happening.'

'Which would consist of –?'

'A confrontation. But there's another version of that – confrontation by proxy. That's why he confessed. Okay, he'd done that before, so the Judas Syndrome was already at work in him, but then something altogether more dramatic happens. Think about it: *someone he's been following gets murdered.* Not just any victim, but Valerie. His Valerie. Think of the mixed emotions. She's been taken from him: an outrage. Someone else has singled her out: a greater outrage. But the logical extension of his power-play – Valerie's death – someone's done that for him; outrage, perhaps, but also relief. Relief and excitement. He has to be a part of that, he can't let it go by. So he says it was him. Maybe he half believes it was. You're eating and I'm not.' Anne forked up some more pasta and, for a short while, they ate in silence.

Finally, Stella asked, 'And the tape?'

'Well, he made the tape before Valerie's death, so his assumption was that she'd get it, watch it, be terrified by it. The question is, what next? He can't follow her any more after this. She'd go to the police, they'd be on the case. He could keep sending her videos, I suppose, but I can't see that being satisfactory for very long – same performance every time, really; same script, same costume. Boring.'

'So you think he'd do what?'

'I think he'd either stop – move on to someone else – or he'd kill her.'

'Which?'

Anne smiled. 'I know you think psychiatry is a question of calculating the odds, but people are unpredictable, especially those you've never talked to, never met and know almost nothing about.'

'Apart from the journal and the tape.'

'Right, so he's a type but not a person. Dealing with type is largely guesswork.'

'So guess.'

Ann poured more wine. She said, 'You've got spaghetti sauce on your chin.' Then, 'I think he's ready to kill.'

'Too cold to snow' might be a fallacy, but that's still pretty cold. When Anne opened the door to the street, Stella stepped out and turned with something to say but didn't say it.

'What?' Anne asked.

'Delaney went to see him.'

'Kimber?'

'Yes.'

'Why?'

'The Judas Syndrome – he thought it was a nifty title.'

'Oh, so it's my fault.'

'It would help if you owned up to that, yes.'

Anne laughed. 'He can see an article in it.'

'That's right.'

'And why not?' Anne asked. 'Do you want to come back in, because it's quite astonishingly cold?'

'No, I'm going. It's not so much that he wanted to write a piece, it's more that I asked him not to.'

'Write the piece or see Kimber?'

'Both.'

'And you have a right to ask that?'

'A psychoanalyst's question.'

Anne shrugged. 'I'm a psychoanalyst.'

'But not my psychoanalyst.'

'So why are you asking all these questions that I'm answering while freezing my tits off and not being paid?'

'He went to see Kimber, he didn't tell me he was going to, and he hasn't told me that he did it. He was working off privileged information, things I'd said to him in confidence. It might well have compromised me. It was sneaky.'

'A sneaky journalist. There's a first.'

'He's *my* sneaky journalist, that's the point.'

'So you feel –'

'Betrayed.'

'That's a big word. Very big word. For Jesus Christ's sake, come into the hall, I've lost all feeling in my fingers.'

'No, I'm going. What should I do? Confront him? Wait for him to tell me? Leave it until the piece appears and act outraged? Tell me as a friend.'

'Your problem,' Anne said, 'is not so much the fact that he's done it as whether he might do it again. My problem is that I have frostbite.'

'So what are you saying – wait and see?'

Anne was closing the door as she said, 'That's what life is – a matter of wait and see.'

Stella walked towards her car. She said, 'Why did I fucking ask?'

*

Bloss was drunk, the kind of settled-in drunkenness that would take a long time to bottom out. He wanted to do some more drinking, but thought he'd better go home to do that. There was a tendency to rashness in him.

He left the Ocean Diner with Kimber at his heels; just the right place for him to be. Sadie and Jamie were getting ready to bed down in the side alley. As he passed, Bloss handed Sadie a ten-pound note. He said, 'There's a good night's sleep in that,' and laughed, bird-like and shrill. Sadie took the money and turned away from the alley, hungry to make a connection.

It was late but the streets were full and the bars were on long licence. The Gate Cinema was showing *It's a Wonderful Life*. In the estate agents' windows, colour snaps of six-bedrooms-four-bathrooms that could be yours for a cool two mill were linked by tinsel streamers.

A girl went by, a pretty bottle blonde, and Bloss nudged Kimber, laughing. 'Could be her.'

Another was wearing a fur hat, a quilted coat and tall heels; a pale, perfectly oval face beneath the hat. 'Could be her.'

Another crossed the road towards them, long-limbed, auburn hair caught by the wind. Good to look at. 'Could be her.'

They were all good to look at.

Bloss took Kimber by the bicep and gave a squeeze. 'We'll do it, Bobby. We'll do it together.'

Stella took a drink through to the bedroom, where Delaney was watching TV. He switched it off when she came in.

'It's okay,' she said, 'keep watching.'

'It was just some cop show. Big Shit Cop was a tough

guy who broke all the rules to get things done, but you loved him for it.'

She smiled. 'That's the way it is with Big Shit Rulebreaker Cops.'

'How did it go?'

'We got there. He was out.' She didn't say 'gone'. She didn't say 'not going back' and she didn't say 'your fault'. There's no virtue in a confession when the confessor has nothing to lose.

'You'll peg him another day.'

'Oh, sure.'

He sampled her drink, then set it aside and drew her on to the bed. He kissed her and she kissed him back, of course she did, but all the time they were making love she was thinking bad thoughts.

31

I will call this one Monica.
I will call this one Nancy.
I will call this one Olivia.
I will call this one Patricia.
I will call this one Rosina.

This is a good place for photographs. My new
adress. I can open the window and photograph them
as they go by. Its a main road. I am looking for a
special one. My friend Leon Bloss and I are looking for a special one. I dont know what shes like
but Ill know her when I see her.

This is different to before.

But he just likes the end of it. Thats how it was
with Valerie and Sophie he told me he just went
out and found someone and did it. That was it. End
of story. Not for me. Ill find someone and follow
her a bit get close and know her a bit and that will
make it different. Make it more sniffy-wiffy more
touchy-feely. Smell the perfume off her hair and
maybe brush her shoulder on the tube or listen to
her making a call on her mobile phone know what
her voice sounds like. Thats what Ill do.

Maybe Ill go and see Nancy being just down the
street. Maybe Ill give her a ring. There was one
today a redhead but I dont know if it was natural
she was wearing a long black coat no buttons just

a belt and the coat opened as she walked and she had on a short skirt and bright colured tights and boots. She was choice. I snapped her as she crossed the road I took three or four. I called her Patricia. Now shes up on the wall. If shes a regular Ill follow her.

Theres another wears a leather coat with fur on the collar and round the sleeves. Shes blonde I think its natural but she wears a red hat woollen what they call a beanie cherry red youd call it. Shes the one Ive called Monica. I dont see her so much but I like the look of her. She went into a shop and bought some CDs. I followed her to her flat which is not far and looked up at the window for a while and saw her looking out she didnt see me. It could be her. Choose her perhaps. She might do. She might well do. But I like Patricias short skirt and I like her red hair.

Its just a step its just one step further.

I had a dream last night. I was flying across London and I could see everyone all the girls Ive ever photographed or followed but they couldnt see me. I was the invisible man. And I could walk through walls but they couldnt see me doing that ether. I could walk through walls and get into where they lived but then I was there and they had gone and I felt alone and sad. It was like a dream I used to have when I was small.

Leon says Ive got to get my giro from a different post office each week then they cant track you. I think Ill give Nancy a ring or I could just go up the street their ten a penny up there. All of them are foreign who would miss them? Their trash.

I wish he wouldnt call me Bobby.

I think Ill go out for a walk. I think Ill go and see who I can find. Patricia or Monica or another.

32

There was frost in the air and a high wind-chill factor when Roseanne Cotter walked into Paddington Green nick. She was wearing jeans, a T-shirt and a light sweater, and there was a touch of blue about her lips and tear-streaks on her face. She was carrying a photograph, a holiday snap of herself and her husband in Majorca. She gave the photo to the desk sergeant.

She said, 'His name's Martin.' Her hand remained outstretched as if she might take the photo back, as if she'd had second thoughts. Then she added, 'The girl on the towpath. All the others. His name's Martin.' She was shivering, but it had nothing to do with the weather.

The local CID lifted Martin Cotter twenty minutes later. He'd been asleep and woke up to a ring of cops round his bed, all wearing Kevlar vests and protective headgear and carrying semi-automatic weapons. He lifted his head from the pillow and looked round as if there might be some simple explanation for this, then realized that there was.

He said, 'Roseanne.'

They kept their guns trained on him as he got out of bed, but he was carrying nothing more than a hangover and a lean stare. Roseanne had told them where to look: they went down to the small basement where Martin kept a DIY workroom. His tools were racked in order of type and size and they gleamed, so although the forensics team would later remove them for testing, no one expected the tools to tell a story.

They also found items of women's clothing, mostly

underwear, all bloodstained, and that was where the story both began and ended.

Pete Harriman fielded the call from Paddington Green detectives, then he and Stella took the Westway flyover and sat in traffic for thirty minutes listening to a radio news show called *Christmas Round the World*. Reports came in of slaughter in the Middle East and a gore-fest in Africa and Harriman laughed out loud. 'Peace on earth,' he said. 'Wasn't that the idea? Goodwill towards men.'

'It was,' Stella told him. 'So far as I understand it.'

'So what went wrong?'

'Listen, he's just a baby. What can he do?'

The squad room at Paddington Green was overheated and the DI in charge, Steve Boston, looked half asleep. Boston was carrying a lot too much weight: a roll of chins, a belly into his lap, pouchy cheeks. He rasped when he breathed and seemed to need to speak in short sentences. 'We matched the clothing,' he said. 'It wasn't difficult.'

'What's your reading of him?' Stella asked.

'Thrill-killer.'

'Has he said much?'

'Brief statement. I thought I'd leave him to you. For the time being.'

'Brief statement saying what?'

'Saying pretty much fuck all.'

'Fingerprints and forensics?'

'Taken prints. Emailed as attachments. Someone in your team called Marilyn Hayes. Sound right?' Stella nodded. 'Forensics whenever, but there's no doubt it's him. No cross.'

'Sorry?'

'Your victim . . .' Boston looked at a report on his desk. 'A cross was taken, cross on a gold chain.'

'That's right.'

'We didn't find it.'

'Yet,' Stella cautioned.

'It wasn't with the other trophies. We're still searching the place, sure.'

'Where's the wife?'

'She's there, at the house, showing them what's what.' Boston gave over to just breathing for a moment, then said, 'All yours.'

Martin Cotter smiled at Stella as she walked into the interview room. He smiled at Harriman as he sat in a chair by the door. He smiled to himself when Stella asked him about Valerie Blake and Sophie Simms.

He said, 'I don't know them. I saw their pictures in the paper, but I don't know them.'

'You killed two women and you attacked three others.'

Cotter looked at the tape. He leaned forward slightly, talking for the tape. 'I was somewhere else.'

'What?'

'The first one you mentioned. The other officers asked about her and about Sophie Simms. When she was killed –'

'Valerie Blake –'

'Yes: Blake. When she was killed, I was in Manchester at a wedding.' He glanced at the tape again, speaking clearly, his North Country accent modulating because he was keen to be understood. 'I think you'll find,' he said, 'that I didn't kill anyone.'

Harriman laughed and Cotter glanced up sharply, his eyes dark. Stella said, 'Bloodstained underwear was found in your workroom, Martin. It matches the clothing taken from five victims.'

Cotter shrugged. 'Not me,' he said.

'What's not you?'

'The clothing.'

'It was there.'

'So you say.'

'Your wife found it.'

'So she says.'

Stella thought she could see the shape of Cotter's defence already. 'What about Sophie Simms?' she asked.

'I was in London, but I wasn't there. I was in a pub.'

'Local pub? Would people have recognized you – friends?'

'No friends. Someone might remember. I was just drinking. They had the telly on. Sports channel.'

Cotter was tall, even sitting down, and slim-hipped. He had fair hair, thinning but worn long; a Celtic band tattoo circled his right forearm. When his fist clenched and unclenched, the tattoo muscle-jumped.

'Your wife thinks you killed them,' Harriman said. 'She came to us. Did you know that? She gave you up, Martin.'

'There's your problem,' Cotter said. He was smiling again. 'She's fucking mad, didn't you know? She likes crack.' He chuckled. 'She's cracked. She's having a crack-up.'

DI Boston was getting through the day on whisky and water, a one-to-five mix, so a low-octane sort of a day. He set his glass down on a crowded in-tray and said, 'I'm right, aren't I? Thrill-killer. That's how we've got him pegged.'

'What did his statement say?' Stella asked.

'Says I didn't do it. God knows why, he's got no chance.'

'He thinks he has. He's going to say his wife put the bloodstained clothes in his workroom and that she's nuts – out of her mind on crack.'

Boston looked startled. 'You're kidding me. The underwear belonged to those girls. There's positive ID.'

Harriman said, 'Yeah, sure. But the point he's going to make is that he's not the only person in the house.'

'He'll say the wife did it?'

Harriman shrugged. 'It might not go like that. He'll say he doesn't know anything about the clothes. So if it's not him, it must be her.'

'Or,' Stella said, 'someone she knows. Someone who's persuaded her to fit him up. The real killer.'

Boston closed his eyes and breathed, *rasp, rasp, rasp*. Maybe he was picturing the courtroom scene, a clever brief, a jury full of frowns. Juries were a notorious wild card. When he opened his eyes again, he asked, 'How clever does he seem to you?'

'Clever,' Stella said. 'There ought to be no way out, but he looked and he's hit on something. Listen,' she added, 'can you hold back on a press statement?'

'For a while, I suppose. Why?'

'It might help us.'

'If he'd admitted to the killings, it would be difficult. The press are all over us on this one. But he's holding out, so there's more work to be done. We'll sit on it for as long as we can.'

'Thanks,' Stella said.

Boston took a sip of weak whisky. He had a thought and brightened. 'DNA,' he said.

'If she can plant the clothing,' Harriman observed, 'she can plant his DNA. Hairs, saliva . . . semen, obviously.'

Boston walked them to the door; Stella could hear his thighs chafing and the thready breath in his chest. She said, 'Know what I think? Revenge gave him inspiration. If he'd had some bad luck, if the clothes had come to light a different way, if someone else had shopped him, maybe he'd've caved in. But it was his wife. Maybe he hates her, maybe not; either way it's betrayal. Also – and here's the trick – she's close enough to him to have a motive. He can see that. So he turned the thing round and made her the target.'

Boston stopped at the squad-room door, breathing like a runner, lit a cigarette and inhaled hard.

Harriman said, 'Marriage really is a two-way street.'

Boston didn't laugh. He said, 'Merry fucking Christmas.'

If it wasn't crack, it was certainly something.

Roseanne Cotter sat in the living room of what lawyers like to call the marital home. The house was part of a cramped terrace and the rooms were small enough without Stella, Harriman and three detectives from Paddington Green being there. Roseanne sat on a chair, facing them, as if being interviewed for a job. The job of witness for the prosecution. She was jumpy and sweating; she picked at loose skin on her fingers; she never looked at anyone for more than a second or two. If smoking had been a spectator sport, she would have been up among the medals. And whatever it was that she used, she needed some now. She wasn't talking. She was too strung out to talk. She coughed through her smoking and cried a little and shook her head as if contradicting their thoughts. The day was drawing in, dusk seeming to gather in the bare branches of roadside trees visible through the narrow window.

Finally, she said, 'I want to talk to *her*.'

Stella was the only woman in the room. She looked at the others but no one moved, then Harriman said, 'Could be the only way.' As if seeking a compromise, he added, 'Leave the tape running.'

The men went into the kitchen and made coffee. One of

the Paddington Green cops went out to his car and brought back a half bottle of Scotch. Harriman accepted a drink, then went down to Martin Cotter's workshop and sat among the rows of carefully arranged, gleaming tools and wondered about the lives of ordinary folk.

Stella said, 'Have you got what you need?' Roseanne nodded. Stella said, 'Okay.'

She went to the window and looked out while Roseanne took out her gear and jacked up. A drawer closing was the cue to turn round. Roseanne was smoking a fresh cigarette. She still looked jumpy, but she didn't look like a woman incapable of speech.

'He says he was in Manchester at a wedding –' Stella gave the day and date. 'A girl was killed on that day.'

'Valerie Blake,' Roseanne said. She drew hard on her cigarette. 'He's right. That's where we were. It was the others, not her.'

'A girl called Sophie Simms,' Stella said.

'No, I don't think so. The others.'

'How do you know?'

Roseanne got up and left the room. Stella picked up the cassette-recorder and followed her upstairs to the bedroom. There was no chair, so she sat on the bed. Roseanne went to a dressing table, opened the bottom drawer and reached under the sheets and pillowcases for a folder. It was full of news clippings. She spread them out on the bed.

'The others,' she said. 'These. These were his. I didn't know what it was at first, then I worked out the dates. The last three: I was sure of them. It was the way he acted. The third one, I was certain about her. See, I'd found the things he took off them, yeah? – took off the first two. It didn't take much working out, you know, all the blood and such. And I remembered the way he was when he came in. I'd never seen him like it except once.'

'How was he? How could you tell?'

'Sexed up. Laughing. He'd had some drink too. But he was laughing, yeah? like he couldn't stop, and he was after me.' She glanced at the bed and Stella got up quickly, as if something had nudged her.

'You can vouch for the wedding in Manchester?'

'Vouch?'

'You're certain.'

'Me and all the other guests. It was his niece.'

'Okay.' Stella hesitated, then said, 'It's going to get bad.'

'I had to tell them. What could I do?' Suddenly, and for the first time, she looked close to tears. 'What could I do – go on living with him? Go on reading the papers and checking the dates?'

'You did the right thing, but it's going to get bad.'

'As long as I can get my stuff.'

'Are you registered?' Roseanne shook her head. 'Okay. Tell them. They need you. They'll think of something.'

'Why did he keep those things?' Roseanne asked.

'Keep what?'

'The underwear, all bloodied up. You'd think he'd get shot of it.'

'Trophies,' Stella told her; then, when she looked puzzled, said, 'Hunters put them up on the wall.'

Stella pictured Kimber's wall, the chilling little stories pasted up underneath each snapshot. Something Roseanne had said came back to her. 'What did you mean: you'd never seen him like it except once?'

'Laughing like that, mad, all fired up.'

'When was it?'

'He raped a girl at a party. Well, not raped as such. She was coming on to all the blokes, thought it was funny. She didn't want him to, though. He had to make her. Everyone watched. He was the same way then.'

Stella stared at her. 'How do you know?'

Roseanne lit another cigarette. She said, 'I was there.'

They avoided the Westway and wound up in a long crawl that stretched from Marble Arch to Shepherd's Bush. Exhaust gases hung in the air, shot through with the hot orange of streetlights.

'He's not for us,' Harriman said.

'We'll wait for the DNA,' Stella told him, but she knew he was right. A Jag cruised out from a junction, broadsiding the oncoming traffic, its driver looking for a kindly soul to let him into the flow. Stella tapped the accelerator and closed the gap, leaving him stranded. Drivers leaned on their horns and flashed their headlights.

'What does that mean?' Harriman asked. 'Thrill-killer. What happens? They wake up one day and think, hey, I know what would be fun?'

Stella shook her head. 'I don't know. Where they come from or what to do with them.'

'Hang them,' Harriman said. 'Shoot them, inject them, fry them, drop them over a cliff, what's that thing they use on mad cows?'

Among coppers, it wasn't an original thought.

33

Leon Bloss lived in a room down by the river on the Isle of Dogs. The room was fifty by forty and had once been a grain loft, then a studio and now a cheap rent because the building was due for demolition. Bloss liked the idea that soon it would cease to exist. He wanted to live his life like a man crossing a river on stepping stones, each stone disappearing as his foot left it.

The TV was on but without sound, the radio was tuned to an easy-listening station, and he was reading a superhero comic from his collection. As a kid, he'd liked *The Punisher* and *Dreadstar* and *Wolverine*. Now it was *The Sandman* and *The Preacher* and *Elektra Assassin*.

At one time in his life, he'd earned the nickname 'Angel' because he had liked angel dust, liked the pictures it painted for him, liked the free-form flying. That time was over, but the business of disassociation stayed with him: the TV was on for the ads; he liked those little stories with their beginnings, middles and ends; the music was to damp down the silence; and the superheroes made him laugh. The world crowding in and not quite making sense was how he liked it; the split focus of dreams.

Oh, Bobby, he thought, *Bobby, Bobby, you're perfect for me.*

Who sent you to me, Bobby? Coincidence sent you. Valerie sent you.

The windows in the grain loft were metal-framed and went almost from floor to ceiling, taking in a great swathe of river. A low-beamed vessel loaded with scrap was chugging upstream, sending out a wide, silver wake. Bloss poured himself a drink. He took it to the window and stood with his forehead pressed against the glass. His laugh and the cries of gulls. There was a sick yellow smear in the sky and the cloud-base was so low it seemed almost to touch the water.

Bobby. You're my delight. Angel's delight.

34

Forensics were working faster now; they were cooking with gas. Maybe they were thinking ahead to the Christmas break. Tom Davison called to let Stella know that Martin Cotter's DNA was a match for the first five attacks.

'I thought it would be,' she said.

'So there's another one nailed.'

'It's not my case,' Stella told him, 'and this guy's tricky. What about the other scenes of crime?'

'Blake and Simms? Nothing. He wasn't there.'

'How much does it mean?' Stella asked. 'DNA at the scene, DNA not at the scene?'

'It's the Bible,' Davison said. 'It's the word of God. Also, it's how I make a living.'

'You could be somewhere without leaving a DNA trace.'

'It's feasible, but very unlikely.'

'How unlikely?'

'Full cling-film body-wrap unlikely.'

'But your DNA could be found in a place where you'd never been.'

'Tell me how.'

'Someone plants it.'

'That's an interesting notion; we could discuss it over a drink.'

'Let's discuss it now.'

'And keep the drink social?' There was a pause before he said, 'Look, this guy Cotter wasn't at your scenes of crime and the mystery man whose DNA *was* at the scenes *wasn't* present at the five previous attacks. Separate events, different guys. That's the testimony I'd give in court. You're not married, are you?'

'No.'

'That's right.'

'What do mean – "That's right"?'

'I asked around. People said you weren't married.'

'Are you?'

'Oh, sure, of course. Almost everyone is.'

Marilyn Hayes put some progress stats down on Stella's desk, then walked across to the drinks dispenser and bought herself a coffee. Something that looked like coffee. On her way, she passed Pete Harriman's desk and brushed his hair with her fingertips. Harriman smiled without looking up.

Stella had noticed lately that there was a lightness in Marilyn's step and a glint in her eye. She wondered about Mr Hayes: whether he'd noticed those giveaway signs. Perhaps he hadn't. Perhaps he'd noticed but didn't care. Perhaps he'd noticed and was biding his time, building a head of anger, working out what to do. She imagined him parked outside Harriman's flat, stranded between tears and fury, watching for silhouettes on the shade. She wondered whether George had ever done that and whether, when he had found out about her affair with Delaney, he had wept or cursed her or wished her dead.

35

Patricia is local. She works for an estate agent near Holland Park Avenue and her flat is in Blanveld Road. She gets a bus to the crossroads then takes a shortcut through the churchyard. Shes tall and she wears that long black coat most of the time and her hair doesnt look natural to me but I dont mind. In places its too red or else theres too much black in it. Shes very pretty you might say beutiful and she has great legs the boots really suit her. I follow her most nights but sometimes another. Or her and another. Sometimes she goes to meet a friend sometimes a man calls at her flat but I dont think hes special to her. He stays the night but then sometimes its a different man. Shes playing the field. If I get close I can smell her perfume – its flowers but with a tang. I like her neck. Ive got seven of her up on the wall and Ive written a story about her. About me and her and how things end. She doesnt know how things will end but I know.

36

He picked her up as she crossed the road from her workplace in the first flush of dusk, going to meet a client in Queensdale Road: walking distance. They went into a ground-floor flat and spent half an hour. He watched lights coming on as they went from room to room.

He followed her back. The agency was glass-fronted and only partially masked by property details. He went to a fast-food place across the street and bought a cup of coffee so that he could watch her at her desk making and taking phone calls. She wasn't wearing her coat and he could see more of her figure. She had good high breasts and her Armani trousers tucked up nicely under her rump.

He watched as they left, one by one. There were five of them and she was the fourth to leave, saying goodnight, putting on the long black coat. When she walked to the bus stop, he joined the waiting group but stayed well back. When the bus came, he waited until he saw her sit downstairs, then jumped on as the doors were closing and went to the top deck.

He was breathing quickly and smiling a secret smile.

He could feel an erection starting. That often happened. He looked out at the streets and the people, all of them going about their business without any understanding of who he was or what he did. He was special, but no one could see that, which was just the way he liked it. He slipped a hand into his coat pocket and felt the steel, cool against his palm.

Ten or more people got off at her stop. He stayed back, putting five bodies between them. He knew where she was going, so there was no need to hurry just yet, but he needed to be close when she got to the churchyard. He measured his pace: fast enough to be gaining on her; not so fast that she might get a sense of him. Stare at someone long enough and you nudge their instinct – make them look up. People who are followed sometimes feel the same close, intimate attention and look round for its source. He didn't make those mistakes. The pro. The hunter. The Invisible Man.

When she opened the gate of the churchyard, he was twenty feet back. The path went directly towards the porch, then curved off to the left. As she went out of sight, he quickened his pace, losing her for a moment, but finding her again as they both walked alongside the church. This was the tricky bit. If she turned now, she would see him. Of course, he was just another person taking the same short cut, no one to fear, but that wasn't the point. To be seen was to lose the game.

The path went between gravestones and leafless trees towards a gate on the far side that would bring her back to the street and within a hundred feet of her door. He hurried now, needing to close the distance. At his back, the lit windows of the church glowed; a choir was singing, clear on the icy air.

Now she was within ten feet of the gate. People were visible in the street, but the churchyard was full of shadows. He came close enough to touch and reached out, lifting a skein of hair with his left hand, using the scissors with his right, then turned immediately and walked off between the gravestones and the trees.

She opened the gate and stepped into the street. She was humming along with the choir.

*

Mike Sorley's cigarette packet read SMOKING SERIOUSLY HARMS YOU AND OTHERS AROUND YOU. Sellotaped underneath that was a strip of paper on which someone had written: *This means us!* He shook out the last cigarette and crushed the pack one-handed before lobbing it into the trash. When he lit up, he coughed for half a minute.

He said, 'We had incident boards up in the parks –'

'At all exits and entrances,' Stella said.

'– but no useful responses.'

'Mostly time-wasters. A few genuine sightings, but they weren't any help.'

'Is this looking like a hopeless case?'

'You mean an unsolved?'

'I mean an unsolvable. Thrill-killing is a nightmare. Somebody who's anybody goes out and kills somebody who's nobody. Finding him is all down to luck. He has to be caught in the act, or make some mistake, or take a risk too many.' He gestured at the files on his desk, on the floor. 'This adds up to precisely fuck all.' He coughed again, his face reddening, and grabbed a fistful of tissues from a man-sized box.

'Maybe we'll get lucky, then.'

'It's what you're hoping for, is it?'

'We're making some progress.'

Sorley laughed. 'Don't tell me that – it's what I'm telling *them.*' He killed his cigarette but took out a back-up pack. 'This guy Cotter has just made things more difficult. He's definitely in the frame for the others, is he? Before Blake?'

'Definitely.'

'So we're out on a limb.'

'Paddington have agreed to wait on a press release.'

'The purpose being?'

'That if we've got two killers here – Cotter and our man

but with similar MOs – it would help us if our man doesn't know about Cotter's arrest.'

'You're thinking copy-cat.'

'Something like that. I'm not sure.'

'It's a long way off a result,' Sorley observed.

'Another week,' Stella suggested. 'Then a review.'

'Another week, then we start to tot up the bills.'

Before she left, Stella said, 'If it's flu, you ought to go home.'

Sorley snapped flame from a disposable lighter. He said, 'Smoking kills germs, it's on all the packets.'

The squad room was empty apart from Frank Silano, who was compiling a statements file. He looked up as Stella came in. 'There's a note here to revisit Duncan Palmer. Valerie Blake's boyfriend, right?'

'There is,' Stella agreed. 'You can delete it.'

'No longer in the frame –'

'Never was, really. He was in New York at the time. He was hiding something, but it turned out to be a woman.'

'He was cheating on her – Blake?'

'He was.'

Silano shook his head. 'Lousy timing.'

'Timing's important, is it?'

'Yeah,' Silano nodded. 'Timing's everything.'

'Are you married?' Stella asked.

'Sure.' He closed the file and got up to fetch his coat. Stella lifted her phone and fumbled for her wallet. She was looking for the case number that the man from Immigration had given her, along with his card. Stefan-just-make-it-Steve.

Silano passed her desk on his way to the door. He said, 'Almost everyone is.'

*

'It's DS Mooney. AMIP-5. Stella Mooney.'

'I remember.'

'I have to clear some paperwork.'

'Tell me about it. I live my life in triplicate.'

'The family we found at the warehouse. I need to sign that off.'

'I gave you my details, right?'

'Yes, I've logged all that. It's fine. I suppose I'm just curious about what happened to them.'

'Deported. It was pretty much a foregone –'

'The mother,' Stella said. 'The mother with the dead child. Did she get some help – counselling, whatever?'

'No. She killed herself.' He had spoken quite quickly and without any hesitation and for a moment Stella wasn't sure what he'd said. Because she didn't speak, he filled the silence: 'She went to hospital, the others went to Maidstone nick.'

'Her husband –'

'Husband and the others – brother, sister, aunt, whoever they were, and the other kid. They took the dead one. That wasn't easy: taking it away from her, I mean. Then they sedated her and kept her in for observation. She got up in the night, took a scalpel from the contaminated waste, went to the toilet, cut her throat.'

'Okay,' Stella said. 'Thank you.'

'She looked about fifty, didn't she? I thought fifty or so. Turns out she was in her thirties.'

'Yeah,' Stella said. 'Thanks. Thank you.'

'The hard part was they wouldn't let the husband see her. He's at the airport, he asks for his wife, they say she topped herself, then they put him on the plane. He went berserk. Had to be put in restraints.'

'Right,' Stella said. 'Thank you. Thanks very much.'

*

Robert Adrian Kimber stood outside the first-floor apartment of the girl he called Patricia and watched her cross to the window to draw the blind. She glanced out briefly and saw a street full of people and traffic, just as always.

She went to another room – the kitchen, because he could see pans on a rack. She made coffee. Those tiny domestic moments were precious to him.

He guessed the layout and supposed that the bedroom and the bathroom would be at the back. He thought she would take a bath soon. In fact he was certain of it. He pictured the whole thing. She undressed, she stood at the mirror, she lay back in the bath, she soaped herself.

He held the lock of her hair under his nose. Flowers with a tang.

37

The Cancer Santa outside McDonald's was taking all the business. Jamie sat on his bag, wrapped in a blanket like a reservation Indian. His eyes were unfocused; or they were focused on something no one else could see. Sadie's fingers were too cold to hit the stops, so she was piping a little three-note tootle. She looked up when Delaney arrived but continued to play.

'Have you eaten?' he asked. She shook her head, still playing. 'Have you got a place for tonight?' She shook her head. *Tootle-tootle-toot.* 'Where will you be on Christmas Day?' It would be featured sidebar to his piece, each of Delaney's street-people and where they'd be on Christmas morning. It was a cheap shot but a selling-point.

'It's just another day of the year,' Sadie told him. 'I'll be here.' She tootled a couple of times, then added, 'Unless Jamie's got it right, in which case, of course, I'll be sitting on the right hand of God.'

They talked for another ten minutes or so, Delaney crouching alongside her, getting a Sadie's-eye-view of the world. With its fake snow and fairy lights and sour-faced shoppers, it didn't seem that great a place. He gave her a twenty. He didn't think she'd buy food with it, or a bed for the night; he thought she'd buy a wrap or a couple of rocks. But dues are dues.

When he got back, the business card he'd given to Robert Kimber was out on the counter, a little blot on his escutcheon.

Stella said, 'It was at his flat when we searched.'

'I see.' There had been rain in the wind and Delaney's clothes were wet. He walked through to the bedroom and found a fresh pair of jeans and a sweatshirt. When he emerged, she was watching the street. He said, 'You took your time.'

'I was hoping you'd tell me.'

Delaney shrugged. 'Okay, I should have.'

'But you didn't. Because I'd told you to stay away from Kimber.'

'There's the problem, you see. You *told* me.'

'How do I know it wasn't you that made him run?'

'It wasn't.'

'How do I know?'

'Look, Stella, you have a job to do; me too. So it goes.'

'An idea that works in your favour.'

'Does it? How's that?'

'What would you say if I asked you to reveal a source?'

Delaney was silent on that one. He felt like a man who had just swum out of his depth. Even so, he kept swimming. He said, 'Now that you know, I'd better tell you this – he was talking to someone by email. Someone called Angel. He mentioned you.'

She looked at him, her mouth open. 'Kimber did?'

'No, Angel. Whoever he is.'

There was a silence to break rocks. Eventually, she asked, 'What did he say – about me?'

'No, it was just a mention. I only had a chance to look at the screen for a moment or two. A fantasist, like Kimber. He asked about Kimber pissing you around: "Leading them a dance," he said. I remember that.'

'What else?'

'Well, he was offering his compliments. Telling Kimber

194

what a good job he'd done. Wanting to compare notes.' He remembered another sentence: '"I would like to go through it with you"; something like that.'

Her stillness was the next thing to violence and her voice was just a whisper. She said, 'You knew this and you didn't tell me?'

'You would have known I'd seen him. And I wanted to see him again.'

'Have you?'

'No.'

'And that's all you can remember – of the emails?'

'Stella, I only had a second to look. I saw your name, that was what stuck in my mind. It was just some crazy man; another crazy man; I bet Kimber's address book is full of them.'

'A harmless crazy-man ring, is that how you see it?' He shrugged. She said, 'We spend our time fine-combing. Forensics fine-comb the scene; we fine-comb the evidence; by and large we come up with something very close indeed to fuck all. This kind of case is the most difficult to get a grip of. Drugs, domestics, gang rivalries, turf wars, all of that – no problem. We either know who did it or we know someone who probably knows. Or else we can do a bit of detecting: of the two plus two makes four sort. We're on home ground. This kind of killing's different.' She remembered what Sorley had said and repeated it to him. 'Somebody who's anybody goes out and kills somebody who's nobody. We're grubbing around. We're looking for anything. And you had this.'

'It's not important,' he said. 'Loonies anonymous.'

'Who was it?' she asked. 'Who was this person and how did he make contact? And what else did he say? And what does he *know*, you fucking idiot? If you had told me straight away we'd've been down there within the hour and taken the hard disk and perhaps we'd've saved –'

She stopped because she had never intended to stay to argue it with him; never intended to bat it to and fro, as if they were having a row about who did the laundry, or cut the lawn, as if they were in a *marriage*, for Christ's sake. She was too angry for that sort of farce. Best to go. Best to get the hell out.

She was putting her coat on, and he was watching her in disbelief, when she found herself saying, 'A woman, an illegal immigrant, her child died, she was suckling it but it was dead, and they were getting ready to deport her but she cut her own throat with a dirty scalpel, and this was no day for me to be hearing what you just told me. And fuck you.'

Delaney had thought that he might get between her and the door, but there was something desperate and wild-eyed about her that made him want to let her go. He looked out of the window and watched the hazard lights on her car flash as she blipped the lock. A moment later, she came into view. Her breath was a plume on the cold air, then she was a smudged silhouette on the side window, then just tail-lights snaking up towards Notting Hill Gate.

38

It was eight thirty; already the stats for the day were a little worse than average and the day was far from over.

The Bank Hill Posse made a raid off-territory and lifted a member of the Random Crew. They took him to a park, nailed his hands to a tree and pistol-whipped him. It was a business issue. No one saw a thing.

A Merc cabriolet was eased sideways by a Freelander. The Merc dipped in and out of the bus lane, came down a gear, and slid in front of the other vehicle as the lights went red. Cabriolet Man got out carrying a wheel-brace and hammered the Freelander's lights. When Freelander Man emerged yelling, he was hammered in the self-same way. He went straight from the tarmac to ITU. Passers-by hadn't noticed the incident.

On Harefield, a local crack-distribution problem was solved when the poacher was stabbed five times in the head. He wasn't dead, but his ability to match one thought with the next was never going to be the same. This caught no one's attention.

In a street just off the Strip, a whore had finished giving head in a car when the client showed her a Stanley knife and offered to leave her face intact if she handed over her earnings from the rest of the day's blow-jobs. She gave him the money but called him an arsehole, so he cut her anyway. She ran down the Strip screaming, her lime-green fun-fur gouted with red. She was invisible and inaudible.

You could call it a worse than average day.

Someone pulled a Brocock makeover in a shebeen and wounded four punters; he couldn't remember why. Four kids of about ten mugged seven oldies in fifteen minutes – a numerical triumph. Stella Mooney walked into the Vigo Street flat and took a punch in the mouth that broke an incisor. People would tell her that she only had herself to blame.

They weren't the Clean Machine crew, that was for certain. They'd trashed the place; they'd had some fun. Anything breakable was broken, the surfaces were tagged, the living space looked as if it had caught the brunt of a small twister. Which is why Stella hadn't stopped to wonder whether they might still be there; but they were. They'd heard her come in and had heard her shout of anger. Things were quiet for a while: a period of recovery. Then she'd lifted the phone and started to make a call and that's when they came out of the bedroom, all threats and laughter and crotch-grabbing bravado. Three of them. Baggies, hoodies, big trainers, face-metal. Here's how scared they were – one of them was on his mobile phone.

Stella was on to the local uniforms. She broke the connection and had dialled triple nine before one of them stepped up and hit her. Just to keep her quiet. Just to give them some time. She sat down amid broken glass, books, CDs, the contents of cupboards and drawers, and backed off fast, using her heels and hands, but they weren't coming after her. She had dropped her bag when she fell, so the guy who'd hit her picked it up, taking his time. The sleeve of his hoodie was decorated with a black serpent design like a tattoo. He lofted the bag as if to say thanks, then they collected a couple of bulging black bin-liners from beside the front door and sauntered out and on to the street, the Untouchables.

They would have gone to the bedroom first, because that's where everyone keeps the portable valuables. Stella didn't have a lot of jewellery, but what she had they'd taken. The bin-liners had held her clothes and shoes: not all of them, just the saleable stuff. The sort of items Stella had seen at the warehouse. But these kids weren't the Clean Machine. They were the Shit Spreaders.

They'd checked out the living area and trashed it. Then they'd gone back into the bedroom and trashed that.

And pissed on her bed.

She made a routine call to the local nick and gave descriptions, then went out on to the street. She could feel the corner of her mouth and the flesh along her cheekbone beginning to swell. There was a hard lump between her gum and the soft tissue of her mouth. She delved with her tongue, lifting the half tooth, and spat it out along with a little streamer of blood. She felt for her car key and it wasn't in her pocket, so it must have been in her bag, along with some cash she'd recently drawn: two hundred pounds. Her credit cards were in a thin wallet that she always kept in her pocket, but the loss of the money stung.

On the main street, vehicles were backed up between three sets of traffic lights, no one going anywhere, a toxic haze wafting back and forth in the cold air. She jogged down towards Harefield.

The roads that ran on to the estate had once been brightly lit – that was for a month or so. Bright lights were bad for business, so they'd had to go. Now the inroads were dark, the DMZ was dark, and the lights of the tower blocks, far back, shone through the gloom like ships at sea.

Her phone went and she checked the screen. It was Delaney, so she pressed hang-up. Two minutes later it rang again and she was about to repeat the process when she saw Harriman's name there. She slowed to a walk and answered the call.

He said, 'I thought you'd be amused to know that Martin Cotter has fingered his wife.'

'Her motive being?'

'He wasn't too specific on that one. His wife,' Harriman added, 'and her lover.'

Stella was looking left and right, in shop doorways, along side streets. Three boys in hoodies: it was like looking for pebbles on a beach.

'Who's the lover?'

'Some joke. Some guy she's been fucking. There's nothing in it.'

'It's clever, though. Accuse the accuser.'

'He *is* clever, didn't you think so?'

'Mostly I thought he was a scumbag who killed people for fun and I'd be happy to see him on a slab.'

He noticed the real edge of anger in her voice, and he could hear a chorus of horns from the tailback. He said, 'Where are you?'

'Out by Harefield. Some lads did the Vigo Street flat.'

She went into a pub and stood at the door to look round. Harriman's perception of background changed to boy-band music, laughter, the electronic warbling of fruit machines.

'Oh, shit. Bad one?'

'They pissed in my bed.'

'You're not looking for them?'

'They were still there when I got back. One of them broke my tooth. *And they pissed in my bed!*'

'Jesus Christ, you *are* looking for them. What do you mean, broke your tooth?'

'Hit me. Broke my tooth.'

She was back on the street, scanning doorways and bus shelters.

'Did you call the locals?'

'Sure. We agreed there was nothing much they could do.'

'Stay off Harefield. I'll come down.'

She said, 'Call for back-up.'

'Don't go on to the estate, Stella.'

'Make the call.'

'Jesus! Look, you're angry, you're not thinking straight, don't do it.'

'Make the call.'

Three lads in hoodies eating kebabs and drinking beer from the bottle.

She stepped out into the road and a motorbike cruising the corridor between the lines of cars stood up on its front wheel. Her eyes were on the lads. One had a pattern on the sleeve about where his bicep would be, a flame-pattern that resolved to a snakehead. She recognized it – the guy who'd hit her – and they recognized her as she made the pavement and turned towards them.

They couldn't believe her. What was this mark doing on the streets seeking them out? This *victim*? She was walking fast, looking straight at them and without the first idea of what she was going to do if she caught up. Suddenly she felt scared, but she'd come this far. Come this far and, for some stupid reason, couldn't bring herself to back off. One of them beckoned, as if to say, *Come on, then, we're up for this*, which is when the patrol car rolled up to the junction between Harefield and the main road, looking for an opening in the solid nose-to-tail.

The car was between Stella and the boys. She leaned down and tapped on the window, showing her ID, and the driver let down the window. The car smelled of bodies and smoke and fast food. Stella pointed. She said, 'We're picking them up – suspicion of breaking and entering.'

The boys edged away towards the dark approach roads, walking slowly at first, looking back to see what was happening, then turning and quickening their pace. The cops looked at Stella, then at the boys. The driver said, 'They're about to leg it.'

'I can see that.'

As she said it, the boys started to run. The second cop activated the roof-bar and the patrol car pulled out and turned against the flow of traffic, hopping the kerb with its nearside wheels canted over, making for the first road into Harefield. Stella ran straight for the DMZ. She was counting on the car catching up with her before she got too far into the estate. The boys were in sight, running hard, heading for the walk-space under Block C.

Stella was sprinting through a garbage-field of junked furniture, white goods, bin-bags, whatever people had tossed out and walked away from. She hacked her leg against a toppled fridge and yelled but ran through the pain. The boys were shadows, slipping into the walk-space. She looked round as she ran. The patrol car was somewhere back on the road, trying to weave and shunt its way out of the gridlock.

She reached Block C and pulled up. The DMZ was dark, though not entirely lightless. There was a half-moon and the sky was almost clear; frost glistened on the scrub grass and on the bald concrete pillars that supported the block. In the walk-space it was total blackout. Someone standing twenty feet back would be invisible, but someone walking in from the perimeter would be a dim silhouette. Either they were waiting for her, or they'd gone straight through to the bull ring.

Stella took a step in, then another, then a third. To begin with, she had been operating on raw anger – *They pissed on my bed!* – but now all that kept her going was the fact that she'd come this far, to the black edge of things.

She thought, I could die here. One day you wake up and it's the day of your death. This could be the day. I could have said nothing to Delaney about finding his card in Kimber's flat, could still be there now, could be eating pasta with a good, red wine, could be expecting to go to bed before bedtime. She thought all this in an eye-blink, and something went past her head with a low witter of slipstream and smashed somewhere off into the darkness.

She said, 'Police officer.'

Her voice seemed to echo round the walk-space; it stuttered back to her, bringing with it a shrill laugh. Then there was a moment of stand-off, then the laugh came again, louder, throatier. Stella caught its direction and walked towards it. She was frightened now. Too frightened to turn and run. Footsteps rattled off somewhere to her left. She circled the sound, wondering if she could still be seen against the faint moonlight out in the DMZ.

A shape drifted in the dark, and she thought: *That ghost again. That ghost, like before.* And, like before, a smell came up to her: beer and the sourness of skin, faint and then stronger and then, before she could turn, she was hit from behind, a wild punch that landed between her shoulder blades, making her stagger. She managed to turn, only to take the next punch on the boss of her shoulder. She crouched, angling her body, and kicked out but didn't connect. She could hear movements though she couldn't tell what they meant or which way her attacker was moving. The laugh came again, on a gust of foul breath, and suddenly she was locked in an embrace. She wrestled but he held her, face to face, his arms pinning hers, and they staggered together and fell, the breath rushing from her lungs, her head smacking the ground.

The darkness deepened and she seemed to lose consciousness for a second. When she came to, she thought something was crawling on her, an animal of some kind, then realized that what she could feel were hands. She hit out and struck something. Until then, it hadn't occurred to her to yell, but that's what she did next. As if in answer, a light played in the darkness – a torch-beam – and a voice said, 'Stella?'

The light settled on her for a second, blinding her, then lifted to shine on her attacker. The face above her was framed in wild hair, the mouth laughing a silent laugh, the eyes wandering, white and bald like alabaster eggs.

The patrol car was parked out on the approach road, roof-bar flashing, radio busy. Stella nodded at the two cops. She said, 'You were a terrific help. I can't thank you enough.'

The driver shrugged. He said, 'We were boxed in. Nothing was moving.'

'Least of all you,' Harriman said. 'It didn't occur to you to get out of the car –'

'It would have been an obstruction.'

'You're an obstruction,' Harriman observed. 'Fuck off.'

Stella's attacker sat in the back of the patrol car. He had foul hair, filthy clothes, a rank smell and a docile smile. He was Beggar Ben. He was Panhandler Pete. There were hundreds of him and some were called Sadie or Jamie. By day, he sat on the streets with his hand out; by night he took to the walk-spaces under the towers with as much strong brew as he could buy.

Harriman had cuffed him and hustled him across the DMZ. Panhandler Pete. He'd laughed that shrill laugh and said, 'I can't see so well. I'm good in the dark.' He wagged his head. 'She came at me. She was after me.'

'Tell the arresting sergeant to give him something to eat,' Stella said.

'Give him a kick in the head,' the driver said. 'We'll have to go all the way with the windows down; he smells like a fucking drain.'

Stella said, 'I'll have to paper this. You're in great danger of not coming out of it well.'

The driver got in, his partner sat in the back keeping his distance as best he could. Panhandler Pete faced the open window and smiled vacantly. His eyes were little moons.

He said, 'I can't see so well. I'm good in the dark, though.'

'You're a statistic,' Harriman told her. 'Unsolved burglary number billion-squillion-and-four.'

'I'd better go back,' she said. 'Check what they took.'

Harriman laughed. 'You don't expect to see it again?'

'Of course not. Insurance claim. The locals will give me a crime number, I'll lie about the value.'

'Are you okay?'

'Broken tooth, face swelling up, gashed shin, took several blows to the body, otherwise utterly chipper.'

'What the fuck were you thinking of, Stella?'

They had worked together a lot and each knew things about the other that would never be told. There were times when he called her Boss and other times when he called her Stella. It was a matter of judgement.

'I was angry.'

'Meaning you weren't thinking.'

'Meaning exactly that. I did start thinking, though, at one point. I thought that I might die.'

They were walking down the main road. The snarl-up

was no better and the patrol car was locked in about twenty metres further down. After a moment, they reached the turn-off to Stella's street. Harriman said, 'Everyone's got you teamed up with that journo. Delaney. I didn't know you still lived here.'

'I have two addresses,' she told him. 'Delaney's and mine.'

'I could come back with you.'

'Help tidy up?'

'Send out for pizza. Open a bottle of wine.'

She shook her head. 'It's okay.' They had paused on the corner; Stella was walking backwards, very slowly, towards the flat. She asked, 'How did you know where to look?'

'I heard you scream.'

'I didn't scream.' Still backing off.

Harriman was wearing a suede jacket with a fleece lining. He zipped it all the way up to the throat and lifted the collar.

As he walked off, he said, 'Oh yes you did.'

39

She picked a few things up off the floor and swept most of the crap into a corner, but, all in all, she didn't have the heart for it. One of the tags on her wall read *Smiff* or *Biff*. The locals rang to say they were on their way. Stella congratulated them on their speed and told them to bring a camera. Tags are a very personal matter.

She put the phone back on its cradle and saw that the answerphone light was flashing. When she pressed 'play' she got George, as she knew she would. He told her that Seattle was just the place for boat designers and that things were going well. In fact, commissions were difficult to avoid and his reputation was spreading.

He said, *I'm going to have to stay here for a while.*

He said, *I need to raise some investment money.*

He talked a little about the weather and the people. He sounded pretty good.

Then he said, *So we're going to have to think about selling the flat.*

The sofa was tagged in red and black. She sat on it cross-legged. Now she was still, she could feel her various pains. The broken tooth, the bruised face, Panhandler Pete's lucky punches, the gash on her shin. She played the tape again. It wasn't sentimentality, just that she'd forgotten his voice, its tone and pitch.

The local cops arrived and took notes. They knew, and Stella knew, that it was a pointless process, but they did it anyway. One was tall, the other short, as if someone with a sense of humour had paired them up. They noted the malicious damage and the tags. They noted the cash that had been in her bag. They noted Stella's descriptions of the boys. They noted the fact that the intruders had gained entry by the less-than-subtle method of kicking in a rear window. The tall one went into the bedroom, then emerged with a faint smile on his face. Stella knew that uniforms called detectives 'the Filth'.

He said, 'It's an epidemic round here. They don't always trash the place, but they certainly did a job here. Must have known your routine.'

'You think detectives have a routine?'

He shrugged. 'When were you last here?'

'Ma'am,' Stella said. No one ever called her that; she hated it.

'When were you last here, ma'am?' He tried to sound amused, but it didn't come off.

'I don't live here all the time. A few days ago.'

The short one was the note-taker. He said, 'So that would be it. You're lucky you didn't get squatters.'

'Squatters would have looked after the place,' the tall one observed. 'Squatters aren't like these people. They're pretty responsible.'

'Except they steal people's homes,' the short one said.

The tall one was having none of it. 'Sometimes the places are empty. Sometimes they're nothing more than investments bought to appreciate in value, I mean, just a way for the rich to get richer.'

Stella said, 'Have you finished?'

They agreed that they had. Stella would let them have a list of what had been taken. They'd circulate the list. They would let Stella have a crime number, so she could make an insurance claim. The tall one was still wearing the smile when he offered to ask the crime prevention officer to call.

She stripped the bed and shoved everything into a bin-bag, but that was as far as she could get. The headboard was tagged: *Biff.* The shower was tagged: *Smiff.* Her underwear was spread round the room and blotched with red. The mirrors bore jokey faces eating giant cocks.

Stella went back to the living space and lifted the phone to call Delaney, then hung up. They'd thrown everything out of the freezer, but the vodka bottle hadn't broken. She found a coffee mug and washed it and poured herself a drink, but it didn't make her feel any better.

George, she thought, *I'm glad Seattle's good for you. I'm glad you're making your way.*

Then there were second thoughts. *Are you? Are you glad?*

Why wouldn't I be?

Because he could be here with you, in a world where you hadn't ever met John Delaney, or a world where you'd met him and sent him on his way.

I didn't love George.

Yes, you did.

Not the way I love John Delaney. It was comfortable living with George, it was easy, it was risk-free.

You were bored.

That's right, I was bored.

He loved you.

I know he did.

He loved you the way you say you love Delaney.

Yes. There was nothing I could do about that.

So here you are, having walked out on Delaney, hearing from George and thinking . . . what?

Thinking I can't go back to Delaney tonight, but I will go back.

He lied to you.

He was doing his job. He needed that story. He'd already written half of it in his head.

But he lied. And he withheld information that could have made all the difference. That's not just a lie, it's close to betrayal.

You're right, I know that.

And there's someone out there killing people and –

I said I know you're right.

In fact, you could probably bring charges against –

Enough. I know all that.

So I say fuck him. What do you say?

But Stella had nothing more to offer on the subject.

40

She taped a piece of cardboard over the broken window and left the flat. The traffic hadn't eased, and cabs would be radioing each other to avoid the area, so she started towards the tube, walking quickly, weaving between the late-night shoppers and the drunks and the party-goers. Before she reached the station, she found a neon-lit doorway and behind it an office the size of a cupboard; on the window was an A4 sheet of paper with CAB printed on it. The office hadn't been there last week and would probably last until just after Christmas. Three men sat on wooden chairs, smoking hard as if to counteract the cold.

Stella showed them her warrant card and they looked worried. When she said she needed a cab, they smiled and nodded and showed her a London map pinned to the wall. Stella pointed to Notting Hill Gate. One of the men nodded to her and left the office. Stella followed. They walked off the main drag and fifty metres down a side road. He blipped the lock on a new Ford. Stella almost laughed out loud: it was so obviously a hire car. She wondered how much the local patrol guys were putting in their pockets. Enough to make Christmas a little more festive.

The driver would know the main-road routes, nothing else, so Stella sat in the front to indicate the back-doubles. The guy might have been a stranger, but there were some aspects of the neighbourhood that hadn't escaped him, and when Stella took them through Harefield, he activated the door locks. They cruised through the bull ring. The LCD on the dashboard showed 'ice alert', but there were still ten or more kids hanging out by the offie and the KFC. They all wore baggies and hoodies and face-studs. She peered out at them and one flipped her the finger.

She called the locals and asked them to check the kids. Maybe the alcopops and the big chicken buckets were courtesy of her two hundred cash. Somebody's cash. These kids were the mules and dealers, the crimeline tyros, the team muggers, the teeny-hookers. Doing time was a matter of time, and they would emerge with their apprenticeships served.

The driver didn't react to her phone call because he didn't know what was being said. Stella asked him where he came from and the question must have contained a phrase he'd heard before because he answered at once, 'Afghan.' She asked him how long he'd been in Britain and he smiled and shrugged. She asked him about the war and he smiled and shrugged. She didn't ask him for his driving licence or his immigration documents or his work permit because she had already guessed how much paper that would generate.

He dropped her at the Ocean Diner, where she started a tab with her credit card, ordered a vodka in a shot-glass with one cube of ice and listened to the friendly sound of the ice cracking as the vodka covered it.

Robert Kimber saw Stella off in her cab, then walked the rest of the way to the tube.

He had waited outside her flat, sometimes catching a glimpse of her as she went to and fro through the rubble in the living space. He'd walked off when the local cops called to take their notes, but stayed within sight of the flat. He was patient. He was used to waiting. The cold didn't bother him at all.

When Stella emerged, he was part of the shadow in a doorway. As she walked off, he was no more than just someone on his way to wherever. When she got to the main street, he was one in a crowd. He could tell her anger from the way she walked, finding the gap, angling between groups, leaning forwards slightly, elbows out. He tracked her, he dogged her. He got close enough to touch.

The locals – the tall cop and the short – had been over-joyed when they got the call. The radio had been full of laughter.

Mooney, a DS, her flat's been turned over. Vigo Street.

She's the Filth?

AMIP-5.

And they've done her flat?

You can't wait to get down there, can you?

Laughter. Voices overlapping. Then:

Clean Machine, was it?

She wasn't that lucky. This lot wrecked the place, so she says.

More laughter. The patrol cops talking to each other:

You couldn't make it up, could you?

Just let me do the paper on this one.

And more laughter. Then control coming back into the act:

Be gentle with her.

Kimber had been browsing on the Bearcat and there it was: Mooney. Vigo Street. It was just chance. A chance he couldn't pass up. He'd smiled at his luck.

Stella ordered another and considered her options. Go to Delaney's. Let herself in. Sleep on the couch. Well, she didn't like the sound of that husband and wife stuff.

Go to a hotel, book in with no case, no change of clothes, show the warrant card perhaps, show the credit card. It looked like that was going to have to be the way, until the third option dropped into the diner: DC Maxine Hewitt and her pretty blonde girlfriend, looking for a post-movie meal and a glass of wine.

They hadn't seen her. Stella took her glass over to their table and sat down. She had forgotten about the way she must look two hours after taking a punch to the face. Maxine stared.

Stella said, 'I need a bed for the night. You'll laugh when I tell you . . .'

Maxine lived at the blowzy end of North Kensington, a new 'town house' row, all brown wood and dark brick, divided into flats. She showed Stella the spare room. 'It's really Jan's workspace, but there's a sofa-bed. Do you want some arnica for your face?'

'You have arnica?'

'Jan has arnica. All that alternative stuff.'

'I'll take it,' Stella told her. 'The bastard broke my tooth – it scrapes the inside of my mouth when I talk.'

'Don't talk.'

'What I really need is a shower.'

Maxine gave her a towel, a bathrobe and some underwear. She said, 'So they really did a job.'

'Tagged the walls and the furniture, smashed what they could, stole what they wanted, pissed in my bed.'

'Jesus Christ. You saw the locals?'

Stella gave her a look and Maxine laughed. 'I know. Vodka, right?' Stella agreed that it was, and Maxine said, 'Okay, Boss.'

Despite the favour of a bed, despite being under the same roof as Maxine and her pretty blonde lover, and despite Stella having spent all evening on the losing side, that 'Boss' put them back on an even keel.

The shower was a clear glass cubicle with a jet that knocked you back. Stella stood under the hard flow of water for a long time before washing her hair. Her face throbbed and the lining of her mouth was raw. She thought back through the moments when she'd walked into the flat, although she knew that being wise after the event led only to anger and humiliation.

Should have got out at once, should have called back-up, should have known better. Shouldn't have followed them, shouldn't have ventured on to Harefield, shouldn't have been working off anger.

She was soaping herself when the door opened and Jan came in. She was wearing a silk robe, pale blue with darker blue edgings. She sat on a wicker chair and applied body lotion to her legs, smoothing and stroking, the robe falling away to the side. She seemed lost in what she was doing. Stella might have thought herself invisible, except that Jan smiled at her as she left, the way an acquaintance might smile as she passed by in the street.

The vodka had a sandwich on the side. Stella flopped on to the couch; she was a little dizzy from the hot water and the booze. She said, 'What time do you get up?' She was thinking of going round to Delaney's, collecting some clothes, talking to Sorley about the new development, about Delaney's withheld information. Except that she wouldn't be able to reveal her source. Was pretty certain she wouldn't . . .

Maxine said, 'It doesn't matter. It's Sunday.'

Even murder squads take a day off.

There was no pretending. Everyone knew about Delaney, Harriman had told her that. Everyone knew that Vigo Street was another life.

She said, 'There are some times when you can't go back.'

She wasn't saying anything about the second man, about Angel and the emails. Her story to Maxine simply concerned one of *those* rows.

Maxine said, 'We've all been there.' Then she asked, 'Can't go back now, or can't go back ever?'

Stella said, 'I love him.' She hadn't meant to, but one minute it was in her thoughts, the next on her tongue. She scraped the soft tissue of her mouth with her tooth when she said it: a warning come too late.

She ate the sandwich. They sat in silence for a while. Maxine was pretty enough herself, with her even features and her brown hair in a bob; maybe her lips were a little on the thin side: not perfect for kissing, Stella thought. There were sirens in the street and late-night voices. Maxine said, 'Where's your husband now?'

'Not my husband,' Stella told her. 'He's in Seattle designing boats and making money.'

'And making friends?'

'I expect so,' Stella said. She knew what Maxine meant by friends.

'So things have worked out.'

Stella agreed that they had. Things had worked out as well as could be expected. 'Sometimes I think back to what it was like, living with George, and I remember . . .' She thought round it for a moment, then said, '. . . that there wasn't much to remember.'

'Is that good or bad?'

'I'm not sure,' Stella said, 'but I know I didn't have to think about it all the time. Think about him, about us, about the *relationship*.'

'Love's hard work,' Maxine agreed.

Jan went through with a face innocent of make-up, her blue robe floating as she walked. She waved to say goodnight.

'Are you in love with her?' Stella asked.

Maxine smiled. She said, 'I like her very much. I'm *in love* with her technique.'

The spare room backed on to gardens. Stella switched off the light and looked out of the window. A fox was standing on a patch of frost-rimed grass, head down, searching for prey. The half-moon and the night-long city glow gave more than enough light. The fox's concentration was intense. As Stella watched, it gave a little bound and nipped up whatever it was: a shrew, a house-mouse, a rat.

London was full of predators and scavengers.

Her face hurt and she felt too uneasy in her mind to sleep, but she lay down in the dark. She didn't have a plan for her life and she didn't have a plan for catching the killer of Valerie Blake and Sophie Simms.

Her mobile rang and she knew who it was. She reached out and switched it off. In the next room, Jan and Maxine were talking, their voices low, barely audible. Then the talking stopped.

John Delaney listened to Stella's voice asking him to leave a message. He said, 'Stella, come home.'

He put the TV on and watched a few scenes from a made-for-TV movie, but he couldn't settle. He went from room to room, as if he might find her there, still angry but ready to forgive, though he wasn't completely sure that forgiveness was the issue.

'Home' was a loaded word and he knew it.

Robert Adrian Kimber was writing. He was using a pen because he felt better connected to the words. Also he liked his handwriting: it was small and neat and unfussy. He liked to keep the lines close to one another, so the text appeared as a solid block of penmanship.

Outside, the girls were still working. Some always moved down from the Strip to the main road at this time of night; they worked the crossroads. There were more police patrols, but there were more punters. The side gate to the cemetery was open, and it was a good place to take the head-jobs and the hand-jobs. The pimps moved down too, keeping an eye on their cash-crop.

Kimber made a cup of coffee and watched them for a while. He remembered Nancy, the working girl he sometimes used, and almost followed an impulse to go out and find her, but he had his work to finish. He drank his coffee, then went back to the journal. He wrote about his luck, about DS Mooney, about how close he'd got.

Close enough to touch.

41

It was late when Stella woke. She put on the bathrobe Maxine had given her and walked into the main room, which was full of light and music: a cold, blue light from the clear day outside; slow jazz, trumpet, guitar, drum-brushes. Jan sat at a table by the window drinking coffee. She went to the kitchen and brought a cup for Stella. In the cold morning light, she looked no less pretty, her blonde hair cut to just below the jaw, her nose small and straight, her features almost perfectly even.

'Max has gone out for croissant and the papers. I have to leave in a moment.'

Stella nodded. It was odd, this glimpse of another life, croissant, coffee, two women with their two-women ways. In the AMIP squad room, Maxine had a reputation for being hard-nosed and owning a sardonic sense of humour. No one really knows anyone, Stella thought – George Paterson, John Delaney . . . Stella Mooney. She smiled to herself and Jan noticed. She said, 'That was a secret smile.' It was an oddly intimate remark, but she spoke without any edge to her voice.

'I was thinking that it's impossible to second-guess people.'

'You knew she was gay . . .'

'Oh, God, I didn't mean that. Just . . . people's lives.'

As if to illustrate the point, Jan said, 'I see my daughter on Sundays. She's three.' After a moment, she added, 'You never know what you're looking for until you find it. Who said that?'

'Someone who'd found it.'

'Sounds right.'

Jan went away and came back in a leather coat with a fur trim round the collar and cuffs. Stella asked, 'When did you know?'

'I've always known. The marriage was denial. Poor man.'

'And the child?'

'Heartbreak.' She said it without a trace of self-pity.

Stella thought that Jan was someone who lived life out in the open with no time for polite evasions. The notion drew her in. She said, 'And how does it feel, the life you've got now?'

She meant 'changes' and 'no going back', but Jan said, 'The here and now or having sex with a woman?'

Stella laughed. 'Both, really.'

Jan crossed to where Stella was sitting, dipped between the lapels of the bathrobe and passed her hand over Stella's breast for a moment, a light touch, cupping her briefly, her thumb just grazing the nipple. Stella didn't move; she was barely breathing.

Jan walked to the door and opened it to leave. She said, 'Well, how did that feel?'

Kimber was just cruising. Sunday was a day of broken routines, nothing reliable, nothing you could count on. He'd been to Patricia's address, but had drawn a blank. The temperature was a couple of degrees below freezing and people were hibernating. He felt restless. He'd settle for anything, anyone, someone who caught his eye . . . but he'd come down here just in case, not too far from home, a café where he could be warm, drink tea, keep an eye on the place. And there she was, suddenly, the one he called Monica, wearing the leather coat with the fur collar and cuffs, her blonde hair almost hidden by a cherry-red beanie.

He grinned as he left the café. He was on the opposite side of the road and walking easily because she was not far ahead. He glanced around, as he always did – at the street, to check on the other walkers, at the flat to check that no one was watching her leave – and a movement at the window caught his attention. He glanced towards it, wary now, and his breath went away for a moment.

A panel van was parked ten feet further up the road. He stepped behind it and looked through from the driver's window to the window of Monica's flat. DS Mooney. Stella Mooney. As if he'd never left her; as if she'd never been away. She hadn't seen him. All her attention seemed to be on 'Monica' as she reached the top of the road and went out of sight.

She stood at the window for a while, her gaze unmoving. She was wearing a white towelling bathrobe, one hand out of sight beneath the lapel.

42

Leon Bloss was very slightly stoned. He knew how to do that, he knew exactly how far to go. It sharpened him up. It made smells and colours just a little keener, a little brighter. A line or two was all he needed. Not to go to the edge, but a step or two off centre.

It was how he liked to be when the time came to kill.

There was a hint of darkness in the sky and the cloud-cover that had come in during the day would make for an early dusk. He watched as Kimber paced back and forth by the window, now and then casting an eye towards the ply-and-veneer coffee table where Bloss had laid out a claw hammer, a whipcord garrotte with a steel bar, a packet of babywipes – tools of the trade, the gear, the kit. Kimber had bought a jacket with a red fleece lining that you could turn inside out.

Bloss said, 'It doesn't have to be tonight.' But he knew it did.

Kimber said, 'I followed her from Vigo Street, then I lost her, then she turned up again plain as day.'

'You told me,' Bloss said. 'We're not thinking about her.'

'No, but she was with Monica. Does that make it difficult?'

'Makes it riskier. Degrees of separation.'

'What?'

'You narrow the distance between yourself and the police. There's a connection, something personal. Monica knows Mooney, you kill Monica, Mooney knows you. It's a pattern; it looks like bad luck.'

'But Patricia's random.'

'Yes, she is.'

'You think that's the way we should go?'

'It's my advice.'

'It doesn't matter much to me. I think I would have chosen Patricia anyway. I've been closer to her. I followed her ten times, maybe fifteen, on the bus, in the street, everywhere. She works in an estate agent's in Notting Hill. She uses a Motorola and her boyfriend is called Ben and I know her routes.'

There were a dozen photographs of her up on the wall – taken in the street, mostly, though there was a long-lens shot of her crossing a park and another taken as she bought something in a shop. A dozen photos and an incomplete story written in silver ink on dark paper. Kimber had pinned the lock of her hair at the very bottom of the unfinished page, the place where the story ended.

'What time does she come past?' Bloss asked.

'Seven to seven thirty, but it's easy to spot her. She walks down to the junction, waits for the traffic, crosses the road, then has a hundred metres before she gets to the church.'

'It's good to have a plan,' Bloss said.

He picked up the hammer and hit the veneer table. The hammer-head went through, buried to the claw. He wrestled it out, working the shaft from side to side, then handed it to Kimber.

'Your turn, Bobby.'

43

Kimber watched her up to the junction, watched as she stood at the kerb waiting for the lights to change, then he went down to join her.

He knew it might not be right; he and Bloss had discussed that. Just one other person taking the same short cut would be enough to spoil things. Luck could go this way or that. She strode out in her long black coat, her short skirt and brightly coloured tights, intent on getting home, having a shower, waiting for Ben to turn up. She liked Ben a lot. He was good news and might go on being good news for some time to come. She smiled at the thought, but Kimber was behind her and missed the moment.

He was tense, almost walking on tiptoe; his hand, in the pocket of his reversible coat, was clutching the shaft of the hammer. His eyes were shining.

The lights were on in the church, glowing dimly through the stained glass, and the choir was practising, descant voices wafting out high and clear over the rumble of traffic. The girl's name wasn't Patricia, of course; it was Kate. Kate Reilly. She recognized the carol but couldn't give it a name. She opened the gate and went through, head down, noticing how the light from the windows glistened on the frosted path.

Kimber was breathing fast, like a runner, but making no sound. He looked back for a moment. People and traffic on the road, an undertow of noise, the choir, the yellowish light from the church, but no one behind him and, when he checked ahead, no one in front.

Close enough to touch.

Suddenly he realized that he didn't know if he would kill her; the act lay in the future, just a moment away but unrealized as yet. His face was flushed and his heart drummed. He wasn't sure how he'd got to this point, the girl ahead of him, his hand on the shaft of the hammer, her death waiting for her just a few steps away. He was excited and fearful at the same time; he trembled as he withdrew the hammer.

Where the path curved away towards the far gate, Kate felt his presence and half turned. Whatever she saw in his face terrified her and she put out an arm to ward him off, opening her mouth to speak or scream. His blow took her at the place where her neck met her shoulder. She said, '*Oh!*' and lost her footing, going down on one knee like a supplicant. Kimber lifted the hammer up over his head and stepped back to get a good swing, then brought it down hard, all the strength of his arm and shoulder behind it. Kate seemed to spring up slightly under the blow, then fell forward, her face hitting his thighs and resting there. Kimber had forgotten what to do next. He stood completely still, with Kate nestling against him.

An hour passed, or it might have been a few seconds. On the street a van making a late delivery ran a red light and tail-ended a Volvo estate that was swinging into a fast, illegal U-turn. The vehicles locked and broadsided on the crossroads: a shriek of brakes, the impact, a moment's silence, then a cacophony of horns.

Bloss came up out of the darkness.

*

He barged Kimber aside, then took Kate under the arms and dragged her off into the graveyard: a dark corner close to the far wall where they were screened by trees and gravestones. He propped her against a tree and stood back. His voice tight with anger, he said, 'Hit her again.' He walked off even further. Kimber didn't notice, but Bloss was wearing latex gloves and a woollen hat pulled down hard to his eyebrows. He said, 'Hit her!'

Kimber knelt down beside Kate and paused a moment, head bowed as if lost in thought, then he seemed to find a sudden source of energy, or fury, and he went at her like a man driving a fence post, until he fell back, panting. Bloss said, 'Now the garrotte: use it!'

'She's dead,' Kimber said.

'There's a pattern,' Bloss said. 'Jesus! We went through this.' Kimber looked at him, struggling to remember. The killing had emptied his mind. Bloss hissed with annoyance. He walked over to Kate and pulled her up by the hair until the back of her head rested against the tree, then opened her coat. He unzipped her skirt, pulled it off, together with her tights and underclothes, and stuffed them into the front of his coat. He threw her boots in among some bushes. Kimber was struggling to remember. Bloss positioned the garrotte, turned the steel bar and stood up. He said, 'Come on.'

Kimber let his head rest against the tree, his face close to Kate's. His breathing was slow now. He felt drowsy.

'Come on!' Bloss started off between the gravestones, heading for the gate. Kimber touched her cheek. Her face seemed to have slipped a little and gone lopsided. Her mouth was open, as if that 'Oh!' were fixed on her lips, and her eyes looked straight into his.

Bloss came back. He punched Kimber hard on the shoulder, just that, no word. Kimber got up and reversed his coat, then used babywipes on his face and hands. He followed Bloss out of the churchyard. They walked up on to the Strip, taking a long loop round in order to approach Kimber's room from the other direction. It was a little early for any real action on the Strip, but a few whores were out to catch the home-going husbands, and the deals were going down on corners and in alleyways.

They crossed a railway bridge and Bloss took Kate's clothing out from his coat and dropped it into the scrub beside the line. He gave Kimber a little nudge, almost a blow. 'Just as well I was there. Your guardian angel.' An edge to his voice. They walked on in silence for a while, then he added, 'The first time's strange, Bobby. The first time's always a little bit strange.'

Kimber had his head down like a man hunched against the cold. He was laughing and crying without making a sound.

The voices of the choir filled the church. The lights were low and the altar-candles made the windows glow, deep blues and ochres.

Jamie sat in a pew halfway back, his eyes fixed on the nativity scene to the right of the altar-rail, a dwarfish Holy Family hemmed in by a pint-sized ox and ass. He knew what was going to happen and he knew it would happen soon: Christ would walk the earth. After a while, his gaze moved to the crucifix behind the altar, the naked God spread like a pinioned bird; then to a window that depicted Christ in glory, his arms spread to receive all who would come to be saved.

Jamie slipped to his knees and said a prayer. He was praying for himself and for Sadie.

*

Kimber had been drinking since they'd got back. He'd gone from motormouth to no comment and back again in a very short time.

Bloss wasn't listening. He was watching the activity out on the crossroads, where a recovery truck was still trying to lift the two locked vehicles and traffic cops were making a hash of diverting the traffic flow. He liked the chaos and the horns and the glass littering the tarmac. He'd done a few more lines and he felt sharp – completely in control. Kimber had frozen and that was bad, a bad moment. Bloss had intended to stay clear of the scene, well clear, but in the end things had worked out fine. Things had worked out to plan.

Kimber's eyes were bright and unblinking. His words came like a river as he relived her death, describing the event to Bloss as he might to a stranger, picking through it, going image by image as if he had the video-tape, freeze-framing this moment, slo-moing that, her turn towards him, his swing of the hammer, her voice saying, '*Oh!*'

'*Oh!*' She said, '*Oh!*' He could still hear it.

44

A covering of snow had fallen during the night. The cloud had shifted and a freeze had set in under a hard, clear sky. White name-stones, white monuments, trees shrouded in white, Kate Reilly's white legs and belly, her white hands, her face dark with blood.

White figures on a white ground were the forensics team quartering the area.

Stella and Pete Harriman stood to one side as Frank Silano directed operations. The stills man and the video man had done their work, but the footprints round the scene weren't going to help and the snow would only make sampling more difficult. The uniformed help were running a no-go tape round the trees and getting a scene of crime tent into place. The police doctor wasn't short of options for cause of death, though he wasn't sure which to nominate, the blunt instrument or the garrotte.

Stella said, 'This is our man. This is him.'

Harriman stamped his feet. He was ankle-deep in snow and feeling it. The locals had called it in less than half an hour before.

Harriman said, 'She was reported at nine thirty. This is a cut-through. How many people must have walked past?'

'She's off the path,' Stella observed, 'and she was covered in snow like the bushes and the gravestones.'

'She wouldn't have looked like a gravestone. She'd've looked like a dead body with a covering of snow.'

'People go by with things on their minds, they don't look left or right.' After a moment she added, 'Get someone to put up a yellow board. For all the good it'll do.' She stared at the body, then turned away, feeling the bile rise. She spoke to Silano. 'Get them to bag her. Do it quickly.'

Kate had been out all night, open to the weather. In that sort of cold, with the earth hard and the pickings few, little scavengers had found her quickly: rats and foxes and crows. Silano zipped the body-bag over her eyeless face.

DC Nick Robson was at the scene: exhibitions officers were collectors and curators. He noted the usual stuff – what there was of her clothing, items in her coat pockets, the boots that a uniformed man had found in the bushes. The garrotte.

Maxine Hewitt sat in a church pew talking to assorted clergymen. They told her about choir practice, that they'd all walked along the path as they'd left, that none of them had noticed a thing. They observed that it was a terrible thing to happen, and so close to Christmas. They said they would pray for Kate's soul.

The Holy Family looked on with nothing to say.

'They sang,' Maxine told Stella, 'they left, they saw nothing.'

'Fucking wonderful,' Stella said. As they walked to the gate, a crow hopped across the graves and on to the path. Stella took a kick at it and it flew up to head height, then glided to earth ten feet away. 'Who's doing the family?'

'Are you asking me to?'

'I am, yes. Take Pete with you.'

There was a wind coming in from Greenland. Down by the crossroads, cadmium and carbon monoxide were little toxic twisters with a bite of ice.

'Thanks,' Stella said. 'For yesterday.' She'd spent the day with Maxine, a walk by the river, lunch in a pub, an afternoon movie complete with chocolate and a half bottle of vodka to sip from. Girls' day out and nothing unusual about it except Stella's sore mouth and swollen face and the after-shadow of another woman's hand on her breast.

'There's always a bed,' Maxine said. 'Tonight, if you need it.'

'I found an outfit in the *Yellow Pages*. Turbo-mop, or something of the sort. Anyway, they're on the case. I ought to go back to the flat. Sixty per cent –'

'– of burglaries recur at the same address within a week. I know. Have you spoken to Delaney?'

Stella wondered how it was going to work out, this new level of friendship between herself and Maxine. Between herself and Jan. She shook her head in answer to the question and Maxine didn't ask for more.

Their cars were up on the pavement by the crossroads, with a police-tape cordon round them to stop the traffic wardens from getting smart. The gutters were thick with caramelized glass from last night's crash.

Stella said, 'I'll get your underwear back to you.'

'It's not mine,' Maxine said, 'it's Jan's.'

Jan who, on this bright, cold morning, was still alive and in the world. Jan the unchosen, going about her business somewhere on what was just another day in her life.

Robert Adrian Kimber looking down on the scene from his window. The cops, the body-wagon, the white-coated technicians of death.

DS Stella Mooney coming out of the church gate as Kimber framed her up, as his camera clicked.

45

Someone had stuck cotton-wool balls to the squad-room windows and draped some streamers over the doors. The ashtrays were full and there were coffee cups and cola cans on the desks, chocolate-bar wrappers and doughnut boxes. You would have thought the party had moved on, except everyone was there, including Mike Sorley, standing in the doorway, the party-pooper with the hacking cough.

There was tinsel round the whiteboard that displayed all-ways-up SOC shots of the corpses of Valerie Blake, Sophie Simms and Kate Reilly. Stella sat on a desk and faced the room and repeated what she'd said to Harriman. 'It's him. It's our man.'

'Which killed her: the blunt instrument or the ligature?' Sorley coughed through his words.

'We're waiting on that. Also waiting to hear whether she was sexually assaulted.'

'Also waiting on forensics,' Maxine supposed.

'Yes. In the meantime, it's door-to-door coverage in the streets close to the scene, field any responses to the yellow board, circulate and sift the crime reports, the usual desk-work, okay? You spoke to the family . . .' This last was to Maxine.

'Normal girl, normal life, normal boyfriend. The parents are out of it: both sedated. It's what you'd expect.'

'Talk to the boyfriend,' Stella said. 'There's normal and there's normal.'

'He could be our man?' Silano was sceptical.

Stella shrugged. 'Someone is.'

When the meeting broke up, Marilyn Hayes handed her a 'while you were away' note. She said, 'Dentist at two, apparently,' and smiled a flawless smile.

Sorley hacked phlegm all the way back to his office, where he took three paracetamol, drank some Benylin straight from the bottle and lit a cigarette.

'Andy Greegan and Sue Chapman are both still on sick-leave with it,' Stella told him.

'Which is why you need me.'

'I don't need you. Your wife does.'

'She's in Dubai.'

'She's where?'

'Pre-Christmas treat. Her brother lives there.'

'So you'd be home alone.'

'Which is why I'd prefer to die here.' He took a lungful of smoke and hung on to it until the impulse to cough faded a little. 'I'd been told to close you down. Now this . . .' He meant Kate Reilly's death.

Stella understood: fresh murder, fresh case, fresh funding. Kate had given her a new lease of life. She handed Sorley the morning update, but said nothing about the second man, about Angel. There was no real evidence of his involvement beyond the emails; however, opportunities had been lost and holding it back made her feel edgy.

Delaney, you jerk.

Sorley had stood in the squad-room doorway in the hope of keeping his bacteria to himself. For just the same reason, Stella was talking to him from the corridor.

She said, 'You could stop smoking; that might help.'

'Only thing keeping me going.' As she turned to leave, he added, 'Why the blunt instrument *and* the garrotte?'

*

233

Sam Burgess asked the same question. He was handling Kate as if she might fall apart at his touch. Stella was watching and, at the same time, trying not to see too much. Kate's empty eye-sockets were crusty and dark. Her face was lopsided and oddly ragged; it looked as if no one had ever lived there.

'You tell me,' Stella said.

'I hate to pun, but it's overkill. The garrotte would have killed her if the hammer hadn't.'

'Hammer?'

'Almost certainly.'

'And it was the hammer that did the job.'

'More or less. There's some evidence to show that she might not have been quite dead when he garrotted her, but she would have died shortly whatever he did next.'

'Valerie Blake was hit with a hammer or something similar, but that's not what killed her. The garrotte killed her.'

'Right.'

'And Sophie Simms was killed with a hammer and not garrotted, though there was a garrotte at the scene.'

'Correct.'

'Now Kate Reilly is killed with a hammer but garrotted for good measure.'

'Don't ask me how his mind works,' Sam said, 'I just deal with the wreckage.'

The preliminary examination had been done. Kate had been combed and probed and swabbed. Giovanni had trepanned Kate and was lifting out the brain. Stella could see the damage from where she was standing, and she was standing a good way back.

'Any evidence of rape?' Stella asked.

'I don't think so.'

Sam made the Y-incision, the long fillet, and began to free up the lung-tree. Stella stayed a little longer to get the gist of it, but there wasn't much to tell. Kate had been healthy, like Valerie and Sophie; she'd had a good hold on life.

Stella said, 'Report tomorrow?'

'By noon,' Sam told her. As she was leaving, he said, 'Merry Christmas.'

The dentist took the rough edges off her broken tooth and told her she needed a crown. She endured the needle and the drill and the fact that he hadn't noticed her swollen face and was putting pressure on her cheekbone as he drilled. She lay back while he worked on her and let her mind take its course.

Why the garrotte *and* the hammer? Why sometimes kill with one weapon and sometimes the other? Why strip his victims from the waist if he wasn't raping them? It was a pattern but a broken one. The only clear impulse was to kill.

Flat out in the chair with a hissy loop tape of Christmas songs playing, Stella suddenly felt a tremendous surge of anger: enough to lift her shoulders from the chair, enough to flex her jaw and make her catch her breath. The dentist felt it and let up with the drill for a moment, thinking he'd touched a nerve.

I'm coming after you, you bastard. I'm going to nail you to the fucking wall.

She shuddered and closed her eyes and breathed out. The dentist put the hardware back in her mouth. The loop tape hissed on.

. . . have yourself a merry little Christmas . . .

46

Tom Davison said, 'Do you make men nervous?'

Stella had the phone hooked under her chin. She was eating a sandwich and reading a series of yellow-board responses. 'Why?'

'You want everything in a hurry. It's not natural.'

'Can we get out of the bedroom, please?'

'And go where?'

'The laboratory would be good.'

A man was seen entering the churchyard carrying a gun, a machete, a crossbow. He was twenty thirty forty fifty. He had black brown blond hair. He was following a prostitute a housewife a black woman a Chinese woman.

'There's a problem.'

'Which is?'

'I'm backed up.'

'I said out of the bedroom, Davison.'

He laughed. 'Look, there's a process. I get items from the scene, items from the morgue. They don't necessarily arrive together. I correlate them. I cross-reference. I go to lunch.'

'You know –'

'Do you ever go to lunch, DS Mooney?'

'– what I'm looking for, don't you?'

'A match with the DNA of whoever killed Blake and Simms.'

'Exactly.'

'But you're standing in line. I have other sergeants with black silk panels who are just as demanding as you.'

It was my husband father brother son. It was the guy next door the postman the builder the vicar. It was the man who sells the Big Issue.

'When will I get a result on this, Davison?'
    'Officially, three days from now.'
    'Unofficially.'
    'Sooner.'

A woman like that is filth sewage disease corruption. Luring men to a graveyard. She deserved all she got. She was struck down by the hand of justice the hand of righteousness the hand of God.

'Any chance of sooner than that?'
    'Same MO, was it?'
    'He caved her head in with a hammer and throttled her with a ligature. She was on her way home from work: looking forward to an evening out with her boyfriend. She was twenty-three.'
    'Leave it with me.'

I saw two men coming out of the churchyard. It was about that time. It was dark and I didn't see their faces. They were average height not young not old not fat not thin. The choir was singing. I don't walk through there myself, it's spooky.

Her mobile had five voicemails and three texts, all from Delaney. She went out into the car park to find some privacy and called him to let him know she was all right. There was no moodiness in her or a desire to hurt. She told him about the flat being burgled but not about the lads in hoodies or Panhandler Pete.

'What are you going to do?' he asked.

'Stay at the flat for a bit. It ought to be lived in. There's a danger of squatters.'

'Okay.' She pictured him at his workstation, the mess of books and papers round his chair, and it pained her. 'Call me,' he said. 'Let me know what's happening.'

'I'll be okay there. It's time I had a clear-out.'

Delaney knew enough to give her rope. Even so he couldn't help but say, 'I love you.'

Harriman walked into the car park with a plastic-packed BLT, a tuna baguette, a coffee grande, two Twix bars, three packs of Marlboro Lights and a forbidden Budweiser. Stella said, 'You read the yellow-board stuff?'

'Not yet.'

'A witness saw two men coming out at about the right time. A local secretary, I think she was. Get her in.'

'Two men?'

'It was about the right time.'

'But *two* men?'

'I know. Get her in, all the same.'

She went back to the squad room with him. He gave the tuna baguette, the coffee, a Twix and a pack of Marlboro to Marilyn Hayes. They sat at her desk to eat. Marilyn reached out and took a crumb from the corner of his mouth.

Maybe that's the way to do things, Stella thought, home-life and love-life as separate events. George and Stella. Stella and Delaney.

Tom Davison came back to her just as she was about to go home.

He said, 'You're right. It's him, whoever he is.'

'For sure?'

'Same traces as we found at the other two scenes of crime, Blake and Simms. No doubt. He didn't leave much but he left enough.'

'Thanks, Tom.'

She would write a brief report and circulate it before she left. Her mind was on that and she was getting ready to put the phone down when she heard him say, 'There's more.'

Something in his voice: an urgency. She said, 'Go on.'

'Your confessor, Robert Adrian Kimber. Him too.'

'Him too meaning what?'

'His DNA's all over the place. All over her. He was there. He was involved.'

She was silent for a moment; there was a faint ringing in her ears like distant voices. She said, 'There's no chance of that being wrong?'

'None,' Davison said. 'Does it fuck things up at all?'

47

'We had him,' Stella said, 'but we let him go.'

'You had no option: he hadn't done anything.' Anne Beaumont was making omelettes while Stella opened a bottle of red wine, which meant that they were neither cop and profiler nor shrink and patient, though Stella wasn't at all sure what the other option might be. Friends, perhaps, except that Stella felt that Anne knew a great deal more about her than a friend had a right to know.

'He's done something now.'

'And he didn't do it alone.'

Stella poured two drinks, took a sip, then sat on a stool by the counter. The wine seemed to go straight to her bloodstream but cleared her head rather than fogged it. 'What have we got? A series of attacks on women, including the murders of Valerie Blake and Sophie Simms.'

'And Kate Reilly,' Anne said.

'Yes, I know, but leave that aside. Martin Cotter's definitely in the frame for the attacks before the one on Valerie Blake. So take those out of it. Blake and Simms were killed by a man we can't identify; we've got his DNA, but it's not on record. Call him Mister Mystery. Robert Kimber confesses to killing Valerie Blake but didn't. Now Kate Reilly is killed by Mister Mystery and Kimber is there at the time.'

'Or Kimber killed her and Mister Mystery was there at the time.'

'So Kimber confessed to a murder committed by Mister Mystery, now he and Mister Mystery are working together.'

Anne topped up their glasses. She said, 'You think Mister Mystery and Angel are the same guy – the one who was emailing Kimber?'

'I do.'

'And Delaney didn't tell you about him. I can see why you moved out.'

'I haven't moved out.'

'No? Where are you living? And why am I cooking for two?'

'I have to live at Vigo Street for a bit. They could come back if the place is empty.'

'Good excuse,' Anne said. She added, 'They could come back anyway. What would you do then?'

'Shoot the little bastards.'

Anne looked up sharply. 'Who's that talking? The thug beneath the skin?'

'You forget,' Stella told her, 'that I'm off Harefield. I'm off the estate.'

'So, you're at Vigo Street, but you haven't dumped him.'

'No.'

'In fact, you still love him.'

'Yes.'

'Okay.'

'Do you know how irritating that is – that *okay*?'

'I'm a shrink. I'm not supposed to comment. Which is what "okay" means – no comment.'

'But you're not my shrink any more, so say what a friend would say.'

'Take your time,' Anne told her. She opened a bag-salad and cut some bread. When they were sitting at the table, she said, 'That was a piece of advice. It comes free.'

*

Turbo-mop had done a great job. The place was clean and they'd swept out the crap, made the bed, collected the CDs, put books back on to shelves, boarded up the window, left a bill. The walls and furniture were still tagged in red and black, but with the debris gone you could almost take the flat for a Brit-art installation.

Stella brought in some essentials: chill-cabinet food, vodka, a baseball bat. She called Harriman and told him about Tom Davison's findings.

'Which is why,' he said, 'you're interested in the secretary who saw two men coming out of the churchyard.'

'You know what I think? I think Mister Mystery killed Valerie. Kimber confessed to it. Mister Mystery got interested in him. He contacted Kimber. Now they're a team.'

'He killed Sophie Simms too.'

'He did, yes.'

'Why the fake rape stuff and the garrotte?'

'Cotter raped his victims, or attempted to; he also used a garrotte. Mister Mystery was trying to replicate Cotter's pattern, hiding his killings among Cotter's.'

'Hiding his killings among Cotter's doesn't account for Kate Reilly.'

'I know. But it's different now. Kimber's with him.'

'So what's his motive?'

'I don't know. Maybe he's just having fun. Maybe they both are. But I know this: Mister Mystery could be anyone. We haven't had a single lead on him, not a jot – he would have been impossible to catch unless he made a mistake. But it's different now. We know Kimber. Find him, we find them both.'

'So you want everyone on the street.'

'You, me, Maxine Hewitt, Frank Silano . . . Nick Robson's been office-bound for a while but probably still has contacts,

Andy Greegan, if he can get out of bed. We've all got a chis, maybe two or three. Talk to them, put pressure on. Intensify the house-to-house, take in a wider area, hassle the operators on the Strip: make them uncomfortable, make them understand that thrill-killers are bad for business.'

Harriman said, 'We had him and we let him go.'

'I've been down that road,' Stella said. 'It's a dead end.'

It was late. She propped the baseball bat up against the wall close to the bed-head and lay down. She felt unaccountably sad. Sad to be at Vigo Street, sad to be without Delaney, sad that George was making new friends.

She fell asleep and had a short, brightly coloured dream in which Kimber sat by her bedside and poured the whole story out to her, the whole truth, but his words overlapped and criss-crossed, cancelling each other out. Behind him, in shadow, stood a man who was singing, his voice soft and true.

She looked beyond Kimber to that dark silhouette and found herself drawn into the song, matching his pitch; a sweet duet. She was singing it when she woke.

. . . have yourself a merry little Christmas . . .

48

A chis, a snout, a grass. The first thing to remember is that they're criminals; they're on the other side. They do it for money and in the interests of self-protection. There's always a trade-off and it's not just the back-hander twenties: it's the tight lip; it's the blind eye.

Stella ran three, one of them Mickey Wicks. The other two were Harefield veterans.

Frank Silano used a couple of bookies. Bookies know most things, and people owe them, which is useful.

Maxine Hewitt called in from time to time on an ex-colleague, now a private inquiry agent. He had a few of his own: it was cumulative.

Andy Greegan wasn't too ill to get out of bed, but out of bed was as far as he could get. No one asked him for the names of his contacts: chis relationships worked on trust and exclusivity.

Pete Harriman found his information among the low-lifes and sleazebags, the pimps, the dealers . . . the hod-carriers of the criminal world. The advantage was they were every-where. They ran between cracks and crevices. The fault line was their natural habitat.

He was in a pub called the Wheatsheaf, half a mile south of the Strip, waiting for a guy called Ronaldo, real name Ronald Nelms. Ronaldo worked up on the Strip and had convic-tions for assault, conspiracy and carrying an offensive weapon, though he hadn't considered it offensive at all, he'd considered it necessary. Mostly the girls could cope with an aggressive punter, but just now and then Ronaldo would have to offer a helping hand. The hand in question wore a sap-glove. It was surprising how quickly a fractured cheekbone and the loss of a couple of teeth could quieten someone down. Harriman had managed to get a GBH reduced to 'affray' and on a couple of occasions had told Ronaldo when to take the night off. It was the way things worked; everyone had dirty hands.

Ronaldo came in looking like a man with urgent business, which he was, though the business lay elsewhere. Time was money, and, with no one to watch, the girls could get a few quickies in for themselves and stash the cash. He took the bar-stool next to Harriman's and said, 'I've got girls on a fifteen-minute turn around. Head-job in a car can be ten. Can we get this done?'

Ronaldo was stocky and wore a thin, shaped beard that he thought gave him an exotic touch, like the gold cross earring, like the diamond stud in his tooth. He glanced round the pub looking for familiar faces and not wanting to find them. There were three guys at the far end of the bar drinking brandy chasers. They wore custom-made baseball caps with their gang tag up front – MAGNA – and a tattoo on the side of the neck with a curlicued 'M'. They were branded; they belonged. Ronaldo thought they were from Harefield, but that didn't matter. The estate wasn't his territory and, anyway, they had their own teams to run.

Harriman bought a drink. He said, 'This isn't close to home, Ronaldo. It's unrelated.'

'Good, because there are wheels within wheels, Mr Harriman, Chinese boxes, know what I mean?'

Harriman didn't but he handed Ronaldo some petty cash. It meant nothing to the guy. It was tokenism, like shaking hands on a deal.

'Recent attacks on women. Valerie Blake, Sophie Simms, Kate Reilly.'

'Not familiar.'

'The last one was the day before yesterday, in the church-yard by –'

'Oh, right, yeah. I saw the action.'

'Bad for business, was it?'

'Yes and no. Too many cops about, but they're not looking our way. Doesn't affect the punters, why would it? Some girl was topped, you're getting tossed off in the back of your Vauxhall Vectra, where's the connection?'

The Harefield team was looking at them and Harriman noticed. He said, 'You know those guys?'

'Nah. They're drugs and boy-gangs. We don't cross over.'

'We had a suspect called Kimber. Robert Adrian Kimber. He walked, but now we want him back.'

'Never heard of him. What makes you think I might?'

'He kills women.'

'Not working girls.'

'Not yet.'

The Magna boys got up to leave, brushing along the bar, solemn-faced.

Ronaldo said, 'Nutters are a different thing, Mr Harriman. Nutters make their own rules, know what I mean?'

'I'm talking to everyone.'

'Okay, and you've talked to me.' He looked at his watch. 'I'm supposed to be clocking them – it's rush hour.'

Harriman glanced up as the Harefield guys approached and saw that all three men had their eyes on the door. They were checking a route to the exit. He had time to say, 'Oh, *shit!*' but that was all.

Ronaldo looked the wrong way – looked at Harriman – and the blade went in hard. His eyes widened and he said,

'Ooof!', then his mouth went slack and his eyes misted. The knife-man was already by the door. Harriman got off his stool, swinging a punch that landed dead-centre on the second man's face; he'd put the motion of his body into the blow and he felt the guy's nose-bone crack.

Ronaldo slipped sideways off his stool, the weight of his body taking Harriman off balance. He hopped back, letting Ronaldo's body hit the floor, then took a step forward, lining up the man he'd just hit. He could see the third man out of the corner of his eye and thought he'd sidestep to move himself out of range, but he was too slow. The beer-glass came round in a tight arc and took him in the side of the face. He felt the glass explode, didn't feel anything for a second, then felt everything.

49

Stella was walking into the hospital as Marilyn Hayes was walking out. Marilyn was wearing clothes that said 'sensational figure, look this way' and men seemed happy to obey. Stella wondered how many of them were headed for the maternity wards.

Marilyn said, 'He lost a lot of blood.'

'I heard that. Is he okay?'

'You know Pete.' She bit her lip and looked away for a moment; the line of her mouth went ragged . . .

Stella said, 'We've got good IDs on the guys that did it.'

'That's great,' Marilyn said. 'That makes all the difference.' Then, 'I smuggled him in some cigarettes and a bottle of Scotch.'

'Yes,' Stella said, 'that sounds just what the doctor ordered.'

Harriman was in a side ward, getting his needs through a cannula and watching TV. He had been practising smiling without pain and gave Stella the benefit. One side of his face was covered by a thick wound dressing, but the bandage went all the way round his head.

She said, 'He really caught you with that.'

Harriman grunted. 'Fucking pub fight. What's the likeliest thing? You'll get glassed. Do I see it coming? Do I fuck.'

'How long are you here for?'

'Tonight. There are still bits of glass coming out of my face. Extruding, they call it.' He puckered his lips. 'Extru*uuuu*ding.'

'Then what?'

'I have to come back to get sewn up. Scar-management.'

'Where is it?'

'Starts under the ear, makes a loop, goes along the jawline.'

'Sounds romantic. Like a duelling scar.'

'That's what I'm hoping for.'

'Does it hurt?'

'Oh, Christ, yes. Hurts like fuck.' The news came on TV and he lowered the sound. 'Is Ronaldo dead?'

'No. He's in ITU. The considered medical response of his consultant was to make him a four-to-one shot. Apparently, the word on the street is that it wasn't personal.'

'Wasn't personal? At four-to-one?'

'It wasn't particularly aimed at Ronaldo. And it certainly wasn't aimed at you.'

'No? It felt pretty *well* aimed to me.'

'It was because he's a chis. They're a Harefield firm, running a few boy-gangs – Clean Machine, that sort of thing, the kids who did my flat, perhaps – and they're having a war on narks. Kids are a network. There are rival gangs. They're all doing drugs and they all need cash, so there are lots of leaks.'

'So it's good to know it could have happened to anyone,' Harriman said. 'Pity it had to be me.' He added, 'Give me a day or two, okay? Then I'm back.'

'They'll never have it, Pete. You're officially on sick-leave as of now.'

'Okay, then – in the squad room but off the streets.'

'Forget it.'

'I'll talk to DI Sorley.'

She laughed at his persistence and shook her head. The newsreader was giving crime stats for the Christmas period and it seemed that crimes against the person were on the increase. She said, 'I only ask this in the interests of good team management, but how serious is this thing with Marilyn Hayes?'

'Seriously fun.'

'Is that what she thinks?'

Harriman looked at her, slightly startled. 'What? Sure.'

'How sure?'

'It's all about sex. It's an adventure. We've talked about it.'

Stella left him another bottle of Scotch. She said, 'Talk about it again.'

50

Sadie made a connection and scored some low-grade hillbilly heroin. She'd been busking most of the day, down among the carbon-monoxide overflow and the street-stain, and she'd made enough for a little, but a little wasn't enough. Jamie was tagging along, though not in the hope of being given a handout. He didn't use drugs, he didn't drink, and, so far as Sadie could tell, he didn't eat. He was wearing a quilted coat he'd stolen from a charity shop and a pair of boots with no laces.

They were heading for the alley by the Ocean Diner, a place to sleep, a place to freebase. It was nine thirty, too early for the restaurants to be emptying, too early for the movie- and theatre-goers to be back on the streets, but late-night shoppers were everywhere and Sadie panhandled people as she went, doing a little dance of interception in front of the ones who looked rich or pissed or lost, her litany unbroken: *Spare some change please spare some change could you spare some change please have you got any spare change cheers mate cheers mate merry christmas merry christmas merry spare some change please* . . .

Jamie muttered an invocation of his own, too low to be properly understood. Sadie thought he was getting crazier. He was a liability, sitting a few feet away while she played her tiny penny-whistle repertoire, talking to himself, following her like some dumb animal on a lead. She was aware of people walking a little oxbow to avoid him. She thought it would be a good idea to offload him, to cut him loose, but she wasn't sure how best to do it.

Sadie walked past the diner to the alley, feeling in her pocket for the scorched strip of tinfoil and her gear. Her attention was all in one direction, but when she heard the voice, she looked up. A woman's voice.

They were further down the alley, two men and a woman. It took Sadie a moment or two to work out the dynamic of the group, then she could see that it was a mugging. The men were crowding the woman, backing her up to the wall. She was handing over her bag and her mobile phone, arms out as if in supplication. They stood, a tight little triangle, with no need for words. Everyone knew what was happening, everyone knew what to do next, even Sadie, who was preparing to have heard nothing, seen nothing.

Jamie ran past her, his laceless boots flapping. The muggers looked towards him. There seemed no need for them to run, but that's what they decided to do, heading for the far end of the alley where it opened out on to a side road that would take them back to the crowded pavements of Notting Hill. The woman yelled something and one of the muggers turned and ran back. He grabbed the front of her coat, pulled her towards him and hit hard. She bounced off his punch and Sadie saw a little spray of blood go up from her face; then the man pulled her back – dragging her against the force of his blow – and hit her again.

You can run through Notting Hill Gate without bringing too much attention to yourself, but not if you're a man carrying a woman's handbag. The first mugger had taken out the purse and wallet, so he let the bag drop. Jamie was fast, but not in those boots. He came out of the far end of the alley in time to see the men rounding the corner. In a couple of minutes they would be down into the tube and gone. He gazed after them, breathing hard, then gave a little sob of distress, childlike, before going back to pick up the bag.

The woman was wearing a white leather jacket and a pale blue scarf. She came towards Sadie, walking crookedly, as if she were naked. Her nose was out of true and blood was running from her mouth. Her eyes were unfocused. Sadie stood back to let her pass. The woman's scarf and jacket carried splashes and trickle-lines of red. She neither looked at Sadie nor spoke to her, but walked slowly out into the street as if unsure of which direction to take.

Jamie came back carrying the woman's bag. He was muttering under his breath and grinding his teeth, flicking glances over his shoulder as if the muggers might come back; as if he hoped they would. He punched the wall and Sadie leaped back. She hadn't seen this before.

She said, 'All right?' And then, 'Take it easy.' Jamie slid down to the floor and tucked his knees up to his chin.

Sadie picked through the bag's contents, but there was nothing she wanted, nothing she could sell. Some make-up, tissues, a set of door keys on a casino-chip key ring, a letter, a receipt for a Patek Philippe wristwatch. Maybe the door keys would come in useful, even though there was no address to go with them. She put them in her pocket then, as an afterthought, dipped into the bag's interior pockets and a smile lit her face. Paydirt was a credit card in a zipper compartment, shiny and new and brimming with potential.

On the front of the card, a name: Ms Lauren Buchanan. On the reverse, a signature: rounded, careful letters devoid of flourish or style.

Her clothes were from the skip and thrift-shop collection, she smelled very slightly of piss and her hair was rank, but she asked for a bottle of Scotch and a bottle of brandy in a firm, clear voice and put down the card with confidence.

The guy in the liquor store put the booze into a bag and ran the card. Sadie said, 'You do a cash-back service?'

He said he didn't.

She said that was okay and signed Lauren Buchanan in a neat, characterless hand.

There were a dozen stores still open for business in the arcade and she visited them all, buying things she didn't want but might be able to sell, each time asking for cash-back. When Delaney appeared on the scene, Sadie was carrying a store bag in each hand and looking for the next place to try. Cash-back wasn't a service anyone had been eager to provide and, of the dozen stores, four had called the police. She looked at Delaney and the look said money. He handed her a twenty and they walked together for a while.

'Don't ask me any more questions,' she said.

'I'm just checking on you,' he told her. 'Checking to see how you are.'

'How do I look?'

'Prosperous.'

She laughed. 'I had a good day. It's getting closer to Christmas.'

As they reached the diner, a patrol car drew up and two cops got out, one tall, the other short. They laughed when they saw Sadie laden with her bags, but the good humour didn't last. They'd met street-sweepings before, freaks like this with pink and green streaks in their hair and metal in their faces. Sadie turned to run and one of them got round to block her; he shouldered her into the wall. A bag fell from her hand and the bottles of booze smashed.

Delaney said, 'Hey.'

The cops took him for a bystander. They ignored him. The tall one held Sadie by her hair while the other cuffed her, then they shoved her into the car. Her head knocked the side of the roof.

Delaney said, 'Take it easy.'

The tall cop shut the car door, looked at Delaney a moment, then sauntered back. He said, 'Some sort of problem?'

'You don't have to treat her like that.'

The tall cop smiled. He continued to look at Delaney for a while, as if waiting to make sure that he'd said everything he was going to say. Then he leaned forward and said, 'Fuck you, okay?'

Delaney said, 'Where are you taking her?'

'That was "fuck you", in case you didn't hear.'

'What's your name?'

The cop wasn't expecting it. He had already started towards the car; when he turned back, his look was a slow burn.

'Because,' Delaney explained, 'you might well be seeing it in print.'

The cop stood very close. His breath was smoke-and-burger with a little dental decay built in. He said, 'Are you obstructing me in the course of my duty, I wonder? I'm not sure, so I'm going to give you the benefit of the doubt.' He backed it up with a little, blunt-fingered poke to Delaney's shoulder, then walked to the car, got into the passenger seat and slammed the door hard. His eyes were still on Delaney as the driver tripped the roof-bar lights and cut out into the westbound traffic.

Delaney found Jamie standing at his elbow. Jamie said, 'Where's Sadie?'

'She'll be okay,' Delaney said.

Jamie was looking up and down the street, though he must have seen them take her, must have seen them muscle her into the car. He was shivering but not with the cold.

'Where's Sadie, where's Sadie, where's Sadie, where's Sadie . . . ?'

51

The Notting Hill police computer made a little incident-tree. It started with a rough-sleeper called Sadie Brooks who had used a credit card stolen from a Ms Lauren Buchanan and from there went to a mugging reported later that evening by a Mr Duncan Palmer. The little electric connections then went Duncan Palmer – Valerie Blake – AMIP-5 – DS Mooney. Stella picked up the tree as an attachment to an email sent to her by DS Gerry Harris, the same cop who had done her a favour by spotting the fact that the Clean Machine had burgled Valerie Blake's flat.

Harris had added a message: *This probably means nothing, but your name appeared on my screen. We're doing lots of this sort of business just now. This week – Muggers, 96: Christmas Spirit, nil.*

Stella called to get more details and learned that Lauren Buchanan had been too traumatized to report the incident herself. The officers who called at Duncan Palmer's flat were able to get only the sketchiest description of her attackers. A female beggar had been picked up for using Buchanan's credit card, but after it became clear that she'd had nothing to do with the attack she'd been released with a warning – it wasn't worth the paper overload. Ms Buchanan's bag had been found and returned to her once the contents had been listed.

Stella was interested to see on the list a receipt for a Patek Philippe wristwatch.

Maxine Hewitt was reading over Stella's shoulder. She said, 'Nothing in it for us.'

'He's engaged to Valerie Blake, she's attacked and killed. Now his girlfriend's attacked.'

'But not killed. It was just another mugging, wasn't it?'

Stella shrugged. 'Seems that way.'

'So it's a coincidence.'

'It warrants a visit,' Stella said. 'Here's another thing: Palmer doesn't know we know about Lauren Buchanan. I want to see the look on that bastard's face.'

It was not one look but three: puzzlement followed by surprise followed by anger. No hint of embarrassment.

Palmer said, 'She's in bed. She can't get up.'

DS Harris had faxed over the trauma report from Paddington A & E. Stella said, 'Facial bruising, broken nose, possible hairline fracture of the cheekbone. Nothing about broken legs.'

'It's where she feels safe.'

'Perhaps we could meet her later.'

'She's given a statement.'

'And so did you,' Stella reminded him, 'but it made no mention of Ms Buchanan.'

'It's nobody's business but mine.'

'You didn't tell us that Valerie Blake had been burgled, did you? You didn't tell us because you didn't know. You were in America, ducking her calls. Not just because you were lying to Valerie, but because you were lying to Lauren too. Difficult to field a call from your fiancée with your mistress at your elbow.'

Maxine could hear the edge of anger in Stella's voice and wondered briefly about its source. Like everyone on the AMIP-5 team, she knew something of Stella's relationship with John Delaney, and something of George Paterson. She said, 'We traced some of Valerie's stolen property.'

Palmer said, 'It should go to her parents.'

'It will,' Maxine agreed. 'There were some things in her pockets. A letter to you. You might like to have it; it's not required as evidence.'

The letter was in Stella's pocket, but she didn't produce it. Instead, she showed Palmer the petrol receipt from Heathrow that had been with it. 'She drove you to the airport, didn't she?'

Palmer shrugged. 'And so –?'

'And so she waited while you checked in and – what? – had a coffee with you, kissed you goodbye, waved you off. And you met Lauren Buchanan air-side.'

'Valerie's dead,' Palmer said. 'I don't see how any of this matters.'

'Not much at all,' Stella said. 'I just wanted to establish how much of a bastard you are. We need a word with Lauren before we go.'

She was just as Harriman had described her when he'd followed her to the jeweller's: tall, blonde, slim, sexy, but her body language and the look on her face added other attributes: scared, intimidated, hurt. She had brought her duvet with her and sat wrapped in it while Stella asked her about the attack.

Lauren said that, yes, there were two men. That she didn't know them. That she didn't think she'd recognize them again. That she felt violated. That she felt as if she would never be able to go out again. That London was a violent place full of disgusting people and that the police didn't seem to give a damn. She was sitting next to Palmer on the sofa and hanging on to his arm with both hands. He seemed to lean away from her a little and he wore a stretched smile.

'You can see how she is,' he said. 'If there's nothing else you need –'

'There are victim-support schemes,' Maxine observed.

'We'll be okay,' Palmer said. 'We'll be fine.'

'That's good,' Stella said. She reached into her pocket. 'Here's the letter. Valerie's letter. It might have been evidence, so I'm afraid we read it. She asks what's wrong and whether you're having second thoughts. She tells you she loves you. There's more.' She dropped it into Lauren's lap. 'You could read it together.'

Maxine drove but she didn't speak. Stella let it ride for a while, then said, 'You think I did the wrong thing?'

'Tough to say. He's a bastard; she's traumatized. Maybe it evens out.'

'She must have known about Valerie Blake. The wedding was planned. She waited for him air-side, then they went off on a jaunt.'

'Pretty crappy thing to do,' Maxine agreed. 'But maybe he made promises. Maybe he said it was just a matter of finding the right time to tell her, that he felt trapped, that once the whole marriage thing had started he didn't know how to stop it.'

Stella remembered Jan saying: *I'd always known. The marriage was denial.*

They drove out into Holland Park Avenue. Maxine said, 'Maybe she really loves him and doesn't care what it takes. We've all been there, haven't we?'

Now Stella was the silent one.

52

She had called a local decorating firm and they had said yes, sure, no problem, and hadn't shown up. She didn't mind. She was beginning to like the graffiti-tagged walls and furniture.

Delaney was leaving messages but not at the squad room, not too many and none pleading or sad. Just: 'Take care' and 'Call when you're ready' and 'Are you okay?' She thought it was a clever ploy and wondered what he was really feeling. Then it occurred to her that perhaps the messages meant what they said.

You think so?

Well, why not?

Okay, so what about you? How do you feel?

I love him, I miss him, but now that I'm not there . . .

You wonder what's keeping you away.

That's right.

You still have the keys to his flat. You could walk in any time.

Or I could send them back.

What would Anne Beaumont say: your one-time shrink?

Easy. She'd say fear of commitment, fear of making the wrong choice, nostalgia for George and a relationship based on fondness and trust, the dubious wisdom of going straight from one relationship to another . . .

And what do you say?

I say exactly the same. I also say I love him and I miss him.

And the problem is . . .

That the situation I'm in . . . that we're in . . . what has to happen next . . . It requires forgiveness.

And you're not good at that.

Not particularly. Forgiveness is a virtue. I didn't grow up with it.

She was breaking eggs into a bowl when he called. She saw his name on the screen and picked up.

He said, 'You have to eat, don't you?'

They met at the Indian restaurant and sat at the window table. There were fairy lights round the colour photo of the Taj Mahal and snowflake patterns on the windows. In the street, a few flakes of the real stuff wafted down and disappeared.

Delaney said, 'We're going to need some rules, you were right about that.'

'Your rules or my rules?'

'Our rules.'

They had some things to catch up on. She told him about the Shit Spreaders and the pissed-on bed and Panhandler Pete. He put out a hand and turned her face to the brighter light from the street. The bruise was a fading yellow-black roundel. He said, 'The front line gets nearer all the time. Inside five years you'll all be carrying guns.'

'So the tabloids tell me,' Stella said, and smiled.

They let the conversation meander, edging away from trouble. They talked about Delaney's time in Bosnia, a real front line, about the healing properties of arnica, about his piece on street-people and Christmas. He told her that Sadie had been arrested and advanced the opinion that some cops were sadists, pricks and shitehawks.

When the bill had been paid, he said, 'What do we do now?'

'You mean next. Not now but next.'

'Okay. Next.'

'I'm not sure.'

'Will you tell me when you are?'

She laughed. 'You'll be the second person to know.'

'Who'll be the first?'

'Me.'

She meant to say more but somehow found herself on her feet, bending to kiss him, a kiss that fell hard on his mouth, then emerging into the light fall of snow. She had walked from the flat, wanting to give herself time to think, but now she looked round for a cab. There were plenty but all taken. She was walking fast, jostling her way between the late-nighters, the clubbers, the liggers, as if distance would prevent her from going back to say the right thing. She was halfway home before she jumped a bus.

So how did that go?

I'm not sure.

Any signs, any clues, any hints?

We split the bill. But his keys are still on my key ring.

Shes just like all the others doesnt look doesnt notice thinking of other things. She went to meet a man in a resterant and she walked there and back which was great. I got really close yes close enough to touch. They did me a favour those boys who robbed her it took me straight to her in Vigo St. Its a basment and you can see down into the main room from the street and you can see the bedroom window from the patio at the back. You get into the patio from a side entrance in the next street then go into someone elses then over the wall and your there. She has the blind down but you can see shapes. In the main room she cooks and reads and watches tv. I have to walk up and down and then go round the block but its quiet and

nobody notices. The patio is dark and theres a
wheelie bin to get behind and I dont have to worry.
She walked fast but I could keep up and there were
lots of people for camaflage. She didnt know.
Shes just like the others.

Delaney stopped by the Ocean Diner and looked down the
alley. A couple of kitchen workers were sharing a spliff. He
took a little tour of the Gate and found Sadie sitting next to
a cash machine and playing carols to the queue of people
waiting to draw money. Jamie was next to her, wrapped in
his quilted coat, face buried.

Delaney said, 'Is it a good pitch?'

'Some look guilty, some think I'm taking the piss. It evens
out.'

'The police didn't charge you?'

'Too much trouble.'

Jamie said, 'The Lord in His own time.'

Delaney handed Sadie some money. He said, 'Tell me
what happened.'

Sadie spun him a little story about the arrest, the crowded
charge room, the overnight cell, the cops and their funny
ways. It wasn't entirely true, but she thought it might be what
he wanted to hear. She told him about the mugging, how the
woman had been so cooperative, so passive, until the men had
started to leave. Then she'd called to them – bad-mouthed
them, it seemed – and one had run back and hit her. Sadie
laughed sourly. She said, 'Tidings of comfort and joy.'

Snow was settling in Jamie's hair. He said, 'We shall see
Him. The fire and the rose will be one.'

Stella pulled the blind in the bedroom, undressed, and stepped into the shower. She washed the residue of jet-fuel and

diesel droplets and factory fallout from her hair, massaging her scalp, then stood with her back to the water-flow, head tilted, face raised, smoothing the shampoo away with both hands. She could feel the place where Delaney had snipped off a lock of her hair to show how easily that might be done – a little clump that fell short of the rest. She pressed out the soap and felt the gap under the fingers of her right hand.

Under the fingers of her left hand.

It was as if she had stepped off a cliff in the fog. She felt herself falling, her hands reaching to clutch and finding only the glass sides of the shower cubicle. Then she was sitting down, her breath a hard knot in her chest, the water hitting the shower tray with a sound like thunder-rain.

She reached up to feel her hair again, her hands shaking. A clipping gone from the right side. Yes. And surely – couldn't she feel it? – a clipping gone from the left.

53

In the Jumping Jacks Casino, Leon Bloss was riding his luck. He had already doubled his stake, and now he'd found a blackjack soft hand – trey, deuce, five and the ace of hearts. In a soft hand, aces count eleven. The dealer wore a badge stating that she was Louise. She had a little retroussé nose and her hair was raked back in a pony-tail so tight that it doubled as a face-lift.

Louise flipped her hand and showed a seven and a ten, which left her with one foot on the boat and the other on the dock. She hit the seven-ten and turned a five. Bloss's eyes, bright blue, regarded her with icy pleasure. He said, 'I'm here to make you unhappy, Louise.'

Bloss left his money on the baize: all of it. Louise paused slightly and glanced at him, but he shook his head: *Let it ride.* She shrugged, almost angry, and dealt the table another hand. Bloss caught blackjack, a diamond/club combination. No one on the table could match that sort of heat. Louise turned a pair of queens.

Luck only holds for so long and Bloss knew that. He also knew that a winning streak is something like a freak of nature: there's no explaining it and no holding it back. Between those two notions, caution and belief lay side by side. He split his winnings and waited for new cards. He looked up at Louise and smiled his thin-lipped smile, but she avoided his gaze.

On the CCTV monitor his smile was slightly blurred, his eyes blank. The casino boss, Billy Souza, was watching the play along with two colleagues, a man and a woman. The man was tall and deceptively slim, given the heavy nature of his work. The woman was Arlene Pearce and she was the scrutineer. Arlene could spot within five minutes whether someone was counting cards. Everyone thinks they've got a system, but card-counting is the only way to beat the house short of marking, and no one gets away with that. If the counter needed to be shown the door, there were several guys on hand to do the job. One of them was the tall man sitting alongside Souza. His name was James Charles Dooley and he liked to be called JD because he felt it gave him status.

JD had no status at all with Billy Souza. To Billy he was the hired help. They watched Bloss build twenty through five cards while Louise went tits up on the first hit. Souza leaned forward and spoke into an intercom system that connected to the House Manager's earpiece.

He said, 'Relieve the dealer on Table Fifteen. Tell the punters it's her break. Hold up the play.' To JD he said, 'Ask that shitheel to spare me a moment.'

Arlene said, 'He's not counting, Billy.'

'You're right. He's not a gambler, he's a lucky hitter.'

'You know him?'

'Oh, yes, I know him.'

JD gave Bloss a rack to carry his chips in and walked him into Billy Souza's office. Arlene had moved to a second, smaller room where the CCTV monitors were set up in a more utilitarian way: a room designated for observation. She shared it with the man who watched the doors and the rest rooms. In the ladies' room, two women in designer chic were staring down at themselves in a hand mirror while they did a few lines. Billy didn't mind, but he liked to know who was breaking the law. Knowledge is power.

Souza flapped a hand at JD and waited until the door closed behind him before saying, 'Hello, Leon.' Souza's one-time dark good looks had spread and coarsened a little with age, and you could see the grey in his hair, but he was still at the top of his game. The casino was just part of it. He had other interests, other sources of income.

Bloss sat down with the rack of chips on his lap. He said, 'I was on a little roll there, Billy.'

'You'd already halved your bet. What were you going to do, halve it again?'

'That's right. Which would have left me with a grand on the table.'

'Let's see where you'd've got to.'

They turned to the monitor and looked at Table Fifteen where a new dealer – a man with a chubby face and a red bow tie – was snapping cards from the shoe. A fake blonde in a rhinestone choker was sitting where Bloss had sat. The dealer turned her a ten and a three and she tapped her cards. He turned her a two and she tapped again, drawing a king.

Souza laughed. 'You're up a grand, Leon.'

'Her cards aren't my cards.'

'You believe in fate.'

'I believe my luck is my luck. She's got her own luck and it sucks.'

'I called you a few times, Leon. I left messages.'

'Which is why I'm here.'

'You took your time.' An edge had crept into Souza's voice.

'Things to do.'

'Is that right? Well, there's something I want you to do for me. You know that. We talked about that.'

'I know. I've been preparing the ground, you know what I mean? It's a question of timing.'

Souza had a bottle of Scotch on his desk. He poured two glasses and pushed one across to Bloss. He said, 'It's perfect timing for me.'

Bloss gave a little sigh of irritation. 'I'm the technician here, Billy. I have to set things up my way.'

'But I'm paying the bills. Paying you.'

'Pay someone else, then.' Bloss drank his Scotch in one and rapped the glass back down on the desk.

'I don't think so. We're talking about sorting someone here. We're talking about killing him. You think I want to run round London asking likely people if they fancy the job? We've worked together before, Leon. There's an understanding.'

'It's a question of exposure, Billy. There's a rhythm to these things.'

Souza threw up a hand. 'I don't want to hear about that. Don't tell me about that. None of my business.' There was a silence between them, then Souza said, 'Don't let me down.' The words carried a heavy freight of threat.

'Give me a couple of weeks?'

Souza shook his head. 'I'm going to talk to him. I'm going to talk to him one last time and we'll see where we get. My opinion? We'll get precisely fucking nowhere. Now, you don't need to worry about the ins and outs, Leon, it's a need-to-know basis. But I'll say this much. It's a supply issue. It's an export issue. I've got clients who look to me, and I look to this man. They expect me to deliver, I expect the same of him. If I've got to go elsewhere, I'm going to have delays, I'm going to have risk, I'm going to have expense, and I'm going to have a dissatisfied clientele.' Souza sipped his drink. He seemed lost in thought for a moment. 'But maybe he'll come round.'

Bloss laughed sourly. 'I'll have been to a lot of trouble for nothing if he does.'

Souza shook his head. 'Maybe. But I don't think so. I think he'll be a loose end, a loose cannon. Something fucking *loose*. Which cannot be allowed, Leon.'

'When will you talk to him?'

'Tonight. After that, I'll let you know.' He gestured towards the rack of chips. 'Here's a word of advice. Don't take that money back to the tables. Luck's a butterfly.' He seemed pleased with the idea. 'Know what I mean?' And he fluttered the fingers of both hands.

Arlene's eyes flicked round the monitors and she saw Leon at the cashier's grille. She went back into Billy Souza's office and helped herself to a Scotch, then leaned across and kissed Billy on the mouth. It didn't cost her anything and he liked it. He was a kisser. Sure, she thought, he was fifty-plus, but he still had his hair and not too much of a paunch, besides which money compensates for a lot.

'There are no heavy-hitters in tonight,' she told him. 'Let's go home.'

He got up but gestured for her to stay. 'I'm going out. If there's trouble, JD will have it covered.'

'I could come round later. Make some food.'

Arlene had established herself in the bedroom; her current move was to annex the kitchen. Bedroom, kitchen, and the rest of the house would naturally follow. Wives inherited – this was her thinking.

Souza nodded and smiled. 'Okay. I'll call you when I'm back.'

He was laughing inside. He was thinking, *No chance, bitch*.

54

Stella had asked for a presence on the Strip, and a couple of two-man patrols cruised back and forth from time to time. It made the shebeen-gaffers edgy, was a definite irritation to the sex trade, and left the dealers standing alone on corners and in side streets. Frank Silano made a little tour of the pubs and clubs in the area, letting people know what all the activity meant. As soon as the cops found what they were looking for, he said, they'd be gone. And they were looking for Robert Adrian Kimber. He showed a police photo. No one knew the guy, but they all said how happy they would be to turn him in and go back to business.

Silano had also seen his bookies, but it seemed that Kimber wasn't a betting man.

Maxine Hewitt had spoken to the inquiry agent, who had put the word out, but no words had come back to him.

The dealers were silent; this wasn't a man who used what they had to sell.

The pimps and hookers looked at the photo and shrugged: who knows? Who would remember?

One of the whores was called Nancy and she shook her head like the rest. The cop showing her the photo was a uniform seconded for the house-to-house, and, though he noticed that Nancy had nice tits, he didn't catch the tight little smile on her face when she said, 'No.'

After two or three hours, the patrols moved on and punters on the Strip could get cut-price liquor, a wrap or a blow-job – maybe all three – just like before, while Robert

Adrian Kimber sat in his room down by the crossroads and thought about how it had felt to kill Kate Reilly and how it might feel to kill someone else.

He thought every time would be different. Different and better than the last, but no time would be quite like the first. Now he dreamed it up again, eyes closed, feeling breathless and feverish.

Bloss sat in the room's only other chair, drinking whisky he'd bought on his way, and watched Kimber lost in a world of blood and thrills. How lucky to have found this man, he thought, and how easy to move him from confessor to killer. It wasn't much of a journey; it took only the smallest leap of the imagination for someone as close as Kimber had been. A nudge had been enough.

He went into the bathroom. Kimber's hair brush was lying by the sink. Bloss plucked a swatch of hair from the bristles and put it into an envelope, then the envelope into his pocket.

When he went back to the main room, Kimber appeared to be sleeping. Bloss said, 'I have to go, Bobby.' He said, 'We'll talk soon.' He waited a moment, then added, 'I'll call you.'

Kimber might have nodded; might have been falling into an ever deeper sleep.

55

It ought to be DS Mooney. It ought to be her. She ought to be next. The next one. She walks fast but not fast enough to stop me getting something off her. A clipping. I couldnt smell scent on it but I could smell her. She sits up late and drinks. She falls asleep on the couch. I got a photo of her with the man in the resterant they were sitting by the window. He always calls me Bobby he shouldnt do that. Ive told him about following Stella and he says good but wait. He says wait before you do anything. No one calls me Bobby. She will be next I think. But different not his way not in the street where theres no time. They already broke into her flat so thats what people will think. The police. Theyll think burglars. Stella I was close enough to touch. Your next.

56

Billy Souza had made a call from his car, but Oscar Gribbin's phone was off. Or else Oscar had seen Billy's name come up on the screen and dumped the call. That made Billy angry and, since he was already pretty annoyed with Oscar, he was edging into danger areas. Edging into the red.

Oscar lived in a five million pound mansion off Holland Park. It was after nine in the evening and the staff had left, so no one was picking up the phone. Billy went there anyway, but the alarm system was primed and the floodlights snapped on as he approached, all of which said no one home.

He started a tour of the casinos. He went to Irving's and the Portland and Stars and Stripes, then he went to Aces Up and Kavanagh's and Slowhand; he had enemies in all those places and it wasn't a comfortable expedition. He finally found Oscar in the Palm House, about to go two grand down at craps. He had a blonde by his side who was half his age, half his weight and wearing a cocktail dress that brought to mind the words 'cock' and 'tail'.

Oscar rolled five and three followed by snake-eyes, and shrugged his shoulders. Then he saw Billy and shrugged again. They went to the bar and found a couple of seats on the horseshoe, away from the barman, away from the punters. Oscar gave the blonde a fistful of chips and sent her off to play.

'I was going to call you.'

'I know you were,' Billy said. 'But here I am.'

Oscar was a short man with a long bank balance and the

confidence that went with money. He said, 'I was going to call to say that you'll have to count me out, Billy. It's been okay, we've all made some money, but it makes me jumpy, you know? It's been five times now, five shipments, and sooner or later something's going to fuck up. A Customs and Excise search, a leak from the other end, a piece of bad luck, who knows?'

'You see' – Billy spoke as if he'd been interrupted mid-sentence – 'the thing about this kind of operation is that it takes investment money to set up and it takes time. You were part of the set-up process. You were in pole position. Seed money, it's called. It was a sizeable amount.'

'People come, people go,' Oscar advised. 'I have business decisions to make: this is one of them. No more iffy shipments for a while. I've put a stop on illegals already. Too many are getting lifted and it's a worry; if immigration start going back along the chain, sooner or later they find me. I'm taking a rest. Talk to me again in six months.'

'No, Oscar, you're not listening. I don't have the time. Apart from the money invested in you, there's the way things work, the routes, the channels. Changing all that – it's not an option. I've got clients who want delivery now. I need you to green-light those shipments. I'm losing business, losing money, losing face. It can't go on.' Billy was smiling, even though he'd said it all before.

They were drinking Scotch. Oscar signalled for another round, and they sat in silence while the barman poured. Oscar signed a tab for the drinks; he said, 'That's all there is to it, Billy. I'm out.'

'I can't allow it.'

Oscar gave a chuckle, indulgent, dismissive. 'Find another shipper. They're ten a penny. Rust-buckets are putting in at British ports every day and offloading drugs and whores and illegals and guns. Same with trucking companies. Put the word about. You'll have offers coming out of your arse.'

Billy lifted his glass. He was gripping it so tightly that the whisky trembled along its surface. He said, 'I'm asking you, Oscar. Help me out.'

'No can do. End of story.'

The blonde was in sight at a roulette table and looking excited, as if the numbers were falling for her. She was betting birthdays, lucky numbers and the countdown to Christmas with a side bet on black. Billy said, 'She seems lively. Friend of your wife's?'

Oscar laughed. 'Don't go there, Billy. Think of the things I know about you. I might even have a tape, you know?'

'A what?'

'A tape. We had a meeting at my house, remember that?' Oscar smiled. 'I used to be in the insurance business.'

Billy dropped his head and stared at the moulding on the bar-rail. He was holding on but only just. It wouldn't be clever to kill Oscar Gribbin right here and now, but it would be one hell of a fucking pleasure.

Oscar said, 'Hey, Billy, let's not part on bad terms, yeah? It's a great scam, but I have to get out while I'm ahead. I take the risk, I carry the merchandise. You buy, you ship, you sell on, fuck it, you don't even *see* the stuff.'

Billy put his drink down. He said, 'I can see how you feel.' He put out a hand and they shook.

The blonde waved her arms and bounced with glee as her number came up – days to Christmas, lucky seven.

Billy got into his car and took some deep breaths. A tape. A fucking tape. Gribbin was almost straight, that was the problem. He liked a little on the side, but the roots didn't go deep. It wasn't a way of life, that was the fucking *problem*.

He was a dabbler, an amateur, he was someone who made tapes.

Bloss came on the phone straight away. Billy said, 'I talked to him. He's not open to suggestions.'

'Find a new shipper,' Bloss said. 'Just cut him out of it.'

'He's cut himself out. That's the point. That's why he has to go. He said no to me. Said no – to *me*. I got a whole operation up and running, now he's pulling the pin. Fuck that. Here's something else: here's the kicker. He's got a tape of me.'

'What do you mean, a tape?'

'A tape. A fucking video. Us talking, him and me – talking business.'

'Are you sure?'

'You think I want to second-guess him on this?'

There was a silence, then Bloss said, 'Okay, Billy.'

'Good.' There was a pause, then Billy said, 'What are we talking here?'

Bloss named a sum. Billy named another. They went to and fro for a while, as they had expected to, and met more or less in the middle.

'Make it soon, okay? His wife's away on a winter holiday.'

'I need some time, Billy. I need to get some background, you know – habits, when he's usually in, when he's usually out, where he goes.'

'It's okay, you can short-cut all that; there's someone ready to help.' Billy gave Bloss a mobile number. 'Just call. You'll know his schedule, you'll know when he's back home. You can pop up and see him. Just ring the bell.'

57

It wasn't drugs or whores or illegals – it was guns.

Billy Souza had made good connections in the Balkans, in the Czech Republic, in Russia. He also had growing market input from Australia, South Africa, Israel and Switzerland. Albania has a population of three and a half million people and four million guns; Billy made quite a few trips to Albania. All the ex-Soviet bloc countries had rich pickings: one big arms bazaar selling ex-military weapons, each with its own low-level price tag.

Generally speaking, guns were an optional extra for the people smuggling drugs and girls, but Billy had decided to specialize. It had started as a sideline to Jumping Jacks because he'd had a reason to be at the buyer's end of the market, but then he'd seen the potential. Every hard man in London wanted a shooter. Every crew member, every low-life, every robber, every dealer, every pimp. No gun, no class. No gun, your arse. The revenue from weapons almost equalled the take from the casino, and, after the overheads had been covered, it was gross profit: no tax.

Billy had picked his shippers with care, or thought he had. Two truck companies and Oscar Gribbin, who was a perfect choice because, in addition to illegals, he shipped metal and metal goods. With the National Criminal Intelligence Service, Customs and Excise, Interpol and the National Firearms Tracing Service all on the case, that kind of camouflage was a good idea.

Oscar had been right to say that the guns never came

near Billy. They were pre-sold long before they ever reached the UK. JD and a couple of managers organized the next stage of the journey, when the weapons were moved from London, Liverpool or Hull to wholesalers in seven cities. From those locations, the guns went to smaller outlets: the armourers.

The office of Leon Bloss's armourer of choice was a table in the Wheatsheaf, or at least that was where you made your first contact. Slipper Wilkie had five mobile phones, each for a specific purpose. Certain clients had one number and one only. The divisions had to do with different aspects of his business, though his fifth was an eyes-and-ears phone and rang only if there was trouble. The pub was central, neutral, and there was a racket of muzak and fruit-machine-tunes that meant only those at the table could hear what was being said. Wilkie spent twelve hours a day working, eight on the phone. He was having a 'yes-no-okay' exchange with someone when Bloss sat down at his table with two glasses of Scotch.

Wilkie was stylish. He had expensive blond streaks and a lamp-tan, looked late thirties, obviously kept himself in shape. His clothes were casual but pricey. He finished his call, put another on hold, then turned to Bloss. 'Is it going to be used?'

An unused gun could be returned. Maybe you wanted to frighten someone or show class. Maybe it was for a robbery and no one would get clever or brave. Return the gun and you'd get half your deposit back. A gun that had been fired was a different proposition. There would be a forensic trace. If you were going to use the gun, you had to pay for the gun.

Bloss shrugged and said nothing. Wilkie took that to mean *used*. He said, 'Any preferences?'

'Glock forty-five or something similar. H & K; Beretta nine mill . . .' Bloss added, 'Spare clip with it.' It was unnecessary, but, when it came to his work, Bloss was a cautious man.

Wilkie nodded and named a price; Bloss nodded back. Wilkie said, 'Where do you want to pick up?'

'Walk through Holland Park tomorrow afternoon at four,' Bloss said. 'Come up from Ken High Street.'

'It's out of my way.'

'It's good for me.'

'Anywhere away from cameras is good. Plenty of places.'

'Holland Park,' Bloss said.

Wilkie shrugged. Another of his phones rang and he lifted it, but waited for Bloss to leave.

Out on the street there was was cutting edge to the wind, but it came with a mish-mash of burger fat and exhaust gas and puke. Bloss thought it might be nice to get away for Christmas. In fact he thought it might be essential.

58

Mike Sorley's programme of self-doctoring was going pretty well. It involved a twice-hourly cigarette linked to an hourly shot of whisky and it had certainly brought a glow to his cheeks. The regime allowed for paracetamol on the side.

Stella had picked up her breakfast coffee from Starbucks and gone straight to his office. She was talking to him about replacement officers, fitting the details of her request in between his coughing fits. He had got his coffee from the squad-room dispenser and considered it to be the only real long-term threat to his health.

He said, 'I've got this fucking flu on the run.'

'It certainly sounds that way,' Stella agreed. Sorley laughed and coughed, coughed and laughed. Stella waited for him to recover. She touched her hair, feeling for the missing lock; it had almost become a nervous tic. In the shower, washing the shampoo from her hair, she'd been certain, but now she wasn't so sure. The lock that Delaney had snipped was an obvious absence – high to the crown of her head. The other was lower and seemed slight, and that was when she could find it at all. Her hair was layered; there were other ragged ends. Maybe it was a form of wishful thinking: *Follow me, you bastard, I'll nail you.*

When Sorley got his breath back, she said, 'I need some money, Boss.'

'I thought you had a look on your face.'

'An inducement. Unofficial.'

'How much?'

'Five grand?'

Sorley lit his nine thirty cigarette. The nine o'clock had petered out in the ashtray. He said, 'Try a grand. Go higher if someone looks like biting.'

'I want the word to spread. A grand won't get it far.'

'Okay. Say it's five and if someone makes an offer, give them a grand on account.'

'And let them whistle for the rest.'

'Exactly.'

'It doesn't help my reputation – for the next time.'

'It doesn't help mine when I'm standing in front of the commissioner, cap in hand.'

'Okay,' Stella said. Then, 'It's not all I need.'

Sorley grimaced. 'Oh, good.'

'Silano's in for Greegan and Marilyn Hayes is covering for DC Chapman, but now Pete Harriman's on sick leave and I need more bodies on the street. Someone knows who Mister Mystery is. We need to keep asking questions, keep talking to our sources.'

'He's out there,' Sorley told her.

'He is. Which is why we need to be out there too.'

Sorley looked at her and shook his head. 'What?'

'I'm agreeing with you.'

'About what?'

Stella thought back along the conversation, looking for the fracture in logic but unable to find it. She said, 'Are you delirious or am I tired? Who are we talking about?'

'DC Harriman,' Sorley said and gestured towards the squad room. 'He's out there.'

The dressing had been removed and the scar was a barbed-wire tracery that went from just under the earlobe to halfway along his jawline. Stella took him out into the corridor and they stood by the drinks dispenser, like all office conspirators.

'Where were you when I came in?'

'In the car park,' Harriman said. 'I saw you arrive.'

'In the car park –?'

'Talking to Marilyn.'

'Of course. Have you been cleared?'

'Totally.'

'By the doctors?'

'By DI Sorley.'

'If you're on sick-leave, I can replace you and get someone who's fit.'

'I'm fit.'

'Yeah? You look like a Frankenstein offcut.'

'I didn't say beautiful, I said fit.'

'What did Marilyn say?'

'She thinks it looks distinguished.'

'Well, it distinguishes you from guys who haven't taken a beer glass in the face, that's for sure.' Harriman laughed, then fell silent. Stella said, 'Why the car park?'

'She's talking about leaving her husband.'

'Of course she is, you fuckwit.'

'Do you think she means it?'

'Does she say she'll leave him before Christmas or afterwards?'

'Before.'

'She means it.'

Harriman sighed. 'I thought so.'

Stella said, 'Organize a door-to-door on Harefield. As many uniforms as Notting Hill can spare. Issue mugshots of Kimber. Let's see if anyone at his old address wants to earn a Christmas bonus.'

'Someone always knows,' Harriman said, the murder-squad truism.

'You're right,' Stella said. 'Mister Mystery knows.'

Mister Mystery walked through Holland Park, starting from the Kensington High Street side. The last light showed as a thin lilac glow in the western sky and people were leaving before the gates closed at dusk.

He remembered when he'd done this before, walking the park, finding a place to hide, a place on Valerie Blake's jogging route, feeling the weight of the hammer in his pocket and the weight of his heart banging his ribs. He thought of Robert Kimber, also waiting for Valerie, waiting to follow her. He thought of the way life had somehow arranged to bring them all together at just the right time.

Slipper Wilkie was sitting on a bench close to where the path went into woodland. Bloss sat down with him and they waited for a couple of strollers to get clear. The gun was in a small document case along with the spare clip, all packed in bubble-wrap. It was a Glock ·45. Wilkie passed it over, took an envelope in return, then walked away.

Bloss called Billy Souza on his mobile. He said, 'The girl will be with him, yes?'

'She'll be there. She's your way in.'

'It's important. She's needed . . . the way I'm going to set things up.'

'For sure,' Souza told him. 'You ask, I deliver. Make sure you do the same.'

'She won't take a walk. She knows she has to be there with him?'

'Jesus Christ!' Billy's voice took on an edge. 'What did I just say? She's been told. She'll be there.'

Billy Souza put the phone down. Bloss sat on, watching the dusk settle. It was his favourite time of day.

59

He made a call to the number Billy Souza had given him and the blonde picked up. She called him Maria and said she couldn't talk just then. Half an hour later, she called back and said, 'We're at the Belvedere and he's just asked for the bill. Give it half an hour.'

'What do I do?'

'Ring the bell.'

'You're expecting a friend, are you?'

'We're expecting a man with some very high-grade Charlie.'

'This would be your contact, not his . . .'

'Of course. He's not expecting to know you.'

After leaving the park, Bloss had gone to a pub on Kensington Church Street and had a few whiskies. The place was crammed with people who were on their way to parties or were between parties or had started out for a party but decided to go no further. They were shoulder to shoulder and face to face and back to back, yelling to be heard over the music. Bloss had a stool by the wooden window-shelf that ran the whole perimeter of the pub. The reflections of faces in the windows seemed to mingle with the faces that passed in the street.

He didn't mind making the hit, and the fee he and Souza had agreed on was good money, but it was too much action in too short a time. He'd make a plane reservation to a warm place. Anywhere that was somewhere else.

He drank off the last of his last whisky, shouldered a small rucksack that contained all he needed for the night's task, then pushed through the crowd and started up towards Notting Hill Gate.

Oscar Gribbin looked up smiling when Bloss walked in behind the blonde, but his smile faded fast when he saw the gun. He looked from Bloss to the blonde and back again. He said, 'You fucking slag.' Then, to Bloss, 'Name your price.'

Bloss was dressed for business – industrial overalls zipped to the chin, a woollen beanie, cotton gloves, rubber overshoes. He said, 'It's not like that.'

It was a big room in a big house, lots of pale wood and leather, plasma screen, style-supplement paintings, a freestanding, three-foot-square plain glass aquarium on glass stilts right in the middle. It was a feature. Luminous fish cruised amid forests of weed.

Oscar knew what they meant: the overalls, the rubber shoes. He said, 'Is it Billy Souza? Tell him I'll bring the stuff in for him. Tell him we're back in business.'

'See,' Bloss said. 'It's easy if you try.'

'Tell him no problem.'

'Tell him yourself,' Bloss said, and smiled encouragingly. Then, 'Where's the tape?'

Oscar looked towards the plasma screen and a steel-fronted cupboard below it. Bloss nodded and Oscar hurried across to get the tape. He put it down on a glass and steel table. Everything shiny and transparent.

'Play it,' Bloss told him.

It was genuine. Oscar and Billy, Billy and Oscar. Talk of guns and dates and offshore transfers. Oscar ejected it and slipped it back into its cover, eager to do the right thing. He handed it to Bloss, who sapped him with the Glock, putting him down hard on a dove-grey leather sofa.

Oscar said, 'What?' but the word came from a long way off and his eyes had slipped out of focus.

Bloss's rucksack had contained the overalls; he'd changed before going in. It also held some other, basic equipment: duct tape, plastic handcuffs, a lock-knife, a hammer. When Oscar was cuffed and gagged, Bloss turned to the blonde. He said, 'This is going to look like a burglary, like I had to make him tell me where the stuff is. Maybe you should leave.'

She said, 'I know where the stuff is.'

'Meaning?'

'It's a burglary, right? Someone has to burgle.' A little flush had come to her cheeks and she was smiling. 'What are you going to do to him?'

'Go,' Bloss told her. 'Take what you like.'

He opened the rucksack and removed a plastic envelope, inside of which was a green contamination suit. The overalls, the rubber shoes, the beanie, the gloves – they were fine first protection against shedding DNA. Wet work was a different issue.

He put the suit on over his overalls and snapped the press-stud fasteners. The legs ended in plastic foot-pods that went over his shoes and there was a hood with a draw-string. He removed his cotton gloves, put those into the rucksack, and pulled on a pair of surgical gloves, working his fingers into the latex. He was a workman getting ready for the night-shift.

The blonde said, 'Jesus. Jesus Christ.'

Bloss told her to go and this time she went.

Oscar was speaking from behind the duct-tape gag. Bloss knew what he was saying even though the words were faint and distorted. He was saying, 'Please.' He was using a lot of words but they all added up to 'Please.'

Bloss opened the lock-knife and stabbed Oscar a few times in the fat of his thighs. Oscar arched and tried to back-pedal but there was nowhere to go. He wanted to scream, but that's difficult to do breathing through your nose and choking on your own saliva. Bloss held his man down with one hand and a knee. He stabbed his biceps. When Oscar turned over to protect himself, Bloss stabbed his buttocks. Oscar flipped like a fish and fell on to the floor.

Bloss stepped back and caught his breath. In the same moment, the floodlights came on in the driveway and the doorbell rang. Oscar's eyes bulged and thin, thready sounds emerged from behind the duct tape. Bloss hit him across the temple with the gun and Oscar's eyes rolled to show the whites.

There was a moment when everything seemed to be held on a drawn breath, then Bloss left the room and went upstairs, moving fast but silently. The blonde was standing by a back-bedroom door: the master bedroom. She said, 'Who?' He waved a hand to shut her up. Then he went into a bedroom that overlooked the front of the house and made a curving approach to the window so that he could see without being seen. Out in the street, people were singing carols, barely audible thanks to Oscar's double-glazing, a well-organized charity group with their accordion-player, their Santa hats and their antique lanterns. The doorbell rang for a second time. As he watched, a man and a woman, with lantern and collecting box, moved back from the front door of Oscar's house, pausing in the hope of getting a response, then turned and set off back towards the street. Bloss watched them down the drive and out on to the street. His laugh was almost silent, *huh-huh-huh-huh*. The blonde was behind him at the door. She said, 'What?'

'They've gone,' Bloss told her, and she moved away,

heading for the master bedroom and whatever she could find there.

When Bloss got back to the living room, Oscar Gribbin was on his feet, leaning heavily against a roll-top desk on the far side of the room. His trousers and shirtsleeves were dripping blood and he was shaking like a man with a fever. The handcuffs had restricted him and he'd worked hard to get the desk open and pull out the drawer above the writing-space in order to get the gun, a neat Smith & Wesson .38. He was holding it with his handcuffed hands, trying to support the barrel with his left while going for the trigger with his right, but his fingers were tangling.

There was no time to get across the room. Bloss shot Oscar, taking him lower and more to the side than he'd intended, putting the bullet between rib and hip. The force of the shot half turned Oscar and brought him to his knees, but he held on to the gun. Bloss got off a second shot as he crossed the room; it went to the side of the throat. Oscar was down now and fighting for breath; he heaved himself up on knuckles and knees like a sprinter taking to the blocks. Bloss stood over him and shot him in the back of the head. Oscar came unstrung; everything left him and he seemed to sink into himself.

Bloss kicked Oscar in the side, then in the thigh. He said, '*Bastard!*' Oscar was supposed to die that night, yes, but the weapon should have been the hammer. A gun broke the pattern. Bloss had needed the gun in order to be able to control the situation when he first walked in behind the blonde, but that was all. Now he'd had to use it and that made a mess of things.

He looked round and the blonde appeared as if on cue. She was wearing a full-length ranch mink and holding a diamond bracelet. She put the aquarium between herself and Oscar like a child peeking at a scary TV show from behind a sofa. Trickles of blood seeped round the glass pillars.

Bloss joined her, still wearing the transparent contamination suit, which was slick with blood. He looked like something newborn. 'Did you find what you were looking for?' he asked.

She held up the bracelet. 'Wifey must have taken the rest of the good stuff with her.' She was speaking to Bloss but looking at Oscar, who was on the floor, legs spread, body arched. He looked like a skydiver braced against the wind. She said, 'I have to get to the West End. There's a cabbie going to say he took me straight from the restaurant to a club. The doorman saw me go in an hour ago. Him and some friends.'

Bloss nodded. He said, 'Billy set it up.'

'That's right.'

'Okay. I'm going to mess the place up a bit.' He took the hammer from his bag of tricks and moved a step or two away from her as if making for a further room, then swung round and hit her on the turn, laying the hammer sideways against her temple. She walked a pace or two, her knees buckling like a drunk's, and he hit her again. When she went down, he pulled her back to the aquarium and propped her against one of the glass stilts, then put the garrotte round both her neck and the stilt before taking up the slack with the steel bar. She seemed to leap as he put both hands to use on the bar. Her body shook and her heels rattled the floor. Her eyes popped and there was a sound in her throat like the sea dragging stones.

Bloss worked on her until he was sure, then sat back heavily, shoulders slumped. His fingers ached. After a moment, he got up and went round to face her.

He flipped open the mink coat, pushed her dress up and stripped her below the waist.

He stood over her and let a little of the hair from Kimber's brush fall on the fork of her legs. Then he trashed the place.

The blonde had been right: there didn't seem to be much to take that was portable. Cufflinks, some costume jewellery, three or four hundred in cash, some silver. Oscar had been carrying a wallet stuffed with notes and credit cards, which Bloss had already lifted. He put everything into his rucksack, along with the document case, the hammer, the knife, the gun and the spare clip.

When he left, the blonde was still sitting upright against the glass stilt, her smile a rictus, her teeth grouted with red.

Luminous fish were shoaling towards the light.

He took a bus and then walked, anonymous among the happy, the sad, the bored, the bereft. Among the drunks and the jokers, the pickups and the bustups.

He strolled to the centre of Hammersmith Bridge and stopped to admire the view. Reflections of the lights from riverside pubs flexed and danced in the water. Aviation lights of planes chased each other down the flightpath to Heathrow. The rucksack went in with a small splash: the contamination suit, the overalls, the knife, the hammer, the cufflinks, the silver . . . everything but the cash. The cash was okay to keep. And he kept the gun.

He walked to a street phone and called Billy Souza.

Billy said, 'How did it go off?'

'Just fine,' Bloss told him.

'Our friend?'

'He left. He won't be back.'

'The lady?'

'She went with him.'

'That's good,' Billy said. 'And the tape?'

'There was no tape, Billy.'

A pause, then, 'You're sure about that?'

'He would have told me.'

'You're sure?'

'I know he would have told me. Also, I searched the place.'

'It was a con.'

'I'm afraid so.'

Billy sighed. 'Stupid to bluff on an empty hand.'

There was activity all around, kids going by in search of another party, arguments on the run, someone throwing up in a McDonald's doorway. A couple of beggars were working the late crowd: a girl with a penny whistle and a skinny guy with red hair, wrapped in a quilted coat.

Bloss said, 'I'm thinking I might go away for a bit.'

'Okay,' Billy said. 'Call by for what I owe.'

'That would be cash, right?'

'Sure. Cash.' Just before Bloss hung up, Billy added, 'Listen – good job.'

Bloss called into a bar for a drink. The music was loud enough to paralyse small mammals. It was good to be lost in that noise and the bar-lights and the lives going on round him as if nothing had happened. The barman brought him a large Scotch and pointed to the tariff chalked up on a board.

Bloss patted his pockets. In one, his wallet, in another, the video-tape and the diamond bracelet.

60

The blonde and Oscar, Oscar and the blonde, side by side on the squad-room whiteboard, his sky-diving-in-death pose, her big red-and-white grin. The blonde's name was Ellen Clarke and she'd been identified by a credit card and a driving licence. Apart from the name, she might as well have been a Jane Doe. A set of house keys were still waiting to find a lock and there was no 'home' among her mobile phone contacts. Frank Silano was working through the numbers that did appear and getting a lot of hang-ups.

A small crowd of rubberneckers had gathered: the AMIP-5 team, with their Twix bars and crisps and cartons of coffee. Marilyn Hayes looked for a moment, then walked back to her desk, giving a little hiccough. Stella sat on her desk to talk. She asked for any ideas.

'He follows the girl,' Maxine said, 'intending to kill her as he'd killed the others, but something goes wrong, maybe the street's too busy, she doesn't walk though any parks, whatever, so he follows her home and kills her there.'

'Not home,' Silano reminded her. 'She didn't live there. The sorrowing wife lives there.'

'Where is she?' Sorley asked. He was standing in the door-way, trying to keep his bacteria to himself. 'The sorrowing wife?'

'On a plane home from Meribel,' Stella told him. 'And what' – she turned to Maxine – 'he has to kill the boyfriend too?'

'Seems logical to me.'

'Why not choose someone else? Someone who does walk through parks, someone who isn't making things difficult? Why go into a house where it's likely there'll be another person around? It's not the MO.'

'He works off obsession,' Harriman offered. 'Isn't that what we think? He targets women. We saw the photos in his Harefield flat. He chooses them, singles them out. Something had to go wrong for him sometime. So he kills them both.'

'Him? There are two of them,' Sorley offered, 'we've established that. Kimber and Mister Mystery.'

'We don't know that they were both there,' Stella said. 'We have to wait for Forensics. But let's assume they were. Okay, they torture the man – multiple stab wounds to the thighs, the biceps, the buttocks. What does that say?'

'They want something – hiding place for the valuables, combination of the safe, that sort of thing,' Maxine said. 'It's a common pattern.'

'Yes, it is. But it doesn't fit.'

'Or maybe it was nothing more than opportunity,' Maxine suggested. 'They follow the blonde' – she glanced at the crime report – 'Ellen Clarke, she goes to the house and they haven't had their chance yet, maybe she changed her route, maybe she doesn't usually go to this house –'

'Maybe she's usually Tuesday and Thursdays,' Silano said, 'but the wife's away, so –'

Maxine nodded. 'Right, yes, so they catch up to Ellen at the door, grab her, go in with her, he's there –'

'Oscar Gribbin,' Stella said.

'Right, and so he's got to be killed too. And while they're there, hey, it's a big house, this is a rich guy, why not rip him off? So they hurt him to make him tell them where the money is.'

'And is the girl dead?' Stella asked. 'Have they killed her yet, or is she watching all this? And why did they use a gun on him but garrotte her?'

No one had an answer for that.

Side by side on the whiteboard, side by side on the slab. Sam Burgess was also looking for answers. He worked on Oscar and the blonde together because they were related in death; they were part of the same problem.

'There are things here you already know,' he told Stella. 'He was tortured – fifteen wounds in all, none of them lethal, none deep, all to fleshy parts of the body.'

'It's a means to an end,' Stella said.

'I know that. I've seen it before. The torturer wants information – where do you keep the money, where do you keep the valuables? – and eventually the victim tells him. Some probably tell him almost immediately, but torturers like to have their fun, also they like to be sure, so the treatment continues for a while. Then the torturer makes the victim open the safe or whatever, and leaves. The victim's tied up, combination of shock and blood-loss results in death. There's a difference here.'

'Which is?'

'He was stabbed, then shot very soon afterwards.'

'So Gribbin caved in immediately, told him where the cash was, and the guy finished him.'

'That's what I'd say if it was just him. Rich man, big house, familiar pattern.' He paused and looked across to where the blonde lay waiting her turn. 'Except for her, of course.'

'Yes,' Stella said. 'Except for her.'

*

Tom Davison had some more immediate answers, one of which was that Oscar Gribbin had been the first to die.

Stella sat at her desk, her shoulder lifted to wedge the phone while she papered Sam Burgess's early findings. She said, 'Are you sure?'

'It's in the blood patterns. He lost a lot, she lost almost none. The house has a heavily varnished wood-block floor, no soak factor. His blood-flow crosses the room to the fish-tank thing and keeps going. When she dies, she's sitting in his blood, it's on the backs of her legs, it's on the underside of the fur coat. Ergo, he'd been shot before she was backed up to the glass pillar and throttled.' He paused. 'Why was she wearing a fur coat indoors?'

'Who knows? Early Christmas present, perhaps. I've never had a sugar daddy, so I wouldn't know. He was stabbed fifteen times, so there would have been blood before he was whacked. You're sure he was first to die?'

'Viscosity of blood, amount shed from stab-wounds versus amount shed from major trauma like the head-wound; also size of room, positions of bodies. Trust me, DS Mooney. It may be gore to you, but it's bread and butter to me.'

'No DNA results yet, I suppose.'

'You're kidding, aren't you?'

'Anything on the bullets? Any fingerprints?'

'Fingerprint elimination's under way. The bullets are with a specialist unit.'

'Okay. But how soon for the DNA?'

'I'll rush round with the results as soon as they turn up.'

'Don't fuck me about, Davison, I've got a weird situation here and I need some answers.'

'About Kimber's DNA and Mister Mystery's DNA – you need to know if they're both at the scene?'

'That's right.'

'Look, I'm serious. When the results are in, I'll bring them over. Do you ever eat Chinese food?'

'You're married.'

'Who told you that?'

'You did.'

'Then it must be true.'

The call that had come through on Stella's mobile during the squad briefing had been from Delaney. She picked it up on voicemail as she walked across the car park.

Hi, it's me. Just wondering, trying to keep my distance, not making a very good job of it . . . so let's meet up. I'd sort of thought we might go somewhere for Christmas, now I don't know what to do. What to think. Give me a call. I love you, but I hope you know that.

I do know that. And I don't know what to do either. Or what to think.

Her windscreen was frosted over, so she got in and ran the heater for a few minutes. The ice-melt and her own tears blurred her eyes.

61

Trixie Gribbin had a ski-tan, blonde streaks and a cleavage like wash-leather. The tan was tight over her cheekbones and her eyes had a little upwards slant. Trixie was being looked after by several friends in a house only slightly larger and more expensive than her own. The friends wore designer everything and sparkled when they moved. They brought coffee and cake, then settled into chairs to observe proceedings. When Stella told them to leave, they looked affronted and stayed put. Frank Silano was a little less polite. They left their coffees as if expecting to return before they cooled.

If Trixie had been crying, she'd put her make-up on since the last tears flowed. Stella said she was sorry. Trixie said she was sorry too, and that she had an appointment with her lawyers in an hour, so maybe they could get through things quickly. It was tough talk, but there was a quiver in her voice.

Stella was holding a copy of the crime report from the local cops. The housekeeper who had found Oscar and Ellen was still in recovery. Trixie had given an initial report of missing items that she had described as bits and pieces of silver and a bracelet. There was an existing photograph and full description of the bracelet taken for insurance pur-poses, though without the technical details it came down to four strands of diamonds on platinum with a snake-head clasp and was entered by the insurers at fifty thousand pounds.

'It was the only thing not in the safe,' Trixie said. 'I'd meant to take it, but I forgot.'

'And the safe is in the basement.'

'Bolted to the floor. It's faked up to look like a cupboard. You open the cupboard, there are some trinkets. Take out the back and there's the safe.'

Stella looked at the crime report again. 'Jewellery and other items to the value of a quarter of a million pounds.'

'If that's what it says.'

'I don't know how much you've been told about the manner of your husband's death –'

'He was tortured.' Trixie's mouth gave a little twist. Out of nowhere, she said, 'I knew about the girls. There were always girls.' Stella and Silano waited, but Trixie went on as if she had never interrupted herself. 'To make him tell where the safe was.' Stella nodded. 'But they didn't go near it.'

'So he didn't tell them,' Stella observed.

'That doesn't make sense.' Trixie shook her head. 'That's not Oscar.'

'Are you sure?'

'He would have told them. Oscar would have told them.'

Silano asked, 'What makes you say that?'

Trixie looked at him. 'Who do you think he was – James fucking Bond?'

Silano said nothing.

'It's not a question of being brave,' Trixie said, 'not a matter of holding out or being tough. He'd've told them, because we're insured and, anyway, what's a quarter of a million to Oscar?'

One of the sparkly friends came back to remind Trixie of her appointment with her lawyers. Stella said, 'We might need to talk to you again. And we'll need a photo of your husband.'

Trixie gave her a mobile number. She said, 'There are framed photos all round the house. Take what you want.' Then, 'Tell me about the girl.'

'We don't know that much,' Stella said. 'She's been identified. We're still making inquiries.'

'What name?' Trixie asked.

Stella shrugged. It would be in the papers. She said, 'Ellen Clarke.' Then, as an afterthought, 'Did you know her?'

Trixie shook her head. 'What was she like to look at?'

Stella thought of the plum-dark, swollen face, the insane red-rimmed grin. She said, 'Young. Blonde.'

'Pretty?'

'I expect so.'

Trixie gave a laugh that brought her to the edge of tears. 'There were different girls, but they all looked the same.'

It wasn't her house, but she walked to the door with them. A taxi was waiting in the driveway. She put on her coat and walked out to the cab. Before she got in, she said, 'Do you know who they looked like?' Stella knew the answer. 'They looked like me. Like me when I was young.'

Trixie was right: a quarter of a million was nothing much to Oscar Gribbin, which was one of the reasons he was on the 'obbo' list with Serious Crimes. While Silano went to talk to someone on the SC Squad, Stella called in on Anne Beaumont. Only one of them had mixed motives. Silano wanted to know about Gribbin's connections. Stella wanted answers to questions, some of which had to do with Kimber and Mister Mystery, but others were closer to home. She had telephoned from the car on the off-chance and been told, 'Come now,' so she'd dropped Silano at Notting Hill and driven down to Knightsbridge.

'It's Christmas,' Anne said. 'They forget their neuroses and their crumbling relationships and jet off to the ski-slopes.'

'Though some return early,' Stella observed. She told Anne about Oscar and the blonde and the sorrowing wife.

Anne thought for a moment, then said, 'I don't know.'

'Know what?'

'I don't know what to think. Were they both at the scene – Kimber and Mister Mystery?'

'Forensics might tell us but forensics take time,' Stella said. 'Shall we have a drink?'

'It's early.'

'It's Christmas.'

Anne took an open bottle of Sauvignon Blanc from the fridge. 'Are you drinking too much?'

'Almost certainly.'

Anne poured two glasses of exactly the same size, a non-critical gesture. 'It's as if there were two separate events,' she said: 'a burglary with associated violence and a killing that demonstrates the same pattern as the attacks on Blake, Simms and Reilly.'

'We've considered that – Ellen Clarke is the real target, she's followed, there's no opportunity to kill her until she reaches the house, and Gribbin is a complication.'

'So they're both murdered out of necessity, but whoever kills them decides to rob the place – why not? – which is where the torture of Gribbin comes in.'

'Yes. Except the safe was untouched, though the wife is certain that he'd've told them whatever they wanted to know.'

'Who wouldn't?' Anne sipped her drink and paused, sav-ouring the gooseberry tang, then nodded as if the wine had been a good idea after all. She said, 'We ought to be thinking about it as two separate events. His death, her death. One we recognize, one we don't.'

'But they're connected.'

'I know. Pretend they're not. What do you get?'

'Tell me,' Stella said.

'I don't know. I'm asking you – you're the cop.'

They finished the wine without finding an answer. Stella said, 'Delaney wants us to go away somewhere for Christmas.'

'Will you?'

'In case you hadn't noticed, I'm tits-deep in a multiple murder case.'

'He doesn't want you to go *away*. He wants you to go *back*.'

Stella smiled. She said, 'I'd worked that much out for myself.'

'Think of them as separate events.'

'The killings?'

'Yes, the killings.' Anne paused. 'Also a life with Delaney and a life without.'

62

Pete Harriman was waiting for her with a fistful of reports. He said, 'I'm paper monitor. This is doing my fucking head in.'

'I took Silano because the last thing a sorrowing wife wants to see is evidence of extreme violence, and you're it.'

Harriman handed over the reports. 'Crime report update, scene of crime analysis, budget summary from DI Sorley who's obviously close to death, memos from everyone, confirmation of the five-k reward on Kimber, yellow-board responses – all crap – emails from Serious Crimes and Forensics, ten while-you-were-away notes, lots of luck, I'm on my lunch break.'

Stella watched Marilyn Hayes watching Harriman as he made for the door. After a moment's indecision, Marilyn got up and followed him out. Stella sat at her desk and sifted the paper Harriman had given her. The budget summary went into the bin, the rest she skim-read, looking for new information. After about ten minutes she got to the crime scene update where Oscar Gribbin's 'personal effects' had been listed: whatever he'd had on him at the time of death. Stella read through, then called Harriman on his mobile. When he answered, she heard the end of his last remark tagged on to his response to the phone: '. . . it's okay, we'll talk. Hello?'

'Where's DC Hewitt?'

'Running the door-to-door on Harefield.'

'Okay, you're standing in for her.

'What's happened?'

'Oscar Gribbin had a five hundred pound casino chip in his pocket. Jumping Jacks. Last port of call, maybe. Or fairly recent, anyway. Definitely worth a look. I'll need Maxine for a briefing, then we'll get down to the casino later tonight.'

'Take me, Boss.'

'Forget it.'

'It's *overtime!*'

'Call her in, Pete, and get yourself over to Harefield. You can take your scar down there and wear it with pride.'

Maxine was dressed for the estate, so she'd stopped off to change. Stella had wondered whether the diesel jeans were an in-joke. She sat with a coffee and waited for ten minutes until Maxine emerged from the bedroom in a black trouser suit – narrow pants and a frock coat.

'You look like a gambler,' Stella told her, 'riverboat style.'

'I like to put people at their ease.'

Stella said, 'Look at my hair, here at the back.'

'What am I looking for?'

'Delaney took a snip of my hair, to show how easy it was.'

'Easy for Kimber?'

'Yes.'

Maxine peered; she raised her hand and ruffled Stella's hair a little. 'I see it. He took a chunk, didn't he?'

'Where?'

Maxine touched the right side of Stella's head. 'You're layered, so it doesn't show all that much.'

'I thought it was the other side,' Stella said.

'No,' Maxine said. Then, 'Don't worry. No one would know.'

*

They were going unannounced, but Stella had done some background work. They knew that Billy Souza ran Jumping Jacks and they knew that he'd been under suspicion a number of times. In police terms, 'under suspicion' meant 'guilty as hell but no proof'. DS Gerry Harris's name had appeared on a number of reports and Stella had called him a couple of times, but he was out of the office, so she'd emailed and left it at that. Harris was fast becoming her main man at Notting Hill Serious Crimes Squad.

As they walked out to the car, Stella asked, 'How did it go?' She meant the Harefield door-to-door.

'We showed the mugshot,' Maxine told her, 'and we mentioned the sum of five thousand pounds. Harefield Estate is a refuge for the deaf, dumb and blind.'

'Even the straight ones?'

'Especially the straight ones. The scared ones. The ones behind the B & Q door-chains.' As Stella opened the car, Maxine added, 'You'd think they'd be glad of five grand, what with Christmas coming up.'

'What's Christmas,' Stella asked, 'if you spend it in intensive care?'

Jan returned twenty minutes after they'd gone. She made herself a drink, then found the note that Maxine had left for her. She walked to the window to draw the curtains, drink in one hand, note in the other.

Kimber looked up as she stood framed by the window, the light behind her, head bowed to read. He knew her real name now. Someone had called out to her as she was leaving work: 'We're going for a drink, Jan.'

But Jan had said no. Jan had taken her usual route home, the route Kimber knew so well. Jan with her fur-trimmed leather coat and the bright red beanie. Jan with the even features and the mouth made for kissing.

Jan who had been close enough to touch.

Billy Souza wasn't available to them. It was JD who told them this. He was wearing a dinner jacket and a hard smile. Stella smiled back and suggested that Billy make himself available within the next ten minutes. JD's glance went a fraction above Stella's head, and she turned to look at the CCTV camera, transferring the smile to whoever might be watching.

To Billy.

Maxine waited until JD had walked away, heading for the rear of the gaming room, then said, 'How much can I lose at blackjack and claim back on exes?'

'Pretend you're asking Mike Sorley,' Stella said. Then, 'Why?'

'I know the dealer. She was my chis for a while. Used to fence a bit, hook a bit, hang out with some tough types. Last saw her when she was a club hostess, but that was a year ago. I thought she must be doing time.'

'And here she is, offering us an inside edge.'

'Exactly.'

'Don't lose.'

Maxine laughed. 'Tell me how.'

Louise hadn't been opposite a strong winner since the night Leon Bloss's soft hands had caused Billy to haul her off the table. She had been dealing a house advantage all night, but now she looked up and saw bad luck coming across the room. When Maxine sat down at the table, Louise dealt her a ten-seven, which made her feel a little better until Maxine tapped for a card and drew the three of hearts. The blackjack table isn't a place for catching up with old acquaintances, so when the house paid twenties or better Maxine took her chips and laid down a card of her own: a business card. Louise swept it up with the rest: the fast fingers of the professional dealer.

The locals had been back into the murder house and collected a few photos of Oscar Gribbin. In the one Billy Souza was looking at, Oscar was at some charity function, wearing a dinner jacket and a cheesy smile. He said, 'I know him, yes. He's a punter.'

'Know him well?' Stella asked.

'Well enough to extend a line of credit, not well enough to call him by his first name.'

'It's possible that he was here on the night he died.'

'Who knows? I think he came in one or two nights a week.'

'Alone?'

'Look,' Billy said, smiling expansively, 'if there's trouble, I know about it, if someone loses heavily, I know about it, if someone hits a winning streak, I know about it. Most punters call in, win a little, lose a little more, then go home. What do I know? I'm running a business.'

'The reason we're here,' Maxine said, 'is that if your casino was Oscar Gribbin's last call before going home, the killer might have followed him from here. Maybe he won heavily, maybe someone saw that.'

'I don't think he was here,' Billy said. 'Not the night you mentioned. No.'

'He had a Jumping Jacks chip in his pocket when he died.'

'Means nothing. People keep them as lucky pieces.'

'A five hundred pound chip.'

Billy spread his hands: so what?

Stella said, 'If he was here that night, then it's probable

that he was with a girl. Tall, blonde, pretty, name of Ellen Clarke.' The only picture Stella had seen of the blonde was the scene of crime shot, but she thought 'pretty' was a more than even bet.

Billy smiled. 'Who knows?'

'You have CCTV, don't you?'

'Night by night. It records over.'

'You have security staff.'

'If he threatened a dealer, they'd remember. Other-wise –'

Stella said, 'What time do you open for business?'

'Noon.'

'DC Hewitt will be back at ten tomorrow. Have your staff here, everyone, dealers, cashiers, security, scrutineers, waiters. We'll need to talk to them all, show them the photo, ask them what they remember.'

'I could ask them myself,' Billy said.

'It's a kind offer,' Stella said. 'Ten a.m. No sick-notes.'

As they were going through the gaming room, Louise looked up. Maxine raised her hand as if to scratch her chin, but with thumb and little finger extended: *phone me*. Louise snapped a card from the shoe and dealt someone a losing hand.

Stella got into the shower and washed her hair. She felt for the missing lock. She could feel it, then she couldn't. She put on a thick bathrobe, walked through to the main room and went to the window to look out. A sleety rain was falling. The late-nighters were going by, heads bent against the wind.

She had tried to feel him, feel his presence – if he was really there, if he was really following her – but no instinct had made her turn, or had sent a shiver across her shoulders.

No goose had walked on her grave. After a while she let down the blind and went through to the bedroom. She took off the robe and put on a big T-shirt. It was part of George's uncollected wardrobe. She put out the light. Unusually, she fell asleep almost at once.

She dreamed she was dancing with someone, though she couldn't see his face. They turned and turned in the dance. She gripped his arms as he gripped hers. Her hair was flying.

She doesnt know. I dont have to follow I just wait for when she comes back. I wait up the street then I go over the wall and get behind the wheelie bin. The blind was down but you see shapes. She came in and took something off then put something on. You can see shapes. She puts the light out when shes got into bed. Its a bedside light. The room goes dark but there she is. Shes in there. Shes sleeping. Sweet dreams Stella.

Leon Bloss was sitting in a car two streets off the Strip and talking to a trader. In fact people called him the Trader. This man knew about all sorts of merchandise, but mostly he knew about gemstones. He also knew about risk. He turned the four-strand bracelet in his hand and it caught the glow from streetlights, giving back a soft blue gleam.

He said, 'Is there a call out on this, Leon?'

Bloss shrugged. 'There will be.'

'Then best to keep it for a while. You know that. If the cops are interested, it'll have to be broken, in which case the price drops.'

'I need to cover some expenses,' Bloss said.

'You'll take what you can get?'

'I'll have to.' Bloss gave a chirpy smile. 'Christmas on the way . . .'

'I can raise you ten-k on this. Maybe fifteen. Minus my commission.'

Bloss knew this meant that the Trader could raise twenty. He said, 'I'll take eighteen, no commission.'

The Trader was a big man, broad shouldered, maybe six-four, dark complexioned. He gave Bloss a sorrowful look. 'You don't sound as if you're in a position to cut deals, Leon. You sound like a man on the move.'

'You're right. I could move on. Take it somewhere else.'

The Trader laughed. 'Don't shit me, Leon. That's your plan, is it? Where are you going to take it – Harefield? Stonebridge? Some dudes down there be more than happy to do business with you. They'll take your fucking bracelet and shoot your dick off instead of saying thank you.' He had small hands for a big man. He slipped the bracelet over his wrist. 'Fifteen,' he said.

Bloss shrugged. 'Fifteen.'

It was the sum they'd both been reaching for. The Trader said, 'A few days. I'll call you.'

He drove Bloss down to the tube at Notting Hill, facing down the faint-hearted in the one-lane rat-runs, the bracelet half hidden under his shirt cuff. It threw a glitter when he swung the wheel.

63

The Jumping Jacks logo was the knave of hearts and the knave of diamonds, each set against a bright white playing-card. The neon version was mounted on the wall of the casino. At night, the jacks hopped and bopped in alternating rhythms. At ten in the morning they were as dull and lifeless as the staff lined up outside Billy Souza's office. Billy had taken the morning off, so JD was deputizing. His method of doing this was to walk with a roll to his shoulders and rarely blink. He went for a stare-out with Frank Silano, which made Silano laugh out loud.

'Is there CCTV in Souza's office?' Silano asked.

'Works the other way.' JD was now eyeballing the croupier at the head of the line. 'We look at them, they don't look at us.'

'Recording devices?' JD shrugged. Silano said, 'Who runs electronic surveillance?'

'Woman called Arlene Pearce. The scrutineer.'

Arlene took Silano through to the room next to Billy's office where the CCTV cameras were racked and showed him the mikes. She showed him that they were deactivated: flick-flick, red light on, red light off. When they emerged, Silano asked her to lock the door, then he took the key.

They went through the staff one by one, as if they were shuffling a deck, looking for an ace to match the ten. And there she was, Louise, her pert nose, her vicious pony-tail, lighting a cigarette and saying, 'I'm clean, I'm straight and I'm earning. Leave me alone.'

Maxine showed her Oscar Gribbin's photo.

Louise said, 'Okay, he's a punter.'

'When was he last in?'

'He doesn't play blackjack. A couple of days ago, maybe. He's regular.'

'What's his game if not blackjack?'

'Craps, I think. Not sure. Roulette?'

'Who runs those tables?'

'It depends.'

'All right. We'll ask JD.'

'Ask Arlene, she'll know.'

Maxine nodded and Louise started to get up. Maxine said, 'You didn't call me.'

'Nothing to say.'

'I might need some eyes and ears in this place.'

'Find someone else.'

'I don't need to.'

Louise sighed. She said, 'I call you, never the other way round.'

Gerry Harris raised Stella on the third try. She had been waiting to hear from Tom Davison, but Harris had interesting news of his own.

'One of your guys was over here. Silano?'

'That's right.'

'I was out, but someone took a message. He was asking about Oscar Gribbin. And now I hear you're having a look at Billy Souza.'

'How do you know that?'

'Are you kidding?

'You have an interest in Souza?'

'Yes. And what's fascinating here,' Harris said, 'is that you go from Gribbin to Souza.'

'Gribbin gambled at Jumping Jacks. That's the connection. Not much to it. It occurred to us that if Gribbin was in the casino the night he died, the killer might have been there too.'

'It's not the connection,' Harris said. 'Not the only connection.' Stella was silent. 'Gribbin's an importer of metal goods, everything from scrap to vehicle bodywork and parts. Customs were looking, they tipped us off, we started looking too. We think Gribbin realized this because the only time we jumped him he was clean.'

'You think he was sidelining.'

'That's right.'

'Sidelining what?'

'Illegals at first.'

Stella saw the little group cowering in the warehouse, the upturned faces, the mother with the dead child at her breast.

'At first –'

'It's profitable, I mean, it's big business, but there are risks. Mostly your cargo is volatile. It has a mind of its own. It can tell tales.'

'It can die,' Stella added.

'Yes, that's right, it can.' Stella heard the snap of a lighter and waited for Harris to get his first lungful down. 'We suspected him, but we never got a line on him – contacts in the countries of origin, finance, that sort of thing. Then he stopped, we were pretty sure of that. After a while, though, he started gambling at Jumping Jacks. Became a regular.'

'And so?'

'We were looking hard at Billy Souza. We still are.'

'And he connects – how?'

'Gribbin was a carrier, pure and simple. He moved merchandise around the world. But if he was carrying contraband of some sort or another, he needed a supplier and a distributor. Gribbin hauled the cargo, but someone had to buy it – the importer.'

'And you think that's Souza?'

'Could be.' He paused. 'DS Mooney –'

'Stella.'

'Right, Stella, I'll have to rely on you to keep us up to speed on this. It's your murder, but it's our ongoing investigation.'

'I promise.'

'Okay.'

'So what's the cargo? What do you think he's importing?'

'Guns.'

The call from Tom Davison came in at the end of the day. He said, 'I've got what you want, DS Mooney.'

'Tell me.'

'Better than that, I can show you.'

'Davison, you're persistent, that's all I can possibly say in your favour.'

'No, I *can* show you. I've got it with me right here.'

'Where are you?'

'Sitting in the car park. Mazda sports with the engine turning over.'

64

Pete Harriman had a few stops to make. The first was to the pub, where Marilyn Hayes was waiting for him. They talked for fifteen minutes. The second was to out-patients, where a nurse checked his stitches and told him he was healing nicely. The third was seven floors up and through corridors that smelled of disinfectant and death. Ronaldo was out of ITU and in a private ward and the girl with him wasn't a nurse, unless nurses arrive naked under a full-length fur. Harriman waited while she buttoned up and sidled out.

Ronaldo said, 'Don't go far.'

'All the comforts of home,' Harriman observed. He showed Ronaldo a picture of Oscar Gribbin and got no response, which was pretty much what he'd expected. The Strip is home territory to some, a foreign country to others. Next he showed a picture of Trixie Gribbin's bracelet.

'The last time you asked me a question,' Ronaldo observed, 'I got a blade in the fucking kidneys. I'm paying for minders to watch my girls, which means that the girls are having to compensate. They're giving head so fast they nod in their sleep.'

'I need to hear about the bracelet. Someone's going to want to offload it.'

Ronaldo looked at Harriman's stitching and laughed. 'You didn't see them coming either, did you?' The laugh died. 'Have you found them yet?'

'Magna,' Harriman said. 'We know who they are.'

'Do me a favour, Mr Harriman. Leave them alone. I'm

thinking of taking a little trip over to Harefield when I'm back on my feet.'

'Is that right? Friends of mine in the Drugs Squad fully expect to find them in possession of a very large amount of scag.'

'They don't carry.'

'They would be on this occasion.'

Ronaldo shook his head. 'Here's a deal. I'll ask about the bracelet, I'll put people on to it, okay? You leave those cunts on the street.'

Harriman smiled. He gave Ronaldo his card, just a reminder, then walked out into the corridor where the girl was waiting. He said, 'This must be your night off.'

The Mazda sat low to the road and cornered hard. They went down from Notting Hill towards Hammersmith, taking red lights on the second beat and lane-switching like Mad Max. Stella said, 'So this is the family car.'

Tom Davison was late thirties and good-looking in a professorial sort of way. He had a mop of dark hair, slightly tangled, and wore combats and big boots to go with it. It was a style and it suited him.

He said, 'No. Honda Accord, two kiddie seats, stained upholstery.'

'Where are we going?'

'Chinese food, remember?'

Stella had no idea why she'd got into Davison's car. She should have simply said, *Give me the reports*. They hit Hammersmith Broadway and slalomed through the home-going traffic, Davison finding a neat line into King Street. She said, 'Give me the reports. I can get out anywhere here.'

He pulled over, put on the hazard lights and handed her

a large brown envelope. 'Okay. I'll call you in the morning and talk you through it.'

She didn't get out. They sat together in silence for thirty seconds while cars lined up to get round them, flashing and hooting. She said, 'There's a place in Chiswick High Road that cooks without MSG.'

Davison nodded. 'I know. That's where we're going.'

It was early and the restaurant was almost empty. They ordered a bottle of wine and Stella took out the report. Davison said, 'You only need that if you haven't got me.'

'Tell me.'

'Oscar Gribbin was shot three times, the third, fatal bullet being to the back of the cranium, though either of the others would have done the job eventually by way of blood-loss and shock. Ellen Clarke was garrotted. Technically, she died of asphyxiation, though there was a good deal of collateral damage to the thorax, etcetera, etcetera.'

'I got all that from the PM report.'

'I know. I'm just putting in the background. There were significant differences from the earlier killings. To begin with, there was a gun involved. That's new. One pretty obvious difference is that Oscar Gribbin was there at all.'

'Other things were familiar.'

'The way Clarke was killed and partially stripped.'

'That's right.'

The waiter came back with the wine and asked if they were ready to order. Davison said, 'The usual.'

Stella looked at him. 'You come here a lot?'

'All the time.'

'Bring the family here?'

'The kids love chow mein.'

'What's the usual?'

'It's what everyone eats in Chinese restaurants. The bullets were from a Glock forty-five, bound to be an illegal import, I suppose. There were no fingerprints, but there was DNA.' He took a sip of wine. 'Robert Adrian Kimber, all over the place, thick as autumn leaves. We found hair: a very large and helpful amount.'

'Kimber killed them both?'

'On the evidence, you'd have to think so.'

'Mister Mystery?'

'Well, now, that's the interesting part.' Davison took a sheet of paper from the brown envelope and put it down on the table. 'Quite often scene of crime material gets passed around the lab, this guy might run the tests, or that guy. I've done all of yours. It must be your phone manner; that or the black silk panels. It's allowed me to see a pattern.'

Davison pointed to the paper: he'd made a little evidence-tree.

'Valerie Blake dies and we get Mister Mystery's DNA. Sophie Simms dies, we get the same thing. We could isolate these two because the guy that was responsible for the earlier attacks on women got caught.'

'Martin Cotter. We think Mister Mystery was trying to make his killings seem part of Cotter's pattern: using a garrotte and so forth.'

'Right. So we have Blake and Simms, both killed by Mister Mystery. Then Kate Reilly is murdered and we find Robert Kimber's DNA at the scene. And Mister Mystery's. And here's where I begin to see a difference. Mister Mystery is being very careful. He knows about forensic tracing. He's probably wearing latex gloves and I bet he's wearing some kind of tight coverall hat. The chances are he thinks he's leaving no trace at all. What he doesn't know is that it's almost impossible to perpetrate that level of violence and not shake a few cells free, a few hairs. He's tricky, but I'm trickier.'

Davison topped up Stella's glass. He was talking, she was drinking.

'At the Reilly scene, there were the usual scant leavings from Mister Mystery, but Kimber's DNA is all over the place. In fact, it looks pretty certain that Kimber did the killing. So, while Kimber is taking virtually no precautions – possibly because he doesn't know any better – Mister Mystery is trying to leave none.'

The last point on the evidence-tree said *Gribbin/Clarke.*

'So now we come to this. Where Kimber's DNA is thick on the ground.'

'And Mister Mystery's?'

'He must have thought he was away clear. Almost nothing. Next to nothing. Infinitesimal.' He smiled. 'But then infinitesimal is my stock-in-trade.'

'And you can place him at the scene?'

'God knows what he was wearing, frogman's outfit, I should think. But he couldn't go out like that, could he? Had to take it off. And when you remove clothing, you shed DNA. I can put him by the front door, both inside and outside the house.'

Stella picked up the evidence-tree and stared at it. 'And your theory is?'

'Christ, I haven't got a theory. I'm a scientist. Theories are guesswork; science is fact.'

'Here's a theory of mine,' Stella said. 'You're not married, are you?'

'No,' Davison said, 'I'm not. That's a fact.'

65

Jan leaves work. Jan walks to the tube. Jan stops
to buy a paper or she goes to the 7/11 for some
bread or something today she bought salad and
soup and toothpaste. Jan goes three stops then
changes then goes five stops. She wears the red
wool hat so I cant clip her. Jan goes out in her
lunch break too and thats when I can take photos.
Jan walking down the road Jan going through the
park Jan waiting for a take away coffee Jan close
enough to touch. Sometimes I close my eyes and I
think about Patricia except she was really called
Kate Reilly I found out from the papers. I think
about Kate Reilly but I change her into Jan or into
Stella so its the same and Im following and Ive
got the hammer and its just the way it was the same
things happen and I get the same feelings but when
I do her when I kill her its Jan. Or its Stella. I
havent told Leon Bloss about this because he says
we must stop for a while but the thing is Ive only
just begun. Its new to me. Not the thinking about
it. I used to think about it all the time but its
different when you think about it after youve
done it. Its different because you know what it
really is you know what its really like. When I
think about Kate Reilly its really good but its a
memory. Ive done it and its over. When I think
about it and pretend its Jan or Stella I know Ive

got it ahead of me and I get really hard and have
to hand myself off but even then I go on thinking
about it. Leon Bloss doesnt understand about following. He knows about the killing but he doesnt
know about my way of doing things. The following
and the photos and the clippings and being close
enough to touch. He keeps saying wait and I will
wait but only until the time comes. Now Ive done
Kate now Ive got Kate under my belt sort of thing
I know that theres a right time for this sort of
event. Its when the following isnt enough and the
clippings and the photos are not enough. When the
story I write about them needs a proper ending.
Before I met Leon Bloss the stories were instead.
There was the following and the photos and the
hair clipping and the story was the rest of it.
Now the story is just a beginning. No not a beginning its a plan. A guideline. Yes its a guideline
like people have for making a film. A senario. I
always thought Stella would be next but sometimes
I think it must be Jan. I dont know how to choose.
Perhaps something will choose for me. Perhaps
either Jan or Stella will choose by doing something or being somewhere but I havent reached it
yet – I havent reached the moment when I have to.
Leon Bloss says wait but I know I have to. Hes got
no right to tell me just because he was the person
who showed me how to. He started me off with Kate.
Now its up to me.

Stella leaves work and she goes to Vigo Street
or she goes to the pub first and I can follow or I
can wait for her at her home. I know Stella better
because she questioned me about Valerie Blake but

that makes things more difficult. With Jan I can sit opposite her in the tube and she doesnt know me I can go right up to her and stand behind her in a shop. Jan shares with someone which means I would have to do Jan like I did Kate in the street or somewhere. Stella lives alone at Vigo Street so I could go in. I could go in to her which makes for a different way of doing things. More time. More things to do. With Jan theres the risk and thats another thing thats exciting too. Ill think about it. Ill write some stories. Some guidelines. Yes. A senario. Yes.

66

Stella woke in the dark to the sound of someone speaking and thought it must have been herself. She got out of bed and went to the window, but there was nothing to see. She walked naked into the living space and looked out from there, but the street seemed empty. She switched on a standard-lamp that shed a yellowish glow like snow-light. A cab cruised past. Somewhere off on the high road a car alarm started up, then cut out. Her coat was on the sofa and she put it on in place of a robe. She found a drink and sat on a kitchen stool, her elbows resting on the worktop.

Let's try to make sense of this. Mister Mystery thinks he's leaving no DNA trace. Kimber's leaving lots. MM's being careful, Kimber's not. Or doesn't know he should be.

So why doesn't MM warn him? Why doesn't he say, 'Do like me — wear the full-body condom and a pair of tights on your head'?

She took a slug of her drink. She wanted vodka but could find only whisky.

Let's go further back. MM wants us to think his killings are the work of Martin Cotter, that's why he half strips them — because Cotter had a sexual motive. And that's why he uses a garrotte. But Cotter's been kept under wraps, nothing in the papers, nothing on TV.

Right. So as far as MM's concerned, we might still be thinking of his crimes and Cotter's as being by the same man.

Right. And if we did think that, given the DNA evidence, who would we think that man was?

We'd think it was Robert Adrian Kimber.

Exactly. Kimber confessed to Blake's murder. MM read about this. He contacted Kimber. Then he and Kimber killed Kate Reilly, Oscar Gribbin and Ellen Clarke. Each time MM tries to leave no trace. Each time Kimber leaves half a ton.

Especially in the Gribbin/Clarke case.

You would think it was a master–apprentice thing, wouldn't you? Old hand teaches the new hand. Thrill-kill as a diploma course. Except the master doesn't seem to have noticed that the pupil is making a very basic mistake.

Or has noticed.

What?

What did Anne say? Think of them as separate events. Okay, let's do that. One: we've got a killing that has the Blake/Simms/Reilly MO all over it. Two: we've got something else entirely. A double murder with an opportunist robbery.

Here's something else. Mister Mystery doesn't know that Cotter has been arrested, sure, but he also doesn't know that he's been shedding DNA. As far as he's concerned, we think that Kimber did Cotter's work, and killed Blake and Simms and Reilly, and was responsible for Gribbin and Clarke.

Two separate events. So look at the individual deaths: the victims. Go all the way back and work forward. Where does the pattern break? Who's the odd one out?

Oscar Gribbin.

Stella spoke out loud. She said, 'Jesus Christ, I know what this is.'

From the bedroom came the sound of a footfall. Stella was caught up in her thoughts and registered it only after a beat or two. Then the door opened. Tom Davison took a step into the room, then stopped. He said, 'Are you going?' She looked puzzled, so he added, 'You've got your coat on.'

'Couldn't find a robe.'

'Cupboard in the bathroom.'

He made a move in that direction, but she said, 'It doesn't matter.'

Davison fetched a glass and helped himself to some of his own whisky. He said, 'Don't feel bad.'

'Why do you say that?'

'You're sitting up at almost four a.m. drinking whisky and looking gloomy.'

'I was thinking.'

'Gloomy thoughts.'

'No. Work stuff.'

'Productive thoughts?'

'So-so.'

She knew that what Davison had said over dinner had started the train of thought that had led her to what might be a solution, but she didn't feel inclined to share the outcome with him. Maybe it was mean-minded of her, but he wasn't the person to talk to on this. That would be Harriman or Sorley or Maxine Hewitt.

Or John Delaney.

Davison said, 'I've got an early start.'

'Me too.'

'So come back to bed.' He leaned over and kissed her. 'Because I like what you do there.'

She kissed him back, touching his cheek with the palm of her hand. She said, 'I'd better go.'

'Will I see you again?'

'I don't think so.'

'I don't think so meaning "I haven't decided" or –'

'There's a complication.'

Davison sighed. 'I thought there might be.' He drank his whisky. 'It's a shame. I liked you on the phone and I like you even better now.'

Stella said, 'And I like you,' but he didn't seem to hear her; he wandered back into the bedroom and sat on the bed. She followed him in and found her clothes on the floor. He looked away while she got dressed.

67

The streets were bright with frost; Stella's footprints were a dark spoor. She stood on Chiswick High Road hoping to find a cab, but the night traffic was trucks and party-people. A patrol car cruised by looking for drunk drivers. Stella dialled Delaney's number and got his answerphone, so she dialled his mobile and he picked up almost at once.

'It's four a.m., where the hell are you?'

He laughed. 'Freezing my arse off in an alley. It's called research.'

'You're with the street-people. Your street-people.'

'They do this every night. I'm doing it just the once. As a lifestyle, it leaves a lot to be desired.'

'Don't tell me you've been panhandling the public as well.'

'A particularly aggressive beggar. I ought to be arrested.' She heard him speak to someone, a reassurance, then he came back. 'Jesus, it's cold out here. There's one hell of a frost.' A little silence fell, then he asked, 'Why did you call?'

'Couldn't sleep.'

'Come and sleep with me.'

'In an alley?'

'Tomorrow.'

The light of a black cab was visible fifty yards up the road but moving fast. Stella said, 'I'll call you. Don't get frostbite.'

He said, 'Okay, sure,' but it seemed to come from a long way off.

She flagged the cab and gave the Vigo Street address.

*

Sadie had made a connection late the previous night : a good score. She was hunkered down in her bag and feeling no pain. Jamie wore his quilted coat inside his bag and had pulled everything over his head. He was awake and singing softly to himself.

. . . have yourself a merry little Christmas . . .

There were three other rough sleepers in the alley apart from Sadie and Jamie. The Ocean Diner was open all night and the sous-chef came out a couple of times with a handout. Delaney ate some cold potato wedges and slugged from the hip-flask he'd brought with him. The others watched this but didn't crowd him. They seemed to have some help of their own, mostly chemical. They were wary of him anyway. He was the guy with the cassette-recorder and the mobile phone. He was also the guy with the pocketful of money.

He had a new goose-down bag and thermal skin-wear. He had ski gloves and fur-lined knee boots. He had a pricey apartment less than half a mile away and a vestige of a social conscience.

Stella sat in the back of the cab and stared out at London's homeless and rootless and witless. The city was never calm, it never settled into sleep.

Does it matter?

You tell me.

It was just a fuck.

Oh, really?

Listen, I liked him. Davison. He's a nice guy, he's bright, he made me laugh. In another life –

Shut up, for Christ's sake. Don't tell me that stuff. Save it for yourself. What are you going to do?

Morning-after pill.

I know that. I mean what are you going to do —

It was just a fuck.

— about Delaney?

I don't know. Give me a lead.

Okay, in the short term, do you tell him about tonight? In the long term, are you staying or leaving?

I need some time. I've got a murder case to solve.

Sure. What are you going to do?

Listen, I think I know what it is. I think I know what Mister Mystery —

Sure. What are you going to do?

A couple of days. Let me leave it just a few days.

Until Christmas?

Okay, yes, until Christmas.

You're full of shit.

I expect you're right, but that's the deal.

And are you all right with this? Tell me how you're feeling?

Listen, it was just a fuck.

No, it was a test.

Oh, yeah? Testing what?

You, Delaney. You and Delaney. The whole thing. And it was stupid.

You think so?

It was stupid.

The storefront windows were bright with neon and star-burst stickers. There was a queue outside an all-night fast-food place and a drunk was sitting propped up in a bus shelter. Boys in hoodies and girls wearing blocky heels and fake fur. London streets at 4 a.m.

Okay, it was stupid.

She felt like crying, but that would have been the easy thing to do.

*

329

She switched on all the lights and took a fast shower. There was something about sounds you make in the early hours of the morning, in the pre-dawn dark – doors closing, water running – they were louder, they had a strange sort of shock value. She got into bed but it was a lost cause, so she got up and made coffee, then started putting together some notes for the squad meeting she would call later that morning.

She wrote the name Mister Mystery and remembered something Tom Davison had said. *He's tricky, but I'm trickier.*

I know what you're doing. I'm second-guessing you now. I'm closer than you think.

With first light, the frost hardened as if the sun were ice. A ragged flock of birds drifted through, looking for a place to settle.

Leon Bloss watched the gulls settling at the river's edge, searching for carrion. He was thinking things through. He would collect his fee from Billy Souza, pick up fifteen-k on the bracelet, then make sure that Robert Adrian Kimber took the fall. After that, Christmas in the sun.

But don't think it hasn't been fun, Bobby. Don't think I haven't enjoyed myself.

Delaney sat with his back to the wall of the Ocean Diner and watched the hard, grey light spread into the alley. He was chilled, bone-deep. He wondered how people lived like this, not one night but every night. He wondered how long he would wait for Stella to make up her mind.

It's easier to stay away, isn't it? Coming back means back to stay . . .

*

Stella finished her notes and suddenly felt tired. She got into bed and lay flat out, as if she had fallen there from a height. Patterns from the window-blind, like lines of water droplets, shimmered on the wall. She had some admissions to make, some owning up to do.

It was just a fuck. But here's a thing – he was pretty good. Pretty good in bed.

Robert Adrian Kimber was asleep in his room just off the Strip. His journal and his silver-ink pen were on the floor by the bed. He had slept all night, untroubled, dreamless.

In the cemetery opposite, the city's scavengers hunted between the cold stones of the dead.

68

Pete Harriman said, 'It's a set-up. He's the fall-guy – Kimber. Is that what you're saying?'

'That's right.'

Stella was sitting on a desk at the front of the AMIP-5 squad room, drinking the cooling coffee she'd brought in with her. The first few swallows had washed down the morning-after pill. That was before she'd called the squad meeting.

'Which is why,' she said, 'Kimber's DNA was so prevalent at the Kate Reilly murder and at the murder of Oscar Gribbin and Ellen Clarke. Mister Mystery is happy to let Kimber implicate himself by DNA.' She looked at Marilyn Hayes and asked, 'Anything more on her, by the way – Clarke?'

'Nothing. We've done cross-searches until we're dizzy. It wasn't her real name or no one cares or she's alone in the world.'

'Her mugshot went up to the Strip,' Frank Silano observed, 'but none of the girls knew her. Or no one would admit to knowing her. The fact that the photo clearly showed she was dead didn't help.' He shrugged. 'Maybe she was a honey-trap, or she just got unlucky.'

'Either way,' Stella said, 'we have to separate the Gribbin killing from the others and look at it as a pro-job. It's the only reasonable thing to do. We have to think of Mister Mystery as a technician – a hit-man. There's a link between Oscar Gribbin and Billy Souza. We ought to look at that.

We're dealing with traceable people here and possibly traceable motives. We're dealing with villains and crooks, people we know about, people we can anticipate. If this was a hit, someone ordered it. Go back to the street, go back to informants, look for business contacts in this, look for antagonisms, look for feuds old or new. Maxine, talk to your chis at Jumping Jacks again – the blackjack dealer.'

'Okay.'

'Marilyn – Souza is very probably linked to gun imports. Search computer records for any likely imports involved in a crime or seized by Customs, see where you get, feed in all the names, ask anyone on any police computer-link for anything that looks connected.' Marilyn nodded. She was sitting on the opposite side of the room from Harriman, which hadn't escaped Stella's attention.

'Okay. Anything on Kimber?' No one responded. 'Keep trying. At least we know what he looks like.'

The meeting broke up, leaving a litter of paper cups, sandwich packs and chocolate-bar wrappers. Stella drank the rest of her coffee. It tasted rank.

Mike Sorley had developed the habit of attending squad meetings by standing at the far side of the room. Sometimes he didn't even turn up: the leper of AMIP-5. The sound of his coughing travelled all the way up the corridor from his office, which itself was pretty much a no-go area. Stella stood by the door and watched him flick through the notes she'd made the previous evening.

He said, 'You think he was planning this all along – Mister Mystery?'

'I think he saw an opportunity.'

'Here's a possibility.' Sorley had put down Stella's notes and was looking from the post-mortem findings to the lab report. 'Sam Burgess makes the point that when they combed Ellen Clarke for evidence, they found a substantial amount of Kimber's hair. He queries it as unusually large. So this guy's not just leaving a DNA *trace*, he's leaving something more like a *trail*.'

'You mean it's not just a case of Mister Mystery allowing Kimber to be careless.'

'Sure.'

'The DNA was planted.'

'In this case – yeah, maybe.'

'Kimber wasn't at the scene.'

'Didn't need to be.'

'More than that,' Stella said, 'I guess Mister Mystery wouldn't want him there. It's a different operation, different way of doing things. Kimber would be asking why.'

'He'd want to know what was going on,' Sorley said. 'After all, he's not a hit-man, is he? He's not someone with a logical purpose. Hit-men get paid.'

'You're right,' Stella said. 'And Kimber does it for love.'

When Stella came out of Sorley's office she saw Pete Harriman further down the corridor with Marilyn Hayes, looking like a man who'd just stepped backwards into a bear-trap. Marilyn was standing very close to him and talking in a rapid, low tone. When his mobile rang, Harriman grabbed for it and walked a few paces off to take the call. Marilyn turned and went back to the squad room, hitting the door with the heel of her hand. As Stella walked by, Harriman closed the call. He said, 'That was my chis.'

'Saying what?'

'Saying that he wasn't saying anything over the phone. I'll go down to the hospital.'

'Okay,' Stella said, then, 'I see you talked to her.'

334

Harriman sighed heavily. 'It was just . . . you know – a little affair, fun for everyone, something and nothing.'

'It was something. I don't think it was nothing.'

Ronaldo was hooked up to three lines and looking less than happy. His skin had a yellowish tinge, except round the eyes, where it had the dark bloom of a bruise. There were no girls in fur coats, though the TV was turned to a race meeting and Ronaldo was getting his fun by posting phone bets with his bookie.

He pointed his mobile at the screen as a leggy bay cantered up to the start. 'Can't lose,' he said; 'want me to get something down for you?'

'You look like shit,' Harriman told him.

'They patch me up in ITU, send me down to a ward, I get some fucking virus. Hospitals are death traps. Final Word.'

'What?'

'Name of the horse, Final Word. I know the trainer. I also know it's going to win.'

'There's a fix on?'

Ronaldo laughed. He said, 'Trust me.'

'I'll have fifty quid,' Harriman said.

'It's ten to fucking one.'

'Just the fifty.'

Ronaldo shrugged, then speed-dialled his bookie and laid the bet, fifty for Harriman, a grand for himself. He said, 'There's a man they call the Trader. Real name Lexie Bramall.'

'His real name's Lexie?'

'That's all I've ever heard him called. He's got your bracelet, trying to lay it off.'

'Trying to?'

'The word is it's linked to a murder, so people are being just a tiny bit cautious – they're also being cheap, which is most of the problem.'

'It *is* linked to a murder. Tell me about the Trader.'

'You're wondering if he killed someone for the bracelet, is that it?'

'I'm wondering if he killed someone.'

Ronaldo shook his head. 'I very much doubt it. Anything's possible, but each to his own, you know? Trader's a middle man, that's his living. He doesn't get involved in the heavy stuff. He's a specialist: second-hand and used items. Contraband, Mr Harriman. He doesn't go after the goods, goods come to him.'

'Where will I find him?'

Ronaldo shrugged. 'I haven't got an address. Someone will know; I don't.'

'Where would *you* find him?'

'He does a bit of trading up on the Strip, sometimes.'

'Who with?'

'Whoever wants to buy. The Chinese like to show a bit of class. So do the Yardie boys, you know, get a Rolex or a gold chain, whatever. Nothing like this bracelet, though. He won't get rid of that in any shebeen.'

'How often is he up there?'

Ronaldo looked weary. 'I don't fucking know. It's Christmas, that'd be his busy time, don't you think? I expect he's all over the place.'

Harriman stayed to watch the race. Final Word was brought down by a loose horse at the fourth. Ronaldo closed his eyes and settled back into his pillows. He said, 'You're a jinx, Mr Harriman. You're bad news for me.'

Harriman took fifty pounds from his wallet and dropped

it on the bed. Ronaldo looked at it sourly. 'Jinx money from a jinx copper,' he said. 'You'd better keep it.'

'Okay.' Harriman scooped the money up. 'Keep smiling.'

69

Bloss wanted to give Kimber a sedative. He wanted to give him a Seroxat sandwich or a Prozac pie or maybe a baseball bat to the side of the head would do the job. Kimber was wired, he was running on high-octane fuel, walking the perimeter of his room, and talking. Talking, talking, talking.

Bloss had been trying to break into the flow. He'd said, 'Sure of course, me too –' and 'Listen, we'll do it, we'll definitely do it –' but it was like surfing against the wave and now he was just waiting for Kimber to wind down. He was dealing with a man who had needs, a man with a mission. The mission was to kill someone. It might be DS Mooney or it might be a girl called Jan, but whichever came first, Kimber told him, the other would follow. And then another, and then another.

As he walked the room, Kimber was smiling.

Over the season of peace on earth and goodwill towards men, shootings in London had been running at about three a day and pretty much all of them had involved handguns or small automatic weapons. Shotguns barely figured: they had been the weapon of choice once, but that time was long gone. You might use a shotgun for a punishment shooting, use it to tear someone up, fuck up their legs perhaps, but shotguns weren't cool.

With that number of shootings and that number of handguns, it was difficult to single out a make. The dudes that hung out – the dudes that liked to show class – they had their likes and dislikes. The dudes liked Walther PPKs, they liked Brococks for their cheapness and availability, they liked the weapons coming in from Romania and the Czech Republic, especially the Scorpion machine pistol, and the dudes liked Glocks too, Glocks were solid, but where they scored them and who from was another matter.

Marilyn Hayes found several standard references to *guns/ illegal import/models/country of origin*, but nothing that came with a crime number until she fed in the area reference NHG on the off-chance – *Notting Hill Gate* – and came up with an incident that had occurred almost on the doorstep.

It involved some dudes. Dudes in a BMW parked just off the Saints – Retro Man and his associates. The report told her that two men in the Beamer had died at the scene and a third had been declared dead on arrival at hospital. It told her that the killer had taken a bullet in the side and had spilled his gun before running from the scene. Well, not running: hobbling. Glock Man. He'd left a trail of blood for more than half a mile, twice tried to hail cabs, jumped a bus to the horror of its passengers, and finally had run into a pharmacy off the Portobello Road and started sweeping up sterile dressings from the counter before passing out. Officers at the scene had found the weapon still underneath the car. It was listed as a Glock 21, .45.

Marilyn took the report to Stella. In doing so, she skirted round Harriman's desk, even though Harriman wasn't there. She had paper-clipped a charge-sheet to the report, together with a note to say that Glock Man, whose name was given as Eric Keith Fellows, was on remand awaiting trial.

Harriman called in from his mobile five minutes later. He said, 'Lexie Bramall. People call him the Trader. He's trying to raise money on the bracelet.'

'Is he Mister Mystery?'

'I doubt it. But he's trying to find a buyer, so he knows the guy.'

'Probably,' Stella said. 'Unless it came to him at several removes. Let's hope not. Okay, find him.'

'Easy to say.'

'He'll have convictions, he'll have a record, ask Marilyn, she's records and reports.'

Harriman hung up. Stella redialled and jumped through the hoops necessary to gain an interview with Eric Keith Fellows.

Dark came in early, though it was city-dark, first gunmetal cloud with a bilious, yellow tinge to its edges, then a deeper dusk and a sky slick with sodium, with neon, with halogen.

Stella sat in a prison interview room and made certain offers to Eric Keith Fellows. Since he'd killed three men in broad daylight there wasn't a hell of a lot of leeway, but, given that the men in question had extensive records of violence and intimidation, she was able to raise the notion of 'retaliation' or 'response to threats'. What Stella wanted in return, she told him, was the name of the armourer who had supplied the Glock 21. Fellows listened carefully to what Stella had to say, then he told her to fuck off. He told her no deal. He told her that just talking to her was bad enough and that he had no desire to die.

Later that night, Harriman took Frank Silano on a tour of the Strip. Although it was early, they looked in on some casinos and some drinking clubs and they talked to a few people, though the people in question weren't eager to talk back. No one had heard of the Trader. Harriman had spent a few uncomfortable moments with Marilyn Hayes, who had supplied an address that didn't exist and a mugshot that was six years out of date. They showed the mugshot. No one had seen anyone like that.

Robert Adrian Kimber had the wide-eyed look of a man who hadn't slept for days, who might never sleep again. Since Bloss had left, he'd been drinking, but the booze didn't seem to make him sluggish or to muddy his thinking. It fuelled him. It made his blood sing.

He pulled on his coat. He put the hammer in his pocket.

70

Maxine Hewitt had spent her day talking to informants and was pretty sick of the lowlife, but that didn't mean she was eager for some highlife. She wanted a bath, a DVD and a curry. Jan took two glasses of red wine into the bathroom, where Maxine was showing not much more than a nose and a knee above water-level. When she saw the wine, she sat up. She put out a soapy arm and took her glass.

'Something simple-minded,' Maxine said. 'Not a cop movie.'

They talked about the day they'd had and drank their wine. Jan said, 'I could get into that bath with you,' but when Maxine smiled and drew her knees up to make room, Jan just kissed her and left, returning a moment later with the bottle. 'Back soon.'

'Simple-minded,' Maxine said, 'but not soft.'

'Funny?'

'Not sure about that.'

Jan laughed. 'I'll call you from the video store.'

'No,' Maxine settled deeper into the bath. 'I trust you.'

The café opposite Maxine's flat was closed. Kimber was watching from the far side of the street, where there were parked vehicles and a row of plane trees. He hadn't been early enough to pick her up at her office, but he'd waited by the tube and followed her home. The blind was up and he was able to catch sight of her from time to time; in fact he'd seen both of them, but it was Jan he focused on, Jan who starred in his little part-written story. The story with no happy ending.

The street was lit but dimly. The few people who passed on foot walked fast, heads lowered, hands in pockets. Kimber didn't know what would happen next, but he hoped to get lucky and he wasn't cold, not at all cold, waiting out there in sub-zero temperatures. He was warm, his cheeks flushed like those of a man with a fever. He thought he'd give it an hour. Maybe the other one would go out and he could find a way of getting into the flat. Ring all the bells, wasn't that what you did? Say you had a delivery for someone . . . And then you had to be quick, you had to be ready. He took the hammer out of his pocket and looked around. There was no one on the street. He used the hammer on the bole of a plane tree. It made a sharp sound, with a plangent undertone: a little, ringing echo. Instead of putting it back into his pocket, he threaded the shaft under his belt and let it hang from the head. It felt good. He liked the way it knocked his thigh.

As if the thought had its logical extension in Jan, Kimber looked up and saw her pass the window wearing her hat and coat. He stepped back into the deeper shadow close by the tree. There were three side streets between Maxine's flat and Ladbroke Grove. When Jan emerged, he waited until she had rounded the corner into the second street before he started after her.

Sadie was wearing seven layers, the outer of which was her bag wrapped round like a cape. She and Jamie had spent the day playing north side/south side with the tube security men. It was warmer down there, and the crowds were funnelled through the exits and entrances, which made them easier to beg from, but you got moved on. The trick was to leave by the south-side stairs and come back down the north side, then wait for some bored security man with a grudge against the free-living to kick you back up to the street.

Sadie had left Jamie for a couple of hours while she panhandled the trains themselves. This involved buying a ticket, which Sadie liked to think of as an investment programme, part of a business plan. There were tourists on the trains and they either looked at Sadie as if to suggest that, in their country, she would have been treated to a lethal injection, or they shelled out.

There had been some shelling out and Sadie had taken her share to a good connection off the Grove, where she had bought some crack. Sadie hadn't used crack a lot, but she thought it was a fuck of a rush and that was just what she needed.

Her crack pipe was a Fanta can and her refuge was the dark sub-street area of a basement flat on Bassett Road. She pushed open the letter box and listened for a TV or music or conversation, but the place was silent; she could see down the depth of the flat and there was no chink of light from the hallway doors. Maybe the occupants were away for Christmas. Maybe they were skiing the black runs at Cœur Cheval. Sadie settled into the shadow at the corner of the basement. She was doing a black run of her own, fast and very high.

Jan chose a ghost story and an urban comedy, then went to a wine shop and bought a very superior bottle of Bordeaux. There was no big occasion apart from the fact that this was her first Christmas with Maxine Hewitt and she felt lucky in that. They were good together. She wasn't sure whether Maxine was in love with her – not give-your-life-move-mountains love – but there was definitely something good going on and they were great in bed and she had started out taking it day by day, but now she was taking it week by week.

There was a sliver of moon low in the sky, seeming to stand just above the multicoloured shop signs, and the lights on each side of it were planes banking west for Heathrow. Their jet engines melded into the traffic blast and the thrash metal from alcopop bars and the All Nite's mushy muzak.

Jan loved the city noise, the round-the-clock stuff. She felt part of it.

Kimber had been a browser in the video store, a connoisseur in the wine shop. He had stood next to her as she read the blurb on the case of the ghost story; he'd watched with interest as she chose the Bordeaux. Now he was tracking her as she walked back towards the flat. The Grove was a conduit of noise and light, but the side street was empty apart from a couple walking swiftly away and rounding the far corner.

Jan thought, *Maybe I can start to think month by month; why not?*

She pictured Maxine in the bath, the way the soap bubbles had slipped along her arm to her breast as she'd reached for her drink.

She was halfway down the street, walking in tree-shadow.

Kimber reached under his coat and slipped the hammer from his belt: a cross-draw, left to right. He needed five long steps to reach Jan, maybe six; to be a pace back from her, the right distance to allow for the swing. He took two big strides, raising his hand.

Sadie came out of the basement, turning towards the Grove, and walked into him. She took a step back but somehow kept her balance, swaying slightly. Kimber said, *'Ah!'* and stumbled sideways, his foot turning on to the ankle. He hopped and reached with a hand to save himself;

the hammer clattered to the pavement and he sat down, groping for it, looking up at Sadie, his face turned to the glow from the streetlight. He picked up the hammer and got to his feet, leaning back against a tree. Sadie walked closer and peered at him, puzzled, trying to work out what had just happened. She said something, but neither was sure what it was.

Kimber laid a hand on her shoulder. Sadie watched the hammer go up in a bright arc. A street-level door opened in the house above the basement, there were voices, people walked down five steps to the pavement and stood a few yards away from Kimber and Sadie. You might have mistaken them for one group, some looking back to the house to say their goodbyes, while one couple stood a little apart, his hand on her shoulder, her face turned to his, as if continuing a conversation they had started earlier.

Kimber walked away, slotting the hammer back into his belt, moving with a light, limping tread on his twisted foot. He went past Jan's flat but didn't stop. He walked up to the crossroads, past his own room and took a loop to come down through the Strip from Kensal Rise. It was a good place to get lost. There was a walk-up shebeen with a night-long poker game in the back room. Kimber went in and sat in a corner with a drink, letting the migraine-music batter him.

She saw me.

He stayed there for an hour, then started down towards his room half a mile away. Nancy was cruising the cruising cars as Kimber came towards her, his body swaying slightly as he favoured the injured foot. She stopped and watched. He looked the way he looked in the police photo; he looked the way he'd looked on those occasions when he'd been a full-sex-no-rubber trick. Just for a moment, the pink and lime-green neon on the Starlite Massage Parlour seemed to spell out five-k in big, bright figures. She thought maybe she'd follow him, find out where he lived, call the cops, hold out her hand for the money.

But not if she wanted to keep her looks. Not if she wanted to see Ronaldo's smile.

Kimber was a few feet away, his head down, talking to himself. A car pulled up and Nancy leaned in, unbuttoning her coat to offer up the merchandise. She gave the price for a blow-job and the punter said that would be fine. She got into the back seat among a litter of CDs and Coke cans and winter-break brochures.

She saw me.

He crossed the street and walked the few steps to the side gate of the church. He was taking the same path but going in the wrong direction, telling the story backwards.

Here's where he and Bloss had left the churchyard, here's where he had rested a moment, his face close to hers, and noticed her mouth in that sloppy 'O' shape, here's the tree where they'd propped her and here's where Bloss had dragged her off the path.

Here's where he'd struck her, once at first, then hard and again and again, feeling light and powerful and good.

Kimber stood on the path with the soft lights from the church window cast around him. Then he backtracked to the tree in the corner of the churchyard, beyond the gravestones, and sat down with his head resting against the trunk.

She saw me. I'll have to find her.

He imagined Jan drinking her wine and watching her DVD and not knowing. Not knowing how close. He felt sick. He felt profoundly unhappy.

71

Stella and Harriman were sitting in traffic on Shepherd's Bush Green. Either the Cancer Santa had moved down from McDonald's-at-the-Gate to Flame Burger-on-the-Green or there was a crew of Cancer Santas working the west London punters.

Harriman said, 'I'm at a bit of a loss.'

'Sometimes,' Stella advised him, 'it's a good idea to look for the signs.'

'What signs?'

'If you don't know, I can't tell you.'

Harriman was driving and eyeballing the tailback like a man looking down the barrel of a gun. 'I thought she just wanted some time off. You know, change of scene.'

'And what she really wanted was a life-change.'

There was a gap in the contraflow; he pulled out and gunned the car fifty yards down the wrong side of the road, then went for a gap between a builder's truck and a family Ford. The builder's truck weaved out towards him in a tight little fuck-you curve and both vehicles stopped. There were three guys in the truck. They had big hands and small eyes. Harriman put an arm out of the window; he was holding his police ID.

He said, 'Back up or spend the day in a cell.'

They cruised along the Goldhawk Road towards the mews where Mickey Wicks had his lock-up workshop. He said, 'I didn't see any fucking signs.'

Stella thought back to George and the day he left. She said, 'I can understand that.'

The patio heaters were arranged in a triangle and throwing a big blue and orange glow. Mickey was rewiring the dashboard of a top-of-the-range Lexus, looking confident amid the cords and cables. His confidence dropped when Stella told him what she wanted. He said, 'We had an arrangement, Mrs Mooney.'

'You're right, we did. But this is out of the ordinary, you can see that.'

'I can give you hints, but I can't give you names, *you* can see *that.*'

'Hints won't do it. I need solid information, Mickey. I need names, addresses, phone numbers and the wife's maiden name.'

'I don't know anyone called the Trader.'

'Yes, you do,' Harriman said.

Mickey looked at him. He said, 'I heard about your accident.' He didn't laugh, but there was laughter in his voice. Stella hadn't seen that before: Mickey the humorist. It gave her pause for thought. Harriman looked away and the muscles jumped in his cheek.

'Lexie Bramall,' Stella said.

'No.' Mickey shook his head.

'Lexie Bramall also known as the Trader, big guy, dark complexion, shifts stolen goods, a percentage-man, a dealmaker, a broker.'

'I can't help you.'

Stella guessed that the Trader had big-money connections and some risks are just risks and others are a way of getting nailed to a door. She said, 'Okay, forget him. Someone imported a batch of handguns recently, one of which was used in a turf-war shooting up in the Gate. Three men died, the shooter's in the Scrubs, his name is Eric Keith Fellows.'

Mickey was sitting in the passenger seat of the Lexus like someone expecting to be driven somewhere. Hoping to be driven somewhere. He said, 'Go on.'

'Who's the armourer?'

'Would I know that?'

Harriman went out of the lock-up, got into his car, sat with the door open and his feet on the cobbles of the mews and made a call to the AMIP-5 squad room. He asked for stolen-vehicle information updates and gave his current location, speaking as if to the deaf.

Mickey said, 'Make him stop.'

'I can't,' Stella told him. 'But you can.'

Harriman was giving top-decibel details of the Lexus and a good number of details concerning Mickey Wicks. The term 'friend of the family' was used.

Mickey said, 'I'll make you a deal.'

'Maybe.'

'The deal is you don't come back here. You don't talk to me again. Our deal is over, that's the deal.'

Stella said, 'Okay.'

Mickey said, 'There's a guy called Slipper Wilkie runs an office out of the Wheatsheaf two days a week, I don't know which days, he's the gun-man, he's low profile but he's high usage, everyone from Harefield to Stonebridge, even the Yardies use him, only does quality gear, rent or buy. I don't know about Glocks or any other fucking make or brand but if it came into west London he's probably your man, and a merry fucking Christmas to you.'

He ducked his head, slightly breathless, refusing to meet

her gaze. Harriman was silent, looking back into the lock-up with a half-smile creasing his eyes.

'The Wheatsheaf's no good to me. I can't lift him from there – I might as well post fliers. What I need is a few hours alone with him before anyone knows he's gone.'

Mickey passed a hand over his eyes. He said, 'You don't care whether I live or die, do you?' Stella waited. 'He works out of Harefield.'

'The armoury's on the estate?'

'That's what they say.'

'Ever done business with him?'

'Are you kidding?' But he turned his head fractionally as he spoke.

'I could make a call, Mickey, and sit here with you until a search team arrives, and if they found an illegal weapon in here I'd have to arrest you. Then we could start working back through the stolen-vehicle register for the last five years and choose a few at random. We'd probably be right half the time.'

Mickey was silent for a long time. He was making a calculation, a careful assessment of the odds. He said, 'Is there some way you can cover me?'

'We've been talking to a lot of people. Every officer on the squad talking to every informant they have. This seems to be generally known because it's how DC Harriman got that face. In theory, we could have got this information from any one of ten or fifteen people.'

Mickey shook his head. At fifteen to one, the odds weren't nearly long enough. Even so, he named a block on Harefield and gave a number. He said, 'Now fuck off, would you?'

Stella said, 'It's a deal, Mickey. I won't be back.'

'Good.' Then he added, 'You're a bastard, Mrs Mooney.'

She thought he was probably useless to her now anyway.

72

She saw me. Shes a street person a dirty girl she
sleeps out so Ill just keep looking till I find
her. Its not right. Its not the way to do things.
Jan or Stella not this person I dont know. I would
never have followed her or clipped her shes a down
and out shes no one. I dont know if Jan looked
back. The dirty girl knocked into me and I said
something and she said something and I dont know
if Jan heard and turned round perhaps she did and
then she might have seen me. I have to hurry to get
her out of the way. The dirty girl has to go before
anything else can happen. I dreamed of Kate last
night. Kate Reilly. What happened was I went to
the churchyard after that stupid street person
bitch fucked things up and I went to sleep there
leaning up against the tree and I dreamed it all
again right from the moment I first saw her. It
happened in bits — the dream it was like scenes
from a film. Seeing her in her long coat with her
red hair and then following her past the church
and taking a clipping. Then going after her in the
churchyard and hitting her. And I was looking at
this from somewhere else but I was doing it too
like there was me watching and me doing it and it
could have been a film but I could smell things. I
could smell her hair it was flowers with a tang.

He walked through the alley by the Ocean Diner, but the only person there was a skinny man in a quilted coat talking about Jesus.

He went into the underground at Notting Hill and Queensway and Holland Park and Lancaster Gate. He spent some time in the subway passages beneath Shepherd's Bush roundabout.

He crashed a few squats and looked at the vacant faces in vacant rooms, the groups round jury-rigged stoves in littered kitchens, the bodies sharing a mattress. It didn't occur to him to wonder what he would have done if he'd found her in such a place. He just wanted to find her, kill her, get back to normal.

He tried the cashpoints and the burger bars. He elbowed through the crowded streets, looking left and right into doorways. He tried the parks and the patches of green with their dog shit and cans and condoms.

He even went down to the Harefield DMZ, though he knew it was dangerous territory. He looked among the rusty white goods and the junked sofas, the burned-out cars and the rubble of ex-rental TVs.

Sadie wasn't there. Beggars, buskers, panhandlers, junkies, drunks, some with a mouth organ or a guitar, some with a message written on a strip of cardboard, some with a doped dog, some deep inside their bags, some deep inside themselves, but no sign of Sadie.

She saw me.

And she had, of course, but it meant nothing. Sadie had been off her face. Out of her head. Away in space. Kimber couldn't have known it, but she wouldn't have recognized the Queen of England.

He walked back across the DMZ. He hadn't eaten, but he'd get a burger and eat on the move. He'd keep looking.

353

He knew it was just a matter of time. They had territories. Street-people kept to what they knew.

Stella and Harriman were driving down a Harefield approach road on the other side of the estate. Their car wasn't a Beamer, it wasn't a Merc, it wasn't an American classic and it wasn't a rust-holed Mondeo, so they were fairly easy to spot. Harriman was saying, 'Are you sure –?'

Sadie emerged from the walk-space under Block C and made for a subway that would take her under the traffic flow. She was in need. Crack was for her, no question, but she needed more of it more often. It was the answer. It was the ultimate 'okay'.

A London winter's afternoon, the light fading back to the horizon, darkness seeping in, snow flurries on the wind.

73

Harriman was saying, 'Are you sure you want to do it this way?'

Because lifting an armourer on Harefield would normally be a two-day op with an SO19 gun squad taking the lead. SO19 are the specialists, they're the technicians. They look at maps and plans, they send in a covert surveillance team, they run a trial op in similar terrain, they devise code designations for the north, south, east and west faces of the target building. Snipers occupy vantage points. Calculations are made about the number of occupants, their location, their routes in and out. No one would have wondered whether these occupants might be carrying weapons, given the fact that Slipper Wilkie was an armourer. The assumption would be 'yes' and 'many'. The standing orders for such an operation are 'extreme prejudice' and 'centre-target'. You didn't shoot to wound. An inspector or someone of greater rank oversees operations and procedures: everyone in Kevlar, everyone properly deployed. They probably wait for the early hours when they might expect people to be asleep or stoned. Then it's go.

That's the way it would normally be done. On this occasion, Stella and Pete Harriman were driving across the west perimeter of Harefield on their own in an alien car and with no visible back-up.

With no back-up, visible or otherwise.

'Wilkie doesn't know we want him,' Stella said. 'There's a police presence on Harefield most days. Kids dealing. Gang fights. We could be here for anything.'

'We could be here to get shot.'

'You know how tough it is to mount a raid on Harefield. Almost impossible to get close, also no chance of co-operation, so where's your stake-out, where do you situate your snipers, how do you carry out surveillance? Here's another problem – too many of the local cops earning some extra. Even with a complete information shut-down among the SO19 crew, the chance of a leak is high. Look at the history of drugs raids on this estate – by the time the action-men are abseiling down the blocks, the place is clean.'

Block D, Mickey Wicks had said. Stella parked in the bull ring so as to give no immediate indication of where they were going. When they entered Block D, they could have been taking the lift to any one of twenty-five floors and even then might have backtracked through the sky-high walkways that took you from landing to landing.

Of the four lifts, one was functioning; it even had an internal light. Stella and Harriman rode it to the ninth floor in a miasma of piss, puke and food gone bad. It moved slowly and it made noises like trains coupling.

Harriman said, 'Everyone has a gun, we allow for that. But this bastard's got a room full of them.'

'You think we should have made a weapons-application?' Stella was being wry: you have to paper those requests. Sorley would have wanted the whys and wherefores.

'Maybe we should have made a connection and bought a couple. Everyone else does.'

'I'd like to have a gun,' Stella said. 'And a couple of stun grenades. And a family-size can of CS gas.'

'We have each other,' Harriman observed.

Stella laughed. After a moment, she said, 'Element of surprise.'

Harriman sounded waspish. 'Good, yes; hadn't thought of that. Obviously, we've got the bastard cold.'

Which seemed to be more or less the case, because as they approached Slipper Wilkie's door it opened and a black girl in a white fun-fur came out, saw them and froze. Stella put her hand on the door, holding it open a fraction in case the locks engaged. Armourers have locks and they have hinge-bolts and they have steel-plating. Harriman put a finger to his lips. The girl held her hands out sideways to demonstrate innocence and spoke in a whisper.

'I ain't carrying.'

Harriman was whispering too. 'Slipper Wilkie.' She nodded. 'Where is he?'

'In the bedroom.'

'Is he alone?'

'He is now.'

'Mobile.'

'What?'

'Give me your mobile phone.' The girl didn't move. Harriman said, 'Unless you want to become his close friend and associate on the charge-sheet.'

The girl handed over her phone.

Harriman said, 'Goodbye.'

It was three deadlocks and a Banham; you could take the steel-plating as read. Stella closed the door gently. Harriman went into the bedroom ahead of her, his body tensed. There was a silence, then she heard him laugh, because Slipper Wilkie was lying on the bed bare-arsed, smoking a spliff.

Stella leaned against the door-jamb and smiled at Harriman. She said, 'You see?' He smiled back. They were both still smiling when Wilkie took a gun from underneath the pillow and pointed it lazily at Stella.

He said, 'You're fucking dead.'

Harriman was standing left of Stella but still close enough to be covered by Wilkie's field of fire. He said, 'Where the fuck do you think you're going with this?'

Wilkie laughed. 'Me? Let's talk about *your* next move.'

He sounded good, but he was making things up as he went along. The dope wasn't helping, his heart-rate was up and little paranoid thoughts came at him like moths at a lamp. He got off the bed, the joint dangling from his lips. He stood a moment, then crouched down and placed it carefully in an ashtray, as if he intended to come back to it later.

He said, 'Get down on the floor.' Stella and Harriman stayed upright. He said, 'Get down on the floor or I'll fucking shoot your knees off.' As they lowered themselves, he added, 'Sit on your hands.'

Wilkie's jeans were over a chair. He leaned against the side of the bed and got into them one-handed, standing up to zip. He pushed his feet into a pair of trainers, then backed up to a closet and took out a padded windcheater and put it on, switching from right hand to left with the gun. At that range, it made no difference; you didn't have to be steady or think about good aim.

Stella said, 'It might not be what you think.'

'Sure.' Wilkie wagged the gun, indicating that they should move away from the door.

'If we were busting you, we'd be a gun squad. We'd be mob-handed.'

'You're in my way.'

'What are you going to do? Go for a drink and pop back later in the hope that we'll have gone?'

'Shut up,' Wilkie advised her.

'Is this clever?'

Because he couldn't think of anything else to do, Wilkie stepped in and hit her with the gun, then stepped back. He'd been striking from above and had taken her across the scalp with the barrel-end and the metal had lifted a patch of skin. She could feel a dribble of blood starting up and rolling towards her left eye.

Harriman said nothing. He knew when to keep quiet. Stella moved aside and Wilkie opened the bedroom door but didn't go through. Now the moment had arrived, he had no idea what to do next. He'd shown them the gun, he'd hit the bitch, no way to backtrack from that.

Stella saw the indecision and knew what it meant. *He's deciding what to do. He's deciding whether to kill us. And it won't take much.* A blood-bead seeped out of her hair and ran down her cheek. *Do something. Do this . . .*

She stood up and backed off a little, at the same time moving round to confront Wilkie directly. She said, 'Here's what's going to happen now. I'm going to arrest you and take you to Notting Hill police station, where you'll be charged with assault and possession of an unlicensed firearm.'

Wilkie looked at her as if she couldn't be real – a little dope-dream, a spliff-spook. He glanced down at Harriman and his look seemed to say, 'Can't you tell her? Doesn't she know how to behave?'

Stella took a step nearer. She held out her hand for the gun. Wilkie stepped in too, bringing the gun up but not to surrender it. He extended his arm and the barrel met Stella's forehead, metal on bone, so that she stopped dead and stood still. Harriman watched but didn't speak, as if a word, any word, might tip the scales. The room rang with silence.

After a moment, Stella said, 'You can do this – you can

put the gun down and then I'll arrest you and certain things will happen. We can talk deals. You can listen to what I've got to say and you'll find out what I want. Or you can shoot me. In which case you'll have to shoot him. And then your life changes completely.' She said all this with her head tilted slightly backwards under pressure from the gun.

Wilkie didn't speak because he didn't know what to say. And when Stella lifted her hand very slowly and moved the gun from her head, but kept hold of it, tugging slightly, he didn't know what to do. Until he let go of the gun and he knew he'd done the wrong thing.

They walked out to the landing, Wilkie wearing plastic cuffs and a sorry expression. The lift was on their floor. Harriman thumbed the button and the doors shook, then opened with a clatter. Stella said, 'I don't think so,' and they took the stairs.

Wilkie said, 'I could have killed you.'

'That's right,' Stella said, 'you could have.'

'You talked about a deal.'

'We'll talk about it more later.'

As they crossed the lobby towards the bull ring, a great crash came from the lift shaft and the floor-indicator light went out. Wilkie laughed out loud. He said, 'How did you know?'

'I used to live here,' Stella told him. 'I used to breathe the same air as pissrags like you.'

74

'And the deal is what?'

In the interview room Wilkie looked oddly put together, with his jeans-but-no-underwear, his shoes-but-no-socks and his coat-but-no-shirt. The blond-streaked hair was perfectly in place and had the shellac glint of lacquer. Harriman had organized a little whip-round in the squad room and raised ten cigarettes. Wilkie was smoking them one after the other and the room carried scrolls and scarves of blue.

Stella indicated the tape. She said, 'Of course, anything you might do or say to help us in the course of our inquiries will be reported to the court and might possibly assist them in their consideration of any sentence.'

'What do you want to know?'

'A Glock forty-five calibre handgun was recently used in the commission of a murder. We want to know whether you supplied the weapon and who to.'

'You think I sell guns?'

'I know you sell guns. There's a search team in your apartment as we speak. They've found sixty weapons ranging from handguns to machine pistols and a large quantity of ammunition. You sell guns. Did you supply the Glock?'

'The flat isn't mine. I'm renting it.'

Stella said, 'DC Harriman is leaving the room. Interview temporarily halted at eighteen twenty-seven.'

She switched off the tape. Harriman hadn't moved. Wilkie said, 'What?'

'Let's not start off on some long and tedious journey,

because we're just going to end up back at the start. You sold a Glock recently. Who bought it?'

'I'm not the only armourer in London.' As he used the word 'armourer', Wilkie glanced at the tape.

'You're the only one sitting in a police interview room talking about a deal.'

'What's the time-scale?'

'Three days. Maybe four. Less than a week.'

Wilkie fell silent. He could have been deciding whether to come clean, or simply enjoying a little after-rush from the spliff. Stella was trying not to look as if his answer mattered much, but she knew it was crucial. Wilkie was right. Mister Mystery could have got the gun from a number of sources, though geographically Wilkie was most likely. But if Wilkie had sold a Glock forty-five within the last week, then the chances were strong that it was the murder weapon. There had been only two other shootings on Stella's patch in the last five days and they were black-on-black drug disputes, one involving a Mach 10, the other an Uzi machine pistol.

'Will I walk?' Wilkie wanted to know.

'You heard what I said for the tape.'

'Yeah, I heard. Will I walk?'

He was talking about police bail, about being back on the streets in time for a drink at the local. Stella said, 'It's not up to me.'

'So what kind of a fucking deal is it if nothing's up to you?'

'Give me ten minutes.'

'Okay,' Wilkie nodded and lit another cigarette. To Harriman, he said, 'I'm going to need some more of these.'

'I'm clearing this with you,' Stella told Sorley. 'The tape will be off, obviously, but it's possible that questions will be asked afterwards.'

Sorley spread his hands. 'So there might. Don't worry about it. Set the bail figure high.'

'It won't make any difference to him.'

'No, but it'll look good.' Sorley was drinking from a plastic cup. It could have been coffee, it could have been Scotch or medication. Maybe it was coffee with a slug of Scotch and a dash of medication. 'You went down there without any back-up and without asking me.'

'Officer acting on information.'

'Officer acting like a fucking idiot.'

'It wasn't a problem.' Sorley looked at her, cocking his head, and laughed. She said, 'If Wilkie comes good for me, we'll have a name and a face. In which case, I'll need more manpower.'

'It's okay.'

'And more money.'

'That's okay too. It's all okay.'

Stella looked at him, the cherry nose, the sunken eyes. She said, 'Are *you* okay?'

'Terrific. Benylin, ibuprofen, Strepsils, Scotch.'

'Cigarettes.'

'Cigarettes,' Sorley agreed. He smiled benignly. 'How many guns did they find in this bastard's flat?'

'Upwards of sixty.'

'Down on Harefield.'

'That's right.'

'It's a war zone. The United Nations should move in.'

Stella named a sum for police bail and Wilkie pretended to be outraged. He made a show of including the bail price in their deal and Stella just said, 'No,' and shrugged a lot until he'd finished busking.

The tape wasn't running, but he asked for it to be removed

from the cassette, then he said, 'A guy called Leon Bloss.'

Stella asked him to spell the name and, when he had, Harriman left the room. Stella asked for more and got the details of the meeting at the Wheatsheaf and details of the drop.

'Out of the way of CCTV,' Wilkie said. 'Holland Park.'

Stella felt a chill. 'Where in the park?'

'He waited on a bench up by the trees.'

I'll bet you did, Stella thought. *Happy memories. Valerie Blake jogging by, you moving out of cover . . . I'm getting close to you now. You don't know how close I am.*

'How do you know this guy?'

Wilkie shook his head. 'You meet people.'

'What does he do?'

'No idea.'

'You're lying, Wilkie.'

'Why should I know that stuff? He's around. I've met him. Do I want his life story?'

They'd done their deal, she had nothing left to offer and nothing with which to threaten, so she let it slide.

Harriman came back after twenty minutes and said, 'Nothing,' which meant that Leon Bloss hadn't shown in any computer trace.

Stella turned to Wilkie. 'Slipper, we're going to do some computer-imaging with your help. It had better look a lot like the man in question.'

'What's it to me?' Wilkie said. 'He's yours now.'

They took a break. Only Maxine Hewitt and Marilyn Hayes were in the squad room. Stella sat with Maxine while Marilyn called round to find someone to make the computer-image.

Maxine said, 'Do you think it's him?'

'He picked up the gun in Holland Park.'

'Open space, no –'

'CCTV, I know. It's the only sale Wilkie made last week. The only Glock.'

'It's not a cert.'

'It's a very good bet. We'll have him in.'

'Oh, sure.' A pause, then, 'Are you okay?'

'Fine. Why not?'

Maxine's laugh was an echo of Sorley's and she cocked her head in just the same way. Stella said, 'What?' Maxine reached into her bag and took out a make-up mirror. She held it up to Stella's face. The blood from her scalp had dried and begun to flake, three little rivulets gathering at the point of her jaw. She picked some off with her fingernail.

'I thought he was going to kill us,' she said, 'both of us. Just for a minute, I really thought that.'

It was Bloss. Stella couldn't have known, but it was him for sure, the strange, Oriental features, the thin line of the lips, dark hair balding from the forehead. She thought the eyes must be wrong, such a high, thin blue, but Wilkie shook his head. The eyes were what he remembered best. Stella recalled a saying about blue eyes, something straight from the old wives' handbook – you were looking at the sky through the skull.

The graphics artist printed off fifty copies and Stella posted several round the squad room on windows and doors. She left a copy on every desk. She asked Marilyn to liaise with DI Sorley about new personnel and to arrange for Bloss's likeness to be transmitted to police stations nationwide but with special emphasis on west London. Finally, she pinned the portrait up on the whiteboard, right in the centre, so that he was surrounded by the scene of crime photos of his victims, the bloody wreckage, the blank stares, the heavy-limbed dead.

So there you are. Mister Mystery. Whose blue-eyed boy were you?

Slipper Wilkie was getting restless. He'd been bitching at Harriman for half an hour. When Stella walked into the interview room, he looked relieved. 'I just need to make a couple of calls, raise the bail money, get out of here, okay?'

'Not really,' Stella said. 'No.'

Wilkie looked at her, slightly puzzled, a half-smile on his face, as if he hadn't quite understood. 'You said you'd talk to someone. Fix things . . .'

'I did – my boss. DI Sorley.'

'Good. So we're set.'

'DI Sorley wasn't able to agree to police bail, in part because you were found with sixty-three illegal firearms in your possession, and also because there's a strong reason to believe that a weapon sold on by you was used to murder a man named Oscar Gribbin, but mostly, DI Sorley tells me, because he expects that there would be a high risk of your absconding.'

There was a silence. Wilkie lowered his head. He was shaking like a man with a fever, and the muscles in his forearms were jumping. When he looked up, his eyes were showing the whites. He said, 'You're dead.'

'I found it hard to disagree with DI Sorley, but my reasons for refusing police bail are slightly different. They have more to do with being pistol-whipped and having a gun jammed against my head.'

Harriman was standing very close to Wilkie now. The man looked like someone on the verge of a seizure, breathing hard, the veins in his neck cording and pulsing.

'You're dead, bitch.'

'Also, you're an arsewipe, Wilkie – and there's the most convincing reason of all.'

'You are dead. You're a walking dead person. I guarantee it. You've got my promise. However long it takes, you cunt, you're mine, you're *meat*.'

'I've heard it before,' Stella said. 'I'm still here.'

She walked out of the interview room and along the corridor to the squad room and sat down at her desk and put her head in her hands.

She hadn't heard it before – not quite like that.

75

People went back to source. Officers went back to the pubs and the clubs, the minicab caves and the strip-o-ramas. Maxine Hewitt went back to Jumping Jacks. Louise said, 'I break at ten.'

They met at the bar, where CCTV picked up their images but not what they said. Louise sighed. 'The whole place is on-screen, didn't you know that?'

'So tell them I looked at your statement; there was something I needed to clear up.'

'I'm a good dealer. I've got good hands. I've been clean for a year and I don't give head in alleys any more. Don't fuck it up for me.'

'When does your shift end?'

'Tonight? One o'clock.'

'And you get home –'

'Twenty past. Half past, maybe.'

'Give me an address.'

'Jesus Christ, Mrs Hewitt.'

'But we could talk here if you prefer.'

Louise had given an address in north Fulham: a custom-built low-rise in a back street surrounded by offices and small workshops. Maxine was parked at the door when she arrived. They walked in together, but Louise disappeared without speaking. Maxine helped herself to a drink and waited for Louise to come back. When she did, she'd showered and changed out of her dealer's uniform. She topped up Maxine's glass and gave herself a drink and smiled. That was new. Maybe it meant, I'm on your side now. The smile faded fast when Maxine showed her the computer-image.

'You know him.'

'Yeah.' She sighed. 'Leon Bloss. This isn't going to be good.'

'Why not?'

'He used to work for Billy Souza.'

'Used to?'

'He was security. Like JD.'

'Have you seen him recently?'

'A couple of days ago.'

'A couple?'

'Four, five, a week, I'm not sure.'

'Can you peg it by what was happening that day?'

'All days are the same. I deal blackjack.'

'You saw him at the casino?'

'That's right.'

'Why was he there?'

'Christ, I don't know. Must've been to see Billy. He won some money, quite a lot of money, then JD picked him up at my table and took him upstairs.'

'You say he used to work for Billy. Why did he stop?'

'Well, first Billy took him off house security and upped him to minder.'

'His own minder – Billy's?'

'One of three. I don't know exactly what happened. I think some punter came up to Billy in the car park. You'd be surprised how many think the wheel's fixed or the cards are stacked. No need, of course. The only sure thing about gambling is that you can't win, not in the long run.' Louise shrugged. 'Things got difficult and Leon took the guy apart. Really hurt him. They put him in a car and dumped him outside A & E somewhere the other side of London. The next day, Leon didn't turn up for work. Billy had fired him.'

'Who told you this?'

'It went round the casino. Came from one of the other security guys, I expect.'

'The guy never made a complaint. The guy Bloss hurt?'

'He couldn't.'

'He died?' Maxine asked.

'Not as such. He's away with the fairies. You're going to talk to Billy about this.' Maxine nodded. Lousie wrapped her arms around herself as if she were cold. 'I thought it was too good to last.'

'While I was waiting for you,' Maxine told her, 'I visited every table in the place, spoke to every croupier. After you left the bar, several others took a break. I spoke to them too. Billy won't know where it came from.' Louise nodded, but it wasn't a nod of agreement or belief. 'Give me your number here, and your mobile. If I need to speak to you again, I won't come to Jumping Jacks.'

Louise wrote the numbers on a Post-it note. She said, 'He used to give me the shivers, Leon Bloss.'

'Why was that?'

'There was a story he did snuff.'

Maxine looked at her. 'Snuff . . . what? Videos?'

'No, no, not that . . . Contracts. Snuff.'

'He killed for money?'

'I heard it. I didn't say it was true.' She was silent a moment, as if thinking back, seeking clues. 'He would look at you and there was no one there. No one there behind the eyes.'

Maxine called Stella from her car. Stella was in bed but not asleep. She was listening to the radio and reading and drinking coffee and trying hard to be distracted from the insistent thought that Vigo Street was becoming a permanent address again.

She said, 'There are firms, we know that. There's a tariff. Rates for a broken leg, rates for a kneecapping.'

'Rates for a bullet in the back of the neck and another through the heart,' Maxine suggested.

'Exactly.'

'She didn't say that Bloss was a member of a firm.'

'Well . . . there are freelances too.' Stella turned the radio off. 'Leon Bloss is our man. The connections are too close to mean anything else.'

'Best if I didn't go back to Jumping Jacks. My source there is getting very edgy.'

'I think we'll see Billy Souza at home. He won't like that. But I'll take Harriman or Silano.'

Maxine pulled up outside her flat and looked up to the window. The light was on. When she got in, she found Jan asleep on the sofa and baseball on the TV. She knelt down and kissed her lover softly on the lips.

Without opening her eyes, Jan said, 'Where have you been?'

'Among the low-lifes and the high-rollers.'

'Did you win?'

'In a way.' Maxine got up and went towards the kitchen.

'Are you having a coffee?'

'Tea.'

'Me too.' When Maxine brought it to her, Jan said, 'There's something I've been meaning to say.'

'Okay.'

'I love you. You don't have to say it back.'

Maxine did say it back. She didn't quite mean it, but she said it anyway.

76

To most people, money simply means bank balance or pay packet or mortgage. It means credit card or cheque book or cold cash. To others, though, it's a concept. There's no question of having too much or too little; it's not that kind of commodity. It comes in planks and tranches. It comes in multiples. It lies offshore like a small, independent state or it takes flight, a jet-stream of blurred figures setting off for somewhere safer or more profitable.

It was the kind of money Billy Souza dealt in. It had given him an apartment in Putney Wharf and the consumer durables that went with it. It made him powerful and the power showed as arrogance. When Stella showed Leon Bloss's picture to Billy, she'd been expecting deadpan, but what she got was a broad smile.

'Leon Bloss,' Billy said. 'I'm not surprised.'

'Not surprised by what?'

'That you want him. He's trouble, that's why I let him go.'

'How long did he work for you?'

'About six months. House security at first, then personal protection. He was good, but he was heavy-handed.'

Stella had taken Pete Harriman with her; she'd decided that the scar worked to her advantage. Harriman had been looking down fifteen floors to the traffic backed up on Putney Bridge. Now he said, 'Nearly killed someone, we heard.'

'Not while he was working for me.'

'That's the story.'

'No. Wrong.'

Stella asked for background, but Billy didn't have anything to offer. She asked for history, but it seemed that Billy didn't feel the need to know where his staff came from or where they went after they'd left. He did, of course, have an address for Leon Bloss and he was happy to hand it over, though he suspected it might be a little out of date. Stella suspected the same.

She said, 'Here's the problem. When we last spoke, I was asking about a man called Oscar Gribbin. He was murdered.'

'I remember.'

'He gambled in your casino.'

'Many people do.'

'Now we're here again to ask about Leon Bloss. Know why?' Billy spread his hands and shrugged. 'We think Bloss killed Gribbin.'

Something happened then: Billy's gaze slid sideways before coming quickly back to meet Stella's; there was a fractional pause that he tried to fill with a cough. He said, 'I don't understand.'

'What I said?'

'What you mean.'

'It's an odd coincidence. A client murdered by an ex-employee.'

Billy paused, regaining his balance. 'I have a casino full of clients. And everyone is someone's ex-employee.'

Harriman asked, 'Do you see him?'

'No.'

'He gambles at your tables.'

'I'm not surprised. He knows his way around.'

'So you might have glimpsed him on CCTV.'

'I don't do that. People do that for me.'

Stella put a few copies of the computer-image down on

a vast, glass coffee-table. 'Give those to the people who watch the screens. If they see him, call us.' Stella thought it was a pointless request, but it would seem odd not to have made it. Souza smiled faintly and nodded, but let the pictures lie.

They joined the northbound on Putney Bridge. Harriman said, 'We should just lift him.'

'On what grounds?'

'He's a gun-importer. Gribbin was a carrier. Bloss used to be Souza's minder. Bloss killed Gribbin.'

'We think all that. We don't know for sure. And there's the Serious Crimes Squad to consider; they're still building a case. We're on a different track. We need Bloss for Valerie Blake and the rest. Serious Crimes need Souza out and about for a while. They have to find the money and that'll be off somewhere, a BVI account, several trips through the laundry. People like Billy Souza aren't easy to box up. They've got intelligence networks, they've got fallback positions, they have their places swept for bugs on a weekly basis.'

'For some you look in the court records,' Harriman suggested; 'for others you look in *Who's Who.*'

'Exactly.'

'What's BVI?'

'British Virgin Islands,' Stella told him. 'No place for you.'

Billy Souza drove along by the river without bothering too much where he was going. For a man who thought of money in block-units, Billy was carrying a large amount of change. In his business it was called shrapnel: the sort of stuff that punters collect from change-counters in polystyrene cups and carry from one fruit machine to the next.

It didn't matter to Billy where he drove because any pay-phone would do. The one he found was standard issue: whores' cards and a strong smell of piss. He made a long-distance call, got referred, made a second, listened to an answerphone message, made a third. He said, 'You know who this is?'

The man taking the call had a slight Slavic burr to his voice, but his English was near-perfect. All business transactions are negotiated in English, the international language of opportunism and deceit.

'I know who.'

'All shipments go on hold as of now.'

'I'm not sure we can do that.'

'It's not a request.'

'We're backed up here, you understand?'

'Your problem. Make a shipment and it'll be backed up here, because no one's going to be making any collections.'

'You have a difficulty.'

'It's just temporary.'

'I think I can find a buyer for your consignment.'

Billy thumbed shrapnel. He said, 'Give me a month.'

'A month is a long time. Markets are opening up everywhere.'

'Give me three weeks.'

A pause. Then, 'Okay. Three.'

'I'll call soon. Don't call me. Not the mobile, not the office.'

'Okay.'

The man on the other end of the phone had already made a mental note that involved notions such as chains of evidence and dominoes. He thought, *This guy's in trouble. This is no one to do business with.*

He said, 'No problem.' And because his English was so good, he added, 'Season's greetings.'

Billy used more shrapnel to call Leon Bloss. He said, 'Time for you to be gone.'

'There's a problem,' Bloss suggested.

'This DS Mooney . . . she's as close as dammit, close so it makes no difference.'

'Close –'

'They've got you down for Gribbin.'

'That's impossible.'

Billy had been holding it down for over an hour. Now it hit the surface, rising. 'No, it's not fucking impossible, because I heard the bitch say it to me. Don't say impossible, you moron, they want you for it. They showed me a fucking picture of you, like a photofit. They'll have it in the press, they'll have it on TV: you'll be headlines, you'll be on every screen in the fucking country. Someone's given you up, my friend, and she's going to nail you, this Mooney. She's on your fucking trail. So listen – it's time for you to leave. I don't want you around. Take a break. Go a long way off.'

'That's the plan. That's what I intend to do.'

'Do it now.'

'I haven't had my money.'

'JD will bring it over. Don't come near me. Don't come anywhere near. You're the plague to me; you're the Black fucking Death.'

Bloss hung up. He walked to the tall windows that looked out to the river and watched snow flurries drifting above the surface of the water. He made a phone call and booked a plane ticket in the name of James Hill, which was the name on the passport he had bought in Chinatown a couple of days earlier. He thought he needed two days. Two days to set things up and then to get clear.

His flight was for four thirty on the afternoon of Christmas Eve.

77

Maybe she'd moved on. Maybe she'd decided that the wage-earners and home-owners of Notting Hill had given all they were going to give. Maybe the weather had finally pierced to the bone and she'd looked for a refuge, some warm place where you could get food and methadone and make good connections for later.

Kimber had been out since early morning. He'd seen a lot of street-people but not Sadie. He'd seen the skinny guy who talked to himself but not Sadie. He felt miserable and slightly unwell, as if he'd eaten something bad. He thought about Jan and the moment in the street when he'd quickened his pace, feeling the shaft of the hammer knocking his thigh. He thought about Stella, the yard with the wheelie-bin for cover, the shapes on the shade. He was out of touch, that was the problem. He was losing contact.

A girl with a dog, a girl with piercings, a man with a card-board sign, a man with a mouth organ, a girl sleeping against a shopfront, a man playing a plastic traffic cone as if it were a didgeridoo. But not Sadie.

Jamie sat where he and Sadie usually sat, his hand out, talking to himself. He wasn't the kind of beggar people liked: he was pitiable but in a remote, unconnected sort of way. This meant not many people gave, so Jamie hadn't eaten much for a few days. He felt light-headed and the chill went deep, but he was content. Except he missed Sadie. She had slept alongside him near the grille in the Ocean Diner alley and then left early. She was unhappy, Jamie thought.

She was out of sorts, a bit distant, but everything would come right soon, when Jesus turned up, when the Saviour appeared.

Just a few days.

Nick Robson was a good exhibitions officer, but he wasn't a street cop. He read the reports and he kept a tidy room. Every item that had a bearing on the case, the contents of victims' pockets, objects found at the scene, whatever was handed on from the morgue or Forensics, anything that might appear as evidence in court – it was bagged and labelled and shelved.

Sue Chapman would have been the officer who kept a record of all this on computer and ran checks from time to time. Except Sue was in recovery, Marilyn Hayes was her stand-in, and, of course, Marilyn was also in recovery thanks to Pete Harriman's emotional miscalculation. Which is why Marilyn had missed what Nick Robson had just picked up.

Stella looked at the evidence bag Robson had placed on her desk, along with two reports. The highlighted passages made their point clearly. She said, 'When did you notice this?'

Nick leaned down and pointed at the time-code on the report. 'Today.'

'I should have seen it,' Stella said. 'We all should have seen it.'

In the bag was an item taken from Oscar Gribbin's pocket at the scene of crime: a gaming chip from the Jumping Jacks casino. The first report noted it. The second report was the incident-tree that Gerry Harris at Notting Hill Gate nick had emailed to her. It included a list of items logged by the station officer as having been in Sadie's possession at the time of her arrest:

Penny whistle
Twelve pounds, seventy pence in cash
Book: *Sophie's World*
Sleeping-bag
Key ring, two keys, tag from Jumping Jacks casino

Maxine's chis, Louise, showed all the signs of someone who'd had a bad night. The biggest clue was the one-tab overdose of ibuprofen and coffee so strong it made your pupils dilate. Stella set her cup down and said Lauren Buchanan's name as if it were a question.

Louise nodded. 'She worked at Jumping Jacks . . . I don't know . . . a year? Bit less?'

'Tell me about her,' Stella said.

Louise looked at Maxine, who said, 'Sorry. We have to know this stuff.'

'She was a croupier, mostly roulette. She had a bit of a thing for Billy at one time. They had an affair. It didn't last long. She was a problem to him.'

Stella let Maxine take over. There's a rhythm to handling a chis: you learn when to push, when to wait. Maxine said, 'How big a problem?'

'Wouldn't let go. But it was a bit more than that. She started following him around, sending texts and emails, hounding him, you know.'

Maxine waited for the rest. Louise poured herself some more coffee; Stella thought her heartbeat must sound like a road-drill.

'Billy warned her off. It didn't work. So he threatened to have her killed.'

'How do you know?'

'She told me. They took her somewhere, out of London, you know, the country somewhere, and they put a gun in her mouth and told her to stop.'

'Billy did this?'

'No, not Billy. Of course not Billy. Leon Bloss.'

Maxine nodded, as if to say, 'Go on,' but Louise fell silent for a while and Maxine let it ride. With her face naked of make-up and her hair down, Louise looked younger and not nearly so tough. Stella noticed the touches in the flat that gave the girl away: a framed photo of an old couple who must have been Louise's parents, some silk flowers, some retro CDs.

'It was odd, but she stayed on at the casino for a couple of months after that. I expected her to leave. Then she started having an affair with a punter –'

'Which is when she left?'

'Soon after.'

'What was his name?'

'I don't know. He wasn't much. I mean, he wasn't really a gambler. Came in with a few guys after a party, I think. Then one or two evenings after that, but again with friends. Lauren made it clear she was interested, and he started coming in on his own, but mostly to see her. He didn't like to lose, and you can't gamble if you feel like that.'

'Was it serious between them?'

'Serious for her, but then it always was: like with Billy.'

'But not for him –'

'He was up for it, you could see that. But I think it was all about sex. A lot of the punters think that. You're a casino girl, you must be a red-hot fuck.'

'What was his name?' Stella asked.

'I don't know. I mean, I never heard it, not his last name.'

'But his first name?'

'Duncan.'

78

Kimber searched through the day and into the night. He'd been further afield – up to Kilburn, down to Kensington, out to Marble Arch. He'd gone into Soho but without any expectations. Soho had its own brands of beggar: either cool and disengaged or matted and mad.

She saw me. She saw me.

He'd walked the length of Ladbroke Grove five times and seen the same sad sacks each time. He'd walked down Bassett Road, getting close, getting too close, to Jan's flat, but the basement areas were empty, save for the usual detritus of cans and bottles and newspapers. He knew about the Ocean Diner and the handouts from the sous-chef because he'd seen it happen, so he'd visited the alley from time to time but found only the kitchen staff shivering and smoking

It was movie and pub time, unless you were late-night shopping. In the Shepherd's Bush subway a man was playing the fiddle, very slowly; outside 'Snow's on the Green', another was selling last month's *Big Issue*. Every twenty feet someone said, 'Spare some cash, please, any spare change, please . . .' Kimber returned to home ground. He went into McDonald's, bought whatever came first on the menu and sat by the window to eat it. When he bent his knees to sit down, the shaft of the hammer rode on his thigh.

Sadie wasn't John Delaney's only street contact, but she was the best. For one thing she liked to talk and, when she did, the stories were lucid and usable. Delaney suspected that not all of them were true, but she knew how to earn the twenty he had waiting for her. She had been his chosen companion on the night he'd slept out: Sadie and the loopy Jesus Man. Now Delaney had a deadline and there were still a few gaps in his account of street-people at Christmas, but he hadn't been able to find Sadie, not last night, not tonight.

Kimber's and Delaney's paths had crossed a few times during the course of the day. Now they were pretty much looking at each other but seeing only Sadie's absence. Delaney was opposite McDonald's, in a pub with a view of the street. It was close to where Sadie and Jamie most often sat. He knew that Sadie might be making a connection, but he thought he would try this patch of pavement for a while, then move on to the alley by the Ocean Diner.

As Delaney bought his second beer, Kimber finished his burger and went back on to the street. The wind had risen a little, and the cold seemed to get behind his eyes. Slow snowflakes settled in his hair.

It was another two hours before he found her. She was in the Ocean Diner alley and she was alone and she was dead.

He stood by her, holding the hammer, not knowing what to think. Her eyes were wide open and a line of puke ran across her chin. He checked her pulse, but it wasn't necessary because she was stiff, her arms and legs rigid, her neck locked. She had looked like someone asleep, though she was lying on top of her bag rather than inside it. The light in the alley wasn't good, but Kimber could see it was her: the pink and green streaks in her hair, the nose ring, the lip-spike. The swallow on her neck, when he rolled her sideways, was rigid in flight.

He had come to kill her and she was dead and he just stood there, the hammer in his hand, wondering what next. He raised the hammer to strike her but saw the pointlessness of that. He kicked her hard in the ribs, as if he found some sort of strange consolation in that for the time wasted, for being sidetracked, for the moment when Sadie had come between him and Jan. Then he left her.

A woman called the cops when she heard the noise – when she heard the noise and saw the madman in the alley. Her husband was all for doing things the London way: don't listen, don't look, keep walking. But she stood at the entrance to the alley and heard the wailing and saw the crazy man dancing around what seemed to be a body. Dancing and wailing and beating the wall with his hands. She thought she might have just witnessed a murder.

The cops didn't think that. They thought the obvious: that Sadie had OD'd, and they were right. They called an ambulance for Sadie, because that was procedure, and they called an ambulance for Jamie because that was necessary. His head was bleeding where he had rammed it against the alley wall and his knuckles were bleeding from the punches he had thrown at the brickwork. To prevent him hurting himself any more, the cops held him down while he howled like a dog.

No one held Sadie, but then, in her life, very few people had.

Delaney heard the noise and saw the ambulance lights. A crowd had assembled as crowds will at such times and a long tailback formed as cars edged round the ambulances, drivers and passengers rubbernecking for a glimpse of the action. He watched as the paramedics loaded Sadie into an ambulance. She was shrouded in a red blanket, but Delaney knew who it was because Jamie was there, shrieking and baying and slapping himself in the face.

'Where are they taking her?' Delaney was talking to one of the cops.

'Do you know her?'

'Sort of. I know her name.'

The cop took a few details, realized that Delaney had little to offer, then said, 'Saint Mary's.' Delaney wasn't intending to go there; he needed the name of the hospital for his feature. The cop said, 'Do you know her friend?'

Delaney shook his head. 'I've seen them together, that's all. Will you be following this up – trying to contact her people and so forth?'

The cop nodded. 'I expect so.'

Delaney handed the man his card. He said, 'Maybe you could update me.'

'Sure. Why not?'

The ambulance doors closed on Sadie, and they closed on Jamie. The watchers shuffled off to go about their business, the tailback thinned, the late-nighters continued to shop and drink and dine.

Robert Adrian Kimber went back to his room by the Strip. He was feeling a little better, a little more himself.

Stella had a key to Delaney's flat, but he had never been to Vigo Street before: he just knew the address. He parked up with the engine running and waited until she got home. It was late and she was carrying a pizza box, holding it two-handed because there was a rising wind. He saw her go into the flat, but didn't follow her at once; instead, he stood in the street and watched as a light came on in the living area. She threw her coat on to the sofa, poured a drink, unpacked the pizza. He thought that seeing her off guard might give him a clue to the way she was feeling, but, as he looked down at the room and Stella in it, he knew that the feelings under consideration were not hers but his. He knew he loved her, but wasn't sure how much or how unselfishly.

It was very cold and the street was empty. Stella took some papers from her bag and spread them on the worktop, perching on a stool and reading them while she ate. At one moment, a sheet slipped to the floor and she leaned down to get it, her sweater riding up to show an inch or two of flesh at the waist, and he realized it was erotic, this watching. It had to do with her unguardedness, the possibility of what she might do next.

She finished the pizza and threw the box into the garbage. She shuffled the papers into a pile and took them with her to the sofa, where she started to make notes on the uppermost page. Engrossed in her work, she looked capable and occupied. She looked like someone who lived alone.

There was a delay before the door opened. A circle of raw wood surrounded a recently installed spyhole, so Delaney guessed the delay had less to do with caution than that it was his face on the other side of the glass. She opened the door and drew him in and kissed him.

They made love in the bed Stella had once shared with George and that didn't matter a bit; she just wanted him nearer and deeper. There was a lamp that shed a low light, making their bodies seem warm and dusky. They didn't speak when they made love and they didn't speak for a while afterwards. Delaney got up and went to the kitchen, where he opened cupboards and drawers until he found what he needed for coffee. Before he went back to the bedroom, he lowered the blinds.

He told Stella about Sadie and she asked, 'What happened to her?'

'Overdose by the look of things. That's what the cops thought. Her friend was there: guy who hung out with her. He was going nuts.'

Stella nodded. She didn't want the coffee because she was slightly drunk and feeling loose-limbed and hazy after their love-making. Her eyes closed a moment.

He said, 'I feel bad about it.'

'Why? What's it got to do with you?'

'As if I'd been looking for the prime-time payoff.'

'What?'

'My piece. The article I'm writing. What could be better than to end with a death? The perfect Christmas package.'

'They take those risks,' Stella told him. 'They live that life.'

She closed her eyes and slept. Delaney lay awake; he went into the next room and found the pages she'd been reading while he'd watched from the street. For just that reason, they seemed to carry a little erotic charge. He sat down with them and his coffee. After half an hour, he went into the bedroom and woke Stella up.

'This woman, Lauren Buchanan.'

She laughed. 'You don't know when to stop, do you? Those are confidential police reports.'

'Lauren Buchanan –'

'Go on.'

'It was Sadie who saw her getting mugged. Sadie who stole her credit card.'

Stella sat up. 'Of course . . .' Stella hadn't put Delaney's street-person together with the girl who'd taken the casino-chip key ring. 'It was, yes.'

'I saw Sadie just after she was released. The cops never

charged her. She told me about it: about the mugging. She said that the woman just stood there; she seemed almost cooperative.'

'Shock,' Stella said, 'or maybe she'd heard of non-resistance, the best way to avoid getting stabbed. You lose your wallet and your watch, you keep your life.'

'And then, when they started to leave, she called to them. One of them came back and hit her: really beat her.'

'She thinks they're going, she calls them bastards, they find the time to show her just what bastards they really are.'

'Sadie didn't think it was like that. She didn't say the woman yelled at them or called them a name; she said: "She called to them."' He shuffled through the reports and found a certain page. 'She's an obsessive. Had an affair with this guy Souza, wouldn't leave him alone until he threatened to have her killed.'

Stella thought about it. 'You think she was calling them back.'

'I do, yes.'

'Because they hadn't done the job properly.'

79

By night, the Ocean Diner was neon shadows and slow music, a place to be alone, a place to be picked up, a place to hang out. By day, it was different: brighter music, brisker movements, people doing business.

Stella and Duncan Palmer were doing business of a sort. The diner was neutral territory, an attempt to put Palmer at his ease and allow him to talk freely: good for business, Stella hoped. She was trying to get information without giving any, or without giving too much.

'Her name came up, simple as that. We weren't thinking about her, but there she was suddenly. A croupier at Jumping Jacks. And we learned a few things about her that made me want to talk to you.'

Palmer spooned up froth from his coffee. 'Such as –?'

'She had an affair with Billy Souza, the guy who –'

'I know who he is.'

'People said she fastened on, that he found it difficult to get rid of her.'

'Billy Souza is a well-known bastard.'

'We know that. Billy's not under discussion here.' Stella paused. 'Would you have married Valerie Blake? Is that what you intended to do?'

They both knew there was no way back from that question. Stella had chosen a window table since it was furthest from the bar, the music, the waiters. Palmer turned his head, avoiding Stella's gaze. It had been snowing on and off for days, sometimes leaving a thin covering that was muddy ice-water within the hour. Now the flakes were thicker and more frequent, they were snow showers. Crystals touched the window and stuck and dissolved.

'It's a problem,' Palmer said. He didn't speak again for several minutes. Stella waited; she knew these rhythms; in the interview room, she would have watched the tape counter revolve, checking the time-lapse in case there was an awkward question from a defence barrister. Finally, he added, 'It was a fling. A pre-wedding fling. You're about to settle down, I don't know, make a life with someone and you think about all those women out there . . . And you reckon one more time, just one, I deserve it.'

'A binge before the diet,' Stella suggested.

Palmer shrugged. 'I went to the casino after a stag party. The whole idea was to pick up some girls. We were all a bit drunk.'

'And you picked up Lauren.'

'Not that night. But she came on to me.'

'So you went back. When you'd sobered up.'

'We went out, we had sex, she was keen, I saw her a few more times.'

'And Valerie?'

'And Valerie what?' There was a challenge in his voice.

Stella said, 'I'm not being judgemental, I'm just asking questions. Things were going on as normal – with Valerie. You were making arrangements for the wedding and so forth.'

'It was set for a week after my American trip. I'm past the stage of making excuses,' he said, 'because there aren't any available to me. A pre-wedding fling: you've heard of such a thing . . .'

'Sure, of course, it happens, why did you take Lauren Buchanan to the States?'

'It was what you suggested – the way she was with Souza. To begin with, it wasn't much; over-affectionate behaviour, wanting more of my time, wanting to give me sex non-stop, as if she could keep my attention that way.' He laughed sourly. 'Which, by and large, she could. Then it got heavier. Talk of being in love with me, making plans. She never told me to leave Val, but she'd talk about how it could have been if . . . and how great it would be if . . . If we'd met earlier, if life were different, if Val met someone else.'

'If Val died.'

'She never said that.' He spoke without having caught a hint of the meaning behind Stella's remark. He was still in the dark.

'In the end, I took her to America in the hope that I could end things that way. She asked to come, but didn't make an issue of it. She just said it would be our time together, something she'd always have to remember.' He smiled. 'That sort of shit.'

'You believed her?'

'Listen, I could see she was over-keen, but I hadn't really started to worry all that much. She knew I was getting married.' He seemed suddenly angry. 'Also she was a hot fuck.'

'Casino girls are,' Stella remarked, 'or so people say.'

'In America, it got worse.'

'In what way?'

'Talk of how terrific we were together, that it was crazy to let something so good go to waste. Then she began to say things that made it seem as though a decision had been made: what terrific luck that we found each other before the wedding, how Val would get over it. She was living in a world apart. If I tried to talk to her about it, tried to make it clear that I *was* going to marry Valerie, that Lauren and

I *were* going to end, she just went quiet, as if she couldn't hear me.'

'What did you do?'

'I was in the middle of a business trip. I thought I'd sort things when we got back to England.'

'How?'

'Tell Val. Only way out.'

'And then that wasn't possible.'

'I'd been ducking her calls, you guessed that when we first spoke. I didn't even know about the burglary. I could tell I was running into real trouble with Lauren and it was all I could cope with – that and five meetings a day. I didn't want to hear Val's voice.' He stopped and gazed out at the snowfall a moment. 'I never heard it again.'

'And Lauren,' Stella remarked, 'is still with you.'

'No. Well, yes, she is, but she's going.'

'Is she?'

'What have I got to lose?'

'Then why hasn't she gone already?'

'The mugging. It really fucked her up. She's terrified to go out, she's seeing a counsellor, Christ, she didn't get out of bed for a week.'

'So even with Valerie dead, you didn't want Lauren.'

'Even less, in a way. I wanted her gone. I expect this sounds crass, but I expected to marry Valerie and I wanted to marry Valerie. I thought we could make a life together.'

'You told Lauren this.'

'She went crazy. I mean, one minute crying, the next throwing furniture at me. She pretended she was pregnant. But it didn't matter and she could see that. She had nothing to threaten me with.'

'Then she got mugged.'

This time, Palmer did hear the edge in Stella's voice. He

looked at her, eyes wide. 'You think she beat herself up?'

'I think she got someone to do it for her. I think she knew how to do that, knew who you talk to if you want something like that done. I think she talked to a man called Leon Bloss.'

'He pretended to mug her, this man?'

'No, someone else did that. I think Lauren spoke to Leon Bloss about Valerie.'

Palmer was motionless. He seemed to be breathing in without breathing out; he started to shake his head as if he could erase the thought or render it null.

'Where did she live – before she moved in with you?'

'She's got a place in Queensway.'

'Do you have a key?'

He nodded. 'I've been going there to fetch things for her: you know, clothes and so on.'

'I'll get a search warrant,' Stella said, 'but I'm assuming I won't need one for your flat.'

'What will you be looking for?'

'A connection between Lauren and Leon Bloss.'

Palmer put a hand to his mouth, as if he might be sick. 'You really think she did this?'

'I'm sure of it.'

'My God,' he said. 'My God . . .' Staring at her wide-eyed.

Stella took out her mobile phone and speed-dialled a number. Pete Harriman answered. She said, 'Where is she?'

'Here with us,' Harriman said. 'Interview Room One.'

80

Stella sat down with her. She said, 'We know pretty much everything, Lauren. We know about Leon Bloss.'

Lauren smiled. 'There's nothing to know.'

'You worked with him. He was for hire: Billy hired him. You hired him.'

'Leon told you this, did he? You've talked to him, you know where he is.'

'There's no way out of this for you, Lauren, no way back. The damage is done.'

'Aren't you supposed to charge me?'

'We're just talking, for the moment. There's lot to get through.'

'Aren't you supposed to charge me or let me go?'

Maxine sat down with her. She said, 'What puzzled us was the other deaths. The other women. But then things came clear, because DNA is like a witness for the prosecution who stands up and says, "He was there. He did it." The connection's easy to see: you, Bloss, Valerie.'

Lauren was smoking and drinking coffee from a thin plastic cup. She held it by the rim to protect her fingers and sipped cautiously. She said, 'I met Duncan at the casino. That's all there is to it. We're in love and we're getting married. It was a great tragedy, what happened to Valerie, but in a way it was a blessing.'

'A blessing?'

'It saved everyone from a life of sadness. Aren't you supposed to charge me or let me go?'

Harriman sat down with her. He said, 'It must have seemed easy. It must have seemed simple. You wouldn't even be there when it happened. You'd be in America.'

'And I was. I was in America when Valerie died. That's the point.'

'We know you paid Leon Bloss to do the work, Lauren. How much did you pay him? What's the going rate?'

'You say you know . . . so prove it. Show me some proof. Shouldn't I have a lawyer here with me?'

'You can have a lawyer, of course you can.'

'I don't need it. You have to charge me or let me go.'

Stella sat down with her. She said, 'I talked to Duncan. He told me he wants rid of you.'

'You'd say anything.'

'You were a fling, he told me. It didn't even have to be you. Just someone to screw because soon he'd be married, soon he'd be on the leash. A bit of excitement before he settled down to a wife and family. He walked into the casino, there you were, you liked him, he liked you. Fine. You were his bit of spare, his bit on the side, surely you knew that. You were wham-bam, Lauren, you were fuck and forget.'

Lauren got up and walked across the room, then turned and walked to the other side, moving briskly, as if she were crossing a road against the traffic. She stopped and stood with her face very close to the wall.

'You would say that. It's what you're supposed to say.' She was trembling slightly – Stella could see the quake in her shoulders. 'You're supposed to charge me or let me go, haven't I got that right?'

Frank Silano sat down with her, but he was the night-watchman. He put the tape on and listed those present but didn't ask any questions.

Stella was in with Mike Sorley. 'She's been given rest periods, food and drink and so on?'

'All by the book.'

'Been offered a lawyer.'

'She has.'

He looked at the transcripts. 'You've had her since late morning, it's now six thirty, you're not getting anywhere, are you?'

'Not so far, not really. I might need an extension.'

'It's all conjecture,' Sorley said. 'What about Bloss and Kimber? There's more of a return in that. We know we can nail them: there's DNA.'

Sorley had requested additional officers and wanted to be sure that his money was being well spent. The AMIP-5 squad room was now three squad rooms and there were fifteen extra officers allocated to the task of finding Leon Bloss and Robert Adrian Kimber.

'There's a media team making sure that we get maximum coverage, we've got an extensive house-to-house going, we're still working the Harefield Estate where Kimber used to live, we're trying to get Bloss through employment records, local tax offices and credit card companies, we're trying Blosses and Kimbers in the phone book in the hope of finding relatives, it's thorough so it's slow.'

'You can have her tonight and tomorrow until the twenty-four hours are up. Ask me about an extension then, but I'm not sure. You've gone off a bit fast here. You've jumped the gun.' Sorley shook a cigarette from a packet that bore the legend SMOKING CAUSES LUNG CANCER AND OTHER SERIOUS RESPIRATORY ILLNESSES. It was a lot of information for the space available. He lit a cigarette, but he didn't cough. The box of man-sized tissues on his desk was unopened. 'You had a search team in at her flat?'

'And at Palmer's.'

'Find anything?'

'Still looking.'

'You've no evidence for this, Stella; you're working off a maybe.'

Stella said, 'No, I'm right.' Then, 'Are you feeling better?'

He smiled. 'Cigarettes and whisky,' he said, 'that's the way.'

81

JD delivered Bloss's money to the Isle of Dogs, as promised. He said, 'Billy wants you gone.'

'I'm going.'

'Wants you gone now.'

'I know that. There's something I have to do.'

'Wants you gone tonight.'

Bloss sighed. He said, 'I'll be gone soon enough.'

They were standing close to the tall windows. JD took Bloss by the arm, his fingers curling hard into the bicep. 'This isn't advice, you cunt, this is what to do. It's a message from Billy.'

Bloss said, 'I understand. I've got it.'

'You'd better.' Freckles of JD's saliva dotted Bloss's face.

'Sit down,' Bloss said. He smiled and wagged the envelope that held the money. 'I don't need to count this, do I?'

'If you like.'

Bloss tossed it down on to a table. 'I don't think I do. Have a drink. You're not working tonight, are you?' He was taking the heat out of things, making it clear he would do as he was told.

JD sat on the sofa and took the glass of Scotch that Bloss offered. He'd done his work, he'd put the frighteners on, and he'd got the result he needed. Now he could relax a little. He said, 'Billy's well pissed off with you.'

'Tell him not to worry.'

'He has to be protected.'

'Of course,' Bloss agreed. 'Wait there, I'll get the tape.'

'What tape?'

'Billy didn't tell you?' JD looked puzzled. 'A tape I took from Oscar Gribbin: it shows Billy and Gribbin doing business.'

'You're joking.'

'Billy asked me to get it for him. I got it.'

Bloss walked past the sofa and into the screened-off bedroom area. He found the tape and took it back, lobbing it on to the sofa so that it fell next to JD, who picked it up. Bloss had also brought a hammer and the garrotte. JD was removing the tape from its cover when he realized that Bloss hadn't come back into his sight-line. The adrenalin rush got him halfway to his feet before Bloss side-swiped him with the hammer.

JD made a sound deep in his throat and sat back down; he slumped sideways. Bloss straightened him up and put the garrotte in place, taking up the slack. JD's arms rose, as if to go to his throat, but then fell again.

Bloss put his back into it.

When he was done, he straightened up, massaging his bicep where JD's fingers had bitten in, then walked round to confront the man directly. He said, 'Don't fucking talk to me like that.'

He stashed most of the money in a drawer alongside the videotape of Billy and Oscar Gribbin, then put in a call to the Trader. He said, 'I'm going to be up near the Strip.'

'You're trouble,' Trader told him. 'Big time. The whole fucking world's looking for you.'

'Have you made a sale?'

'No.'

'I need that money.'

'Then you'll have to take what you can get. The bracelet's unmarketable. You know why.'

'So who's going to buy it?'

'I'll buy it. It'll have to be broken, it's the only way.'

'How much?'

'Two grand.'

Bloss was silent for a moment. He was trying to hold in his anger. Finally, he said, 'Two? No, ten.'

'This bracelet has to be broken quickly. I don't know what the stones will make. I can give you five. We stop there.'

'Five,' Bloss said. 'But I need it tonight.'

They met in the shebeen where Kimber had holed up. There was a poker game in the back room; it might have been the same poker game. Bloss took the five grand without saying thank you. The Trader was eager to be away. He said, 'They've got you down for it. This cop definitely wants you for it – Mooney.'

'I know. She's not a problem.'

'No?' The Trader downed his drink and got up. 'She certainly talks like one.'

'She's nothing,' Bloss said. 'Trust me.'

There was a light covering of snow on rooftops and parked cars, but the hookers and the dealers were still out on the Strip. Business wasn't great, but people had needs whatever the weather. The neon cut patterns in the snow.

Bloss was talking to Kimber as one enthusiast to another. He was telling him to kill Stella Mooney. Kimber told him about Jan and the problems he'd had, but added that all was well now; all was possible. He mentioned the flat near Ladbroke Grove and the flat at Vigo Street. Bloss was looking for a lead, a way of turning things his way.

'There's a difference. You remember telling me about going into Valerie Blake's flat, that you thought about waiting for her to come back, about being able to take your time.'

'Yes.'

'Jan lives with someone. If you do Jan, it has to be like Kate Reilly. You'll have to find a place, an opportunity, the right moment. Look what happened the other night. Look at the risk you ran. Stella Mooney lives on her own. You can get in; you can wait.'

'I've been following Jan. I've been getting ready.'

'You followed Stella.'

'I've been thinking more about Jan.'

'You could be there when she gets back. Be there in the dark, Bobby. Maybe you could hide and watch her until you're ready. No one to see you, no one to interrupt.'

Kimber said, 'Yes, I could.'

'Think of yourself in the dark, waiting, where are you –?'

'In the bedroom. The bedroom's at the back.'

'You could be in a closet or under the bed.'

Kimber said, 'Yes, I could.'

'You hear the door open and slam. She's back. Maybe she's going to have a drink or make something to eat. You could open the bedroom door a little and watch her doing that.'

Kimber said, 'Yes, I could.'

'But whether it's early or late, she'll come into the bedroom, won't she? Maybe you'll have a lot of opportunity to watch her, maybe just a little, but she'll come into the bedroom, to change her clothes, perhaps, get undressed, or to go to bed, and you could be there to watch.'

Kimber said, 'Yes, I could.'

'And then you come out of hiding. And there she is.'

Kimber said, 'There she is, yes.'

'This is just you, Bobby. Not us together. I have to go away for a while.' Bloss put the Glock down where Kimber could see it.

Kimber nodded. He said, 'Yes, I could do that, couldn't I?'

'You could, Bobby. Yes, you really could.'

Bloss walked through Notting Hill towards the tube, a face in the crowd, no one of note. He had bought a hat and a scarf and he bowed his head against the wind, hat low, scarf wound round.

It was almost midnight, almost Christmas Eve. The last tube trains would be full of drunks and people trying not to notice drunks. Tomorrow Stella Mooney would be killed by Robert Adrian Kimber and the investigation would hit a wall; her death, cops on leave, tens of thousands of people at airline check-in counters . . .

He passed a TV rental store and saw pictures of a small war taking place somewhere, of soldiers wearing bandoliers, a plane on a strafing-run. A moment later, his own face appeared, but by that time he had passed by.

A skinny boy in a quilted coat was sitting backed up to the glass and steel frontage of ToyMart. He said, 'Christ is coming, the Lord is coming.'

82

Stella, Maxine, Harriman and Stilano: the team. In the squad room they went into a huddle over coffee and chocolate, they talked tactics. Lauren Buchanan was still refusing a lawyer. People did that; it was a form of denial. Once a lawyer looked in, you had to start thinking of 'proceedings' as 'official'. Stella had put Sorley on notice of a probable request for an extension, but he was still shrugging that one off.

Harriman and Maxine had both been in with Lauren that morning, which meant Stella would sit down with her next. She said, 'How does she seem?'

'Like someone holding out,' Harriman said.

'You can talk about Valerie Blake, you can even talk about Leon Bloss, but you can't talk about Duncan Palmer. Palmer's a minefield.'

'Same as yesterday,' Stella said, 'so that's the way in.'

'She's just fooling herself,' Silano said, 'about Palmer.'

Stella shook her head. 'She believes it – herself and Duncan Palmer. She can see the future.'

Lauren had put on some make-up, but the interview room light cast shadows and her eyes looked bruised. Stella sat down and switched on the tape. Maxine was in as observer.

'We're going to keep talking until we get somewhere,' Stella said.

'There's nowhere to get to.' Lauren lit a cigarette reflexively.

'I've spent the last hour or so talking to Duncan Palmer. He told me what a pain in the arse you are, how he couldn't get rid of you, how he only took you with him to America to keep you quiet.'

Lauren smiled. 'Yeah, right.'

'He knows the whole story now. Duncan – he knows it all. That you talked to Leon Bloss, came to an arrangement. That Bloss killed Valerie for you.' Lauren drew hard on her cigarette, making the paper crumple. 'You can imagine what he thinks of you now. At first, you're just a free fuck, up for it, a last-minute sex-spree. Then you're a drag, you won't let go. Then Valerie's killed and you're digging in, he can't get rid of you. Now there's Bloss and what you told him to do. Duncan hates you, Lauren, of course he does. He never really liked you all that much, but now he hates you.'

'All this ... all this is ... you don't know, you know nothing.' Lauren turned away and shook her head. 'You're supposed to say it. What else would you say?'

Stella stood in the squad room and stared out at the snow. Since early that morning, the fall had been heavy and the wind strong. The cars in the car park were coated, completely white, and the fall was drifting in corners.

Her mobile went and she checked the display. Delaney. He said, 'Are you spending Christmas with me?'

'Or are you spending Christmas with me?'

'You've got interesting wall-murals, but I've got a Christmas tree.'

'Are you serious?'

'About what?'

'The Christmas tree.'

'Of course.'

She laughed. 'I'll have to go back before I come to you,

collect some things. I don't know how late I'll be. There's a fair chance I'll be working tomorrow –'

'Just come.' He'd noticed that she'd said 'back' when referring to Vigo Street. Not, I'll have to go home, but I'll have to go back.

'Okay.'

He said, 'I love you.'

'I love you.'

But there's something I have to tell you about a man called Tom Davison. Something you're not going to want to hear.

Sorley caught her on her way through the squad room. He said, 'You're going to have to let her go.'

'There's some time.'

'A little. Do you expect to get anywhere?' Stella shrugged. 'No. She's going to walk, Stella.'

'I know she did this. She paid Bloss to kill Valerie Blake.'

'You may be right. I expect you *are* right. Only problem – there's nothing in your favour. You moved too soon. As long as she goes on stonewalling, it's just a theory.'

'Unless we find Bloss.'

'Does that seem likely just now?'

Stella was silent on that one.

She asked Marilyn Hayes to do the paperwork: time and circumstances of Lauren's arrest, time and circumstances of her release, then collected some thin, bitter coffee from the squad vending machine and went to her desk. She picked up a few emails; she found a Twix bar deep in a drawer.

There's an hour before I have to let her go. She can sit there and sweat, the bitch.

As it happened, Stella didn't need an hour. Twenty minutes later Nick Robson came back into the squad room with a couple of members of the search team that had spent the morning at Lauren Buchanan's flat. He was holding a small plastic evidence bag.

He said, 'You might want this. It's uncontaminated from the search site; don't take it out of the bag.'

Stella looked at the item inside. It wasn't necessary to remove it. The engraving on the cross was clear: VB.

When she went back to the interview room, Lauren had brightened her make-up and was wearing a cheery smile.

'Is there more, or can I go now?' she asked.

'There's more,' Stella said. She switched on the tape but didn't speak. Instead, she held the evidence bag up so that Lauren could see the cross. Harriman was sitting at the table now, next to Stella. He told the tape what was happening and he described the object in the bag. A gold cross engraved with the initials VB.

'Did you really need to have this?' Stella said, 'I think you did. A token. An indulgence. The winner's medal.'

Lauren looked at the cross for about a minute; she didn't blink.

'Do you want to talk about it?' Stella asked. 'Because if you do, I'm here to listen.'

The tape turned.

'You could help us. We're looking for Leon Bloss, the man you paid. Maybe you could tell us where to find him.'

Lauren shook her head. She was crying.

They left her alone for a while. They gave her some time; time to despair. Maxine and Silano went for coffee and sandwiches.

Harriman said, 'This Bloss is a piece of work.'

Stella gave a sour laugh. 'I can't disagree.'

'He takes a contract from Lauren Buchanan to kill Valerie Blake. He takes a possible contract from Billy Souza to kill Oscar Gribbin. He kills Valerie in a way that makes it seem she's one in a string of other victims – clever-clever – then Robert Kimber comes into his life and he realizes that if Billy Souza activates the contract on Gribbin, he's got a ready-made patsy.'

'He thinks ahead. He's a pro.'

'He needed Kimber to kill, didn't he – to start killing?'

'So that his DNA would be at a murder scene, yes, but more than that – he had to make Kimber authentic. The man had already confessed to Valerie's murder and been shown the door. If Bloss was going to put him in the frame for Gribbin's murder, he needed him to actually *be* a killer and needed us to *know* that. Whatever evidence we held back, Kimber would be completely accurate about the details of Kate Reilly's death because he'd killed her. After that, we wouldn't have had him down as just a victim of the Judas Syndrome.'

'The what?'

'Shrink speak.'

'So Bloss kills Gribbin and thinks he's away clear. Someone looking hard enough might make the Gribbin–Souza–Bloss connection, but who'd be looking? Kimber's DNA is all over the shop and he's already wanted for Kate Reilly's murder. Case closed. Merry Christmas.'

'Gribbin's girlfriend was a piece of luck. Bloss could work her into the mix – not only Kimber's DNA but an MO that goes back to Valerie Blake and then to Cotter's victims. Bloss doesn't know Cotter's been caught. Maybe he thinks that, if he stays lucky, and if we're looking to clear our files, we might decide to charge Kimber with the lot, including Valerie Blake. Couldn't be better.'

'What do you think he said to Kimber?' Harriman asked. 'Said to him?'

'Bloss. What did he say to start him off: to make him kill Kate Reilly?'

'I don't suppose it took much,' Stella said. She was remembering Kimber in the interview room, his fantasies of death, his gloating smile. 'Just a whisper or two. Just a hint of the pleasures to come.'

Harriman looked at her. She was smiling, as if she'd made a poor joke, but a shiver ran through her.

Stella and Lauren; Lauren and Stella. They took rest breaks, they had coffee. Neither spoke. They sat together for a long time. Dusk was coming in, a smoky light filtering through the snowfall. It wasn't by the book, this sitting and saying nothing, but Stella had a feel for it.

Lauren said, 'I thought it was the right thing to do.'

Stella switched on the tape. She gave details of those present and the time.

'It was the *only* thing to do,' Lauren added, nodding as if backing her own opinion. 'It's what they all do, when you have to put someone out of the way. Billy, Leon, JD, all the hard men; it's what they do. It's not so unusual. I knew that if she wasn't there he would forget her, because that's what happens. People forget.' She looked at Stella. 'You must know that.'

Lauren went on talking; she talked for almost half an hour. She gave them a number for Leon Bloss that registered as 'discontinued'.

The street-people had gone to ground. The luckiest had found a refuge or a squat; the worst off were rolled in their bags under bridges or in subways. Jamie was in church, the place where he most wanted to be. He sat at the back and off to the right, where he could hear the choir at practice without being seen. The voices thrilled him; they opened portals to God. When he looked towards the choir stalls, he could see, in the stained glass, the risen Christ surrounded by angels.

It was the church where Kimber had murdered Kate Reilly.

When the voices came to an end, Jamie got on to his knees, then on to his stomach, and lay down in the space between the pews. No one could see him there. He pulled his bag over and took a hassock as a pillow. Long after the choir had left and the church had been dimmed to a single light above the altar, Jamie could hear the rustling of the wings of angels.

83

Leon Bloss packed a bag, then he made a phone call. He pressed buttons to go from one recorded voice to the next. The seventh voice told him that due to blizzard conditions, there were no flights leaving Heathrow Airport. Calls to Gatwick, Stansted and Luton produced the same result. He switched on the TV and got the news and weather. It seemed the country had closed down; the country had seized up. He called the ferry ports and was told that there was a gale blowing in the Channel; all sailings had been postponed, but, if the weather improved, ferries would be putting to sea the next day.

He made a provisional booking for the three o'clock sailing for Le Havre on Christmas Day, then stood by the windows looking at the white-out on the river and wondering who had fixed this for him, who had organized this kind of luck. An odd warbling sound broke the silence and he turned fast, not knowing what it could be, then realized it was JD's mobile phone. JD sat motionless on the sofa. He'd been there all night and he wasn't looking so good, his lips drawn back in a fixed grin, his face plum-dark. Bloss took the phone from JD's pocket and looked at the display.

Billy Souza calling.

He let it ring out, then went to 'Inbox' and found fifteen missed calls, four of which were from Billy. Bloss was filled with a sudden rage that made him grind his teeth and clench his fists until his shoulders shook. He kicked out at JD's legs and then again, kicking and screaming, making the body hop and sway, until his fury slackened. He should be gone by now, on his way to the airport, check-in would have been in an hour, take-off in three. He wondered when JD had been missed and reckoned it must have been late morning. He would have been expected to arrive at the casino at ten, would have been missed by, say, eleven, and the first calls would have been made then. Now it was one o'clock and JD had been out of touch for two hours. At first, Billy would have been more annoyed than concerned. JD had a girl, and they would have checked with her, but she wouldn't have expected him to come home every night or say where he'd been. Soon, though, Billy would remember the errand he'd given JD the previous night.

Take Bloss his money; tell him to leave now.

Bloss had phones of his own, but the numbers had changed since he worked for Billy Souza. If they wanted him, they'd have to make a house call. He thought it through: JD is late, Billy tells someone to put in a call. No reply. This happens a couple of times, then they phone the girl. She doesn't know where he is, so she puts in a call and a few minutes later someone from Jumping Jacks does the same. Billy starts to get angry: he needs JD on the job because the casino is about to open. He tells them to keep trying, but they keep getting JD's message. Finally, Billy puts in a couple of calls himself. Then he thinks back.

Take Bloss his money . . .

He went into the bedroom and collected his bag, his money, his fake passport, the videotape. He put in his copies of *The Sandman* and *The Preacher* and *Elektra Assassin*. The bag was a carry-on size rucksack – he hadn't planned to stand around in baggage-reclaim halls being stared at by CCTV cameras. He shouldered the bag and left without a backward glance. There was nothing of Leon Bloss in the place, nothing that could identify him or provide a trace.

Except, perhaps, JD, lolling back on the sofa cushions and black in the face with laughter.

Jamie had slept for a while and dreamed of angels, their muscular wings and their perfect voices singing of the coming of Christ. When he woke, the echoes of those voices were still there, wafting among the roof beams.

He walked down the aisle to the rood screen and then up to the altar. The table held a small crucifix about a foot high, Christ hanging there, nailed and racked. Jamie picked it up and looked at it closely. He put the crucifix under his padded coat, holding it trapped with one arm, and smiled a secret smile.

84

It had been easy for the hoodie-boys and it was easy for Kimber, because, all in all, properties are easy to break into; even easier if dark falls by four o'clock. Stella had put in a call to a house-security firm who had never called back. Christmas was their busy time: Christmas and summer holidays. Kimber hit the same bedroom window that the boys had hit, used his hammer to knock open the same window lock, climbed in the same way.

He pulled the blind against the weather and stood in the dark for a moment, breathing deeply. He could smell her smells. The bedroom light was on a dimmer switch. Kimber turned it on low and made a tour of the room. Everything was there, just as he'd imagined it: clothes in a closet that was fronted by a long mirror, other clothes in drawers, perfumes and make-up and creams, bits and pieces of inexpensive jewellery, personal items – *personal*. He had brought a little bag with him. Bag of tricks. He put it on the floor, took off his outer clothes and draped them over a radiator, then went through into the larger room.

A street light was shedding an orange glow into the living space. He walked around it, as if claiming possession, then sat on the sofa for a moment, just where he'd seen her sit, but it wasn't really where he wanted to be. He helped himself from the fridge, a little snack; he helped himself from the vodka bottle, a little nip. Then he went back to the bedroom.

He opened jars and tubes, sniffing, sampling. He stripped off and opened the closet. Her clothes were his. He put on a sparkly top and a short skirt, a pair of black silk trousers, a backless dress. None of it fitted: he had to leave zips unzipped and buttons unbuttoned, but he turned this way and that in front of the long mirror, in the dim light, feeling the material against his skin just as she had. He opened the drawers and put on her underwear. He applied some body lotion and a little flourish of lipstick.

He smiled at his image, the blond hair flopping to the side, the grey-green eyes, the lips a little too pink.

It was okay to switch on the bathroom light, because there was no window. He breathed deeply, wanting to get all there was of her: the hot, perfumed smells, but most of all he wanted some taint, some earthy scent of Stella herself. The odour of her faeces or her menstrual blood. He took a shower, using her gels, her sponge, taking it into his crotch, over his buttocks. He washed his hair with her shampoo and rubbed in some of her conditioner.

After a while he went back to the bedroom, walking naked. He'd brought with him the clipping of her hair, a photo of her approaching the AMIP-5 offices, and a little story he'd written about himself and Stella, silver pen on black paper. He pinned them all to the wall. The story included everything he'd done so far but also mentioned that he climbed naked into Stella's bed, smelling the lingering perfume on the covers and on her pillow, so that was what he did next.

With the cover pulled up to his chin, he waited for Stella to come home so the story could end.

The London streets were nothing but headlights and snow-light. The sky had come down to a point just six feet above the heads of the home-going crowds and if you looked up from Notting Hill Gate towards Bayswater, you saw what seemed to be a tunnel with white, flowing walls, lit by beams racked back for miles. On roundabouts and at junctions, there were pile-ups and broadsides and sideswipes. Drivers stood bare-headed in the blizzard, exchanging insurance details. A chorus of horns was sounding across the city.

Jamie held the crucifix up for the drivers to see and the metal seemed to shed droplets of white light. He held it up to passers-by as they walked into the near-horizontal snow; they dodged and sidestepped. He held it up to anguished shoppers crowding the stores in search of that post-last-minute gift; security men hustled him back on to the street. He held it up in the cafés and fast-food facilities; the customers studied their plates with unusual interest until he went away.

And he was shouting – to be heard over the traffic, the muzak, the indifference – *He is coming the Lord is coming Jesus is coming* . . .

The car drivers and the shoppers and the diners had him down as a crazy, another of the looney-toons bastards who made life uncomfortable for a moment or two, but if Jamie was deranged, he was also strung-out, angry, half starved, abandoned and desperate. He knew that Christ's appearance on earth would change everything; it would salve the wretched of the earth. It was something he had to believe in because there was nothing else to hand.

On the snow-covered streets, he ran back and forth, slipping and stumbling, crossing roads, weaving between cars as they nosed forward, showing the crucifix and its dangling man to everyone he met. On Christmas Eve, for a man like Jamie, it was a last hope. Why shouldn't it be true?

Even in that weather, even at six in the evening on the day before Christmas, AMIP-5's complement of extra officers were going door-to-door on Harefield, making follow-up calls and calls to doors that hadn't opened first time round. They showed pictures of Robert Adrian Kimber and Leon Bloss. Sometimes people shook their heads, sometimes they invited the officers to fuck off.

The weather was having an effect on business. Just as the Strip was clear of hookers and dealers, so the bull ring and the Harefield approach roads were white waste lands. Out on the DMZ, the shapes of abandoned hardware were muffled under snow. Business was being done indoors, and the presence of cops on the estate was making everyone jumpy. Triple locks were being thrown and lights were being switched off. The high walkways were swept by the winter-wind and the cops tramped round cursing their luck.

Marilyn Hayes was going home for Christmas, which was the last thing she wanted to do – and the last thing she'd expected to do. Pete Harriman had tried to intercept her; he wanted to say something, but he had no real idea what. Sorry, perhaps, or I didn't get it, or I never promised you a rose garden. Marilyn had brushed him off with a look. Now she got into her car and gunned the engine.

I thought it was something special. I thought it was something different.

She jabbed the accelerator, shimmied, turned to line up with the exit, floated sideways and hit another car with a slam-crash sound that allowed her to know that real damage had been done.

She wasn't going back into the squad room now. She made a call on her mobile and said, 'I've just hit your car. I think it's a bad one.'

Stella stood side by side with Marilyn and looked things over. She said, 'You're right. It's a bad one.' The driver's-side window was smashed; there was glass all over the interior of the car; the door itself was buckled and jammed, a flat scissor-blade of metal protruding into the driver's space.

Marilyn said, 'I'm really sorry, Stella.' Her own car had damage to the entire side, but nothing that would render it undrivable.

Stella smiled, meaning: forget it. She glanced at the mascara runs on the other woman's cheeks, then looked away. She said, 'It's okay. Go home, Marilyn.' She didn't say Happy Christmas.

Harriman looked at her. 'What?'

Stella shook her head. 'Nothing. There's ice in the car park. She hit my car.'

'Is she all right?'

'Was she hurt? No. Is she all right? I don't think so.'

She made a call and told Delaney what had happened.

'I'll come and get you.'

'No. I don't know how long I'll be here. We've charged someone, there's the paperwork . . . I'll get a cab or cadge a lift, go to Vigo Street, then come on to you.'

'Okay.'

'It could be really late.'

'Okay.'

'Don't wait up.'

85

London was white.

Things were freezing over and closing down. The elevated sections and motorway approaches were thick with accidents or abandoned vehicles. Emergency services were having emergencies of their own. This is what extreme weather could do. What it couldn't do was stop the parties. There were parties in houses, in pubs, in clubs, in bars and – in back-ups that stretched from the city to the suburbs – there were parties in cars.

Leon Bloss cruised the streets until he found the party he was looking for just off Kensington Church Street. It was a big house and you could hear the music through the double glazing. When Bloss looked up he could see something going on in every room: people dancing, people drinking, people finding ways of getting close to each other. He backtracked to a wine store and bought a bottle of champagne, then leaned on the bell until a girl in a green dress opened the door. He held up the bottle and laughed, she laughed back and let him in: everyone was someone's friend. Bloss thought he would quite like to be hers, because of her strawberry-blonde hair and her wide smile. She wasn't a terrific looker, but her smile knocked you out.

He found the kitchen and opened his champagne, then found a glass and wandered through the party, pouring for other people now and then, laughing at people who nodded and laughed back at him. It was a big enough party for there to be degrees of separation; some people knew each other well, some a little, some not at all. He talked to a few people on topics that no one knew much about, he danced on his own or in a little group, he circled, looking for the girl in the green dress.

The black cabs had gone home early, already garaged and washed and spruced; minicabs were somewhere on the end of a phone that rang into oblivion.

Maxine Hewitt stopped by Stella's desk and said, 'Forget it. They'll never answer. I'll give you a lift.'

'It's out of your way.'

'A little. What are you going to do – ski?'

Mike Sorley went through looking fit, smoking a cigar and carrying eight store bags with fancy handles. His paper was in order: Lauren Buchanan in police custody for three days, then in front of magistrates, then, for sure, on remand to Holloway. It was something. It wasn't Bloss and Kimber in adjoining cells, but it was enough for a while.

Stella and Maxine soft-footed it over the car-park ice and Maxine drove very slowly out on to the road, which had been partially cleared by the weight of traffic.

'I'm going back-doubles,' she said; 'the main roads are solid.'

They talked about anything but the Bloss–Kimber case because they were talked out on that. They talked about everything and nothing while Maxine inched through the rat-runs.

When they arrived, Stella said, 'Come in and have a drink.'

'I don't think so. It'll take me a while to get back.'

'A coffee.'

'No, it's okay.'

'There might be a duty-call for tomorrow.'

'I know, I've warned Jan. She understands.'

Stella got her keys out. She said, 'Have a good Christmas.'

In her flat, the phone had just stopped ringing. As she crossed the street – the wind whipping her face, sirens whooping in the surrounding streets – her mobile was going off in her bag, but she couldn't hear it.

The girl in the green dress was called Dallas. Bloss said he hadn't heard an American accent. Dallas said, no, she was born in Oxford, but her mother just liked the name. Bloss said he thought it was a terrific name. He thought Dallas was terrific.

'Except,' Dallas said, 'for Kennedy being shot there. And the TV soap.'

They laughed about that. Dallas thought Bloss was a strange-looking guy, with his bright blue eyes and his Slavic cheekbones and his high-pitched laugh, but there was something about him that she liked. She decided that he must be powerful in some way or another, a media mogul, perhaps, or a captain of industry. She had him down as a boardroom slugger. They danced and she liked the way he snaked his hips.

He said, 'You know them – the people giving the party.'

'Yes. No, not really. I came with a friend. She knows them, but she had to leave. Do you know them?'

Bloss shook his head. 'Not really.'

They stood by a window and watched the snow and sipped their drinks. Dallas was happy to get drunk; she wasn't drunk yet, not very, but she was happy to get that way.

'I ought to be in Oxford, with my parents. There aren't any trains.'

Bloss laughed. 'Me too. I came down from Birmingham. I'm stranded.'

'What will you do?'

'Find a hotel,' he said, and saw the look on her face, and knew he was home and dry.

Kimber had been dreaming. He was flying over snow-swept London with his eagle-eye, and he could see them all, Valerie Blake and Sophie Simms, Kate Reilly, Jan, Stella, and all the others, all he'd ever followed or snapped or clipped. He could walk through walls, he could find them in their rooms.

He dreamed he was in Stella's flat, lying in her bed, waiting for her to come home; he dreamed he heard the phone ringing and the call was to say she was on her way; he dreamed that he heard the front door open and close as she came in, then her voice on the telephone.

And then he was awake and it was true.

Stella sat on the sofa, her back to the bedroom door, and dialled Anne Beaumont's number. The answerphone said she was away for a few days, but Anne lifted the phone before the message had finished.

'Not away, then,' Stella said.

'I would have been. Look out of the window.'

'I'm sorry to call. I shouldn't be calling. I slept with someone.'

Anne laughed. 'Nothing like coming to the point.'

'Delaney doesn't know.'

'But you've decided to tell him.'

'What else can I do?'

'Not tell him.'

Kimber got out of bed. He could hear Stella's voice but not what she was saying. He smoothed the covers and patted the shape of his head out of the pillow.

'Would that be a good thing?'

420

'Only you know that,' Anne said. 'The point is, people don't necessarily have to know everything. Truth isn't medicine.'

'You don't usually talk like this.'

'I'm speaking as a friend.'

'What would you do?'

'You mean what have I done in the past?'

'If you like.'

'It depended.'

'On what?'

'On the likely reaction of the person in question. Good reaction, own up; bad reaction, shut up.'

'Is that your advice?'

'Christ, no. You asked me what I did and I told you. I never give advice.'

Kimber had slept with the Glock under the pillow. Now he lifted it out and turned towards the door, catching sight of himself in the mirror, a naked man with a gun and a sleepy smile. He was fine. He would wait for her to finish the call. There was all the time in the world. He put on his trousers and shirt because, naked, he felt at a strange disadvantage. He should see her naked first; he felt that was the right way.

'I'm going to tell him,' Stella said.

'Okay. Did it make a difference – being with this other person?'

'No. Nice guy, went to bed, not sure why, testing, I think ... And nothing. Well, a bit of residual guilt. But no change in the way I felt about Delaney.'

'Sounds okay.'

'Does it?'

'Sounds fine. What do you think he'll do?'

'I don't know.' And she realized that it was true: she

hadn't the first idea and wondered if she ought to know him better than that.

Anne said, 'You know something, Stella, over too many years of listening to people talk and trying not to tell them what to do or how to behave, I think I've reached the conclusion that the best bet is to do what you want.'

'Why?'

'Because you're the only person who knows what that is.'

Stella had been sitting in her coat. Kimber heard her get up and walk across the room. He waited, but there was a pause he couldn't analyse. Stella was dropping her coat on to a chair, deciding whether to have a drink, try to book a cab or pack a few things immediately. In the end, she thought she would have a shower. She was unbuttoning her shirt as she walked into the bedroom.

And there he was. And there she was.

86

Stella could feel herself beginning to faint, her vision narrowing and edged with black, a sound in her ears like a train coming down a track. She knocked the door-frame with her hand, but didn't know how that had happened.

Her first lucid thought was, *Don't faint because if you faint you're dead.* Her second was, *You're probably dead anyway.* Kimber was pointing the gun at her, his hand trembling slightly. He stooped by bending at the knees so he wouldn't have to take his eyes off her, picked up the bag and threw it on to the bed.

'Open it, Stella.'

She pulled the drawstring and upended the bag. He had brought some duct tape and lengths of cord, a pair of scissors and a camera.

Make him talk. Make him talk it instead of doing it.

'There's a way out of this.' She backed off a little, away from the bag of tricks. 'Tell me where Leon Bloss is. Stop now, stop this now, and just tell me where Bloss is and we'll pick him up and you and I can cut a deal.'

His name is Robert Adrian Kimber. Call him by his name. Is he Robert, Bob, Bobby . . . ?

'That's the way, Robert. That's the way out for you.'

Kimber had brought his free hand up to cup the butt of the gun and the barrel wavered slightly. He said, 'There's no way out, Stella. I'm sorry.'

'Don't make things worse. Don't get any deeper. We know about Bloss but we don't know where to find him.

You do. You can tell us. Then we talk about a deal. That's the way it works.'

'I want to get deeper.' Kimber was grinning. 'That's the point, I want to get as deep as I possibly can. You'll see. You'll know about that.'

'What's the point?' she asked. 'I don't understand – what's the point of killing me?'

He looked at her, frowning slightly, as if her question had puzzled him. 'It's not like that,' he said. 'It's not a reason . . .' Then, suddenly impatient, 'Take your clothes off now, Stella.'

He put out a hand to the duct tape and the cords, and the gun gave a little wobble, as if one hand wasn't enough, and Stella realized that it wasn't nervousness or excitement that was causing the unsteadiness, but that Kimber simply wasn't used to guns: he was holding the weapon too tightly, his finger curled hard on the trigger. He shook the gun to make her hurry and she saw his knuckle was white. With that kind of pressure, the gun should have fired or, at least, he would have taken up the trigger-slack.

'Get undressed now.'

It hasn't fired because he's got the safety on.

'Take your clothes off, Stella.'

You think. You hope. But you don't know for sure.

'Do it!'

He was one side of the bed, she was the other. It gave her two, perhaps three seconds, but she didn't make a sudden movement because that would have set off an alarm-reaction in him. She simply turned and walked out of the door, closing it behind her.

Then she ran.

He had tried to shoot, because there was certainly time for that. Maybe he realized it was the safety, maybe he thought the Glock had jammed. Either way, he yanked on the trigger as he was moving after her and the delay gave her enough time to get to the front door and out.

Kimber crossed the room at a run, hitting the arm of the sofa and half falling; when he came up the basement steps, Stella was halfway down the street, running on the icy snow with small, unsure steps. She fell hard and took a second to get up. Kimber was loping after her, somehow keeping his balance, trying to watch Stella and look at the gun as he ran, trying to work out how to release the safety. Stella moved off the pavement and into the middle of the road, where cars had left patches of tarmac exposed. For a brief while, she found a purchase, then slipped again and fell on her back. When she got to her feet, Kimber was a pace or two behind her and there was a car coming towards her, its lights dazzling.

Delaney could see only shapes, one rising in front of the car, the other a little way back and running with a slip-sliding sort of gait. He braked and turned the wheel, drifted into the kerb, then slewed back, fast and out of control, taking one of the figures up over the bonnet and down hard on the other side; then he stopped. Stella only knew that Kimber had been hit, had got up, had run on. She sat on the road, breathless, and watched him making slow progress up the road, running with a hop and a slide as if his hip were out of joint. The Glock was spinning on the ice in the middle of the road. Stella picked it up.

She didn't know it was Delaney and he didn't know it was her, but then he helped her up and she had clear sight of him and her first thought was, *What's he doing here?* Her second was that Kimber was still running.

Turning the car was impossible. Stella simply said, 'It's

him,' and started up towards the junction. Delaney ran with her. They got to the main road and could see Kimber on the other side, about thirty yards down, running lopsided, arms out to keep his balance.

Stella said, 'He's going into Harefield.'

87

It ought to have been business as usual for Jaz. He'd been busted, but his connections had signed on a sharp lawyer and a case had been made for 'possession for personal use'. This was only possible because of some fast chuck-and-flush action on the part of Jaz's girlfriend. It depended what you meant by personal use; some persons used more than others. Either way, a deal was going to be struck and Jaz was out on medium-to-heavy bail.

All things being equal, he would have been back to supplying half of west London, but just recently Harefield had become a cops' playground: first the visits to Kimber's flat, then Kimber's disappearance and his flat being searched, then the scene of crime cops and the forensics cops and the observation cops and the cops cruising by on patrol just in case. Now the door-to-door, the re-calls, pictures of Robert Kimber being shown; and, on top of that, the weather. That *bastard* Kimber. The *fucking* weather.

Low turnover meant that Jaz was seriously over-stocked and that made him very edgy. After the cops had left for the day, he'd made some calls. Most of his street contacts had said, 'Another day, man. Have you been outside? *Shit!*', but a few were more desperate than that. They'd made it over to Harefield and Jaz had met them in the bull ring; he didn't want a queue of high-usage dealers standing outside his door, just in case there were still some cops somewhere on the estate – overtime cops or heavy-weather cops or non-stop cops.

He was standing in a tight circle with his customers when Kimber ran into the bull ring, hopping and sliding and crying out with pain. Jaz looked at him. For a moment, he didn't make the connection; and when he did he was too angry even to smile. He said, 'Man, I've been waiting for *you*.'

Kimber tried to run through, hobbling, heading for a walk-space under one of the blocks, but Jaz moved in and kicked him high on the hip. Kimber howled and went down hard on to the packed snow. Jaz kicked him again, finding the gut and the ribs; when his man rolled over, he stamped down on his back, then on his head.

Jaz said, 'You fucking freak.'

The street-dealers stood back, watching, thinking this must be an old score, this must be something really bad from the past. Jaz brought his heel down into Kimber's face, then tried to land a second but missed and raked the man's chest. Kimber bucked and rolled, but Jaz was after him, getting kicks into the body. He was finding a rhythm now, he was warming to his task.

Stella held the Glock up, double-handed, elbows slightly bent, knees flexed. She said, 'Police!' Jaz turned. The street-dealers left, moving away quietly one by one, not hurrying but not looking back. When Jaz followed them, Stella didn't stop him. To Delaney she said, 'Call an ambulance first, then my office number, it's on automatic transfer.'

Kimber stirred and sighed, then rolled on to his back and made an attempt to sit up. Stella stood over him with the Glock. She said, 'Stay there. Sit on your hands.' He was bleeding from the nose and from a dozen face wounds; a great clump of hair and flesh had come away from his scalp where Jaz had stamped on him. Rivulets of blood ran down to his jawline and collected at the point of his chin, a thin drizzle.

When he smiled, his teeth were awash with blood and he made little bloody bubbles when he spoke: 'Stella. Stella. Stella. It all went wrong, didn't it?'

The light went out of his eyes as if something had switched off. After that, he didn't speak a word.

88

The party was hot but Dallas was ready to leave. She was nicely drunk and didn't want to go any further with that for a while. Later, yes.

Bloss picked up his rucksack and asked, 'Is it far to go?'

'Down in the Gate, Pembridge Square.'

They walked hand in hand because it gave them stability and they laughed their way down the street. The Ocean Diner was throwing pink and blue neon prints on to the snow: cocktail glasses that filled and emptied and filled. Dallas slipped and almost took him with her, shrieking as they slid sideways like skaters.

She said, 'Hold on, Jimmy.' He'd given her the name on his fake passport. 'Jimmy, I'm going.' She slipped again, laughing helplessly, and grabbed at him and their faces came close. She looked into his eyes, that startling blue, and reached up to kiss him, her Christmas Eve one-night stand.

Bloss thought he would phone the ferry in the morning and see whether the three o'clock sailing was expected. If not, he'd go to the ferry port and wait; take the first boat going anywhere. He was angry because he ought to be in another country, away clear, and the anger must have shown in his face, because Dallas pulled back for a moment and said, 'What's wrong?'

He shook his head and smiled. 'Nothing. Everything's fine. I met you.'

*

At her flat, they made love and Dallas thought Bloss was a by-the-book man – go here and do this, now go there and do that. She didn't mind; at least it was a book he'd read. She got up and went to get a drink. Bloss looked round at her room and found his anger growing: the collection of soft toys, the poster of a dolphin leaping against a setting sun. What luck had brought him to this stupid girl's bedroom in a snow-locked city, what black chance, what killer destiny?

Dallas came back empty-handed. 'There's nothing to drink. I was expecting to be at my parents. I thought there was some red wine, but there's nothing.' She looked cheated.

'It's okay,' he said. 'Coffee or something.'

'I really fancy a drink.' She got into bed beside him. When he didn't reply, she added, 'Once you've started to think about it, you know . . .'

He could feel the edge of anger again and fought it down. Was she really asking him to –

'There are a few places in the Gate.' She kissed him and made a girlish face. 'Don't you want a drink?' He shrugged. 'I do. I *really* do.'

Bloss got out of bed and put his clothes on.

Dallas lay back against the pillows, giving him a good view of her breasts. She said, 'It won't take you long.'

A & E had been at full stretch all night – minor car-crashes, broken bones from falls on the ice, road-rage victims, pub fights, alcoholic poisoning, the usual Christmas heart-attacks – but Kimber was a police priority so a senior charge nurse and a trauma consultant had taken him on. Two police officers stayed with him the whole time; they were in the cubicle, they were in X-ray. In any case, had Kimber tried for freedom he would have been towing a hospital gurney, because he was cuffed to the frame.

The consultant told Stella that Kimber had major abrasions to the face and head, a broken nose, a fractured cheekbone, extensive bruising of the upper body and three cracked ribs. Stella informed the two officers that they wouldn't be getting home for Christmas. She put in a call to Mike Sorley, who asked, 'Did he tell you where to find Bloss?'

'He's not telling us anything. He's not speaking. I've got two coppers with him, they have my number.' She paused. 'They also have yours.'

'Oh, good.'

'I'll have a go at him tomorrow. He won't be out of hospital until then.'

'He'll speak. Eventually, he'll say something.'

'Will he? I'm not sure.'

'He knows where Bloss is. He'll want to cut a deal.'

'Maybe. I wouldn't count on it.' Stella had seen the light fade from Kimber's eyes. 'I think he's gone somewhere.'

'What?'

'Somewhere inside his head.'

'Jesus, Stella.'

'I don't know,' she said. 'I'll try again tomorrow.'

She would wait until Kimber had left A & E and gone into a side ward with the two officers. Delaney waited with her. He said, 'I knew you'd never get a cab. I called the squad room, they said you'd left, I called the flat, but you didn't pick up, I called your mobile and it went to message. The main roads are fucked, but no one's using the back-doubles.'

'Do you know what luck is? A combination of circumstances.'

They were in the relatives' room, the place where people face up to bad news. He put his arms round her and held her tightly, his face in her hair. He said, 'It scares me to think about it.' When they pulled apart, he said, 'I love you, Stella.'

She thought she should tell him, there and then, because a bad-news room might be just the right place.

'There's something –'

One of the officers assigned to Kimber came in to say that he was in a ward and had been given a knockout drop.

Delaney said, 'Let's go home.'

89

Jamie walked the streets of Notting Hill in his padded coat, his hair clotted, his beard a tangled scrub, holding up the dying Christ to anyone who passed.

His Christmas message was, 'All will be well and all manner of things will be well.'

Leon Bloss stepped left to avoid him and Jamie went the same way; Bloss stepped right and Jamie stepped right. 'All will be well –'

The anger rose in Bloss like bile, a hot gusher. He shouldered Jamie, but the prophet staggered, then stepped back, gripping the crucifix, bringing it close to Bloss's face. Important to get the words out, to finish the message.

'All will be well –'

Bloss spat his anger out, a gobbet of phlegm that hit the man on the cross. He palmed Jamie aside, then walked on towards the late-night liquor store. Jamie stared. For a moment, he was inhabiting a vacuum where energy, action, loathing and fury were all in abeyance; then they rushed in to fill the space. To fill Jamie.

Bloss felt a blow to his head and managed to half turn before it properly took effect, then the force of it ran through him and he was on his knees like a man at prayer. Jamie stood over him and the crucifix flashed in the storefront light as it rose and fell. He was hitting wherever he could, Bloss's skull, his face, his neck. Blood geysered up from a split artery to soak Jamie's face and arms, but he kept striking, anger and outrage behind every blow. Striking for

Christ. When Bloss toppled, Jamie went down with him, hammering at the man's face, at the mouth that had defiled, at the eyes that refused to see.

They were out in the open, close to where Sadie and Jamie had always sat, the shops, the fast-food places, the pubs. Some people came out of the Ocean Diner, two men and two women. Jamie was sitting on the pavement panting from the effort he'd put in. The foursome paused, not sure what they were seeing, then they took in the great halo of blood round Bloss's mashed face. One of the women started to scream.

Jamie said, 'All will be well. And all manner of things will be well.'

Whatever the right time was, it wasn't when they were making love. Stella held on to Delaney and kissed him hard. He laughed at her eagerness, but it excited him; he didn't consider that it might proceed from fear or guilt.

He got up afterwards to fetch some water and, when the phone rang, Stella assumed it must be for her, so she picked up the call on the phone by the bed. It was and it wasn't. The caller asked for Delaney. He said, 'Detective Sergeant Harris.'

Stella said, 'Gerry, it's Stella Mooney.'

It took Harris a moment to make the connection. 'And is there a John Delaney there?'

'Yes.'

'Okay. Before I speak to him, are you . . . is there an involvement here, between you and him, I mean?'

'Yes, there is.'

'Okay. Not that it matters much, at least I don't expect it does, but it's best to have things straight.'

'What's the problem?'

'We've got an unlawful killing at Notting Hill Gate. The attacker had John Delaney's business card in his pocket. This guy is pretty disorientated. He's a rough-sleeper by the look of it. We found the card and thought Mr Delaney might be able to shed some light.'

'We're a street away,' Stella said. 'We'll come up there.'

'You know the Ocean Diner?'

'Yes.'

'You'll see our scene of crime tent.'

Delaney told Gerry Harris what he knew, which, they agreed, wasn't much: the names Sadie and Jamie, some fragments, the story of a night spent on the street for research purposes. Harris said, 'Don't worry about it. This is all pretty straightforward. We might find a record, we might not. Someone knows who he is.'

Jamie had left the scene in a police car, accompanied by a forensics officer. Drenched in blood and with the murder-weapon still clutched in his arms, Jamie was a forensic gift.

Halogen lamps had been set up inside the tent and seemed to be drawing thick columns of snow down into their beams. Shadows lurched on the blue screen as the technicians went about their business.

'Who's the victim?' Stella asked.

Harris shook his head. 'No ID of any sort. No wallet, no credit cards . . . Take a look if you like.'

Stella stepped inside the tent and stared down at the man lying there, the wrecked face amid the great patch of blood-soaked snow.

Harris said, 'He really fucked the guy up, that Jamie.'

You couldn't say what the dead man had looked like. Even if you'd known him well, it wouldn't have been enough, that one bright blue eye in a churn of flesh, that one view of the sky through the skull.

Stella went back to the street where Delaney was finding shelter in a doorway. He said, 'And –?'

Stella shrugged. 'Some guy. Who knows?'

Dallas had fallen asleep minutes after Bloss left. Now she woke, just before first light, and looked at her watch. He'd gone and that was no surprise. Then she turned over and saw his rucksack on the bedroom floor and remembered how he had wanted to keep it near him. She opened it up. A few clothes, a passport, some freaky comic books, a videotape.

Much later, after she had been able to get a train to Oxford, after she'd returned, and when she could be bothered, Dallas would turn the rucksack over to the police. And because Jamie's victim would still be unidentified a connection would be made: just speculative. And a cop would thumb the video into a VCR and watch Billy Souza cutting a deal with Oscar Gribbin.

And even later than that, a neighbour would notice the smell from the loft down on the Isle of Dogs. The locals would arrive with a hydraulic hammer and take the door out and find what was left of JD still on the sofa, though looking nothing like his former self.

Dallas could feel the first flickering of a hangover. She got up and made some coffee and took it back to bed, but she knew that things would get worse. Her hangovers always started slow, then picked up.

She was glad she'd never had that extra drink.

Stella was standing naked at the window in Delaney's flat. From somewhere in the building came the sound of a guitar

437

playing, slow and bluesy. The snow had stopped. It was the moment before first light, the sky almost clear now, the few patches of cloud reflecting the bilious city glow. As she watched, a thin light spread in from the the horizon, touching the tips of the trees in Holland Park.

I'll tell him, she thought, *I'll tell him sometime.*

Not now.

The End